The scarlet A referenc
main objective of my missi

M000202667

The BIG 3-0. Tonight I was facing down the end of my twenties, determined to get some living in during these last hours. In fact, I hoped the living would carry into the early hours of my thirtieth year.

If I had known, sitting on that barstool, determined to escape my pitiful shell for just a few hours, what awaited me when I was dead . . . let's just say I would have run like crazy the few blocks to The Madam (my old Victorian house, which I was renovating into a wine bar and dog park), barred the door, and hidden under my bed for a week.

Although . . . maybe not. It's funny now that I think about it: I had to die to start really living.

But again, I digress. Back to the mission. It was a fairly simple plan, or at least I thought it was. I was looking for a one-night stand.

Don't judge.

You see, I had led a relatively safe and incredibly boring life for my first twenty-nine years. It's a tale as old as time: I was the small-town Texas girl who married her high school sweetheart. The story veered off track, literally, when a tractor accident widowed me at twenty-seven. My life could have been the inspiration for a sappy country song. Jad—my heart still pulled at the thought of him—was the only man I'd ever been with. You know, WITH.

Moving on had proved difficult, but I hoped that having one crazy night completely outside my comfort zone might be the catalyst to launch me into the life I wanted. A life without fear. A life where I not only dreamed big dreams but lived them. A life without regrets. Well, that last one was a pretty tall order, but a girl could hope, right?

So, in summary, I was a twenty-nine-year-old widow, sitting there with her big-ass martini that she could only afford one more of, trying to work up the courage to troll the bar for some stranger to help her ring in the BIG 3-0.

Happy birthday to me.

Giving one last, longing look at my fellow patrons in the mirror, I gulped half of my martini for courage, returned the glass to the bar, then slowly swiveled my barstool to face the rest of the nightclub.

The Perch wasn't my idea of a meat market, although Owen Carter, the web designer for my soon-to-be-opened business, had assured me it was. I had imagined a dance floor, flashing lights, and crowds of sweaty people wriggling to techno music. Instead, leather sofas and cushy chairs gave it the feeling of an upscale Starbucks. A speakeasy, this was not. Rather than reassuring me with its sophistication, The Perch made me feel even worse about my mission—dirty, somehow.

The notion that I had crossed the enemy's line and was operating in their territory was as hard to shake as the feeling that I was cheating on The Madam by taking a room at the attached hotel. But I could help none of that. The Perch was the closest club to The Madam, and just because the owners of the Dragonfly Hotel were trying to torpedo my business opening didn't mean that I shouldn't be here.

Big and stinky's elbow jostled me out of my reverie. Luckily, my glass sat safely on the bar or I would have been wearing my martini like perfume. If my drink hadn't been so expensive, I would have 'accidentally' spilled it on him. Gin would have been an immense improvement on the wet-dog and body-odor smells wafting from him, topped off with a considerable dose of cheap cologne. He probably thought the cologne masked the other smells.

I looked him up and down, mainly to put off making eye contact with the other patrons. He was huge in both height and girth, and not in an attractive way. His jeans and T-shirt were ill-fitting and decidedly rumpled, and his forehead had a sheen of sweat.

Sympathy for his obvious discomfort welled up inside me. It lasted just about as long as it took him to bump me again when he waved for the bartender. I glared indignantly at him. The bastard hadn't apologized once. I decided to ignore him and get back to looking for Mr. Right Now.

My gaze slid slowly across the dark throng of twenty- and early thirty-somethings in their business suits and little black dresses, or LBDs as the magazines called them. They lounged indiscriminately on the leather sofas or stood in small groups, each one looking more affluent, more attractive, and more at ease than the next.

My slow scan screeched to a halt as I met dark eyes staring intently at me. I shivered at the uncanny feeling that they weren't just staring at me but into me, then I broke eye contact to take in the rest of him.

Holy Mama! He sat on one of the sofas but he still looked tall, or maybe that was just wishful thinking. I like them tall. His dark hair matched his eyes and, while longer than I usually liked on a guy, on him it worked. Boy, did it work. His light skin was a dramatic contrast to his hair and eyes. His dark suit fit like it was made for him, and even this Target shopper could recognize that it probably was.

My lips parted and I sighed involuntarily, thinking of all the things I would let HIM do to me. Unfortunately, I knew I was safe because he wasn't looking at me. Men like that didn't look at girls like me. I could drool, uh, dream, though.

He raised his drink to me in a silent salute. Oh, God! He had caught me staring. I dropped my gaze to the floor, and red flooded my face. Wait! The bar was behind me. He must have been signaling the bartender he needed another drink. I almost slumped from relief. Or disappointment.

I stole a quick glance back at him. He was still looking in my direction. I peeked over my right shoulder to see if the bartender had noticed tall, pale, and handsome trying to get his attention. The bartender was at the other end of the bar.

I reached behind me for my drink and took a quick sip, looking up from beneath my lashes to see if he was still looking in my direction. He was! Unfortunately, in my surprise and excitement the sip became a gulp, and the gin burned its way down my throat. I gave a few small coughs and struggled to keep them from turning into a full-blown fit.

When I recovered, my eyes watery and burning, I glanced up to find him still watching me, now with a slight smile. Mortification battled with amazement. What now? The burning gin had emboldened me.

While I mulled over my next move, a pale, delicate hand cupped his cheek and turned his head away from me, breaking our eye contact. The hand belonged to the woman who sat on the couch next to him. She was quite possibly the most stunning creature I had ever seen. I call her a creature because she was so beautiful, she seemed otherworldly. She was so white she almost glowed, as if made from purest alabaster. The minuscule red dress she wore was the same shade as her flowing hair. So much for redheads not wearing red.

She left her hand on his face, staking her claim. They made such a stunning match I couldn't stop staring.

Oh crap! Crap, crap, crap! Her gaze had turned on me, and unhappy didn't begin to describe her expression.

I decided a trip to the powder room was in order; anything to escape the daggers her eyes were throwing at me. I considered the half-full martini I had nursed for the better part of an hour. The bartender was busy at the far end of the bar, ogling the cleavage of a very Dallas-type girl—big hair, big boobs, and dark tan. I didn't think my barely C cups (on a good day) were enough to drag his attention away from those triple Ds long enough to tell him not to throw away my drink while I was gone. I looked to my left. Big, dark, and stinky was definitely not an option for a drink protector.

Maybe a little buzz was what I needed to move my mission

along. I took a deep breath and finished my martini in four big swallows, trying not to grimace and shudder.

On the way to the powder room, I peeked over to where tall, pale, and gorgeous sat with the redhead. Only he was no longer there. She was sitting by herself, staring at me and looking really pissed.

That was when I nearly mowed somebody down. The somebody had excellent reflexes, his hands on my arms abruptly halting my forward motion before I slammed into him. Damn! My eyes were level with his broad chest, and it was a body that I wouldn't have minded experiencing full contact with.

"Hello, are you okay?" he asked. The deep voice washed over me like warm caramel covering a scoop of ice cream.

"Aaarrrhhh." The power of coherent speech abandoned me when I raised my eyes from his chest to his face. It was Mr. Tall, Pale, and Handsome. I slid my eyes over to the redhead. She looked even more pissed off than before. When I looked back up at him, his lips twitched in humor. Amusement made him more attractive. Amusement at me, which I should have taken offense to, but I couldn't. He was just so beautiful.

"I'm surprised to see you here." His voice, not only the sound but the slight accent, something Slavic maybe, distracted me momentarily from his words. "Surprised, but happy and encouraged by your presence. Of course, if you had responded to any of my calls or letters, I would have been happy to set up an official tour of my property."

Stupidly I stared at him, my brain fuzzy from the martini. Pieces slowly came together in my mind, and the picture they formed wasn't pretty.

"Mrs. Thompson? Laramie Thompson?" he asked. At my slow nod he continued, "Marek Cerny. CEO of Cerny Enterprises. We have been trying to contact you, but . . . never mind. It is good that you are here now."

Caught! I looked down, breaking eye contact until I could

decide how to respond. My gaze focused on my shoes, the cheap black pumps from Target. I had to leave. What had I been thinking? I didn't belong here.

"Mr. Cerny . . ." I trailed off as I looked up at him, only to see that I no longer held his attention. He was scanning the room as if trying to spot someone, and he was . . . sniffing? Judging from his face, he had gotten a whiff of something offensive.

Please, God, just let me die. The odor from big and stinky must have transferred to me during the many bumps. My humiliation was complete. Or so I thought.

"Don't leave The Perch," said Marek with alarming intensity, his eyes meeting and holding mine.

Once again, pinned by his gaze, I could only nod stupidly. After a quick motion to the redhead, he pushed past me and headed towards the bar. I looked to see what had attracted his attention but saw nothing out of the ordinary. Big, hairy, and stinky was no longer on his barstool, but he wasn't my concern.

Marek Cerny was my concern. I had been avoiding letters, emails, and phone calls from him and a Grace O'Malley for months. I didn't intend to deal with them on my night out, so I headed for the club's exit, only to stumble over an end table before I'd made it three feet. The table rocked precariously and I mumbled an apology to it. What was happening to me? A few healthy sips of gin, coupled with an attractive man, and I was stumbling into and apologizing to inanimate objects? I had to get out of here. But first, a stop at the club's bathroom to regroup seemed in order.

I entered the bathroom and thought for a minute that someone else was in there before I realized it was my own fuzzy reflection in the full-length mirror. I had been slightly plump all my life. What polite country people described as big-boned. After Jad's death, the weight had just melted off me. So far, knock on wood, I hadn't gained it back. It had been two years, but I still didn't recognize the thin person who looked back at me. My dress hung on me loosely, as I couldn't seem to bring myself to buy clothes in my new size.

I didn't really need to use the facilities, so to speak, but as long as I was there I might as well. Never waste an opportunity to pee, I thought, and a small giggle surprised me. I'm not sure why that was funny. Just like I wasn't sure why walking had become such a challenge.

I made it into a stall and maneuvered my dress and tiny sexy underwear, bought specifically for this occasion, into the proper peeing position. Another thing I couldn't get used to was not needing Spanx. The benefits of your husband dying young, I thought with another small giggle. I gasped when I realized where my thoughts had gone, and tears filled my eyes. I would gladly be big-boned for the rest of my life to have Jad back. Wouldn't I? I mean, we'd had our problems, but he was the love of my life. Right?

I leaned my head back to keep the tears from running down my face and ruining the free makeover I had gotten at the Clinique counter. I dabbed furiously at my eyes with a piece of toilet paper. It was the good stuff, at least two-ply. I should ask the manager what kind it was so I could stock it when I opened my business, The Whine Barrel. I had decided to name it that since it combined my two loves, wine and dogs. Then I remembered that I might never open The Whine Barrel, and I would probably lose my house in the process. I welled up again. *Pull yourself together, Laramie.*

I was trying to push up from the toilet seat when I heard the tap, tap, tap of high heels. The sound galvanized me into action. I didn't want to be caught crying in a toilet stall on my birthday. How pitiful was that?

I arranged my clothing, flushed, and left the safety of the stall. Dang, it! The other occupant of the bathroom was none other than the stunning creature who had been with Marek Cerny.

She had to be Grace O'Malley, Cerny's right-hand man, er, woman, if rumors were correct. Her glorious red hair and porcelain skin practically screamed, "I'm Irish." I wasn't entirely sure, though. Cerny Enterprises garnered an obscene amount of press coverage that included constant gushing over both Cerny and O'Malley's business acumen. The articles always included pictures of their properties, managers, and employees, but never of them.

She leaned close to the mirror and reapplied lipstick in the same bold shade of red as her hair and dress, her eyes focused on my reflection. I felt trapped, but I couldn't bring myself to walk out of the bathroom without washing my hands. I mean, come on. What would she think of me?

I stepped up to the sink and went through the motions. Turn on the water, wet hands, get soap, rub hands with soap and water for at least twenty seconds. One one thousand, two one thousand, three one thousand . . .

"Would you be all right?" the stunning creature asked with a small frown. Like Cerny—Marek, I thought dreamily—she had only a slight accent. But where his had seemed Eastern European, hers had an Irish lilt. Or maybe all that red hair was making me fanciful.

My whimsy quickly turned to horror at the thought that maybe I had been counting out loud as I washed my hands.

"I'm fine," I replied, deliberately enunciating my words. What the hell, I might as well go for broke. "Are you having a good time tonight?"

Grace O'Malley turned to face me. She seemed to consider her response carefully. "I cannot say that I am. Marek seems quite distracted, and I need his mind fully on the business at hand."

Taking The Madam away from me, I thought, but I stammered out inanely, "That's too bad."

I turned to throw my crumpled paper towel into the trash bin, swayed again, and almost lost my balance. Grace's sudden grip on my arm kept me from falling. Her hands were icy. Cold hands, warm heart, I mused, giggling to myself again.

After reassuring herself that I was steady, she released my arm. "Leaving would be in your best interest. You don't belong here, especially not in this condition."

I wanted to be offended by the "You don't belong here" statement, but wasn't it precisely what I had been saying to myself all night? To my mortification, once again my eyes filled with tears.

Grace heaved a very put-upon sigh.

"Jaysus! Why does everyone have to be so sensitive? Look, this is not the place for you, especially when you are in no fit condition. You couldn't look after yourself if your life depended on it. Which it might."

The last part she said partially under her breath. I heard it, but I couldn't process it. A loud sniffle was my inadequate response. She softened a fraction and sighed.

"My name is Grace, and I'll get you home. You'll come to no harm with me."

I sniffed again, stared at the floor and mumbled, "Thank you, but I'm staying here tonight. I have a room."

Grace gave me a hard look and then nodded.

"That'll do. I'll walk you to your room."

"That won't be necessary," I mumbled to the floor. "I'm going now. Thank you."

I JUST CAN'T CATCH A BREAK

**72 Hours and 30 Minutes
(11:30 p.m. Friday)**

I walked out of the bathroom, putting one foot carefully in front of the other and fighting the odd tilt of the floor that I hadn't noticed earlier. Grace watched me leave without comment. I passed a group of beautiful people who I was sure had never been told they didn't belong in a place like this. Marek was standing at my vacated barstool and didn't so much as glance in my direction as I left the nightclub. He and Grace would probably have a good laugh at my expense later tonight.

I paused in the hotel hallway to get my bearings. When I leaned against a wall to steady myself, a crushing wave of self-pity with a strong undertow of loneliness threatened to swamp me. Here I was, minutes away from turning thirty, with every penny I had sunk into a business that might never open. I couldn't stand up to another woman in a bar bathroom and, for the life of me, I couldn't get laid. Another thing I couldn't do was spend the night in this hotel by myself. I would be miserable when I woke up tomorrow morning and had to do the walk of shame home. Only my shame was that I couldn't find a man to spend the night with.

Screw my stuff upstairs. I checked my watch. The numbers swam, but I had enough time to make it back to The Madam before I turned thirty at midnight. Hell, since I'd only had one of my two drinks, I could afford to treat myself to a taxi. I turned resolutely toward the lobby, but had to put a hand on the wall to keep from falling down.

Damn! Foiled again! Grace O'Malley was standing between me and the lobby, staring at me with a fierce scowl. Apparently, she intended to follow me to my hotel room and tuck me in.

"Grace!" The friendly greeting hailed from behind her.

I was stunned by the sight of the man walking towards us, a broad smile on his face. A smile that froze as quickly as a rabbit caught in a cobra's stare when he saw me. I wouldn't normally consider myself a cobra, but this man had sat in my home just two days ago, supposedly to help me get my business open. Now he was having chummy late-night meetings with the people throwing up all the roadblocks? If I hadn't been so woozy, I might have felt a little venomous.

I didn't know who was more shocked: Grace O'Malley or Dallas City Council member Austin Crockett. Me? I wasn't that shocked. I had known all along that someone powerful must be behind my problems opening The Whine Barrel. I had been shocked when Council Member Crockett, with his too-wide politician's smile, expensive suits, and haircut—not to mention his rugged good-ole-boy good looks—swooped in from out of nowhere to help "our poor little widow." I hadn't wanted to look a gift horse in the mouth, but his help had seemed a little too good to be true.

"I've told you never to come here." With one last look over her shoulder at me, O'Malley grabbed Crockett by the arm and practically dragged him back towards the lobby.

Exhaustion and sadness washed over me. I couldn't think

about this tonight. More than anything, I wanted to be in my own bed, curled up with my sweet pit bull Bo. I wouldn't even begrudge her stealing the covers like she always did.

Now that I couldn't leave the hotel through the lobby, I would have to find another way. I turned and saw an exit sign floating over a door. I was a little fuzzy on the layout of the hotel (I seemed to be fuzzy on a lot of stuff tonight), but I thought it opened to the street out front.

No one was in the hall to see the drunk girl stagger along the wall and then practically fall out the exit door.

An exit door that clanged shut behind me, stranding me in a creepy parking lot on the wrong side of the hotel.

YOU'RE NOT THE BOSS OF ME

**60 Hours
(Noon Saturday)**

A wild, throbbing dance beat reverberated around me. For once in my life, instead of being a wallflower I was on the dance floor, gyrating in time to the deep thrumming of the bass. I was strong, seductive, and alive. All around me, beautiful people moved to the rhythm, sweat gleaming on their faces. An unbearably sexy man wearing tight slacks and a shirt in the same dark shade as his hair and eyes thrust himself into the small space in front of me. As I smiled an invitation, I noticed that a vein in his neck throbbed to the beat of the dance music. When I looked around me, everyone's neck veins throbbed to the beat of the music that wasn't really music at all. It was heartbeats, and all the hearts were beating for me. Waiting for me. Pounding for me. Pounding. Throbbing. Pounding.

I jerked awake. At first I thought the pounding of the heartbeats had woken me, then I realized it was the obnoxious ringtone I had assigned to the most annoying person I know. My mama. The ringtone's purpose was to prevent me from accidentally answering the phone when she called. I needed to mentally prep before I talked to her. If you knew her, you would understand. She was the only person I assigned that ringtone to. Well, it was also my sister Cheyenne's, but she never called me anyway.

I stretched across the bed to the nightstand where the phone blared and, terrified I would accidentally hit accept, touched the decline option on the lit-up screen. The phone mercifully silenced, I fell back onto my pillow with a sigh. God, my head ached! But it wouldn't do any good to lie here. Mama would call back. She was nothing if not determined. Resigned, I eased myself into a seated position on the bed.

What the hell! I wasn't wearing a stitch of clothing.

In the pitch-black room I could just make out the shapes of the furniture. I wasn't in my turret room at The Madam. My chest tightened in panic until I remembered I was in my hotel room at the Dragonfly. My gaze whipped to the other side of the bed. Empty. I wasn't sure if the sigh that escaped me was one of relief or regret.

Had I really thought Plain Jane Laramie Thompson could go out to a fancy nightclub, pick up a stranger, and spend the night with him? In the cold light of day—or rather, in the dark of a hotel room with the most fantastic blackout curtains I'd ever experienced—the answer was no. Even if I had met someone, I didn't think I could have gone through with it. Besides, nothing exciting ever happened to me. I sighed again. This time I knew it was from regret.

I was the very untalented middle child in a family of very talented rodeo stars. My daddy and my older brother, Monty, had been professional bull riders. Mama and my younger sister, Cheyenne, were both barrel racing champions. Mama tried, Lord knows she tried, to make me one too, but I just hadn't had it in me.

Mama always told me, "Laramie, you have everything

inside you to achieve anything you set yourself to. You just have to believe in yourself and really want it."

Sadly, that wasn't true. Mama had finally realized it, too, and hung her dreams on Cheyenne.

But I would not feel sorry for myself. It was my big day, and I had a birthday party to get to at my parents' house. Ten to one odds, Mama had been calling to tell me to pick up my own birthday cake on the way there.

I groped for the bedside lamp and turned it on, illuminating the room. I turned my phone to face me and nearly screamed when I saw the time.

It was 12:05pm! I had less than two hours to make it to the party. The drive from Dallas to my parents' ranch just outside of Faith, Texas would eat up an hour of that time. In a panicked scramble I disengaged myself from the plush comforter and numerous pillows and propelled myself out of the ginormous bed. The room spun, and the infamous big-ass martini from the night before threatened to make a reappearance in the worst possible way. I held myself very still and, after several moments, the nausea passed. The worst of it, anyway. How could one martini, albeit a big-ass one, have done this to me?

The last thing I remembered was . . .

Heck, what was the last thing I remembered?

I tried to clear the fog. My stomach clenched again as I recalled meeting Marek Cerny. Wait, had Council Member Crockett been there? If my last memory was of leaving the hotel, why was I back at the Dragonfly?

No, I remembered something else. I had been walking towards The Madam, and then . . . Had an animal attacked me? No, it had been a man, because he had spoken, hadn't he? Something about regards and a church . . . or was it a temple with a cross? Just thinking about it made my head hurt. And then . . . someone had stood over me right before everything went black. No, it couldn't be.

My stomach lost the fight with the martini. I barely made it to the bathroom in time.

Afterward, I leaned my head against the cool porcelain of the bathtub, which did nothing to ease the pounding. A quick inventory proved I didn't have so much as a bruise on the parts of my body I could see. Aside from the massive hangover, I was fine. Everything after leaving the club had to be a dream.

But how had I gotten back to my hotel room?

Grace! She must have followed me to make sure I made it up to my room. Had I passed out along the way, and she undressed me and put me to bed? And the person I'd seen right at the end? He couldn't have been there.

I wallowed in self-pity for a few moments over my miserable birthday eve and the fact that a woman as gorgeous as Grace had seen me naked. Mortification and self-pity battled each other for dominance before I decided there was plenty of room on this dismal day for both.

My body jerked as Mama's ring tone blared again, more as a Pavlovian response to the caller than from being startled by the noise. I might as well deal with her now. I was thirty today. It was time to face my challenges head on. With no small effort, not to mention queasiness, I got to my feet, wiggled into the plush hotel bathrobe, and trudged towards the ringing phone.

"Hi Mama," I answered, trying to sound awake, cheery, and not at all hungover.

"Where are you?" she asked without preamble.

I jerked to attention. How did Mama know? What kind of radar had tipped her off that I was in a hotel?

"Wha . . ." was all I could force out.

"I hope you haven't started driving yet. We are going to have to postpone your birthday party. Cheyenne got last-minute tickets to the George Strait concert there in Dallas tonight. She and Bradley are going to be staying at some fancy hotel. The Bumble Bee or Fly or some other kind of bug name. Who in their right mind would name a hotel after an insect?"

"The Dragonfly?" I asked faintly.

"That's it. They've got early check-in. They dropped the girls off for me to look after and are already on the road to Dallas. How about tomorrow?"

"Tomorrow?"

"For your party? It wouldn't be right to have your party without Cheyenne. Two o'clock?"

"Um, sure."

"Okay, see you at two tomorrow. Don't be late. Bye."

The phone went dead without so much as a happy birthday. That was Mama at her finest.

Despite the hangover, I moved faster than I had ever moved before. The last thing I needed was to run into Cheyenne and her husband, Bradley, checking in while I was checking out. She would be on the phone to Mama before I could make it out the front door of the hotel.

In the bathroom, which felt more like a mini-spa, I studied my reflection in the large mirror over the sink. I looked like death warmed over. I winced when the comb I jerked through my hair caught in a thick knot at the back of my neck. I untangled the comb and tried to pull it through again. After it stopped in the same spot and wouldn't budge, I pulled my hair over my shoulder to work out the tangle. Something caked the matted hair. When I scraped it with my fingernail, some substance flaked off and fell into the sink. I leaned over to inspect the flakes. They were almost black, with a dark red tint. I pulled the matted hair close to my nose and sniffed it, gagging at its putrid odor. I don't know how I recognized the smell, but I was positive that it was dried blood.

Nausea swept over me again and brought with it a fresh memory of snarling and snapping, and me lying face down on the ground. The scene was so vivid that I dropped the robe and spun around to check my back in the mirror. I sagged against the sink in relief. My skin was unmarred.

Something had happened last night. As I faced the mirror again, I noticed a large bruise on the left side of my neck, several inches below my jawline. The blemish was almost as big as my palm, and the colors in it were a sight to behold. Almost hidden by the rainbow colors of the bruise were two small, white spots about an inch apart. Each spot was roughly an eighth of an inch round, and they had the appearance of old scars. A quick rub of the area made me wince. It was sore, and the marks were slightly raised.

Had I been bitten by the dreaded brown recluse spider? That wouldn't account for two marks unless it had bitten me twice, but it would explain why I felt so bad today. I was warming to the spider theory when I remembered the blood in my hair and the disjointed images from last night.

That brought an even more sinister thought to mind. Maybe I had been drugged. There had been a lot of stories in the news lately about the date-rape drug. Spiders and drugs? It was all too much to think about, especially with a bitch of a headache wreaking havoc with my thought process and my bitch of a sister closing in on me.

I stared at myself in the mirror and noticed something even stranger: my face was devoid of makeup. Had someone washed my face while I was passed out? If so, what else had they washed?

Even though I could practically feel the noose tightening around my neck as Cheyenne got closer to the hotel, I quickly stepped into the shower. As I scrubbed the Dragonfly's coconut-scented shampoo roughly through my hair, I fervently tried not to think about what might have happened to me while I was passed out, or about what I was washing out of my hair. The hair part became more challenging when I rinsed it and the water ran a bright red before it swirled down the drain.

I pulled the entire, sopping wet mess into a ponytail and slid my arm across the counter, dragging all my toiletries into my small black cosmetics bag. I left the bathroom to get dressed. The relaxing spa feeling continued throughout the room, with pale greens and aqua mixed with beige, and it oozed expense and understated elegance. I wished I had thought to take pictures with my phone the night before. No time now.

I tugged on the unexciting clean underwear I had brought for my morning after, followed by my boyfriend jeans and the black, V-necked, long-sleeved tee I had worn to the hotel the day before. I completed the outfit with an orange silk scarf, a nod to the fact that Halloween was only a few weeks off. I had included the scarf to dress up my casual outfit, but now its job was to cover the bruise that most people would think was a hickey. I wrapped it around my neck, letting the ends trail down the front of my T-shirt.

Finally I slid my feet into black leather flats and made a quick round of the hotel room, scooping my few possessions into an overnight bag. Where were my LBD and sexy under-wear from the night before? Another wasted purchase, although in fairness, they had come from the sale rack at Walmart. I frantically scanned the room and saw them neatly folded on top of the dresser. My face burned again at the thought of Grace undressing me. I grabbed the clothes, intending to put them in my bag and head for the door, but stopped when I realized they were damp.

I pondered why Grace would wash my clothes but not hang them up to dry. Then I remembered that Cheyenne was on her way; I didn't have time to ponder. I threw the damp clothes into my bag and backed towards the hotel door, reaching behind me for the handle as I scanned the room for any belongings I had missed. Something crackled under my hand. Frustrated at another distraction, I turned and saw a folded piece of paper taped to the door handle. I hastily pulled it free and unfolded it. Written on the paper in a flowing script that called to mind centuries-old documents under glass were one sentence and a name:

Do not leave this room until Grace or I come for you.

Marek Cerny

The ramifications almost had me running for the bathroom again. Marek had been in the room last night. Not Grace. Had we? Had he? After a moment of deliberation, I decided no to the first. Unfortunately, I was pretty sure that the answer to the second question was yes. He must have undressed me.

I realized that without even making a conscious decision to do so, I had walked back to the bed. Good girl, Laramie, just follow directions as usual. I was thirty today, dammit. It was time for me to start making decisions for myself. I balled up the note, tossed it onto the bed, and walked out of the hotel room.

4

THE MADAM

59.5 Hours
(12:30 p.m. Saturday)

I felt like I was swimming in shark-infested waters as I navigated through the hotel. Thankfully, I made it out of the front door without seeing any of my particular sharks. I had briefly considered slipping out a back door, but the horror of my dream from the night before outweighed the worry of running into Marek, Grace, or my sister.

I heaved a sigh of relief when I reached the sidewalk and turned towards The Madam. Despite a slight chill in the air, it was a gorgeous, sunny day with barely a cloud in the sky. Too bad I hadn't packed my sunglasses yesterday. It was only a couple of blocks to The Madam, but the sun bored into my eyes and intensified my headache. Actually, it seemed to burn into my entire body. That martini had really dehydrated me. That and the vomiting.

The only bright spot in this miserable day was Mama canceling my party. Now I could spend the whole of my birthday in bed snuggling with Bo if I wanted to. I'd have to contact Owen Carter, my full-time web designer and part-time dog sitter, about picking her up. Figuring a quick conversation was better than trying to text while walking, I called him.

"Hey, Owen! I'm almost on my way."

"Since I hadn't heard from you, I figured you were running late, and I'm bringing Bo to you."

My relief at not having to drive to Owen's house in my hungover state was short-lived when he continued, "I hope you had a great time last night. Don't think you can rush out the door without sharing all the juicy details. You can be late to your birthday party."

"Mmm," I responded, while inwardly I groaned. Although I hadn't given Owen any details when I asked him to keep Bo for the night, I suspected he knew exactly what I had been up to. Or at least, what I had been trying to be up to. I got that feeling with Owen a lot. Most people accept the walls you build around yourself at face value. Owen was one of those rare people who seemed to see right through those walls to the core of everything you were trying to protect. It was disconcerting. I hadn't decided if he was intuitive or simply a big snoop who didn't respect boundaries and asked awkward, prying questions that I always ended up answering. I hadn't mastered the art of telling people to mind their own business. People usually just weren't that interested in me, so I'd never had to.

"Great. I'll be there in five. Pour me a glass of wine." Owen disconnected without a goodbye, much less a happy birthday. I expected that from Mama, but Owen forgetting to say the words was a surprise. I wondered if my entire birthday would pass by without someone wishing me a good one. I'm not one to wallow or feel sorry for myself, but I felt like kicking a stone on the sidewalk.

All thoughts of wallowing melted away when I looked up to see my beautiful Victorian looming half a block ahead of me. The Madam. The sight of her never failed to give me chills, and the goosebumps on my arms proved her magic was working. The large house was the very definition of an architectural flight of fancy. But the creamy white paint that covered her expanse, and the pastel shades of lavender and mint that outlined her windows and adorned her trim, brought to mind an elaborate wedding cake rather than a house. Several porches draped the house like swags of buttercream icing, and the numerous pitches in her roof further added to her embellishments. However, the topper was the honest-to-God turret that stood proudly at the front of the house.

I had inherited The Madam from Jad's aunt, Hattie Thompson, who'd gotten a kick out of living in a house that resembled the wedding cake she never had. The colors weren't my choice, but I couldn't imagine The Madam any other way. So confectionary she would stay.

Before I could slip my phone into my back pocket, it rang. Bill Martinez's name and number popped up on the display.

"Oh, what now?" I asked the universe in disgust. Bill was the contractor in charge of the renovations to turn The Madam into The Whine Barrel. He was an exceptionally competent contractor in his mid-forties, and had been one of the few bright spots in the process. But it had been a long week with issue after issue, and I didn't want to deal with another one today.

"Hey, Bill, what's up?"

"What the hell happened since your meeting with Council Member Crockett on Wednesday?" Bill asked, skipping the usual pleasantries.

I did a mental head slap. On Wednesday, I had met with Council Member Crockett and Bernie Wallach. Bernie called himself a community activist, but really, he was just a massive pain in my ass. He was doing his best to torpedo the opening of The Whine Barrel and, unfortunately, was succeeding. Tom Harner, The Madam's closest neighbor, had also been at the meeting. Bill knew that session had ended with the final code inspection for The Whine Barrel being indefinitely put on hold, but I had forgotten to tell him what had happened yesterday.

"I'm sorry," I said. "I meant to call you about it, but last night and today have been crazy. Bernie and Tom dropped by the house yesterday unannounced. It wasn't pretty, and when they left, Bernie was making noises about complaining to Crockett. Why?"

"Whatever Bernie did worked in our favor. You remember Don Williams, the code inspector with the city who has been out a few times? He just called, and wants us to meet him at The Madam for the code inspection."

"The same code inspection that Bernie somehow got held up for the last week? The one Crockett told us wouldn't happen anytime soon—that code inspection?" I asked in disbelief.

"The same. But I should warn you, Inspector Williams is madder than a wet hen about having to do it on a Saturday. Don't be surprised if he nitpicks everything."

"Are we ready for this? I mean, I know the inspection was supposed to have happened earlier this week, but when it got canceled did anything get pushed back or fall between the cracks?"

"Except for a pissed-off code inspector gunning for us, we are good to go," Bill replied.

"Great. What time does he want to meet us?"

"Now."

"Now?" I asked incredulously.

"Now."

"Okay," I replied weakly. "I guess this thing is happening."

5

LUNCH, ANYONE?

**59.25 Hours
(12:45 p.m. Saturday)**

Before I inherited The Madam she had been in Jad's family for over a century, owned most recently by his Aunt Hattie. At the age of sixteen, Hattie had secretly married her high school sweetheart on the eve of him leaving to become a fighter pilot in World War II. His plane was shot down, devastating her. Despite having had many suitors, at least the way she told the story, she had never remarried.

It had always been understood that Jad would inherit The Madam one day. Hattie and I were friendly while Jad was alive and became even closer after his death. She was kinder to me than my own family. Whenever I had needed to get away from Faith and the memories, I'd always had a place to stay. I had felt like a fraud, leaning on Jad's great aunt for support, but I thought that Hattie understood how things had been between Jad and I and hadn't cared. After Hattie's death, a little over a year ago, no one had been more shocked than I to learn that she had left me the house. Hattie's only directive in the will regarding The Madam was to "make her live again."

I often wondered if that sentiment was directed at me and the house was only a means to that end. I can't deny that I quit living after Jad died. Hell, had I ever really lived, even when he had been alive?

But I was trying to change that. I stopped in front of the gate, looking at The Madam with pride. The half-acre yard that wrapped around the front and side of the house was mostly grass, dotted with several large shade trees. My beautiful three-story (not including the basement) Victorian house took up the other half-acre of the enormous lot—enormous for modern-day Dallas standards, anyway. I thought the unique house with its many porches and large yard in an urban setting would make The Madam successful as The Whine Barrel. Every dog owner wants a place to go drink wine with her dog, right? Please, God.

Along with the large house and the even larger yard came astronomical property taxes. Luckily, Hattie had left me some money too. If I didn't turn The Madam into a paying business and ate only every other day, the inheritance might pay the taxes on her for about ten years—maybe twelve, if I moonlighted at a job involving a pole.

I had surrounded the house and yard with a four-foot-tall picket fence painted creamy white, with a chain-link fence snuggled up behind it. The combination fence had cost a pretty penny, but I couldn't take the chance that a visiting dog might escape.

A beautiful wooden gate topped with an oval arch beckoned people and their pets inside. When (if) I received final approval, I'd hang a sign made from the top of a wine barrel, with The Whine Barrel painted in cursive script. My brother Monty had built the gate's arch so that the sign would hang gracefully inside it.

I passed through the wooden gate, giving the latch an

extra tug to ensure it was secure. Taking a second to eye the small six-foot by six-foot chain-link enclosure that customers would have to pass through before entering the yard, I determined that it was ready for inspection, too.

I pulled the second metal gate firmly closed behind me, the loud clang ratcheting my headache up a notch. In sympathy, my stomach rolled. I closed my eyes and took a few deep breaths until the nausea passed. I sent up a prayer of thanks and walked the fifty feet from the gate to the broad front steps of The Madam. My misery eased further when the cool shade of the porch enveloped me. Large, natural-wicker chairs with plump cushions covered in durable lilac canvas were placed at intervals along the porch. They looked so inviting that I considered easing myself onto one to wait for Bill and the inspector.

However, before I reached the front door, the low growl of Owen's classic El Camino alerted me to his approach. Bo's head stretched out of the passenger window, her big, silly, pittie grin covering most of her face.

I dropped my overnight bag between the front porch and the shrubs. I really didn't want Owen to see it and start asking questions.

Just as Owen parked in front of The Madam, Bill and Inspector Williams pulled up. Bill drove a battered red Chevrolet truck, while the inspector was in a white Ford pickup with City of Dallas Code Compliance displayed proudly on its side. What was it with Texas and trucks? Even Owen, who did his best not to fit into the Texas male stereotype, drove an El Camino, which was just a hipster pickup in disguise. I couldn't throw stones, though, as I drove a truck myself.

As I made my way back to the street to greet everyone, I saw that Owen had released Bo and she was happily welcoming her visitors. Bo, short for Bodacious, is a white and brindle spotted American Staffordshire terrier mix I rescued from the high-kill city animal shelter. She was incarcerated there when she became homeless on the mean streets of Dallas. If Bo could tell the story, I'm sure it would involve high drama and assertions that SHE saved ME. Bo was quite the diva, hence the name Bodacious.

I hoped she would behave herself, but I wouldn't bet money on it. She was so excited about the people there to see her—in her mind—that she hadn't greeted me. In fact, if I hadn't known better I would have thought that she was purposely keeping her distance from me.

Owen leaned against the El Camino, his worn cowboy boots crossed at the ankles. He had figured out the code inspection situation and was hanging back so that I could handle it. His ever-present man purse, or murse, as he and I jokingly called it, hung from the strap that crossed his chest. I couldn't help but smile. Owen was an anomaly. One day he wore old-school Converse high tops and the next day battered ropers. Lanky and just shy of six feet tall, with hair and eyes the color of dull copper pennies, he'd come across as a nondescript nerd when we first met. That had probably been his plan, since he'd been interviewing for the web designer position at The Whine Barrel. I had hired him on the spot.

In the months since, his love for Bo had moved him up in my esteem from competent contract employee to dog sitter and, lately, sounding board for my ideas for The Whine Barrel. I'd also noticed that he was a lot more attractive than he had first appeared. If he didn't constantly pester me about my personal life, he would be the perfect employee.

I joined Bill and Inspector Williams by the code inspector's truck.

I smiled at Don Williams, but he only glared at me in return. The gigantic, pearly white smile that usually beamed out of his dark face was nowhere to be seen today.

The Madam was in Don's assigned area. He had inspected several of Bill's projects and the two men always got along well. In fact, Don had stopped by the house several times and given Bill pointers to make sure things would be up to code. Being called into work on a Saturday must have been aggravating, but his attitude seemed to be directed specifically at me.

Bo sensed the tension and used her paw-on-the-leg trick on Don. I mentally crossed my fingers that she could work her charms on him. He reached down to scratch her ears, still glaring at me. "I just want to go on record that I need my job, so I will do what I am told. I don't have to like it or agree with it, though."

"Okay," I said, puzzled. "Don, I am sorry that you had to come out on a Saturday, but this wasn't our doing."

"Wasn't it?" he sneered. "Well, I got a call from my boss, who I guess got a call from his boss, and so on up the chain. Someone with some pull wants this inspection to take place today. It must be nice to have friends in high places. That said, they can make me be here, but they can't make me pass you. No job is worth my integrity."

My heart dropped. Gunning for me was right.

"Don, I won't lie. I'm glad you're here. We need to get the work inspected so we can open The Whine Barrel on time. But we aren't the ones who put off the first inspection, and we aren't the ones who scheduled this one."

Don held my gaze for several seconds. He seemed to make up his mind about something and gave a slight nod. "Let's get this inspection started, then."

He took his clipboard from the truck and walked into the yard, looking at the exterior of the house and taking notes as he went. My heart stuttered when he stopped in front of the shrub that concealed my bag, but returned to its normal rhythm when he moved on.

As Bill and I trailed behind him, I noticed that Bill seemed uneasy.

"Bill, tell me the truth. Did you call in any favors on this?"
I whispered.

Contractors of Bill's caliber were hard to come by. He was
only doing my renovations because of the weight Jad and
Hattie's last name still carried in Dallas. Otherwise, renovating
The Madam into The Whine Barrel would be small potatoes
for him. I knew he and Bernie had butted heads on jobs
before. Nothing would bring Bill more satisfaction than to
complete an end-around on Bernie.

"No, Laramie. I swear," Bill said tersely.

"Are you nervous Don will fail us?" I asked, still confused
by Bill's demeanor. Why was he so distracted?

"Look, right before I pulled up I got a call from another
site. I hate to leave you here by yourself for this, but I have
to go."

What the hell? If anyone could smooth over things with
Don, it was Bill. And if Don had questions about any of the
work done, Bill had the answers, not me. Bill had been with
me every step of the way; he wouldn't walk away now if it
wasn't important. Would he?

"I'm going in," Don shouted back to us as he walked up
the front steps, Bo on his heels.

That was when I noticed the front door was ajar.

I never left the door unlocked. I tried to remember, step by
step, leaving the house the night before. I had been in a hurry
and had been reeling from the meeting with Bernie and Tom.
I must not have pulled it closed behind me.

Bill's phone buzzed. He grimaced when he looked at the
screen. "Look, Laramie, I'm real sorry to leave you in the
lurch like this, but I have to go."

"Okay." I wanted to tell him no, but I couldn't form the
word.

Bill climbed into his truck, pulled away from the curb, and
was gone. I couldn't help but envision a rat swimming away
from a sinking ship.

Owen pushed off the El Camino and came over, looking after Bill's truck. "What the hell was that? Why is Bill leaving when the code inspection is just starting?" He looked as perplexed as I felt.

"At this point, Owen, you know just as much about it as I do."

Short, sharp barks came from inside The Madam. Owen and I smiled at each other. Don wasn't giving Queen Bo the attention she felt she deserved.

Owen walked with me as far as the front door. "I'll wait here on the porch. Unless you want some help in there?"

"No, but be on standby. I'll call you if I need you."

Owen smiled encouragingly and gave me a thumbs up. I squared my shoulders and entered The Madam.

From the door, I could see a good deal of the first floor because of its new, mostly open floorplan. The expensively restored grand staircase was the first sight that greeted visitors. To its right lay a large room that Owen laughingly referred to as the saloon. Bill had created it by combining a parlor and a formal dining room. A wine-tasting bar stretched along the back wall, its wood chosen and finished to match the dark walnut of the staircase. I had to agree that the bar and the glass shelves behind it brought to mind an old western saloon rather than a wine bar. Despite that, I wouldn't change a thing about it.

Tables dotted the open room for guests who wanted to enjoy a glass of their favorite Texas vintage inside, away from the hordes of dogs (hopefully) and their owners enjoying the outdoors. Several small rooms, which could be used for overflow or for intimate events, opened off the saloon.

To the left of the grand staircase, large glass doors opened into the gift shop. I had already picked out boutique-style dog, cat, and (of course) wine accessories to sell. Customers could also buy cases of wine to carry out or be delivered to their homes. The restrooms were behind the gift shop, their entrances underneath the staircase in the saloon.

Unseen to guests, but equally important to the business, were my office, a storeroom, and a kitchen. The Madam's original kitchen had been renovated and would be more than adequate to produce light fare for private events and the bed and breakfast guests, when I got that part of the business up and running.

Don exited one of the bathrooms, finally beaming his usual Don smile.

"Laramie, y'all have done good with this job. Real good," he said before catching himself. "The inspection isn't over, so this isn't a pass yet. I'm just commenting on the work. I am impressed with what I see. Cheryl and I have been looking for a place like this to spend lazy Saturday afternoons." His face hardened at that, probably thinking about how today's lazy Saturday afternoon had gone off the rails. But he continued, "The fact that we could bring Buck with us and let him run around while we try some new wines is a huge bonus."

Don scrolled through pictures on his phone as he talked and held it up to show me an image of himself and a woman who wore a smile almost as big as his. A small white poodle posed regally between them.

"Buck?"

"Yep," Don said. "Don't let the small size fool you. He has courage as big as Texas and the swagger to match."

I smiled back, sharing a moment between dog owners who viewed their dogs not just as pets, but as family members. I relaxed. Everything would be fine.

Bo ruined the moment with a burst of barking.

"She must be in the kitchen," I said, frowning. Bo rarely wandered too far from people who might rub her belly, and she wasn't usually a barker, either.

"Good thing I'm the code inspector and not the health inspector," Don said, smiling conspiratorially.

"Yeah, good thing," I answered, smiling over my shoulder at him as I walked towards the kitchen.

"I might as well come with you. I need to inspect the kitchen, and I was specifically ordered to check the dumbwaiter to see if I think it's a hazard."

"The dumbwaiter? Order from whom?" I asked.

"Passed along by my boss when he told me to come out here today. I'm not sure who it originated from."

I was pretty sure I knew who the order came from, but I kept the thought to myself. "Bill and I have both expressed our concerns to you. We think that with the locks we put on every door of the dumbwaiter shaft, we should meet the code requirements."

Wanting to retain as many of the historical features of the house as possible, I had kept the dumbwaiter system. Its original purpose was to carry trays of food to the upper floors and then transport the empty dishes back down to the kitchen. However, overworked maids had quickly determined that baskets of clothes and linens made the trips between the floors just as easily as trays of food. Basically, it was just a small wooden elevator about two-and-a-half feet wide by three feet tall. There was an opening on each floor, covered by an ornate sliding door.

That the dumbwaiter had been used during prohibition times to shuttle cases of moonshine from the cellar was rarely discussed, at least not in polite society. Now it would come in handy for bringing up wine from the cellar.

I walked through the swinging door into the kitchen and held it open for Don. I wasn't a cook, but I still felt a swell of pride. The industrial appliances and countertops, all surfaced in shiny stainless steel, had somehow integrated well with the old wood of The Madam's original kitchen.

Bo stood on her hind legs, her front paws on the counter below the dumbwaiter. She looked at us, then back at the dumbwaiter, and barked sharply.

"Bo! Off!" I commanded sharply. It was bad enough she was in the kitchen, but I knew the sight of her paws on the counter wouldn't help my cause.

Bo ignored me and whined, her attention focused on the dumbwaiter.

Don joined her and said, "Laramie, there isn't a lock on this door."

"I know," I responded. "I didn't see a need to put the locks on until we opened for business."

Don tried to slide the door open. It didn't budge.

"Come on, Don," I said with a laugh, "put your back into it."

Bo's back paws scrabbled on the kitchen floor as she tried to reach the dumbwaiter's door. I grabbed her collar and pulled her back to stand beside me. Don braced his legs and gave the door a good heave. It held for a moment and then slid open with a loud bang.

A body fell out of the dumbwaiter, rolling onto the kitchen counter and practically into Don's arms. Don flailed backward and the body rolled off the counter and landed with a sickening thud on the floor.

Even with his face twisted into a gruesome mask, I had no trouble recognizing the dead guy.

It was Bernie Wallach.

6

IT'S RAINING MEN

59 Hours
(1:00 p.m. Saturday)

The police officer who sat with me in the saloon while his coworkers tromped through The Madam made me jumpy. But not for the reason you might think.

Plain and simple, Officer Mins reminded me of Jad. Mins looked to be in his late twenties, maybe even thirty. The age Jad had been when he died. Mins' hair wasn't quite as black, his eyes not quite as blue, and he wasn't quite as tall as Jad's six foot two inches. Despite the not quites, he still forced old memories to the surface.

In an effort to get my mind off my dead husband, I tried to focus on the dead guy in my house.

After the body (I tried not to think of it as Bernie Wallach) fell out of the dumbwaiter and we recovered from the first wave of shock, we called 911. Actually, Don called 911 while I dragged Bo out the back door and locked her in a kennel in the back yard.

As I entered the kitchen, I heard Don telling the 911 operator, "I don't know if he's dead. You should get an ambulance here as soon as possible."

The gruesome expression—a cross between anger and pain—frozen onto Bernie's face and the rigidity of his curled body convinced me that he was dead, but I wasn't an expert. Ignoring the roiling in my stomach, I leaned over and placed my fingers against his neck. They encountered cold, stiff skin. My first instinct was to recoil, but I forced myself to search for a pulse. Nothing.

When I pulled my hand back there was a dark, sticky substance on it. I recognized it as congealed blood. *Gross!* But . . . not gross. I stared at my fingers, mesmerized by the red goo. His life force, I thought vaguely. The strangest desire to taste it overwhelmed me.

"Laramie! Laramie!" Don interrupted my reverie. "Did you get a pulse?"

"No."

"Oh man! Is that Bernie Wallach?"

"Yes, it is. Don, we should wait on the porch for the police to arrive." I cleaned the blood off my hand with a dishtowel and tossed the bloody cloth into the trash. I never wanted to use it again.

"I agree," replied Don. As we walked through the swinging door, he looked back at the body and shook his head. "That guy was an asshole, but I still wouldn't have wished this on him."

Apparently, Bernie's particular brand of nasty had touched almost everyone in the city.

We filled Owen in on the body tumble as we waited for the police to arrive. When we told him whose body it was, his shocked exclamations halted and he turned a pale shade of gray. I remembered that any time over the past few weeks when Bernie's name had come up, Owen had fallen strangely silent. Before I could ask him about it, the first police car arrived.

When the two young, male officers stepped out of the car I wondered if they had ever worked with Jad. I must still have been a little woozy because when Officer Mins approached the porch, for a moment I thought he was Jad. I swayed, and Owen steadied me with a gentle arm around my shoulders and a sympathetic smile. He hadn't known my husband, but his constant nosy questions had pried a lot of information out of me over the last few months, so he knew the story. Well, as much as anyone knew except me. There were some things I was too ashamed to tell anyone, prying questions be damned.

I told the officers about finding the front door open when we arrived, something I had thought was an oversight until we found the body. They exchanged looks, but their only questions were whether anyone else was in the house and where the body was. Bo was still creating quite the racket in the enclosure, so I warned them about her in case they needed to go out back. Bo was extremely friendly, but that wasn't the impression most people got when a seventy-pound pit bull ran at them pell-mell. I didn't want any accidents involving their guns and my dog

After they cleared the house, cop jargon for verifying nobody was inside, they determined that Bernie was, in fact, deceased. This came as no surprise to me, but Don sighed. I guess he hoped that I had been wrong.

The officers radioed for backup to secure the scene. They also requested supervisors, homicide detectives, the Physical Evidence Section and, well, just about everyone else under the sun. As additional officers and units arrived, I told my story to a patrol officer twice, and a third time to a patrol sergeant.

By the time the sergeant arrived, the original officers had separated Don, Owen, and me into different areas of the house. I was in the saloon. They moved a table and chair into the gift shop for Don. Owen asked to stay on the front porch.

Unfortunately, this wasn't my first rodeo and it brought back memories of the investigation after Jad died on his family's ranch. Jad had been a Dallas police officer for several years before his death. It was ironic how scared I had been that he would be killed on duty, when in the end it was something as mundane as a tractor that had taken his life.

When an officer dies, there is always the possibility that someone with a vendetta against the officer, or against law enforcement in general, is responsible. That Jad's body had disappeared before an autopsy was performed further complicated matters. His death had been nothing more than a tragic accident but, out of professional courtesy, the Faith Police Department had conducted an abbreviated investigation. I had hoped never to be involved in another death investigation, no matter how peripherally, but here I was.

About an hour after the first officers arrived I opened several cases of bottled water and passed them out. It was a self-serving act of goodwill. Even after drinking three twenty-four-ounce bottles I was still thirsty, and the throbbing in my head hadn't eased.

Don had to be escorted past me to the bathroom, and he looked pissed. His lazy Saturday had taken an ugly turn. But I didn't feel that bad for him. It didn't compare to the last few weeks of my life, and neither of our problems held a candle to Bernie's. During his visit yesterday afternoon—sorry to speak ill of the dead—he had been just as nasty and obnoxious as ever. Had Bernie had the slightest inkling, while railing at me about my plans for The Whine Barrel, that he had less than twenty-four hours to live?

Speaking of the meeting with Bernie, I had glossed over it with the police officers, but I would have to go into more detail when the detectives arrived. If this turned out to be more than just an accident, the police would need to establish a timeline of Bernie's last few days.

I tried to remember exactly how everything had happened so I could give the police an accurate accounting.

Tom Harner and Bernie Wallach had arrived at The Madam around four o'clock on Friday. I remembered that because I had just drifted into a light doze. I didn't normally nap in the afternoon, but I had wanted to rest up for my big night at the Dragonfly.

Their pounding on The Madam's front door woke me. Then Tom followed it up with a phone call. I hadn't spoken to him since the meeting that had ended with the final code inspection of The Madam being put off indefinitely. Before Bernie's crusade against The Whine Barrel started, I'd considered Tom a friend. In truth, longtime acquaintance and recent neighbor more accurately described our relationship; Tom owned the only property whose land adjoined The Madam's. If anyone could claim to have a dog in the fight, it was Tom.

I answered the phone, wildly hopeful that he'd heard something about the status of my code inspection.

"Hey, Laramie! Tom here. Bernie and I are downstairs on your porch. A couple of neighbors have reached out to me with concerns and I would like to give you a chance to address them."

"Sure. I'm upstairs, so give me a little while to make it down."

My hopes dashed at the mention of "concerns," I changed from the sweats I had been napping in to jeans and a T-shirt. Not exactly businesswoman attire, but I hadn't invited them so I wasn't going all-out. I told myself this even as I straightened my tee. Being raised by a rodeo beauty queen makes you conscious of your appearance, no matter how hard you might try not to care.

Bo had been snuggling with me on the bed. She started dancing about as soon as I pulled on my jeans. When I pushed my feet into runners, she did zoomies around my bedroom in anticipation of going outside.

"Okay, let's go!" I said to her.

I cursed my choice of words; she was convinced that walkies or ridies were imminent. I compounded my mistake by opening the bedroom door without restraining her. Bo shot through it, tore through my sitting room, and rocketed down the back stairwell of The Madam.

The Madam's original master bedroom is located on its second floor. But Hattie had converted the top level of the turret and the entire west side of the attic into a bedroom, sitting room and en suite bath for herself. She had used the converted attic for her bedroom and the turret for her sitting room. I had moved my bed into the turret. As small as it was, I loved its 180-degree view of my neighborhood and the Dallas skyline to the south.

The official door to my suite opened onto a third-floor hallway, but I used the servants' steeper stairwell rather than the grand staircase that dominated the middle of the house. I shivered every time I had to go down it—Hattie had slipped and tumbled to her death on those beautifully polished wooden stairs. The next morning, Tom had found her lying at the base of the staircase on the first floor. She was already gone, but at least her body hadn't lain there for long.

As I made the cramped turn in the stairs to the second floor, I heard Bo's dog door in the back entry flap several times with the force of her exit. As usual, she had nominated herself chairwoman of the greeting committee.

I was less than halfway to the first floor when the yelling erupted.

"Pit bull! Vicious pit bull! Get back! Get back!"

I sped the rest of the way down and yanked open the front door to be greeted by the sight of a terrified Bernie backed up against the porch rail. Bo wiggled with happiness at the prospect of a new friend. Tom, who knew Bo was harmless, stood nearby watching the show.

And it was a show. Some people are frightened of dogs.

Then there are the people who just don't like them. Despite
his effort to appear scared, Bernie obviously fell into the latter
category. He couldn't hide his smirk, and his eyes darted to the
sidewalk, hopeful for witnesses to the 'vicious' pit bull attack.

"Bo, go do potties!" I pointed at the yard

Bo refused to leave her visitors, but to appease me, she
moved a few feet away and lay down, sighing loudly. She
dropped her big, block head on her front paws and looked up
at us from beneath her wrinkled brow as if she was the most
mistreated dog on earth. I didn't know who the better actor
was, Bernie or Bo.

"Miss Thompson!" Bernie exclaimed, emphasizing the
Miss even though he knew I was a widow. "That is exactly
why we can't have an establishment such as the one you are
trying to open in this neighborhood. It just isn't safe. Dogs are
dangerous animals. And when you throw alcohol into the mix,
who knows what will happen?"

Bernie won the Best Actor award.

"Now, now, Bernie," Tom interjected, "you know not all
dogs are dangerous. Just look at my sweet Dixie. She is just a
love bug to everyone. But not all dog owners are as responsible
as I am." He shook his head sadly. Apparently, Tom was
gunning for the Best Supporting Actor award.

I've rarely met a dog I didn't like, but I wasn't sure Dixie
was a dog. She looked like a rat terrier and Chihuahua mix,
but acted like a rabid teacup badger. She snapped at anyone
who got close to her, and barked incessantly. Bo was her
favorite target. Whenever Tom and I met on the sidewalk
while walking them, Dixie would hide behind him, growling
menacingly. With Bo weighing a solid seventy pounds
compared to Dixie's soaking wet twelve, Dixie would have
done well to give her a wide berth. Luckily, Bo ignored her.

Tom and Bernie were as different as Bo and Dixie. Tom
was a born and raised Dallasite, while Bernie had immigrated
from New York City some twenty years before. Tom was tall

and good looking, in a used-car-salesman way. Bernie was short, squat, and barrel-chested. Tom's light brown hair fell perfectly into place and never budged. Either caps or years spent in braces had given him perfect teeth, and he had bleached them a blinding white. Bernie's hair was a muddy-colored, unruly mess that grew straight up from his scalp, and his teeth were crooked and stained.

Tom had lived his entire life in the house that adjoined The Madam's property, inheriting it from his mother when she'd passed away several years previously. He wrote literary fiction that had been lauded by the critics and reviewed in *The New York Times*. Bernie didn't live in the neighborhood. He didn't have a dog in this fight. Not even a little rat-dog like Dixie. Unfortunately, the Dallas City Council didn't feel the same.

Bernie lived in an area of Dallas that was an eclectic mix of restaurants, retail establishments and residences. He ran a blog called *Bernie's Backyard*. His sole purpose was targeting people and businesses he had vendettas against. He published whatever information he could beg, borrow, or steal about the owners of the businesses, their employees, and any residents he deemed to be 'bad neighbors.' What he couldn't prove, he suggested in innuendo.

Unfortunately, people love dirt and subscriptions to his site rose. When politicians defied Bernie, he blasted them and called for his readers to do the same. Politicians, being what they are, tried to stay on his good side. They invited him to events, took his calls, and slyly pointed him in the right direc-tion—usually against their opposition—for his 'investigative blog series.' Their support gave him credibility with his read-ers, which in turn garnered him more power. Somewhere along the way, Bernie tagged himself a community activist.

Bernie's backyard was nowhere near my backyard. In fact, the entire downtown area of the city of Dallas lay between us. But he offered his services—for a fee, of course—to neighborhoods that were dealing with sticky issues like businesses or politicians.

That was what really irked me. Someone was paying Bernie to keep The Whine Barrel from opening. I just didn't know who.

"Aren't you going to invite us in?" Tom asked.

"It's such a beautiful afternoon, let's sit out here," I replied, and led the way to a grouping of wicker chairs and a table on the porch. I wasn't letting these two yahoos into my house and validating their bad behavior.

When I had met with Bernie, Tom, and Council Member Crockett just two days earlier, I had agonized over the meeting preparations. We drank my best wine while I delivered an extensive presentation at one of the tables in the saloon. Then I gave them a comprehensive tour of The Madam, including the cellar where my wine was stored. All the preparation, touring, and talking had ended when Council Member Crockett said that the final code inspection was on indefinite hold. He claimed he needed time to review my business plan, my permits, and the "concerns of my neighbors and the other businesses in the neighborhood." *My ass!*

I had met with my closest neighbors before I even started the renovation project. I had taken blueprints and bottles of wine to their houses, sat on their sofas, and explained my vision. While they had expressed the normal concerns, most had tentatively supported the plan and several had shown outright enthusiasm.

The closest business in the neighborhood was the Dragonfly. I had no doubt that they had expressed concerns. With my primary business being a wine bar, and the intent to open the second floor as a bed and breakfast in the near future, The Whine Barrel would technically be in competition with the boutique hotel and their nightclub, The Perch.

While the Dragonfly pretended to be a unique urban hotel, it was owned by a multinational conglomerate, Cerny

Enterprises. The Whine Barrel couldn't compete with them. But the owner, Marek Cerny, had made the Dragonfly his primary residence and had been affronted that someone would open a business so close to his. He had even made an offer to buy The Madam, along with the surrounding land.

Over my dead body. Or my bankrupt body, which was much more likely to be the case. After I turned down Marek's offer, he and his partner, Grace O'Malley, had continued to call and send letters requesting meetings. I had ignored their overtures.

Tom shifted uneasily on his wicker chair and its creaking brought my attention back to the present. Bernie, on the other hand, seemed to feel no discomfort whatsoever.

"We'll do everything possible to keep you from opening this business," he said. "And we'll be successful."

I didn't respond. It was hard not to, but not for the reason you might think. Conflict is hard for me. I always want to smile and make everyone more comfortable. I've mentioned I'm a doormat, right?

"Your aunt leaves you this landmark house in this beautiful, old neighborhood that can trace its roots back almost to the founding of Dallas. Then you want to ruin both the house and the neighborhood by turning this property into a bar that caters to dogs," Bernie continued, baiting me.

I'm ashamed to admit that it worked, and I jumped into the fray.

"This will not be a bar that caters to dogs. It will be a wine store that specializes in Texas wines. Bottles of wine can be bought here and taken home. Yes, the license also allows for on-premise consumption, but I expect the bulk of the wine to leave The Whine Bar without ever being uncorked. In addition to wine, I will sell pet-related items. Owners can bring their dogs here to run about the property, like the city's Bark Parks, but with the added benefit of being able to enjoy a glass of wine and some light food."

None of this was news to Bernie or Tom. It was the exact spiel I had given them just two days before.

"I, I, I," Bernie interjected. "All I hear is I. Don't you care about anyone else but yourself? What about your neighbors? They will have to live with the increased traffic, the barking dogs, and the worst part: drunk drivers leaving your bar. Just consider the danger you are putting these innocent home-owners and their families in."

I wanted to explain to him, in detail, how big of an asshole he was, but I couldn't force the words out. I stopped my hand halfway to my mouth and tried to lower it discreetly back to my lap. I hadn't chewed my nails in years, but the disgusting habit still tried to reassert itself when I was upset.

"Bernie," Tom said in a wheedling tone, "I think we need to agree to disagree about what type of business manager Laramie will be and go inside to see what she has done to the place. Laramie, I know the final code inspection is on hold. Maybe if we like what we see, Bernie will ask Council Member Crockett to schedule it."

"Yeah, have you boarded up the dumbwaiter? What if a kid thinks it's an elevator and gets stuck in it?" Bernie shook his head sadly.

Bernie had harped on the dumbwaiter during the previous meeting with Crockett. In typical politician fashion, Crockett had nodded gravely each time Bernie expressed his concerns. But I had seen his eyes roll when Bernie pretended to get his finger stuck in one of its doors.

I stared past Bernie and Tom while I considered their request, and my gaze fell on the Dragonfly. With its buttercup-yellow paint, white trim around the windows, and red gera-niums in the flower boxes, the hotel looked like an oasis of calm, beckoning me. My resolve hardened.

"Not today, gentlemen. You said you had new concerns to discuss, but all we've done is cover old ground. As for the code inspection, I am pretty sure that Bernie had something to do with the holdup, so I don't think showing you around my place, AGAIN, is going to help. Now, if you'll excuse me, I have somewhere to be."

Tom gaped at my words. Bernie grinned. I'm sure that he was happy he had gotten a rise from me.

Bo stalked with me to the front door, glued to my side as if she expected trouble. I couldn't resist firing one parting shot.

"Bernie, don't come back to The Madam without an invitation. It won't be pretty if you do."

I closed the door, then leaned weakly against it. My legs shook like I had just climbed Mount Everest. In a way, I had. For most people this wouldn't have been a big moment, but for me it was huge. I had just made matters worse, but I didn't care. For once I would go down fighting. I refused to let Bernie, and whomever he was working for, push me around.

———

The buzzing of Officer's Mins' phone jolted me back to the present. It wasn't as if I had threatened Bernie's life in the meeting yesterday, but I had been adversarial. I would skim over that when I discussed it with the detectives. Of course, Tom had been there and would relay his version.

I shouldn't have goaded Bernie, but I had been livid. When the Dragonfly opened two years ago, it obtained a Special Use Permit, or SUP, to operate a business and a nightclub with alcohol sales in the area. The Whine Barrel was small potatoes compared to a hotel and nightclub, and besides, the city had already approved my permits.

Bernie's involvement marked the point when my dreams had come to a grinding halt. I wasn't positive who was paying him, but I had suspicions. Tom, though he acted like a well-meaning mediator with my best interests at heart, was tied with Marek Cerny at the top of my list.

Since Hattie's death, Tom had made several offers to buy

The Madam. He believed I had only inherited because Hattie hadn't updated her will after Jad died. The truth was, Hattie had updated the will, specifically leaving the house to me.

Tom had a lot to gain if The Whine Barrel didn't open. I had sunk every penny into renovating The Madam, getting the business permits, and buying wine stock. If Crockett delayed the opening much longer, I would be in dire straits. I could end up having to sell The Madam, although I would do everything within my power to make sure it didn't come to that.

Once again, police officers interrupted my reverie, but this time they were in suits and ties. The homicide detectives had arrived. The real show was about to begin.

7

WHO KNEW?

**57 Hours
(4:00 p.m. Saturday)**

"Detective . . ." I paused, trying to remember his name.
"Bodwyn," he replied.

"Detective Bodwyn, I've already told you. Lots of people know about the dumbwaiter: Hattie's friends, neighbors, and every workman involved in the renovation."

"I find it odd that the victim—just yesterday—was questioning the safety of this . . . contraption and today the code inspector finds his body stuffed in it."

"I think the better question is, what was Bernie doing in my home? I've already told you the door was open. He must have broken in to snoop around. He was fascinated with the dumbwaiter. Maybe he leaned in too far and fell from one of the upper floors." It was the only explanation I could think of for why Bernie was dead in my house.

"That could be it," Bodwyn replied, nodding slowly. "Do you mind if we look around?"

"Go ahead," I agreed quickly. "Hopefully, you can find something that will explain all this."

"Great!" Bodwyn responded. He slid a document, with the words CONSENT TO SEARCH printed across the top from a leather portfolio, filled in some blanks with the date and time, and printed my name.

"Please sign here," he said, tapping a line on the page with a calloused finger.

"What's this?" I asked hesitantly.

"It just protects any evidence that we find."

"Okay," I said slowly. I wasn't sure why, but the document made me uneasy. A quick skim revealed that though there were lots of words in it, the purpose was in the title. I was giving the police permission to search my property. I had nothing to hide, so I signed it and slid it back to him.

"Great," he said again. "We'll get to it."

"Don't you need me to show you around?" I asked as Bodwyn pushed back from the table and stood.

"No, we have a system and it's better if you stay out of the way."

He nodded at Officer Mins. As Bodwyn walked away, I looked over at the officer. I knew that the nod had been a signal for him to stay with me. But somehow this felt different, like I was being restrained. A ribbon of unease snaked through me.

———

Over three hours had passed since we'd found Bernie's body. Within moments of my signing the CONSENT TO SEARCH form, a battalion of officers sporting PES jackets had marched into the house. They had started in the kitchen with the body. But based on the sounds coming from above, a troop had splintered off to the third floor.

Footsteps on The Madam's porch drew my attention to the open front door. As the afternoon progressed, the saloon had dimmed. The daylight streaming through the entrance backlit the newcomer and created an otherworldly impression. The golden rays outlined his tall, muscular frame and imbued his blond hair with a golden hue. He looked like an avenging angel. As my eyes adjusted and I focused on his features, the feeling grew stronger, rather than diminishing. His icy blue eyes scanned the room and locked on me.

Van Anderson. He had been Jad's best friend and his partner in the Dallas Police Department. He usually made me uncomfortable and a little jumpy, but today, relief washed over me at the sight of him. He would be on my side, if only for the sake of Jad's memory.

Van nodded to me, and then crossed to Officer Mins' table. I couldn't hear their conversation, but when Mins' shoulders slumped, I knew what Van had said. Mins' long, sad look at me confirmed it.

I hadn't wanted to use the cop's widow card. Whenever I told people that I was a widow, which was as infrequently as possible, universal looks of pity crossed their faces. But the reaction was even more dramatic from police officers. It was as if they grew wings and tried to enfold me in them for protection.

That it made me uncomfortable was an understatement. It reminded me that I was a fraud. I had literally been packing my bags to leave Jad while he, unbeknownst to me, lay dying.

Mins chose a new table on the far side of the saloon, putting at least thirty feet between us. He studied a painting of the Texas flag and bottles of wine that hung on the wall nearby.

Van joined me at my table. "How are you doing?" he asked quietly. "And how did Bernie Wallach end up in your house? How do you even know the guy?"

"Not good," I replied just as quietly. "Van, I only met him a couple of weeks ago. I don't know why he was here or how he died."

"You weren't with him when he died?" Surprise, chased by

disbelief, crossed his perfect face. Most people have some type of imperfection, no matter how small. Not Van. Not a single scar or even a pockmark marred his face. I have known him for over a decade and I still find it hard not to stare at him.

"No," I whispered, "the code inspector and I found him."

The sound of voices and tramping feet drifted down from upstairs. Van looked upwards and asked in a low voice, "You found him upstairs?"

"No, in the dumbwaiter in the kitchen."

"Is there a crime scene up there?" Van asked, motioning above us.

"I don't know. They won't let me leave the saloon."

"Laramie, you're the homeowner. They have control over a crime scene, but they can't go through the rest of your house without a search warrant." He rose from his chair as he spoke.

"Van!" I grabbed his hand to stop him from charging upstairs and ordering everyone to get out. "I gave them permission to search the house."

Van sat back down heavily. "All of it?"

"All of it."

"Oh, Laramie, this isn't good." Van looked as nauseous as I felt. "Have they searched the cellar yet?"

"No, why?"

"It isn't important," he replied, waving his hand. "Where were you when Bernie died?"

"I don't know." He arched his eyebrows questioningly. "Van, they haven't told me anything."

Van checked to make sure Mins was out of earshot. The officer's focus was on his phone.

"The detectives probably don't know exactly when he died. They won't have a time frame until the ME gets here—the medical examiner" he explained at my puzzled look. He or she will be able to give them a general idea, based on a visual of the body. The ME will be able to calculate it with more precision when the body gets to the morgue, but the initial estimate will give the homicide detectives a starting point."

"I've gone over my schedule with Detective Bodwyn several times. Bernie and Tom dropped by here yesterday afternoon around four o'clock. They were here for maybe thirty minutes and then left."

"Harner, your creepy neighbor? Why would he bring Bernie Wallach here?" Van asked. He never missed an opportunity to take a shot at Tom. If it was anyone else, I might think that he was jealous of the attention Tom had showed me since I moved into The Madam, but Van still saw me as Jad's wife.

The floorboards above us creaked. Not waiting for an answer, Van waved his hand, giving me the universal 'move this story along' signal. I frowned at him.

I hadn't told Van about the issues with Bernie, or the meeting with Council Member Crockett. His family, the Andersons, have immense social standing and influence in Dallas. If Van had known, he would have viewed it as his sworn duty to fight the battle for me. I hadn't wanted to owe Van anything and would have involved him only as a last resort. Maybe not even then.

That duck was dead in the water now, though, and I had to figure out the quickest way to condense the story. I explained that Bernie had inserted himself in my business plans and that he and Tom had shown up the day before. In the interest of time, I left out Council Member Crockett's involvement. I could bring Van up to speed on that later.

"So Bernie was snide, degrading, and took obnoxiousness to a whole new level," I said, wrapping up the details of yesterday's meeting. "He kept harping about the dangers of my plan—mainly dogs, drunks, and the dumbwaiter."

"The dumbwaiter?"

"He said kids would fall in it."

"Ironic," Van said after a pause.

"Yeah, so Bernie didn't bring up any new concerns and I got the feeling that Tom was starting to side with him. I totally lost my temper and told them to leave."

"What did you do after they left?" Van asked, not meeting my eyes. "Did you do something fun for your birthday?"

I felt the blush crawling up my neck and my eyes watered. Van, of all people, had remembered my birthday. I stared down at our table, unsure how to present the information in the least damning, not to mention embarrassing, way possible.

When I didn't answer at once, Van sighed and leaned back in his chair. "I didn't know you were involved with someone. Give me his name and phone number so he can verify he was with you if the time of death falls in that window." His face was grim.

I didn't understand why Van would look grim at the idea of me dating. He should be relieved at being let off the 'you're responsible for Laramie' hook he had hung himself on since Jad's death. He had made it his personal duty to look after me, taking me out to places or joining me at The Madam. When I realized what he was up to, I put a stop to it. I refused to be anyone's pity project.

Plus, things had always been awkward between us. We came from completely different backgrounds. Van came from old—by Texas standards, anyway—oil money on his father's side. His mother could trace her lineage back for centuries to somewhere in Europe. Van didn't have to work, but he had decided years ago that being a police officer would be fun and had convinced Jad to go down that road with him.

I resented Van for pulling Jad into that life. Of course, it hadn't taken much effort on Van's part. Jad had always been up for an adventure and would have followed him through the gates of hell. I was the only thing Jad ever resisted him on. I had overheard Van trying to persuade Jad, on our wedding day no less, not to marry me. I had never admitted that to either of them.

"I'm not seeing anyone," I mumbled, refusing to meet Van's eyes. "I stayed at the Dragonfly last night and went to The Perch, the nightclub inside the hotel, to celebrate my upcoming thirtieth."

"By yourself?"

"By myself."

"Oh, Laramie." Sadness covered his face like a blanket. "Did you talk to anyone, meet anyone who can verify you were there?"

My face was an inferno.

"I got ready in the hotel room and went to The Perch at about ten o'clock. I'm not sure what time I left. I don't . . . I don't remember much from after I got to the club until I woke up in my hotel room around noon today. And don't look at me that way. I only had one drink." It was a big-ass drink, but he didn't need to know what. "Van, I know it sounds crazy, but I think I was drugged. I remember being in The Perch, talking to people. Then I had this strange dream that I was outside the hotel and that someone attacked me, but when I woke up, I was in my hotel room."

Van was as still as death for a few moments.

"Who did you talk to in The Perch?"

"The owner of the hotel, Marek Cerny. I also met his assistant or partner—I'm not really sure of the exact dynamic there—Grace O'Malley."

"Let me get this straight. You spent part of the evening last night with Marek Cerny? The same Marek Cerny who is trying to buy this land and tear down The Madam so he can expand his hotel? Damn it, Laramie! That guy is the worst kind of trouble on so many levels that you don't even know about, and you go out drinking with him?"

The explosion caught me off guard and I replied shakily, "No."

"No, you didn't hang out with him and Grace O'Malley last night? Christ! She's worse than he is! What were you thinking?" He shot to his feet and almost yelled the last part. Officer Mins stood, prepared to come to his aid. Van held up his hand to stop him, then stood, head lowered, trying to regain his composure.

A guy wearing a PES jacket stepped through the front door. He took in the scene, then directed a question at Mins. "Bodwyn?"

Mins pointed at the staircase. The officer gave Van and me a hard look then headed upstairs.

Van sat down and said grimly, "Tell me exactly what happened."

"While I was drinking my one drink in the bar," I responded, stressing the one, "Marek approached me. I didn't know who he was until he introduced himself. He welcomed me to his hotel but didn't seem too thrilled that I was there. I started to feel the effects of the drink, or whatever, and went to the club's bathroom. Grace walked in a few minutes behind me."

I paused, only now realizing what happened.

"She followed me in there. She was very nasty to me." I heard the whine in my voice. Crap. I sounded like an unpopular girl in junior high talking about the head cheerleader. "She told me I didn't belong there, and that I should leave."

"You didn't belong there," Van replied heatedly.

The people who went to The Perch were from his world and I wasn't. I can't deny that hurt.

"Go on. I need to hear it all."

"My memories are jumbled and fuzzy, but I think I decided to walk home. From there, I'm not really sure which memories are real or drug-induced. When I woke up, I was back in my hotel room." Van's face had morphed from sad to angry, and it was now thunderous. I braced for the worst. "There was a note from Marek telling me to stay in the hotel room. I didn't feel up to listening to a pitch to sell him The Madam, so I came home."

"He was in your hotel room," Van forced out between gritted teeth.

I was saved from responding by the PES officer and Detective Bodwyn coming down the staircase together. The PES officer stepped onto the porch, but the detective stopped at the bottom step. Van rose and crossed the room, hand extended, to greet him. The older officer held up his latex-gloved hands to show they were occupied. One gripped a brown paper grocery sack, and the other a clear plastic bag, the contents hidden by the large white label affixed to its side.

"Van H. Anderson," Bodwyn said, stressing Van's middle initial in the manner of a mother addressing a naughty child. "Why are you here? This is a homicide, not a robbery investigation."

Apparently, Bodwyn wasn't a member of the Van fan club either. If the detective wasn't such a douche, I would get a kick out of it. But he'd raised a good point. Van had been promoted to detective after Jad's death and had recently transferred to the Robbery Unit. Nothing about this situation fell under his jurisdiction.

"Bodwyn," Van said flatly with a nod, "I heard the call come out and decided to come by. Laramie's husband was my partner and best friend. So, you are looking at this as a homicide, not an accidental death?"

Bodwyn's lack of reaction proved that he had known I was a police widow, yet had never acknowledged it. The PES officer returned with another paper bag. When he handed it to the detective, a look passed between them. The officer, relieved of the bag, backed away and leaned against the staircase railing.

Bodwyn ignored Van's question and moved past him to address me.

"So, Mrs. Thompson, we found a few things in the search that we hope you can shed some light on. It would help us with our investigation."

A wave of relief washed over me. They had found something that would help explain what was going on.

"Yes! Anything you need."

A small movement behind Bodwyn caught my eye. Van shook his head at me. I ignored him. I had nothing to hide, and I wanted to help.

When Bodwyn sat down at the table with me, Officer Mins crossed the room to stand next to Van. The sight of the two of them unnerved me, and all the times I'd seen Jad and Van standing together flashed through my memory like a slideshow on fast-forward. They had been almost the same height and build, and their eyes a matching blue. Van's golden blond hair had been the perfect foil for Jad's jet black. I had called them Yin and Yang.

Why was I seeing Jad everywhere today?

Bodwyn thumped the three bags onto the table. He opened the paper bag the PES Detective had handed him and pulled out a length of black material. He laid it on the table in front of me and raised his eyebrows expectantly. I picked up the black dress I had worn the night before. It was still damp, but now that it was unfolded, I noticed something else: the entire back of the dress was little more than strips of fabric held together by threads.

I raised my eyes to Bodwyn's and asked, "What happened to my dress?"

Bodwyn shrugged but didn't answer.

I decided to let the question pass for the moment, but I still needed answers. "This dress was in my overnight bag. When I said you could search my house, it was to find out how Bernie got in and to determine how he died. Not to go through my personal things."

"The dress that you hid in your yard." While it could have been a question, Bodwyn turned it into a sneer.

"It wasn't hidden," I responded, mentally crossing my

fingers. I had concealed the bag, just not in the way that Bodwyn implied.

"The consent to search form that you signed allows us to search the entire property and its contents." Bodwyn opened the other paper bag and removed a dishtowel.

"That's from my kitchen. I wiped my hand on it after I felt for Bernie's pulse," I said, sounding defensive even to my ears.

"You tampered with the body?" Bodwyn asked with exaggerated drama, his eyebrows almost disappearing into his hairline.

Van snorted loudly but, before I could respond to the deliberate misrepresentation, Bodwyn laid the plastic bag on the table and I saw the contents.

"Is that Jad's gun?" I asked, finally angry.

Again, Bodwyn only shrugged.

"Did you get that from my bedside table?" I demanded, my voice rising.

"As a matter of fact, I did," Bodwyn replied with a self-satisfied grin.

"Officer Mins, did you just hear Mrs. Thompson identify all three items, acknowledge that they are hers and were located on her property?"

"Yes," Officer Mins responded regretfully.

"Mrs. Thompson, we're going to conduct our questioning in the homicide offices at police headquarters. You have the right to remain silent."

"Conduct questioning?" Van broke in angrily. "You've been questioning her, and if this is the first time you have informed her of her rights, everything up to this point is inadmissible."

"But Detective Anderson," Bodwyn replied innocently, "I didn't ask Mrs. Thompson a single question. I merely laid out the items on the table and she identified and claimed them. Her *res gestae* statements should be fully admissible in court. If it comes to that. I only asked her about tampering with Mr.

Wallach's body, to which she didn't respond. Officer Mins, did you hear me ask Mrs. Thompson a single question regarding any of the items?"

"No," replied Officer Mins, resigned to his part in all this.

Detective Bodwyn stood up, pushed back his blazer, and withdrew handcuffs from a leather case on his belt. "Mrs. Thompson, please stand up and put your hands behind your back."

I looked helplessly at Van. He clenched his hands by his sides, and although he looked ready to explode, he nodded at me.

"Laramie don't say another word. An attorney will meet you at headquarters. Not one word to anyone except the phrase 'I want an attorney' until he arrives."

Bodwyn paused in the handcuffing process and sent Van a look that could kill. Van stared him down unabashedly.

"If you decide to waive that right, anything you say can and will be used against you in a court of law," said Bodwyn, picking up where he'd left off as the cuffs tightened on my wrists with a ratcheting sound. He droned on about my rights as he walked me through the front door of The Madam and down the sidewalk to the waiting police car.

8

UP A CREEK

56 Hours
(5:00 p.m. Saturday)

The ride through downtown Dallas to the Jack Evans Police Headquarters building was mercifully short. Officer Mins escorted me to the Homicide Unit's offices and locked me in a tiny room about a third of the size of the interrogation rooms shown on television. It also lacked the two-way mirror that no self-respecting TV cop show interrogation room would be without. Instead, I was sure that there was a hidden camera and they, whoever they were, were watching my every move.

From the moment the cuffs went on at The Madam, I had refused to answer any questions. This was harder than it sounds. I had been raised to respect authority, and having been married to a cop made me want to trust them. I hadn't killed Bernie. Surely, if I could just explain it to them, they would understand. But I held firm. Van had tried to warn me before I opened my big mouth. I wasn't going to say another word until the attorney he'd promised me showed up.

A Detective Eyler had been the first cop to try to interrogate me in the small, stuffy room. Bodwyn had stayed at The Madam to continue looking for evidence. Eyler, almost Bodwyn's exact twin in both attitude and cheap suit, had been easy to resist because he was a dick.

Detective Branch was next up. He was probably somewhere in his early fifties. With his easy smile, salt-and-pepper hair and friendly brown eyes he looked like a good father, or just a genuinely nice man. I refused the soft drink he offered and he only nodded, then told me about a murder he had worked where Jad had been the first uniformed officer on the scene. When he offered his condolences, I nearly broke.

The *pièce de résistance* came when he assured me that this was all a misunderstanding and he wanted to help me clear it up. I leaned forward in my chair and opened my mouth to explain but stopped myself just in time. He was playing good cop to Detective Eyler's bad cop, so I repeated my request for a lawyer. After a few moments Detective Branch sighed, closed the folder he had brought with him, and left the room.

Several hours later, I was still waiting for that lawyer. I was scared. I ached all over and I wasn't sure what hurt worse, my throbbing head or my burning eyes. Despite the water I had drank at The Madam, my thirst was overwhelming. In short, I felt like I had been run over by a semitruck and left flattened on a hot Texas highway.

The door to the room opened again and a tall, fit man who could be a model for *GQ* entered. His light gray three-piece suit—I didn't know men even wore those anymore—probably cost more than the entire wine stock I had bought for The Whine Barrel and contrasted startlingly with his perfectly styled jet-black hair. He carried himself with a quiet confidence that showed he was much older than his smooth, unlined face implied. The guy must have had some expensive work done. He had the well-rested, healthy look that only piles of money paid to a majorly talented doctor could buy.

"Hello, Laramie. I'm Andrew Healy. Marek Cerny hired me to represent you. Let's get you out of here."

9

HOWL AT THE MOON

**51.5 Hours
(8:30 p.m. Saturday)**

I'm not sure what Healy discussed with the homicide detectives before he walked into the interrogation room, but when he walked me out, Detective Branch was waiting for us with my purse and cellphone. He looked as if he wanted to say something to me, but after a glance at Healy, he handed over my property without a word.

I didn't know how Marek Cerny had found out about my arrest and I didn't care. That he would use this as added leverage in his bid for The Madam didn't concern me either. I just wanted out, so I would accept his help. For now.

Another detective walked us out of the office and to the elevators. During the wait for it to arrive, I looked him up and down. He wore the standard detective's uniform—an inexpensive suit and a white shirt with the sleeves rolled up. He had discarded his suit jacket and the butt of his semi-automatic peeped out of the holster under his right arm, identifying him as a lefty.

That reminded me that they still had Jad's handgun, which was fine by me. Growing up in the country, I had learned to shoot. It wasn't something I enjoyed, though, and I hadn't fired a gun in years. After Jad's death, I hadn't felt comfortable keeping his pistol. But everyone seemed to expect me to cherish it, so I hadn't wanted to admit that I didn't want the darn thing.

Next to Healy, the detective looked decidedly rumpled. I wasn't sure what it was about the attorney but, even though the detective was armed, Healy seemed the more dangerous of the two. He reminded me of a shark: still, unblinking, beautiful but unnerving, and somehow, you just knew he was deadly. Eerie vibe aside, I was glad he was here. When the police haul you in for murder, you want a shark for an attorney.

The detective rode down with us to the first floor, then walked us out to the lobby and past the guard station. After a slight nod, he turned and headed back to the elevator.

Night had fallen while I was in custody. A bright, full moon hung just above the horizon, its light reflecting off the huge silver police badge on the side of the headquarters building. I took a deep breath that felt as though it was my first full one in hours, maybe all day. I stopped and soaked in the moonlight and the cool night air. I felt better and, lo and behold, my head didn't ache. Finally, the hangover was gone.

While I savored my freedom, Healy continued toward a row of cars parked at the curb in front of the building. Not quite sure what I was supposed to do, I trailed after him. Across the street I could make out the silhouette of the old Sears and Roebuck factory that had been converted to loft apartments. To my right was a gorgeous view of the downtown Dallas skyline. I wanted a moment to take it all in, but I saw that Healy had joined two people standing next to the vehicles.

"The only thing they have on her right now is the gun and the bloody dress," Healy said as I joined the trio. The sight of Marek Cerny and Grace O'Malley stunned me, but I guess it shouldn't have, since Marek had hired the attorney.

Healy addressed Marek. "The preliminary time of death falls into the period that we know she was at the hotel. I presented them with your signed affidavit attesting to that fact."

I had thought Grace was stunning last night in the red dress. But tonight, wearing black jeans, riding boots and a white shirt that buttoned up the front, she was, if possible, even more breathtaking. Marek, in sable-toned pants and a matching collared shirt, looked much the same as the evening before. Basically your run-of-the-mill dark, foreboding, wildly sexy man.

"They will want to talk to you in person at some point. But without ballistics on the gun to prove it was the murder weapon, and with her refusal to talk," they all looked at me like I was a child who deserved a gold star, "they aren't ready to charge her. Yet. It will hang on the forensics from the dress and the ballistics result."

"Bernie was shot?" I asked. I had already gathered that from the mention of ballistics, but I wanted to confirm it.

Healy gave me a curt nod. Then he removed a set of keys from his pocket and, after a silent blinking of lights from a sleek, two-seater silver Mercedes, said, "I'll be in touch when I know more." Without even a wave, the shark folded himself into the low-slung car and drove away.

"I don't understand," I stammered, rushing to fill the awkward silence. "Van was hiring an attorney for me. Why did you?"

Marek and Grace exchanged a brief look that I couldn't interpret, but waves of hostility rolled off her.

"We need to talk," said Marek.

Well duh, I thought. I managed to keep the juvenile sentiment to myself, but just. The events of the last twenty hours
made me feel like a kindergartener in a play directed by adults
who wouldn't take the time to explain the plot to her.

"This isn't the place to do it," Grace interjected. "We need
to be on the move."

"Grace is correct," Marek agreed. "We will talk en route."

"En route to where?" I asked, even as Grace climbed
behind the steering wheel of a sleek, black sedan, and Marek
held open the rear door for me. "I have to call Van and let
him know where I am."

Marek had tensed both times I said Van's name. The first
time might have been a fluke, but I was sure that the second
time meant something. And his reaction had been minor
compared to Van's explosion this afternoon when I mentioned
Marek. How did they know each other, and what had created
the bad blood between them?

"There will be time for that on the way. Get in now, Mrs.
Thompson," said Marek shortly, motioning me into the car.
His formality after hiring the lawyer seemed touchingly old
fashioned, despite his tone. The mysterious accent and the
way he said my last name sent tingles down my spine. I might
collapse into a helpless heap if he said my first name. This
man was sex on a stick. Scary sex on a stick, but that somehow
made him more appealing.

We stared into each other's eyes for a few seconds. Then I
felt the soft leather of the car seat underneath me as I slid
across it to let Marek climb in beside me. How had that
happened? I didn't get in cars with strangers, even sexy
strangers who hired shark attorneys for me. Especially sexy
strangers who hired shark attorneys for me. My, I'm quite
fanciful today, I thought as I tried to tamp down a small
bubble of hysteria.

As Grace pulled away from the curb, I took my phone

from my purse and tapped on Van's name from my recent contacts. Marek's hand covered mine, stilling it before I could hit the connect button.

"That can wait. We need to talk about last night." After a pause, he continued, "I think you were drugged by the . . . guy who sat next to you at the bar. I'm not sure why you would be a target. I need you to tell me exactly what you remember from last night."

Grace had navigated the streets south of downtown and was now taking the entrance ramp for I-30 Eastbound. I had been trying to watch where we were going, but Marek's comments gained him my full attention. I didn't know whether to be relieved that he also thought I had been drugged, or horrified that I might have been right.

"The guy next to me kept bumping me, and he smelled awful. I didn't notice anything else about him except that he was huge. I was trying to ignore him." I paused, not sure if that was what he wanted to know, but Marek nodded for me to continue.

"I remember talking to you and then . . ." I hesitated, meeting Grace's eyes in the rearview mirror. I looked away. ". . . I spoke with Grace in the bathroom. Things get a little fuzzy after that."

"Oh, Christ! I knew that she was going to be worthless!"

"Grace!" Marek warned sharply.

Grace snorted. But wisely, to my way of thinking, she didn't say anything else.

I took a deep breath and continued, "Actually, I thought I was attacked, but I couldn't have been, right?"

Marek frowned, "Why couldn't you have been attacked?"

"When I woke up this morning, I didn't have any marks on me."

"None?" Marek asked with a slightly raised eyebrow. "Not even a bruise?"

"Yes, just one bruise," I replied, fingering the scarf that covered it. I rushed on, "But the attack was brutal and there was blood. There should be more marks. Maybe it was all a drug-induced dream?"

Marek ignored my question. "Do you remember anything after the attack? Did you hear anything else? See anyone?"

"No," I whispered. I thought about the face that had hovered over me, but I knew for sure that had been a dream or a hallucination. Then I remembered something else.

Marek's eyes bored into me. "What is it? You are hiding something."

I decided to part with half of it. "It doesn't make any sense." At his impatient look, I continued, "I thought someone whispered in my ear, "Temple sends his regards," and then something about his cross. A true cross?"

The air in the car turned blue with cursing. They both swore in foreign languages I didn't recognize, but you know bad words when you hear them.

I raised my voice to be heard over the swearing. "Do you know someone named Temple? I don't."

Grace and Marek simmered down on the language, but neither answered my question. Taking that as a yes, I moved down my question list.

"Who found me, and how did I end up in my room?" *Who undressed me* was my main question, but mortification kept me from asking it.

Marek hesitated, but, with a resigned look, responded, "When I noticed that you had left The Perch," at that he gave the back of Grace's head a significant look, "I knew some-thing was wrong, so I checked your room. When you weren't there, I thought you might have decided to go home. I found you. The attackers had left. I returned you to your room and called Grace to put you to bed."

"Oh," I said, feeling vindicated. It was obvious that he was leaving out parts of his story as well. It was just a matter of figuring out how our gaps matched up. I looked at his face, really looked, trying to compare the two faces and features in my mind. Both had dark hair and the same basic bone structure, but where Marek's face was all hard planes and angles, the face in my memory was slightly rounder and softer. Still, with drugs in my system, I could have superimposed the face over Marek's features when he found me.

Marek's words broke into my thoughts. "Did you see the note I left that instructed you not to leave the room until we had a chance to talk?"

I nodded and looked down at my phone, still in my lap.

Marek said a few more choice words under his breath. "Have you told Anderson any of this?" he asked.

"Van? Yes, I told him some of it earlier, right before the police arrested me."

Marek paused, his head cocked to one side, before asking, "What was his theory?"

Theory? Van hadn't had a theory. He had been too busy being pissed off about me being with Marek and Grace. I didn't share that with Marek, but his shrug indicated he already knew the truth. "Mrs. Thompson, I'm not sure how much you know about Van." He paused and grimaced when Grace snorted again from the front seat. "It may not be in your best interest to trust him too far on this issue. He is focused on a much larger agenda. He might have your best interests at heart . . . and then again, they might get overshadowed by other, let's say priorities."

Agendas and priorities? Playboy Van? Not likely.

Just when I thought I couldn't get any more confused, Marek changed directions. "Someone drugged you, attacked you, and framed you for a murder. Do you know who or why?"

I shook my head. When he summed it up like that, it was clear something was going on, but I'd be darned if I knew what. Then, like the moon sliding out from behind dark clouds, the answer became clear to me.

"You."

"What?"

"The only person who has anything to gain by this is you. You've been trying to buy my property so you can expand the Dragonfly. If I'm out of the way, you have a clear path to The Madam."

I slapped my hand over my mouth. Now that he knew I knew, he would have to get rid of me. Just like he got rid of Bernie. Like an idiot, I had gotten into the car with him and then blurted out that I was onto him as soon as the thought crossed my mind. It screamed of every bad B movie ever made. Silly female finds murder victim in her home. Dangerous stranger (and Marek oozed danger) hires attorney to get girl out of jail so that he can lure her into his car along with his henchman, or henchwoman in this case. He murders silly female and dumps her body along some deserted road. I don't know that I would blame him if he killed me. Obviously, I was too stupid to live.

In many a novel I have read the expression 'His eyes blazed.' Honestly, I'd always thought it was crap. I mean, really, how do eyes blaze? Well, it wasn't crap. Marek's eyes turned red for an instant. Oh, damn! This was it! Surely he wouldn't kill me in the back of his car, would he? I didn't even know if this was his car. Maybe he stole it just to murder me in.

A bark of laughter from the front seat broke through my frenzied thoughts.

"Damn! I'm starting to like this kid," said Grace. "She isn't the brightest bulb, but she is mad bold."

"Me?" Marek said. "I no longer want The Madam. I want us to work together. Which you would know if you had returned even one phone call or letter from us!" His eyes had returned to their normal melted-chocolate brown—maybe I had imagined the red thing—and he was clearly trying to calm down. In a quieter voice, he asked, "Why would I have my attorney get you out of jail?"

"I wasn't in jail," I reminded him, although it was semantics. I didn't respond to his assertion that he wanted to go into business together. Why would a multinational corporation want to work with me?

"You needed to make sure I couldn't tie you to any of it." My voice dropped to a whisper. "You needed me out so you could tie up loose ends."

I glanced out my window to get my bearings and saw that Grace had exited the freeway and we were in Deep Ellum. Deep Ellum is an area comprised of several blocks crowded with bars, tattoo parlors, and cafés. The neon signs in windows and over doors created a cacophony of colored light throughout the funky area. It was a busy Saturday night and the overflow of people and parked cars that lined the narrow streets had slowed our progress to a crawl. Seeing a chance to escape, I yanked on the handle and threw my shoulder against the door.

The door didn't give an inch. It was locked and the child safety feature was probably engaged, too. *Smooth move, Laramie.* That was going to leave a bruise, but I refused to give them the satisfaction of rubbing my aching shoulder.

Grace's eyes met mine again in the rearview mirror and she smiled slightly. "Don't try that again." Then, sliding her eyes to Marek, she added, "The kid's got spunk. I'll give her that."

I knew I should take offense at Grace calling me a kid, especially since she couldn't have been much older than me. But in my entire life, no one had ever accused me of having spunk. I felt an odd warmth spreading over me. I tried not to smile back at her when our eyes met in the rearview mirror again, but failed miserably.

"If you two are done having a moment," Marek said acerbically, "I will explain. When you were attacked last night you nearly died. To save you, you were infected with, for lack of better terminology, a virus. Roughly seventy-two hours from the time of infection it will take full effect. So," Marek checked his watch, "we are down to approximately fifty-one hours until life, as you know it, ends. While you were disobeying my orders to stay put, and to further complicate matters getting yourself arrested, I spent the day looking for answers. Of which I have none. And now I find out Temple is involved. Which makes me think you know a lot more than we thought you did. His involvement makes me want to *not* be involved. But until some of this is sorted out, we are moving you to a safe place, where you will remain until I say otherwise. And you are going to tell us everything you know about Temple and the True Cross. Hell, maybe you even asked for the bite."

His voice had risen steadily as he talked until by the end, although not quite yelling, he was on the loud side. He was well and truly peeved. I am an expert at recognizing the peeved state, as I often have the same effect on my mama.

The car jerked to a halt, and I slammed against the seat in front of me.

"We've got trouble!" Grace yelled. She threw the car into reverse and hit the gas. We shot approximately five feet backward before, with a loud crunch, we jerked to a stop again. The roof of the sedan caved in over Grace's head and the vehicle rocked.

Grace bailed out of the car and disappeared. I gasped when the roof caved in again, this time over our heads. From the noise and the shaking, I would have sworn there were two people on top of the car engaged in a fight to the death.

"Laramie! Laramie!" Marek yelled at me as he shook my arm to get my attention. "I've got to get out there and help Grace. DO NOT leave this car under any circumstances. Promise me!" he shouted over the din.

I nodded mutely. How had a fender bender devolved into this melee? Then, just as quickly as Grace had disappeared, Marek was gone. He hadn't seemed to have any trouble with the childproof locks. This time the bubble of hysteria was much larger and harder to tamp down.

Through the open car door I saw reserved, perfectly attired and coiffed Marek brawling with another man on the sidewalk. I considered his order to stay in the car, but he was insane. His talk of viruses and bites, not to mention the events that were currently transpiring on the roof of the car and the sidewalk, convinced me of that. Insanity trumps orders and promises, right?

I slid across the seat and out of the car through the door Marek had left open. I tried to get my bearings, but the crowd that had formed around us blocked my view. The streetlights were suspiciously dark.

The cheers and jeers from the crowd focused my attention back on the brawl. Marek was holding his own. As I watched, he punched the man he was fighting in the jaw, knocking him into a nearby parked car with enough force to dent the door panel.

At a sound from above, I looked up and my breath caught. Grace, her alabaster skin glowing in the moonlight, crouched on the roof of the car. She was faced off against a guy larger than the one Marek fought. When he slashed at Grace with a knife, she easily evaded it and parried in return, the moonlight glinting off the dagger she wielded. Her red hair swirled around her, and she laughed with each slash, clearly in her element. I felt twin stabs of envy and awe. What I wouldn't give to be so fearless.

With the streetlights out, the scene was illuminated by an eerie mix of the moonlight, the neon glow from the business signs, and the headlights of the cars backed up behind the crumpled sedan. Initially I attributed what I saw to the lighting. Then I remembered that Deep Ellum had always attracted an offbeat crowd, and Halloween was only a few weeks away. The men Marek and Grace fought wore fake-fur wolf masks that disappeared into the collars of their shirts.

Something buzzed in my hand and I realized I was still clutching my phone. Van's face filled the screen. I touched the connect button. With Marek and Grace's attention otherwise occupied, I melted into the crowd.

THE VOODOO PRINCESS

51 Hours
(9:00 p.m. Saturday)

"Laramie! Why the hell are you with Marek?" Van yelled by way of greeting.

Bad news travels fast.

"Van! I need help! I got away from Marek and Grace, but they'll be looking for me soon. I'm in Deep Ellum. Can you pick me up?"

"What street are you on?"

I looked around for a landmark and spotted a café where I used to meet Jad and Van on the nights I had driven into Dallas to eat dinner with them. Another loud crash drew my attention back to the brawl. The crowd was growing.

"I'm on Elm, about half a block from The Fried Armadillo. I'll head there and hide in the women's bathroom. Call me when you're out front." I broke into a fast walk.

"No! Too close—they can track you to there. Two blocks past the Armadillo is a shop on the south side of the street named The Voodoo Princess. It's tiny so you have to watch for it. Get there as fast as you can. I'll call LaRue and let her know you're coming. Run! Now!"

The phone line went dead. Heeding Van's order, I broke into a quick trot and, after a few steps without tripping over my feet, I picked up the pace to a slow jog. Half a block later, I pushed into an all-out run. Athleticism and coordination have never been my strong points, but tonight I was flying.

The tops of the storefronts were uneven. The taller buildings cast shadows while the lower ones allowed the moonlight to illuminate the sidewalk. My strides lengthened to the point that it seemed my feet only touched the dark patches and I took flight each time I passed through the moonbeams.

I crossed several streets, barely pausing to check for cars. Ahead, a lone woman stood illuminated by light cast through the windows of a business. Please let it be Van's friend, I thought as I slid to a stop in front of her like a cutting horse in a show arena.

"LaRue?" She didn't move. A quick glance at the store's sign confirmed I was at The Voodoo Princess. Why was she blocking the door to the shop when we needed to get inside and hide?

"I'm Laramie! Van Anderson told me to come here."

Instead of responding, she leveled the largest, shiniest revolver I had ever seen directly at my chest.

I struggled to pry my eyes off the gun and look at her. She was around Van's age and stood five feet nothing, with styled hair the color of a ginger snap brushing her shoulders. It complemented her large amber eyes and, combined with a latte-toned complexion, gave her an exotic appearance.

Remembering the boatload of crazy behind me, I tore my eyes from her and her gun to glance frantically over my shoulder. Fortunately, none of the crazies—Marek, Grace or the wolf worshippers—were on my tail. Unfortunately, the crowd around the wreckage had shrunk, which meant the fight was over. They would be searching for me soon, if they weren't already.

"Either take me inside or let me go," I demanded, without the foggiest notion of where I would go.

She pushed open the door to The Voodoo Princess with her foot then motioned me through it with the gun. She followed me inside and, with accomplished precision, held the revolver in one hand while shutting and locking the door behind us with the other. The barrel never wavered from my chest for even a nanosecond.

She had decided to help me but not to trust me. *Great.*

"Walk to the back of the store and through the black curtain," she ordered.

The shop was tiny—about twelve feet wide by twelve feet deep. The shelves lining the walls displayed merchandise with a decidedly witchy bent. I thought that voodoo and witchcraft were different, but I didn't know what that difference was. I passed dolls, macabre figurines, charms, assorted herbs, and incense in the few steps it took me to reach the black curtain that extended across the back of the store.

My toe caught as I stepped through a gap in the curtain and I stumbled into a room that was probably four times larger than the store. It was equal parts warehouse, kitchen, potting shed, garage and . . . command center? On one side of the space was a desk with several monitors on it. Based on the tableaus on the screens, multiple cameras had been positioned for optimal views of the entrances to the building, street and alley. And . . . I squinted to make out the image on one of the monitors . . . the roof? Why did a novelty shop need that kind of security?

A boxy gold SUV hulked in the middle of the warehouse. I wasn't up on my car models, but I couldn't miss the large Mercedes emblem in the grill. Most of the wall behind the Mercedes consisted of a large, partitioned steel door that resembled a garage door designed for a nuclear bunker. A smaller, person-sized steel door was next to the larger one, hung barn-door style and secured with enough locks and rein-forcements to hold off the four horsemen of the apocalypse.

The petite woman—I still didn't know if she was Van's LaRue or not—followed me, holding the gigantic gun at the ready. She pushed a button on the wall. A door the width of the shop sprang to life and slid closed along the track I had tripped on. It settled into place with a mechanical sigh, covering the opening into the store and cutting us off from the outside world. I wasn't sure whether to be relieved that I was safe from the crazies outside or concerned that I was locked in an unbreachable space with Annie Oakley.

She waved the gun to a small table and two chairs in the middle of the room. The grouping reminded me of the setup in the interrogation room at police headquarters, except that a deck of tarot cards was spread across this table. Not for the first time today, I felt like I had fallen down the same rabbit hole as Alice.

"Sit down," she ordered.

I moved slowly to the chair she indicated and lowered myself into it. She remained standing, keeping a healthy distance between us, her eyes (and gun) trained intently on me.

"LaRue?" I asked hesitantly.

"Yes." She didn't volunteer any more information.

With nothing else to do, I studied her. Even under the industrial fluorescent lighting, she was beautiful, bringing to mind an exotic Tinker Bell. I envied her the striking looks and petite hourglass figure, but not the sadness in the tawny eyes that studied me right back. Although she tried to keep her face expressionless, I could tell that she found me lacking.

Pounding on the back door caused me to jump and let out a small shriek, effectively ending our staring contest. My nerves were frayed from the past twenty-four hours, and a fairy holding a gun on me didn't help. I followed LaRue's gaze to the monitors and saw Van on one of the screens, standing in front of his red Chevy truck. She sidled past me and managed all the locks and bolts on the smaller steel door without lowering the gun.

I wanted to know what her workout was. She had to have quite the arm strength to hold the gun that steady for as long as she had.

Van rushed into the room, not slowing down until he reached me. He pulled me out of the chair and into an embrace before I could protest. In all the years I had known Van, he had never held me the way he did now. A few half-hearted hugs in greeting when Jad was alive and a few side hugs after Jad's death made up our hug history. This type of embrace, with full body contact from head to toe and his cheek pressed against the top of my head, was completely new territory for us. His body was molded against mine and damn, but it felt good. Way too good. And I had thought this day couldn't get any stranger.

"Van!" LaRue's shrill voice broke into my increasingly heated thoughts.

Van pulled back like he had been burned and spun to face her. Her stricken expression confused me until I realized her absurd assumption. I wanted to reassure her that things weren't like that between us. Obviously, Van would never be involved with someone as ordinary as me.

"Thank you, LaRue. I don't know what I would have done if . . . I couldn't have gotten to her in time."

LaRue's expression changed from shocked to mad. "We have to talk," she said between gritted teeth, and motioned him to the farthest corner of the warehouse.

Van squeezed my arm, then joined her. They huddled together; he had his back to me and she faced him, slightly offset so she could keep an eagle eye on me. Her death grip on the gun hadn't relaxed, but she no longer pointed it directly at me.

I couldn't make out all of their whispered conversation, but did hear, "I can't believe you would send her here" and several murmured, "I'm sorrys."

Finally, a slightly hysterical and louder, "She's not right Van! You didn't see her running down the street. Her feet barely touched the ground. You need to figure out how this happened. We have to fix it. One way or another. It's your job."

Someone wasn't happy about a murder suspect being sent to her shop. I wouldn't be thrilled with him either, if the roles were reversed. But . . . I got the feeling that there was more to it than that. And the comment about my running? I had been going fast, but in my defense, I had been escaping crazy kidnappers and wolf worshippers.

"We need to leave. Now!" Van proclaimed.

"Finally, something we can agree on," LaRue replied. She pulled a large, black Coach purse from underneath the monitor console and swung it onto the shoulder of the arm not holding the gun. "If you hadn't blocked the door with that monstrosity, we could take mine. But I guess there's no help for it."

Van strode across the warehouse, navigating around the counters laden with potted plants and jars filled with who knew what—maybe eye of newt. Was that even a real thing? And if so, was it used in voodoo or witchcraft? I still didn't know the difference. With those thoughts, I realized I didn't know anything about anything, and there was the rub.

"Come on, Laramie," Van said. "Marek can't be far behind. We're going through the door and straight into my truck. I'll have you and keep you safe the whole time." He grabbed my arm and propelled me toward the steel door he'd entered through only minutes before.

"No." I braced myself. I must have been stronger than I thought because, despite his forward momentum, he came to a halt and couldn't budge me.

"Laramie," he pleaded, "I'll explain everything when we have you safe, but we are in grave danger right now. We have to leave before they track you here."

The thought that I was putting Van in danger almost made me relent, but then I steeled my will. I always did what I was told. *Good little Laramie.* Already tonight that policy had gotten me kidnapped, involved in a car wreck, and awarded a front row seat at a brawl. I wouldn't get into another vehicle until I knew what was going on.

When I said as much to Van, I'm sure he contemplated picking me up bodily and carrying me to the truck. Then his shoulders sagged, and I knew I had won. We sat at the small table.

"Van! We have to get out of here now!"

"LaRue, if they were coming, they would already be here."

"Who's to say they aren't out there?" LaRue turned back to the monitors, continuing under her breath, "In the dark."

Van ignored her question but closed his eyes briefly at her comment. He opened his eyes and turned his attention to me.

"Laramie, I want to give you answers, but I'm not sure what is going on. Please explain to me why Marek would hire an attorney for you, and what would possess you to leave the station with him and Grace."

"How do you know about the attorney?" I asked.

"Detective Branch called me as a personal favor when you left. Laramie, Cerny is one of those guys who is always around when bad things happen, but they never get pinned to him. The simple fact that he hired you an attorney makes you look guilty."

"Van, I was just so happy when that attorney showed up and walked me out of there . . ." I trailed off. For the first time I wondered why Van hadn't sent an attorney like he had promised. But he motioned for me to continue, and it didn't seem like the time to pick at that bone.

"When Healy and I got outside, Marek and Grace were waiting. They promised to tell me what was going on. Bless their hearts, I didn't realize he and Grace were unbalanced until after I was trapped in the car with them. I tried to get out before the wreck, but the doors were locked. Afterwards, I was able to slip into the crowd while they were fighting."

"Wreck? Fight?" Van's voice rose. He took a calming breath, "We'll get to that in a minute but, first, what made you think they were . . . unbalanced?"

"Remember how I told you I thought I had been drugged last night and dreamt I was attacked?"

Van gave a tight nod. I looked over his shoulder and saw that LaRue was watching us. The hands that had been so steady now trembled, and her eyes were huge. I looked back at Van: he was pale as death.

"Marek believed I was drugged." If Van hadn't looked so shaken I would have taken a dig, since he hadn't believed me earlier. Or at least he had been so busy yelling at me for being at Marek's hotel that he had skimmed right over that part of the story. "When I told them what I dreamt had been said to me, he and Grace practically exploded. He said that I was attacked, and that to save me I had been infected with a virus, but my life would still end."

Van leaned back heavily in the chair and covered his face with his hands.

"See, crazy talk," I said, but my voice faltered. His reaction scared me more than Marek's had.

"Van," LaRue said from the corner. When he didn't respond she said again, a little louder, "Van."

"Just hold on, LaRue," Van said from behind his hands. "Let me figure this out."

"I have it figured out. We need to handle it."

"What is it? Will someone please tell me what's going on?" I was tired of everyone talking in circles around me—first Marek and Grace, and now Van and LaRue.

Van lowered his hands and leaned toward me. "Laramie, this is important. I need you to answer my questions as specifically as possible. Do you understand?"

"Van, I'll answer any question you have," I replied in the same 'I'm talking to a second grader' tone he had just used on me. It went right over his head.

"What did you dream the attacker said to you?"

I had been thinking about this since Marek and Grace's reaction in the car. I was pretty sure I had the sequence right.

"Temple sends his regards. The True Cross will be his."

LaRue gasped. "Temple?"

"Laramie, why don't you believe you were attacked?" Van asked, his voice so low I had to lean forward to hear him.

"Because, besides this bruise on my neck," I said, pulling the scarf aside to show him, "I don't have a mark on me."

"Holy crap!" Van yelled. He shot up so fast he knocked his chair several feet backward.

A click echoed through the warehouse and Van spun to face LaRue. The cocked revolver shook so hard I didn't think she could hit the side of a barn, but it was pointed at us, so I didn't want to test the theory.

"Van, get away from her," she said through tight lips.

Van put himself between us. "LaRue, we have to get to the bottom of this and we have options. Put the gun down."

"I'm not particularly interested in the options," LaRue responded, but she lowered the gun. Fractionally.

When Van turned to face me, he appeared to have aged five years. "How did you escape from Marek and Grace?" Van asked.

"We had the wreck and I ran."

"What did they hit?"

"Other cars. One backed out in front of us and then there was one behind us. I slipped into the crowd while Marek and Grace were fighting these really big guys. Grace was amazing," I enthused, not caring that I sounded like I had a girl crush.

"Two cars . . . an ambush?"

"I hadn't thought of that. I guess that's why you're the cop," I smiled crookedly at him. "I thought the guys were wearing masks because it's so close to Halloween, but that makes more sense. What do you think Marek and Grace are into that guys are attacking them?"

"I think they were after you," Van responded quietly. "What kind of masks were they wearing?"

After me? That didn't make any sense, but Van was waiting for an answer. "They were the full-head kind, and extremely realistic. They looked like wolves."

"Holy crap!" LaRue shouted. Van turned to her and simultaneously they said,

"Werewolves."

WEREWOLVES AND VAMPIRES AND VOODOO, OH MY!

**50 Hours
(10:00 p.m. Saturday)**

"Werewolves," I deadpanned. The last twenty-four hours had been a crazy ride. Why not werewolves? Another bubble of hysteria floated up. I mentally shook myself.

"Am I getting punked?" I asked, looking around wildly for the hidden cameras.

Neither Van nor LaRue paid me a bit of attention. They stared at each other and, although neither said a word, I was sure a whole conversation was taking place between them.

"Someone tell me what's going on. Now!" I yelled.

Van looked at me in surprise. He wasn't used to me raising my voice. Or demanding anything at all, for that matter.

"Van, we have to go! It was bad enough when it was Grace and Marek, but if weres are out there . . ."

"Laramie, LaRue is right. I promise I will give you answers soon, but we must get to the compound. You'll be safe there."

Van's urgency was unmistakable, but I didn't let it sway me. "The compound? Safe? Right now, the two of you sound crazier than Grace and Marek. I'm not going anywhere with you until you tell me what is going on. And who the heck is Temple?"

Van considered for a moment, picked up his chair from where it had fallen, and sat back down across from me. He looked rattled and disheveled, both of which were decidedly un-Van like. I'd seen this guy come off the baseball field after overtime innings played in the hot Texas sun, his blond hair perfectly in place and his uniform spotless. But tonight, his hair stood on end, his tie was askew, and his clothes were rumpled.

This Van scared me.

"Laramie, you aren't on *Candid Camera*. I'm going to tell you some things that will sound crazy. Batshit crazy," he said with a slight smile, to my relief showing some of the 'nothing fazes me' Van I had always known. "You have to listen to everything I, uh, we tell you. It's deadly serious."

"More serious than a dead guy in my dumbwaiter?" I asked, to show him that I could meet and raise him one in the humor department. To prove that, for once, I wasn't going to fall apart. "Hit me with your best stuff, Anderson. I'm thirty years old, for God's sakes, and I've been to jail."

My effort at humor only seemed to dishearten him. "Yes," he said with a sad smile. "But this is far more serious—for the world in general, and you in particular."

"Okay," I said with a deep breath. "I'm ready."

"Laramie, there are things in this world that go bump in the night. Things that you've heard about in fairytales and horror stories. Things that you have nightmares about but, when you wake up, you feel safe because you don't believe they exist. Unfortunately, they do."

"Things like werewolves?" I tried to say it jokingly, but my voice cracked on the word. He couldn't be serious, and I wanted to prove to him that I wouldn't naively fall for it. But I couldn't, because I was falling for it. There had been too much strange circling around me in the last twenty-four hours for me not to believe this—just a little. But I wasn't ready to admit it.

"Werewolves and vampires." With another look back at LaRue, he continued, "There is also a lot more power in witchcraft and voodoo—among other things—than some in the world would have us believe."

"You expect me to believe in vampires, too?" When I said the word vampire, I felt a slight throb in my neck. My hand flew to the bruise. "Van, you know that this is crazy talk, right?"

"Batshit crazy. I warned you that it would be, but that doesn't make it any less true."

"Vampires? Creatures that suck blood and can't come out in the daylight because they will burn to a crisp? And werewolves? People that get all furry and wolfie when there is a full moon?" Several bubbles of hysteria rose and this time I couldn't tamp them down. I heard it in my voice. It wasn't the craziness of the idea that caused my panic, but memories of the brawl. Guys with heads like wolves flooded in moonlight.

"Those weren't masks?" I struggled to get the words out.

"No, honey. And Marek and Grace . . ." Van trailed off.

I considered their paleness, unblemished skin, and ageless good looks.

"Vampires," I whispered.

"Vampires," Van confirmed.

RUN FOR YOUR LIVES

49.5 Hours
(10:30 p.m. Saturday)

"Van! We've got company!"

LaRue's cry echoed through the warehouse, shredding the cocoon Van's talk of creatures of the night had woven around us.

She was pointing at a monitor showing Marek Cerny's dark sedan, now less sleek with its front and rear ends crumpled. The car idled on the street in front of the shop, the vehicle's darkly tinted windows prohibited us from seeing inside.

"We can't wait any longer. We have to go now," Van said to me, but he didn't move. I nodded slowly in response to the questioning look he shot me. I had wanted answers and—except for telling me about Temple—he had given them. Whether I believed him or not was something I could figure out later, when two possible vampires weren't lying in wait for me.

"LaRue, are there any others?" he asked.

"No." LaRue gave the screens one last look before turning

to Van. "But we should stay inside. I think the defenses will hold and we may be safer in here than out there."

"No! We can't chance it. If they get her now, we won't be able to stop The Change."

I knew they were talking about me, but I didn't know what change Van wanted to stop. I remembered Marek's warning about Van, but I felt safer with him than with Marek and Grace.

"What's the plan?" I asked, surprised at how calm I sounded. Maybe I was in shock.

Van looked from LaRue to me then pulled a large, blue steel semi-automatic pistol from the shoulder holster that his suit jacket concealed.

"LaRue, you go out first, open the truck door and slide across. Laramie, you'll go next, then me. No matter what you see or hear, get straight into the truck. If I'm not in the truck in five seconds, shut the door and drive away."

"I'm not leaving you!" LaRue and I said at the same time.

"LaRue, you know I can take care of myself. Laramie, you just have to take my word for it. Five seconds."

LaRue gave a tight nod. I didn't like it, but Van was right; I had to trust him.

We huddled together at the smaller of the two rear metal doors. LaRue held the cannon-sized silver revolver in her right hand, her left ready to open the locks at Van's signal. Van stood close behind me, the blue steel semi-auto in his left hand and my shoulder in a death grip with his right. I knew he wouldn't let go if the Hounds of Hell were on us—or in this case, werewolves and vampires. I was surrounded by guns and we were about to run into an alley where we might or might not be attacked by mythical creatures. I should have been terrified, but it all felt too surreal. How had my world gotten so crazy so fast?

I felt a quick squeeze on my shoulder, then Van yelled, "Go!"

LaRue sped through the locks, pushed the door back on its track, and ran into the night. The squeeze on my shoulder turned into a push and I was in the alley. The interior of the truck gaped in front of me. I propelled myself into it and across the front seat. Then there was a loud bang behind me.

"Van!" I screamed, scrambling back across the seat to get to him.

Then he was in the truck and it was rocketing down the alley.

"It was the door to The Voodoo Princess!" LaRue had to yell to get my attention over the screeching tires and the revving of the large truck's engine. "It closes and locks automatically."

I tried to slow my racing heart, but the truck's rocking as Van dodged the trash cans and dumpsters did nothing to help. The narrow alley was not suited for sixty miles per hour, so despite Van's superior driving skills, I was terrified.

"Brace!" Van yelled.

Ahead of us, a road crossed the alley. My heart rate skyrocketed out of the stratosphere and I lunged for a hold on the dashboard. Van hit the brakes and turned the wheel hard to the right. The truck fishtailed onto the street and slid toward a row of cars along the curb. He worked the steering wheel like a cowboy wrestling a steer and managed to get the truck headed down the road without hitting a single parked vehicle.

A shaky breath escaped as I saw the elevated I-30 highway ahead of us. In a few blocks, we would be on the freeway. I released the dashboard and fell back against the seat.

"They're back there!" LaRue shouted.

I swung around to peer out the back window of the truck. The battered sedan was half a block behind us. Meanwhile, LaRue had climbed out of the passenger window. She sat on the window frame, with only her legs still inside the truck.

"LaRue! Get back in here!" Van shouted at her. He reached across me to give one of her legs a hard tug.

LaRue fell back into the truck but still managed to hold onto The Cannon—as I had started calling the revolver in my mind. I couldn't imagine what would have to happen for her to drop it. In her other hand was a large spray bottle. She shot Van a look that could kill, but stayed in the truck. Mostly. She crouched on her knees on the seat, facing the truck bed, and —holding the spray bottle out the window—continuously sprayed its contents into the night air.

Van made a hard right onto the I-30 westbound entrance ramp. He merged onto the freeway and crossed four lanes of traffic with barely a glance at his side mirror to see if he had a clear path.

LaRue withdrew her arm and closed the window as we swung into the fast lane. "They're still behind us," she said, no longer shouting.

"Laramie, put on your seatbelt," Van instructed me. "They're probably waiting until we get north of downtown to ram us."

His calm statement that we would be rammed met with stony silence from LaRue, so I fastened my seatbelt, equally taciturn. He swerved in and out of traffic as we traveled past downtown Dallas, the truck's speed never dropping below eighty.

"What's in the bottle?" I asked, curiosity finally getting the better of me.

"Wolfsbane oil and distilled water," LaRue responded long after the silence hit the awkward stage.

"Ummmm . . ." was all I could say. Reality had started to reassert itself, and I didn't want to turn the conversation back to vampires and werewolves if I could help it.

"The wolfsbane will keep the weres from being able to scent track us. The water helps disperse the oil onto the air. It also deters vamps, although not to the same extent as the weres. But if they have the vents in their car open, it will make following us unpleasant." Sensing my unease, LaRue suddenly seemed to take perverse pleasure in sharing information with me.

We merged onto I-35 North, leaving downtown behind. At the last moment, and without slowing even an iota, Van took the exit for the Dallas Tollway. I looked back and saw the sedan match the maneuver without difficulty.

"LaRue, call the compound and let security know that we're coming in hot. They should sweep the fence line to ensure no one is lurking outside."

"Will do," LaRue said and took out her phone.

A strange feeling I couldn't identify engulfed me. Anxiety? No. Anxiety and I were old friends. Exhilaration? Was I enjoying the chase? I snuck a quick side glance at Van. He was focused on the road, still weaving in and out of the light traffic on the toll road. A quick thrill ran through me as I was struck by how handsome he was. I mean, I've always known that Van was handsome. I am a woman with eyes in her head. But I'd never really contemplated it because it seemed so far-fetched.

But sitting here in the truck, right next to him, with the adrenaline from the night pumping through me . . . well, nothing seemed far-fetched, not even Van. I relaxed a little and the next time Van swerved around a car, the motion threw me against him. Where our arms touched, I felt a jolt of electricity. He jumped and looked over at me. Had he felt it too? I slowly straightened, but watched the road ahead for my next opportunity to 'accidentally' be 'thrown' against him.

"They know we're coming," LaRue said, breaking into my reverie. "They don't see anything out of the ordinary around the grounds."

"Great, hang on!" Van swerved across two lanes and took the exit ramp that would take us into an exclusive neighborhood north of downtown Dallas.

I knew where we were going now. I should have clicked on

it before, although in my defense I had more important things on my mind—like that crazy vampire and werewolf story, or that jolt of electricity when Van and I touched. But I digress. On more than one occasion, Jad had jokingly (I thought) referred to the Anderson family mansion as The Compound. Despite many invitations, I had always refused to accompany him there. I knew that it was in an exclusive Dallas neighborhood and that the house and grounds were huge, even by Thompson standards.

"We're three blocks out. If they don't make their move now, they'll hit us at the gate. Are you sure it'll be open?" Van asked LaRue.

"Your guys said it would be."

"Then it will be, and they will be there to bring us in." He glanced in the rearview mirror and cursed.

"What?" I asked, bracing myself for the hit that must be coming.

"They've dropped back at least two blocks." Van hit the steering wheel with his open palm.

"And that's a bad thing because?" I asked.

"Because I have no idea what they're up to."

13

THINGS THAT GO BUMP IN THE NIGHT

49 Hours
(11:00 p.m. Saturday)

My first sight of The Compound's gate filled me with dread. The narrow residential road we sped down dead-ended at its iron bars. At the last possible moment the gate opened, and we rocketed between its posts and along a smooth asphalt driveway. Large black shapes hulked along the drive, and it took me a moment to identify them as people wearing riot gear. The Compound had been breached.

"Van!" I shrieked.

"They're our guys, Laramie! You're safe." Van pulled into a garage large enough to pass for an airplane hangar. "You're safe," he repeated after a large steel door closed, sealing us inside.

Events after the car chase were anti-climactic. The attack never came. Security reported that the sedan drove slowly past the gates, as if to make sure we had made it safely inside, then left the neighborhood.

During Van's debrief of his heavily armed and armored guys I reviewed the events of the night. I skimmed over the hug Van and I had shared at The Voodoo Princess and ignored the moment in the truck. This new awareness of him was possibly more frightening than the 'things that go bump in the night' discussion. What I couldn't skip over—it was a small thing, but it niggled—was that Van had said "you're safe" as we pulled into the garage. Not we're, but you're. He hadn't been concerned for himself or LaRue—only me, and I wasn't sure why.

That forced me to consider the talk about werewolves and vampires. I wasn't convinced they existed, but there was something out there. Something that must be worse than anything I could imagine, to force Van to live in a fortress and have an army at his disposal.

I tried to remember everything I'd read about vampires and werewolves; all the movies I'd seen. I wasn't a supernatural buff, so I didn't have a lot to work with. Nothing much came to mind about werewolves, besides wolves, furry, and issues with full moons, but vampires rang several bells. They killed people by biting them on the neck and drinking their blood. I slid my hand under the scarf at my neck and touched the mysterious marks. There was something else . . . *Think, Laramie, think.*

Foreboding filled me when I remembered. They were called creatures of the night. Vampires slept all day and hunted after dark because sunlight would kill them. I had thought the big-ass martini and whatever I had been drugged with explained my misery. But the hangover had miraculously disappeared after sundown.

"Van?" I whispered.

"Yes, Laramie?" The small army had retreated from the garage and Van and LaRue were huddled together, talking. Although he was exhausted, I could see the concern for me on his face.

"Why are vampires and werewolves after me?" My legs gave out and I collapsed to the floor.

I didn't faint; I would have died from mortification. It was just a moment of weakness. Surprisingly, or maybe not surprisingly, it seemed to reassure Van. It was typical Laramie behavior and he knew exactly how to deal with it. He swung me into his arms and carried me through a door to the mansion.

I hate to admit it, but I laid my head against his shoulder, closed my eyes, and reveled in being close to a man. It had been a long time; much longer than the two years I had been widowed. Any guy would have felt good—it wasn't because it was Van. Really. LaRue's footsteps followed us. I ignored her and imagined that it was just Van and me.

That fantasy was abruptly dashed when Van laid me down and LaRue said, "If you want to know what this has to do with you, you need to quit playing the maiden in distress and open your damn eyes."

"LaRue!" Van chided her, but I knew she was right.

I sat up and looked around. We were in a plush, under-stated study that dripped old money. LaRue had commandeered an overstuffed chair across opposite the sofa I was on. Van eased himself onto the coffee table between us and breathed deeply. "Based on what you've told me and everything that has happened since last night, it sounds like you were attacked leaving the club, possibly by werewolves, and Cerny saved you."

"I don't think what Cerny did to her can be classified as saving. I would say he cursed her. It would have been kinder to let her die," LaRue said angrily.

"Why? Why would werewolves attack me? Why would Marek save me? And how am I in one piece when my dress was shredded?"

"I don't know why you would be a target for werewolves, but my guess is that they were sent to kill you. A human can usually be saved from near death by drinking vampire blood.

It speeds up the body's healing process. Marek saving you? Your guess is as good as mine."

Drinking blood? *Ick.* But then I remembered the strange compulsion to lick Bernie's blood off my hand. I pushed the memory away.

"If the human is too close to death, say from blood loss or massive injuries, vampire blood alone can't heal the body fast enough to save them," Van continued. "However, if a vampire bites a human and injects their venom before the human dies, it immediately stops the death process and heals the body. I've never personally observed it, but I've read that the healing can occur in less than two minutes. Broken bones mend, lacerations heal, even severed organs will re-knit themselves.

"Venom, like snakes?" At Van's nod, I said, "But venom is poisonous, it isn't supposed to heal you."

"Vampire venom works a little differently. We aren't sure if it is an evolutionary process in vampires or how exactly it works, but it starts by healing the body it is injected into."

"That's why I don't have any marks on me?" I asked, stunned.

"Yes," Van replied, "except for the bite marks on your neck and the bruise. Normally when vampires bite humans to feed from them, there is a component in their saliva that causes the bite marks to heal almost immediately. Between that and the mind control, most humans never remember being bitten."

"Mind control?" I yelped.

"Yes," Van said, unfazed by the interruption, "but when a vampire bites and injects his venom into a human, the venom burns the tissue at the entrance site. So the bruising at the site will only last until the transformation is complete, but the bite mark will be with you forever."

"Transformation. What are you talking about?" I asked.

Van stared at his hands, unwilling or unable to continue.

After a moment, LaRue picked up the conversation and she didn't pull any punches.

"To vampire. For whatever reason, Cerny, the bastard, decided to change you into a vampire. It takes seventy-two hours, give or take, from the time of the venom injection to change from human to vampire. That's what Cerny meant when he told you that life as you knew it would end in less than seventy-two hours."

"So in seventy-two hours I will have to start drinking blood and wearing extra heavy-duty SPF? Van, what is all this? When did you get involved with vampires and werewolves and, and . . ." I trailed off, at a loss. Van stared at me; anguish contorted his beautiful face.

I shifted my focus back to LaRue, who sat quietly across from me, still holding The Cannon at the ready in her lap, and caught my second wind. "And voodoo and compounds and having a small army at your disposal!"

"I can tell you a little about the voodoo part," LaRue said. "I come from a long line of women who have the talent. Voodoo is considered by many a dark art, but my family has always used it to fight evil. I make a living telling fortunes and selling hex dolls and love potions. Things that most people buy for a laugh and don't really expect to be real or to work. But that allows me to continue the fight to bring a balance to the universe. A balance between good and evil. I've grown up knowing about the things that, as Van said, go bump in the night, and have always known it was my job to fight them."

There was more to the fairy than met the eye. The Cannon should have been my first tip-off. On the other hand, we were in Texas. Here, a woman who knew how to handle a gun was the norm rather than the exception. Thank God.

Van finally spoke. "My family has also fought evil for centuries. Sometimes we are referred to as The Organization. Jad always said that you weren't a supernatural buff, but have you ever heard of Abraham Van Helsing?"

"Yes." I wracked my brain. The Van Helsing name was somehow connected with vampires. Then the shoe dropped. Van. Van H. "Are you trying to tell me that you're immortal?"

"What? No! Abraham was my great, great grandfather. I am definitely mortal."

LaRue coughed. It almost sounded like she said "bullshit" at the same time, but she couldn't have. That would indicate a sense of humor, and I had seen no evidence of that.

"I am," Van directed at LaRue. "My family was, um, gifted or cursed, depending on how you look at it. Along with some of the vampires and werewolves we were given, I guess the best way to describe it would be genetic enhancements back in the forties."

"The forties?" I asked, completely clueless.

"Stop!" commanded LaRue, holding up her hands. "We don't have time to get into this now. Van, we need to talk and make some decisions. This whole history lesson can wait."

Van slowly nodded in agreement, and even I had to admit that I didn't know how much more vampire and werewolf lore I could take in tonight. I had one final question I needed answered, though.

"So, short version. What is going to happen to me in . . ." I checked my watch, "forty-seven hours? Will I drink blood and only be able to go out at night? Will I try to eat small children?" I said this half-jokingly. I still didn't really believe any of this, but then another thought hit me. "Will Bo be safe from me?"

"We don't know," Van replied after a brief look at LaRue. She studied The Cannon intently.

"You don't know? Van, how is it that you don't know when you are obviously up to your teeth in this stuff?"

Van took his time and when he answered, I could tell he had chosen his words carefully. "Vampires and werewolves have different strengths and weaknesses depending on their, let's say, history. We didn't even know that Marek could make other vampires. We thought he, along with the rest of the vampires known to us, had lost that ability in . . ." he trailed off with a glance at LaRue.

"In the forties?" I asked. "Marek doesn't look much over thirty. Grace looks even younger. How old are they?"

"We know Grace is a little over four centuries old because of her documented history. Marek, on the other hand, has kept a lower profile, so we aren't exactly sure, but we think he is even older." Van held eye contact with me. I could tell that he thought that this might be the piece of information that sent me over the edge. It was a close thing, but I was so far into this already I refused to give him the satisfaction.

"I can't wait to hear about these crazy 1940s. But until then, I should just prepare for the worst?" I asked. I wasn't sure when I had clenched my hands into fists, but my fingernails bit into my palms with the effort it took to keep my voice light.

"Not if we can help it," said Van grimly. "Look, Laramie, I've never seen a transformation, and even accounts of them in the Van Helsing library"—he raised his hand to forestall my question—"are rare. From what I've read, the venom starts to take over the body immediately. During the first twelve hours or so after the venom is injected, the victim falls into a vegetative state and the heart slows almost to a stop. If the historical accounts are to be believed, they were often mistaken for dead. We think that this allows the venom to spread throughout the body with less resistance. The victim wakes sometime after the initial twelve hours have passed—still human, but starting to experience the effects of the transformation by sensitivity to sunlight, improved eyesight, hearing and healing, and quicker movement and reflexes. The transformation to vampire is completed approximately seventy-two-hours after the bite, when the venom stops the victim's heart."

We sat quietly for several minutes. I was stunned, unable

to even begin to take in the enormity of what I had just heard. I thought back to how fast I had run in Deep Ellum.

"There are ways to reverse the process during the seventy-two-hour window," Van said.

"Van," LaRue said sharply, "we don't know if it works. It's just a theory. A theory I don't want to hang my hat on. We need to end this."

Van turned on her furiously. "No! That is not happening. This is my responsibility. She is my responsibility. I promised. And besides, for all your big talk and waving around that gun, could you really do it? Because I know I can't."

"Just hold on a dang minute. I don't like this talk about ending IT. Like I am just a thing," I said to LaRue. Then I faced Van. "As for you, what makes me your responsibility? Who did you promise?"

"Who do you think he promised?" LaRue asked, and rather snottily, I might add. "If you don't know who he's talking about then you are even stupider than I thought!"

I'd never been in a physical fight but, after the day I'd had, I had a lot of pent-up pissed off and I thought I could take her, gun and all.

Holy crap! How did I end up on the coffee table? I'd gone from sitting on the sofa to crouching on the table mere inches from LaRue. They looked more shaken than I felt. LaRue, for all her big talk and gun-waving earlier, as Van had pointed out, held the gun limply in her lap.

"Oh, Laramie," Van whispered, "it's happening." He cautiously reached out to help me off the table.

"Jad," Van said quietly after I sank back onto the sofa.

"Jad?" I asked.

"I promised Jad I would look after you."

I looked at LaRue, but she wasn't paying attention to us. Tears coursed down her cheeks. I didn't know what she had to cry about. I was the one turning into a vampire.

"Did Jad know about . . ." I trailed off, unable to say the words.

"Yes," Van replied. Just when I thought he wasn't going to say anything more, he continued. "I got him into it. When we were in college, I had to put down a werewolf who had gone rogue. There is a much longer explanation, but mainly it boils down to the were left the pack and attacked humans. When that happens, they must be stopped. The were's mate didn't agree and followed me back to Austin. Remember that little house Jad and I rented off campus?"

"Who could forget The Bat Cave?" I asked, smiling at the memory. My smile faded as I realized the significance.

"Yes," replied Van. "Nobody can thumb their nose at the other side quite like a spoiled college jock. Anyway, the were attacked Jad, to force me to watch a friend die. Before I could get to them, Jad had her down on the ground in a sleeper hold so she couldn't get her claws or teeth into him."

"So, all those years watching wrestling and then MMA finally paid off?"

"It did that day. I had to tell him everything. Jad wouldn't buy some half-baked cover story that most people fall for because they don't really want to know what is out there."

"People see what they want to see," I replied. Jad had said it often during the years we had been married. Tonight, I realized that I had done the same thing with Van since the day we had met. The strong, serious Van I saw today had been there all along, but all I had wanted to see was the spoiled college jock who I blamed for the problems in my marriage.

"After Jad heard the story, he wanted in on the monster fighting, as he called it. Fortunately—or unfortunately, depending on how you look at it—there wasn't a lot of monster fighting of the supernatural kind left for the Van Helsings to do. Most of the Evils had been wiped out during the war. Plus, after the rift between the Goods and Evils, the Goods had pretty much taken over policing their kind."

"The war? Goods and Evils? I'm confused."

"Ahh . . ." Van checked his watch, "I'm getting ahead of myself on the story. I don't think I should hit you with it all tonight."

"I really don't know how much more I can take in, but I do need to know about Jad."

"Without going too far into it, with the supernaturals policing themselves, The Organization—and Jad, once he knew about all this—were left at loose ends. Then he pointed out that the human supply of bad guys was practically limitless. So we decided to become police officers."

"I always thought you talked him into that," I said slowly.

"No, it was his idea."

During the conversation, LaRue had moved from the chair to a window across the room. She gazed out into the night, her back to us. I wanted privacy for the question I was about to ask, but I doubted she would to give it to us after my table-hopping act.

"Van," I said, my voice low, "do you ever see him?"

My voice wasn't as low as I hoped; LaRue turned to us from the window. The color drained from Van's face. He was convinced I had finally cracked, after everything they had told me tonight. Maybe I had. But I just wanted him to reassure me that I wasn't the only one who saw Jad's ghost everywhere. I wanted to hear that he looked for him in crowds, saw him in dark alleys and mistook other people for him, like I had with Officer Mins today or with Marek last night after the attack.

I opened my mouth to try to explain, but I was interrupted by a clang, followed by a thud. LaRue no longer stood by the window. She was crumpled on the floor with The Cannon next to her.

14

DUMB AND DUMBER

46 Hours
(2:00 a.m. Sunday)

Laue came to in quite the snit. Although in my limited acquaintance with her I hadn't seen her in anything but a snit, so I had a hard time judging where this fell on her snit scale. We had hurried to her side after she fainted. She ordered us (really, just me) to get away from her.

Van and LaRue formulated a plan while I waited in the hallway outside the study. After a couple of minutes, she rudely brushed by me and headed down the hall without a backward glance. While I could tell that LaRue didn't hold me in the highest esteem—I was blaming that on the whole vampire transformation thing—I thought the attitude had more to do with being embarrassed over fainting in front of me than anything else.

Van had filled me in on their master plan. As much as LaRue disliked me, she would still help. That was a good thing, because the plan had two parts and both of them hinged firmly on LaRue and her voodoo skills. Part one boiled down to a ritual that would determine what type of vampire I would be after The Change. Apparently, vampires fell into one of three categories: Good, Evil and Dualistic.

Y'all, let me tell you, I'm a little fuzzy on the particulars but I'll try to explain. It all comes down to your true self. The answer to the age-old argument over whether the human race is inherently good or inherently evil is null. It isn't one or the other. It's both. Most humans are a combination of good and evil, but ultimately, each person has a true self. This true self is either more inherently good or more inherently evil. When changed, people carry that good or evil into vampire form with them and take it to the extreme. In very rare cases, at least according to Van, a being can be Dualistic. Meaning that like humans, they can be either evil or good based on the circumstances, usually what is best for them at any given time.

Unfortunately, you can't tell just by talking to a person whether their true self is good, evil or a combination. Some of the nicest people are inherently evil but are adept at covering it up with a big ole layer of nice. In their defense, some of them truly want to be good and fight the evil every day. In contrast, some of the nicest people don't feel the need to be all showy with it. While they may not come across as evil, no one ever thinks of them as particularly saintly because they just get on with their lives.

I have to tell you, I was a little concerned. I mean, I had never dismembered small animals, but there had been a lot of not-so-nice thoughts about Mama and Cheyenne . . . well, let's just say, I figured the jury was probably still out on me.

My best shot for a normal life was the second part of the plan. Van was hopeful that LaRue could perform another ritual that would stop the transformation. He didn't tell me all the particulars, just that it was very complicated and would "involve a great deal of luck." I wasn't happy to hear that, as I have never been very lucky. I mean, I was widowed at twenty-seven. Although come to think of it, that might have had more to do with Jad's luck than mine. But I digress. Van believed we could stop the process, and as I have never been a big fan of change, I was all for trying.

Completely disregarding the time and, in my opinion, proper business hours, Van had called a private detective his family kept on retainer. I didn't ask if he meant the Anderson family or the Van Helsing organization, and he didn't offer.

Van's conversation with the detective was brief and to the point. He told him to put all other business on hold and throw all his resources into following Marek Cerny ASAP. I only heard Van's side of the conversation, but the detective didn't seem too upset about the midnight phone call, or about being told to start on the job immediately. Either the Andersons or the Van Helsings paid very well.

By the time Van was done updating me and the PI, he was exhausted. Thankfully, his family was either out or asleep because he hadn't gotten a grilling by Vivian, his socialite mother.

Vivian! Vivian and Van's sister Bunny must know about all this. Otherwise, how did Van explain the army outside? Wow. Mind blown.

Van played the part of the perfect host and settled me into the guest room in his wing of The Compound with the promise that we would figure everything out tomorrow. He also made me swear not to leave the house.

I was mad at Van and Jad. But since it is easier to be mad at the living than the dead, my anger was focused on Van. This had to be his fault. Why else would werewolves target me? I didn't have any connections to anyone else in the super-natural world.

I should have been exhausted after the last twenty-four hours, but I wasn't. Maybe it was the adrenaline. Since sleep was not in my future, I decided that a tour of Van's mansion —his wing, at least—was in order. Technically he still lived with his parents, but I didn't consider having a wing to yourself quite the same as squatting in your folks' basement. The Madam was huge, but Van's wing alone dwarfed her. It was decorated with furniture and art that probably cost more than I would ever earn in my lifetime. I didn't envy Van his home, though; while it was impressive, it wasn't in the least bit comfortable or cozy and it made me yearn for The Madam.

When I returned to his study, my gaze lit on a beautiful antique desk in one corner of the room. I hesitated only briefly before I searched it for supplies. Thankfully, a Mont Blanc pen and a yellow legal pad that would serve my purposes perfectly sat prominently on top of the desk. Even though I was mad at him, I felt bad enough wandering around his house while he slept; I didn't want to dig through his desk drawers.

Did that reluctance to invade someone's privacy make me a good person? Would it keep me from killing indiscriminately if we couldn't reverse The Change? I didn't know for sure, but I hoped it was a mark in my favor.

I curled up in an overstuffed chair next to the desk. I'm a list girl. If you need to get something done, make a list. I also apply this method to problem-solving and I needed to do some of that, big time.

Where to start? The elephant in the room—or in this case, the dead guy in the dumbwaiter—loomed large. Not only had someone been killed in my house, but the police liked me for the murder. I was looking at prison if it didn't get solved.

My second and more immediate problem was the turning-into-a-vampire thing. I still didn't know if I bought the bumpy story (what I had decided to call things that went bump in the night) lock, stock, and barrel. But something had happened to me in that alley last night and my life had been pretty strange since then. The two alternatives were that they (Marek, Grace, Van, and LaRue) were insane or that I was. I could believe all of them were except Van. While he had always struck me as an entitled jerk, I didn't get even a whiff of crazy off him.

That left me. Surprisingly, I liked that option. If I was a mental case, then the dead guy in my dumbwaiter and the vampires chasing me probably didn't exist. I could check myself into an institution and take a nice, long rest. Problem solved!

Except . . . It would take something big to make me go so completely around the bend. *Wouldn't it?* Something like a murder? I gasped at the thought. What if I had gone home on Friday night, found Bernie in The Madam, thought he was a burglar, killed him in self-defense, and had a psychotic break as a result? That could account for my complete loss of time from midnight Friday until noon on Saturday. Then I had created the vampire, werewolf, and Van Helsing universe to divert my attention from the guy I'd shot and stuffed down my dumbwaiter!

I shifted in the chair to get more comfortable while I gave that idea some thought. No, I couldn't believe that I had killed anyone, not even a blight on humanity like Bernie Wallach. But maybe the stress of finding Bernie's body in The Madam had caused my break with reality, and if I solved the murder my sanity would return. I liked the idea. With Bernie's murder solved, I wouldn't be facing jail time and, bonus, the whole vampire bunk would dissolve.

Warming to the idea, I tapped the end of the pen against my teeth for a few seconds while I considered how to start, then wrote on the pad:

'Who wanted Bernie dead?'

Well, that would be half of Dallas and some of the outlying suburbs. Also happy to see Bernie's demise would be business owners, neighbors, reporters, and politicians. I couldn't even begin to narrow that list down.

I pondered how to come at it from a different angle. Van's

fancy pen made a satisfying scratching noise on the paper as I wrote:

'Who would benefit from Bernie's death?'

That didn't narrow the list. In fact, it made it longer. All of mankind would benefit from Bernie's death.

Note to self—don't bring up that sentiment if questioned again by the police.

I was attacking it from the wrong angle. Too many people wanted Bernie dead to go down that path, so who would want Bernie dead in my house? I sat up a little straighter. That might be it! I brainstormed several questions, leaving blank lines between each one:

'Who stood to gain from Bernie dying in my house?'

'Who could get Bernie into my house?'

'Who has access to my house?'

Bingo! There were no signs of a break-in, so the last one was the million-dollar question and the answer was surprisingly short. Only Van, Owen Carter, Bill Martinez, and Tom Harner had keys to The Madam.

Van had a key from when he and Jad would stay there when Hattie was alive. Despite Marek's warning that he had an agenda, I couldn't imagine Van murdering Bernie in my house or leaving him there to be found.

I guessed that when Marek said Van had an agenda, he had meant the whole Van Helsing organization's purpose, not anything specific to me. But maybe it was more than that. It had to have been my connection to Van that had gotten me attacked by werewolves. Once again, I remembered Marek and Grace's reaction to my mention of Temple. Damn it! Why hadn't I demanded straight answers about Temple or the True Cross—whatever that was?

I drew a heavy line across the paper several spaces below my list of key holders. Under the line, I wrote TO-DO LIST. Then:

'Ask Van about Temple.'

'Google the True Cross.'

Oh my God. How complete was my break that not only had I made up vampires and werewolves, but created someone named Temple and this True Cross stuff, too?

I contemplated adding a 'Tell Van I've gone crazy' reminder to the list but didn't think it was necessary. His and LaRue's responses when I brought up seeing Jad everywhere convinced me that they already knew I had.

Next on the list was Owen. He had a key to The Madam in case I needed him to stop by to check on Bo. That reminded me that he had taken Bo home with him after I had been hauled out of The Madam in cuffs.

A quick check of my phone revealed numerous text messages from Owen. The first several were different variations on are you okay, what's going on, are you out yet, call me, but then they devolved into just a question mark, sent every thirty minutes or so.

If I called him with an update, he would keep me on the phone forever asking every question under the sun, and what would I say, anyway? Sprung from jail, kidnapped, now free, but I still can't pick up Bo because I have to get this turning-into-a-vampire thing sorted out? No, I couldn't talk, and a text would trigger a phone call from him. At least Bo was being taken care of, and that was one less item for my to-do list.

So, back to Owen's viability as Bernie's killer. If The Whine Barrel opened, Owen would get more exposure as a web designer. He had also agreed to pick up shifts behind the wine-tasting bar and in the gift shop. Were exposure and a few part-time hours enough to make it worth his while to take out Bernie so The Whine Barrel could open on schedule?

But what if Owen had met Bernie at The Madam to try to convince him of the benefits of the business? When the meeting didn't go well, Owen . . . what? Pulled a gun from his murse, shot Bernie and left him in the dumbwaiter for me as a present? No, leaving his body for the police to find would slow down or stop the opening, so that knocked out Owen's motive.

Bill Martinez had a key because he was my contractor. As with Owen, I couldn't imagine that Bill would do anything to sabotage me or the job. But he had acted so suspiciously when Don came by for the code inspection.

The more I thought about it, the more red flags popped up. Bill and Bernie had clashed on previous construction projects. Bill had warned me how difficult it would be to get The Madam finished after Bernie had butted in. What was my relatively small job compared to the much larger and more lucrative contracts Bill stood to gain and work on problem-free with Bernie out of the picture?

I doodled a rocket beside Bill's name with the number one in it, but kept moving down the list.

Next was Tom Harner. Tom's mother, Maria Harner, had worked for Hattie for years. Hattie hadn't trusted Tom and when Maria had lost her battle with cancer, Hattie had asked for Maria's key back on a couple of occasions. He always had an excuse for not returning it. One time it was on the ring with his car keys and the car was in the shop. Another time he had misplaced it.

Whenever I had asked Hattie why she distrusted Tom, she said he gave her the willies. I thought he was attractive and likable. He had always been friendly, and anyone who could love that rat-dog Dixie couldn't be all bad. Tom's possession of a key had only begun bothering me over the last few days, when, instead of helping me with Bernie, he started siding with him.

On the flip side, Tom wanted to buy The Madam. Had he killed Bernie and left him in my house to frame me for the murder, thereby forcing me to sell? The image of Tom in his perfectly coordinated designer clothes murdering someone was hard to conjure. Wouldn't shooting someone and then stuffing them in a dumbwaiter muss you up a little? I had never seen Tom mussed.

The list of people with access to my house exhausted, I was nowhere closer to an actual suspect. I went back to brainstorming questions and wrote:

'Who would benefit enough from keeping me from opening The Whine Barrel that it would be worth their while to hire Bernie to make it happen?'

Marek. He had the most to gain, but he didn't have access to The Madam.

Or did he? Could Marek turn himself into a fog and enter through a keyhole? Maybe he'd entered the house in some nebulous vampire fog and unlocked the door from inside to then let Bernie in.

I slumped in the overstuffed chair. I had gone as far with this train of thought as I could go, until I talked to Van about vampire lore and figured out what exactly Marek could or couldn't do.

Which brought me back to my other big problem. If I hadn't gone crazy, I was turning into a vampire. Why? It all started, if Van's conjecture was correct, with the werewolf attack. Why would werewolves attack me? Van, Temple, and the True Cross were my only clues.

'Vendetta?'

I scribbled it in the margins, as I was out of space on the lined portion of the paper.

Jad had been pulled into fighting bumpies by a werewolf with a vendetta against Van. So maybe one with a grudge against Van had come after me as payback. Could that be what "Temple sends his regards" meant? Was that why Van had talked about everything but Temple? Once again, Marek's warning about Van having an agenda echoed in my memory. Maybe I had dismissed it, and Van as Bernie's murderer, too quickly.

Something that had been niggling at my subconscious

finally surfaced like a cork thrown into a creek. Marek had everything to gain and nothing to lose from my death. So why would he save me?

And what about Grace? She was Marek's right-hand man, er, woman, er, vampire. Maybe she was loyal to him beyond even what he wanted. She had told me I shouldn't be at The Perch, effectively sending me out into the street to be attacked by werewolves.

Grace moved to the top of the suspect list. The more I thought about it, the more convinced I became. She figured if she had me killed, thereby putting The Madam up for grabs, she would be the employee of the year. But she hadn't counted on her boss being too good of a vampire for his own good and saving me. Luckily for her, unluckily for me of course, she was a quick thinker and implemented Plan B, or Plan Bernie. I had seen her in a fight. She didn't need a gun to kill Bernie, but shooting him improved the framing job on me.

And she must have tipped off the werewolves after she and Marek had picked me up from headquarters. She had made a good show of fighting them for Marek's sake, but she must have intended for me to be killed in the fight.

Grace had underestimated me, though, and I didn't blame her. She thought she was still dealing with mousy Laramie from The Perch. But something had given me the courage to run from that scene to save myself. Maybe it was just the self-preservation instinct or the effects of the vampire venom, but for once in my life, I had taken action. Okay, okay, it had been running from danger instead of fighting—but at least I hadn't just stood there and waited to be killed.

I was opening my own business. I had withstood a police interrogation (lame as it was) without breaking. I had escaped from vampires and werewolves. Those were all pretty big things. I was done selling myself short, I vowed. And if Van and LaRue couldn't stop The Change, I would deal with being a vampire.

I was all pumped up with pride and determination. I looked around the dark house. Van had told me to stay put, but I couldn't just sit here waiting for him to wake up and save the day.

I had a damsel in distress to save.

Me.

15

FINDING PROOF

**44 Hours
(4:00 a.m. Sunday)**

I circled The Madam's block twice in the plain black car I had, um, borrowed from Van's multitude of vehicles, before deciding it was safe to go in. I parked in the large, wooden shed that acted as a garage and general catchall behind The Madam. My truck sat in its normal spot, a graveled area a few feet from the building. With Van's throwdown car hidden and my truck unmoved since Friday, I hoped no one would realize I was home. The police hadn't told me not to come back, but I thought it would be better if the house looked undisturbed to anyone who might drive by looking for me.

The shed, which had originated as a carriage house, had large double doors that were difficult to close without help. Of course, since I wanted to be stealthy, one of them broke free from my grasp, swung wide open and bounced off the shed wall with a loud bang that reverberated through the early morning stillness.

Since Tom Harner's house was the only other one on the

block, he was the only person I was concerned about disturbing. His kitchen light shone through the darkness, but Tom left lights on all the time. When no other lights came on, I breathed a small sigh of thanks and wrestled the door closed.

The silver paint of the new-to-me Dodge glinted in the moonlight as I passed it on the way to The Madam's back door. My previous truck had been totaled in an accident six months ago when the brakes failed. Thankfully, I hadn't been injured, and with a bit of the money Hattie left me added to the pittance I got from the insurance company for my old truck, I had been able to buy this one.

I had unlocked The Madam's back door before I realized that I hadn't needed my phone's light to guide my key into the lock. Was the vampire venom improving my eyesight?

The rear door led into a small foyer. To the left lay The Madam's kitchen. Straight ahead was the door to my office, and beside that was the base of the servant stairwell that led up through the second floor and ended at the rear door of my attic apartment. Finally, on the right was the storeroom for The Madam. I needed to check my stock.

The storeroom was windowless, so I felt safe flipping the wall switch. When light flooded the room, I found myself staring at several small nude men with only wine leaves covering their privates. It wasn't as exciting as it sounds. Several cases of my favorite Texas brand, Nude Dude Wines, were in the middle of the room with the men on the labels in all their glory. It was the most nude action I'd had in years.

I conducted a quick inventory to reassure myself that my nude dudes, and the rest of my stock, remained unmolested by the police or anyone else. I couldn't be sure without checking the stock list, but it looked like a couple of cases might be missing. Just great! A murder and a theft. The Madam was at the epicenter of a crime spree.

I opened the door at the rear of the storeroom and stared into the inky darkness the cellar stairs disappeared into. The cool breeze that rose from its depths and my terror of the creepy crawlies that lived down there gave me pause.

The cellar, not something often found in Dallas houses, was the perfect place to store wine as it remained cool even during the hellishly hot Texas summers. Plus, it was rumored that moonshine had been hidden there during prohibition. According to the legend, the tunnels had run from the cellar out to the surrounding grounds. The liquor had been transported in and out of the cellar without entering The Madam, thereby lending the Thompsons some respectability. Not a single trace of a tunnel had ever been found. Still, I kept hoping that some shred of evidence would turn up, for marketing purposes. If I could find proof, it would make a nice addition to the short history of The Madam that would be printed on our wine lists.

No, the middle of the night was no time for a tromp through what was basically a creepy hole in the ground. I closed the door and turned to leave the storeroom, but the memory of Van's question about whether the police had checked the cellar halted my progress. Why would he be concerned about that? Marek's words of warning about Van again rose unbidden in my memory.

I looked once more at the boxes of Nude Dude wine and couldn't help but smile. Its name came from a romantic weekend gone awry, when the vineyard's owner had mistakenly booked into a bed and breakfast that catered to nudists. The first inkling he and his wife had was when they tried to enter the property's hot tub in their swimsuits and were told, "Not unless you're nude, dude" by another guest. They had a name for their next line of wines, and when they found out that the term 'going nude' was also used for shedding one's inhibitions and putting it all on the line to go after one's dreams, the Nude Dude Wines line was born.

Maybe that was what I was doing, I mused as I stepped out of the storeroom and closed the door firmly behind me. I was finally shedding my inhibitions and going after what I wanted, without making excuses. And although the idea of drinking blood made me slightly queasy now, if we couldn't stop The Change, maybe I would come to think of it as drinking a nice glass of Nude Dude merlot.

But that wasn't going to happen if I ended up in jail for murdering Bernie. I needed to look for clues. After chewing a fingernail for a few moments, I decided to start at the beginning and work my way back. We'd found Bernie in the dumbwaiter, so I would begin there.

A rancid smell, like steak that had sat out for too long, permeated the kitchen. I decided to chance turning on the lights. Unlike on TV cop shows, there was no chalk outline on the floor where Bernie's body had landed. Thank goodness. One less thing to clean up.

I felt a twinge. My concern was about cleaning up a chalk outline rather than about someone having died in that spot? Did it mean that I was a bad person and I would be an Evil vampire?

I clenched my hands and mentally shook myself. If I kept tallying my thoughts as good or evil, I was never going to catch a murderer. Or, if my hunch about Grace was right, a vampire murderess. Van and LaRue would work out the ritual to keep me from turning into a vampire, I told myself. Then I wouldn't have to worry about the good and evil thing except in the context of whether I wanted to go to heaven or hell when I died.

Oh crap! If I changed into a vampire, even if I changed into a Good one, would I be damned? I wished I had brought the legal pad and pen with me. I needed to start making an 'Ask Van' list. So far, I was up to food, fog, and now, damned.

Okay, back to murder sleuthing.

Carefully, I stepped around where Bernie's body had lain. The police had left the dumbwaiter door open and, unable to put it off any longer, I looked inside. The box was in the exact same spot as it had been when Bernie rolled out of it, and a blackish goop covered its floor. I recoiled in disgust. Now I knew what congealed blood looked and smelled like.

I tried to remember what blood at a crime scene meant. Had Bernie been alive when he was jammed in there, his blood still pumping? He was a miserable excuse for a human being, but dying alone, crammed into a small dark space, wasn't a death I would wish on my worst enemy.

I searched the first two floors of The Madam without finding anything that jumped out at me as a clue. Not wanting to announce my presence to the neighborhood, I used the flashlight app on my phone. It was slow going. On the second floor, I slid open the dumbwaiter's door and leaned into the shaft. The air was dank and musty and carried the ruined-meat smell. Holding my breath, I lit the shaft with my phone's flashlight. The box still sat on the first floor, but when I looked up, I saw that the door to the shaft on the third floor was open.

On the grand front staircase, halfway between the second and third floors, the rancid smell broke over me like an ocean wave. I gagged. It was much stronger than it had been in either the kitchen or the shaft. I continued slowly up the stairs, breathing through my mouth and dreading what awaited me at the top.

I paused when I reached the third floor and slowly swept my phone from left to right. The staircase opened onto what was little more than a landing, with several small hallways that led to rooms carved out of the attic, including my suite. When The Madam was built, this floor would have housed the servants. The opening to the dumbwaiter shaft was down one of the hallways that led toward the back of the house. A large puddle of congealed blood coated the century-old hardwoods. That was going to leave a stain.

The gore had turned black and resembled lumpy motor oil more than the bright red pools you see depicted on television and in movies. I gagged. The good news was that I hadn't gotten dizzy or fainted, like I normally did at the sight of blood.

Black streaks led from the puddle to the darkened hallway that housed the dumbwaiter. If Bernie had been shot here, he had either pulled himself or been dragged to the dumbwaiter. I followed the trail, being oh-so-careful not to step in it, gagging at the overpowering smell. I would love to say this was because I wanted to preserve the crime scene, but really, I just didn't want Bernie's goo on my shoes.

Yeah, I know. I'm such a girl.

The gory trail stopped directly beneath the opening for the dumbwaiter. I leaned into the shaft and, with a death grip on my phone, shone the light around. No bullet holes or gouges. In other words, no clues.

I sighed in defeat. I didn't know what I had expected to find. Was it too much to ask for the killer to have dropped his *Why I am Framing Laramie Harper Thompson Manifesto*, with his name printed on the top right corner?

Heck, I didn't even know for sure that I was being framed. Maybe the killer hadn't meant for the body to be found in The Madam. Maybe he—or she, if my hunch about Grace proved correct—killed Bernie and had been interrupted before he could get the body out of the house. Then it had been discovered during the code inspection before he could return for it.

The code inspection! It couldn't be a coincidence that the code inspection that had been indefinitely suspended was suddenly rescheduled, and on a Saturday, no less. Who had the horsepower to order an inspection on a weekend? I added a talk with Don Williams to my mental to-do list.

My light flickered across the wall, illuminating dried blood smearing the wallpaper between the floor and the dumbwaiter's opening. Whoever had shoved Bernie in there hadn't had an easy time of it.

Something just inside the shaft shimmered in my light. I tentatively reached for it—on guard for a spider ambush—and touched the dangling strands. They weren't cobwebs. Long red hairs hung from a splinter on the side of the shaft. Who involved in this fiasco had long red hair? Just my number one suspect, Grace O'Malley! Finally, a clue!

I tapped Van's number into my phone to call him to have PES come back out to collect the hairs, but my optimism fizzled before I hit send. I've been called a Pollyanna on more than one occasion, but even I recognized that the evidence wouldn't matter to Detective Bodwyn. Worst-case scenario, he would believe that Van or I had planted the hairs. Best case scenario, he would claim I had tainted the crime scene.

I carefully freed the hairs from the splinter. At least I had something to show Van. They wouldn't prove that Grace murdered Bernie or was behind the plot to turn me into were-wolf chow, but they were evidence that she had been at the scene of the murder. I wound the hairs into a small ring. I would put them in an envelope for safe keeping when I finished the search, but my pocket would have to do for now.

A low creak pierced the silence. The Madam, like many old houses, groaned and sighed more than a grandma climbing out of a recliner. Between the house settling, doors swinging in drafts and small creatures wandering its recesses, I'd woken many a night sure someone was in the house with me. Frozen, I waited for more sounds. When the quiet stretched to nearly a minute, I chalked the noise up to settling and resumed my search of the third floor.

With nothing left to check out down the rear hallway, I returned to the landing, once again careful to steer clear of the gore. Only one room opened directly off the landing, and another hallway ran toward the front of The Madam. I opened the room's door, its iron skeleton key rattling in the lock, and shone the light inside the tiny room that housed the steps that led to the widow's walk which perched on The

Madam's roof. Scuffs in the layer of dust covering the floor let me know that the police had already checked it. I couldn't make out actual footprints and there wasn't any blood, so no clues there.

Stepping back onto the landing, I shone my light around the walls and the openings to the other hallways. That was when I noticed a gouge in the wall that I had missed on my first pass. Five feet off the floor, and directly above the puddle of blood, an uneven crater about three inches in diameter marred the plaster. I crossed to the hole and illuminated it.

Leaning in closer to examine the area, I shuddered at the small dark spots and black lumps on the wall around the crater. I didn't have to be a forensics expert to know that they were blood splatters and body matter. I recreated the scene in my mind. For the bullet and spray to be on that part of the wall, the shooter must have been standing at the top of the stairs and Bernie standing where the congealed blood now pooled on my floor. Had the killer entered the house with Bernie, or had he snuck up on him here?

As I pondered Bernie's last moments, a stair creaked somewhere below. I prayed fervently that it was just the house settling and not the killer returning to the scene of the crime. Geesh! I'd given myself the willies. I tried to chuckle at my silliness, but it stuck in my throat.

Another stair creaked. It wasn't settling. Someone was in the house.

16

WINING

**43 Hours
(5:00 a.m. Sunday)**

Another creak sounded, closer than the last. I thought (hoped) that the intruder was at least one floor away. I quickly switched off my cellphone's light and swept my outstretched arms through the darkness. If I could find my way back to the small room I had just checked, I could lock myself in and call 911.

After a couple of steps, my fingers brushed something. I ran my hands over it and felt only smooth plaster. *Dang it!* I had no idea if the door was to my right or left. I held my breath, listening intently.

A staircase step creaked, followed by the solid thud of a shoe on the landing. Could I hear someone breathing or was I imagining it? Should I launch myself toward it and send him tumbling down the stairs? With my luck, I would miss him and catapult myself down the stairs instead. If the intruder was here to kill me so be it, but I didn't intend to do the job for him.

Clothing rustled nearby, followed by a light step. He was getting closer.

If I could momentarily blind him with my phone's light, maybe I could find the room and lock myself in. Holding my breath, I pressed the button to turn on the device's screen and then jabbed the flashlight icon.

In the feeble light, I saw a large figure brandishing a crowbar over his head. I screamed. The intruder yelped and froze mid-step. I swung the light around crazily until I saw the door less than a foot to my right. In a burst of inhuman speed I pulled the key from the lock, turned the knob, and practically fell into the room. I slammed the door behind me and got the key into the keyhole just as something collided with the door. It shook, but I was able to hold it closed. I turned the key, locking the door just as the knob started rattling. Bam! Something struck the door again. These doors and locks were made to last, but not to withstand an assault.

"You better get out of here! I called 911 when I heard you come in the house! They should be here any minute!" I hoped the bluff sounded more realistic to the intruder's ears than it had to mine.

The rattling of the doorknob stopped. "Laramie?"

"Yes?" I responded hesitantly.

"Oh, thank God! Laramie, it's Tom. Open up."

"Tom?"

What was Tom doing sneaking around The Madam in the middle of the night wielding a crowbar? I considered my options. I didn't trust him, but I also didn't want to call 911 unless forced to. I'd had enough of cops for one day.

"A loud bang woke me up earlier, then I saw what looked like a flashlight moving around. I thought kids from the neighborhood had broken in to see the crime scene. I let myself in with the key that Hattie gave me."

Tom fell quiet. Did I believe him? Not really. The pause stretched out between us.

"I'm so sorry I scared you," he added. "I was only trying to protect the house. I hope I did the right thing."

He had access to the house, and I needed to question him if I wanted to solve Bernie's murder. But how could I trust him not to kill me as soon as I walked out the door? I thought fast.

"Tom, hold on a minute. I need to call the police and let them know it's okay." I turned up the volume on my phone and punched three random numbers, hoping the sound would carry through the door and convince him I'd dialed 911.

"Hi, this is Laramie Thompson at 2769 Rowan Lane," I said into dead air. "I called about five minutes ago and told you someone had broken into my house. Yes, that's right. I was so scared! You can disregard the call. My neighbor, Tom Harner," I raised my voice on his name so he would think that the police had a record of it, "came in because he thought I was an intruder. Yes, he's standing right here with me. We're both fine. Oh, they're just a block away? No, really, tell them thank you. I'll call back if I need them. It's nice to know they're so close. Thank you for your help tonight, goodbye."

I said a quick prayer to the gods that if Tom was the murderer, my fake call had worked, and unlocked the door.

Stepping carefully from the room, still using my phone as a flashlight, I located the nearest light switch and turned it on, illuminating the whole ghastly scene on the other side of the landing. Tom faced me, wincing in the sudden glare.

"Thank God it's you," he said, releasing a pent-up breath. "When I didn't hear any giggling or talking, I knew it wasn't kids. My imagination got the better of me and then—well, you know what they say about murderers returning to the scene of the crime."

"Yes, I've heard that too." I fought the inane urge to smile and put him at ease. I wanted him off balance.

"Now that I know that both you and the house are okay,

I'll say goodnight." He turned and saw the gore. "What the hell happened here?" he blurted.

"A murder," I deadpanned.

"Oh," Tom said. "I heard they found him in the dumb-waiter shaft. I figured he fell and thought maybe the murder talk was just the police covering their bases since he was hated by, well, everyone."

I gave Tom the once-over. As the saying goes, he looked green around the gills. Until I saw him brandishing that crowbar—the one he still gripped tightly—I couldn't have imagined bookish but still *GQ* Tom killing anyone. Now I wasn't so sure. His reaction seemed genuine, but how was I really supposed to know?

"Tom," I said, placing my hand on his shoulder, "Let's go downstairs and have a glass of wine. You look like you could use it."

He was on my suspect list and, no matter how ill he looked, I needed to question him. I made sure that he and his crowbar stayed ahead of me the entire way down the stairs.

I settled us at the large kitchen island with a carafe, aerator, two large wine glasses and a bottle of Nude Dude shiraz. The kitchen made me queasy, but it was a calculated move.

Being a red, the shiraz needed to breathe and pouring it through an aerator into a carafe was the best way to speed up the process. Yes, it was a tense situation and I might be forgiven for letting some things go by the wayside. But drinking red wine without letting it breathe? We weren't savages.

I uncorked the bottle and poured the shiraz through the aerator, watching it stream through its small holes and cascade down the sides of the carafe. I imagined that my interviews with my suspects would need to follow the same principle. Strain out any impurities—or lies—and swirl the story around in my head, plumping it up until it became its true self, not the flat version they were trying to sell.

I poured a taste into Tom's glass and nodded at him to do the honors. While Tom swirled, sipped, and gurgled, I considered how to proceed. Although he claimed the shed door had woken him, Tom was freshly shaved and his pistachio polo and khaki Dockers were perfectly pressed. He appeared relaxed, which was a little odd considering what had happened upstairs. Tom was a good-looking man but a little too smooth. For the first time, I agreed with Hattie and Van. He was creepy.

After he completed the ritual, he smiled and motioned for more shiraz. "This is excellent," he said, in obvious surprise. "I thought it was a gimmick wine. You know, one where more time was spent naming it and working on the label than actually went into the vinification."

"I wouldn't carry it if I wouldn't drink it," I replied.

"I should have given you more credit."

I paused to organize my thoughts. I had to ask the right questions to progress with my investigation. Unfortunately, I had no idea what the right questions were, this being my first murder and all. Finally, because I didn't have any smooth interrogation moves, I decided the direct approach was best.

"Tom, why do you want to buy The Madam?" I asked.

He stopped mid-sip and stared at me.

"Where did that come from?"

"Someone got murdered in my house yesterday and I'm the prime suspect. The police didn't give me the impression that they are looking for anyone else, so I figure I need to."

"So I'm your suspect?" Tom asked incredulously.

"Actually, I don't have a suspect yet," I said, mentally crossing my fingers at the white lie. Grace was as good as behind bars in my mind. At least she had been until Tom brought a crowbar to the party. Unlike the police, I needed to be open to multiple suspects.

Tom eyed me silently over the rim of his glass. Just when I

was sure he was going to walk out, he took another sip of wine and started to talk.

"You know I grew up in the house next door, right?"

I nodded.

"The very small house next door," he said wryly. "I would visit The Madam with Mother and was awed by it. When I was at home, I would stare out the window at this place and make up stories about it. I think the house inspired me to become a writer."

"Well," he continued with a wave of his hand, "awe probably isn't the right word. I felt an affinity to it. Hattie always made me feel at home. Oh, she could be harsh, but she lived her life without regrets or excuses, convention be damned."

Harsh wasn't the way I remembered Hattie, but I smiled at him encouragingly.

"When Hattie passed away after the accident, I thought that she had left the house to me. We were always close."

In a pig's eye.

"When I found out you inherited The Madam, I was hopeful we might come to an arrangement. You never had much interest in the place when she was alive, or even in living in Dallas."

"I never had any interest in living in Dallas but, like you, I felt a connection with The Madam the first time I saw her," I said. "More than that, I needed a fresh start in a new place. Hattie gave me that by entrusting The Madam to me."

"Do you think that Hattie would agree with turning the house into a business and all the changes you've made?" Tom appeared genuinely curious.

"I'm not sure about the changes, but she would agree with the business. Hattie always said that The Madam needed more activity and people. She told me, on more than one occasion, that she was wrong to keep her for herself, but that she didn't have the energy to open her to the public."

"Hattie was never herself after Jad died. Van and I would

both visit her, but it wasn't the same as when your husband would stay with her for days on end."

His eyes watched me intently for my reaction. I would have loved to correct him regarding his assumptions about the problems in my marriage; unfortunately, I couldn't. I struggled to keep my expression neutral.

"I always thought that Hattie wanted the house filled with family, not with paying customers. I don't mean that as censure," he added when I looked up sharply. "When Marek Cerny made you an offer on the place, I knew I could never compete with him. My books are selling, but I don't have the wealth of a corporation behind me. So I was very happy that you wanted to stay, even if you were turning the house into a business. If I must live next door to a bar, I would rather it be yours than Cerny's."

"Wine bar and dog park," I murmured, then smiled brightly at Tom as I gathered my wits. He had just torpedoed what I thought was his motive for killing Bernie. If I had to sell The Madam to pay my legal fees, he knew I'd take the highest offer. He would lose The Madam as a buffer between his house and the Dragonfly. He wouldn't be framing me for Bernie's murder if it meant forcing me to sell to Marek.

Tom must have misinterpreted my overly bright smile because his smile in response was just a little too smarmy. I considered, for about a nanosecond, flirting with him to see if I could get answers that way, but quickly discarded that idea. I was worse at flirting than I was at investigating murders.

After another sip, Tom sat his almost empty glass down on the island's countertop. Bingo! Wine should loosen his lips more than my flirting any day. I topped up his goblet and waited for him to take another mouthful before I continued with my questioning.

"So, who do you think brought Bernie on board to try to sink my business?"

Tom jerked, causing his shiraz to slosh dangerously in his glass.

"Wha . . . what do you mean?"

"Bernie didn't live in the neighborhood. Right before I was due to open, he showed up out of the blue and suddenly everything was tied up in red tape. Someone had to have brought him in, and it had to benefit Bernie." I sipped my wine, letting that sink in before I continued, "I wonder what they offered him?"

"Oh," said Tom, regaining his composure. "I see what you mean. I never thought about it quite that way before." He paused and swirled his wine around in his glass, making a big show of considering the question. "My bet would be on Cerny. He wants your property for himself and has the money to bring someone like Bernie on board."

"I agree." Tom was right, in a way—Marek looked like the obvious choice. But his behavior over the last twenty-four hours wasn't that of someone who wished me ill. "But if the delayed inspection that Bernie finagled had pushed the opening back even a few more weeks, I would have run out of money. All Cerny had to do was wait me out. Then he could have picked up The Madam for a song. So why kill him?"

Tom pursed his lips, then suggested, "Maybe Bernie wanted more money?"

"I can't see that as an issue for Cerny. He could probably pay Bernie off ten times over without it denting his pocketbook. Maybe Bernie threatened to go public?" I said, thinking out loud.

"Bernie, go public?" Tom laughed nervously then added, "That could be it."

He seemed to stare into his wine glass intently, but then I noticed he was surreptitiously watching me through his lashes. I was on to something, but what? If Tom had brought Bernie in and then Bernie threatened to expose Tom, what was the worst that could happen? I would be mad, and it would make for an uneasy neighbor situation, but it wasn't worth killing someone over.

I was stumped. Tom either didn't know anything or he wasn't saying. Either way, I didn't think I was going to get anything else out of him.

Another thought occurred to me. It was a long shot, but what did I have to lose?

"So, you don't think Temple brought Bernie in?" I asked and watched Tom closely for a reaction.

He jerked again, and this time some of the dark red wine sloshed over the side of the glass, landing on his pastel polo and soaking into the light-colored fabric. Oh, that was going to stain—just like Bernie's blood on my hardwoods.

"Who is Temple?" he asked.

"Oh, just someone else who has expressed an interest in The Madam," I lied, hoping he would let something slip. "You haven't met him?"

"No," Tom could barely get the word out. "I didn't know someone else was trying to buy the house. How much has he offered?" He attempted to set his wine glass casually on the counter, but his hand was shaking and its base rattled against the stainless steel.

I thought he was lying, but then, so was I. Maybe the thought of another player in the game had really shaken him up. I stayed silent for several moments, hoping it would make him uncomfortable enough to start talking.

I'm sad to say, the tactic worked better on me than on him and I was the first to break. I had been saving my trump card for last because it would end the evening—or morning, as it were—on an unpleasant note. But me going to jail would be more unpleasant than pissing off a neighbor, so I went for broke.

"What keeps bothering me, though, is how did Bernie get in?" I asked.

"What do you mean?"

"There were no signs of a break-in. Someone with a key brought Bernie into the house and then killed him. Only four people have keys besides me."

"Are you asking if I killed Bernie?" Tom asked incredulously.

I felt very small, but I held my ground. "Did you?"

"Laramie," Tom stood and pulled his jacket on over his stained polo shirt, "Bernie was a huge pain in your ass but, while I like you a lot, I'm not willing to commit murder for you. I know you're tired. I'll see myself out." He dug around in his jacket pocket and placed a ring with two antique keys on the kitchen counter.

"Don't forget to lock the door after me." He walked out of the kitchen, through the back door, and disappeared into the early morning darkness.

17

ENEMY TERRITORY

42 Hours
(6:00 a.m. Sunday)

I re-corked the wine and rinsed the glasses while I pondered my next move. I considered calling Van but decided that since he wasn't blowing up my phone because I left The Compound against his orders, he must still be asleep. Not wanting to wake him was only partially altruistic. The next part of my plan would be easier sans Van. Easier, hell—if he knew, he would forbid it. I was done asking people for permission. But I wasn't above taking the easiest route possible to my objective.

So, what was it that Van would forbid? My plan to step into the enemy's lair. Or, in this case, the enemy's office. I wasn't sure what office hours vampires kept, but I would be really surprised if they included early (or maybe late, for them) Sunday mornings. I was going try my hand at a little breaking and entering, or B&E as it's called it on TV, at the Dragonfly. Maybe I could find something that linked Grace to Bernie, or at least gather some of her stray hairs to see if they matched the ones in my house.

I kept on my boyfriend jeans but exchanged the top I'd worn for the last twenty-four hours for a different black, long-sleeved T-shirt and my flats for a pair of Skechers. While I had managed an amazing run down Elm Street in my cute flats after my escape, I didn't want to tempt fate or a broken ankle if I had to flee the scene. I transferred Grace's hair (I was sure of it) into an envelope and put it in my purse to give to Van when I saw him. Then I shoved my purse under the front seat of my truck and my keys in my pocket as I left The Madam. I wanted everything ready in case I needed to make a quick getaway. I walked to the hotel, since I was sure the parking lot had cameras.

Less than fifteen minutes later, taking the 'hide in plain sight' approach, I walked into the hotel like I belonged there. If anyone stopped me, I'd flash my room key from Friday night and keep going. Luckily, the lobby was empty of both hotel personnel and patrons, and the doors to one of the two elevators just past the front desk were open. I crossed the lobby's expanse at a brisk pace and practically dove into the metal box.

When the doors opened again I was on the second floor, where conference rooms, hotel offices, and Cerny Enterprise offices were all located. I had to make this quick. Even if the offices weren't occupied, surely someone was watching a video feed of the hallways. I crossed my fingers that he or she was on a coffee break.

A poster board sign on an easel—probably left up from last week—proclaimed that the *Marketing for Tomorrow* training was in the Cattail Room, with an arrow pointing down a hallway to the elevator's left. Hoping that I was right in my assumption that the conference rooms would be on one side of the hotel and offices on the other, I turned down a hallway to my right.

As I cool breezed down the hall, I slid Jad's lock-picking set out of my pocket and eased the rake out of the holder.

Mindful of security cameras, I kept the tools hidden in my hand. I scanned the plaques beside each door I passed. I would start with Grace's office and then, if I wasn't interrupted, move to Marek's.

This floor of the hotel was decorated in muted natural greens, blues and browns with occasional pops of iridescent colors that I could only assume were supposed to bring to mind dragonflies. It worked on me, anyway.

After I passed several offices that seemed to be hotel specific, I reached a large glass door flanked with windows. Looking in, I saw a reception area with two wooden interior doors on its far wall. One door had a gold plaque with Grace O'Malley printed on it big as day, the other had Marek Cerny emblazoned on it. Neither had a title.

I inspected the lock and relief washed over me. It required a traditional key, rather than an electronic card. My skills ran only to old-fashioned locks. Jad had learned how to pick locks around the time he started at the police academy, and had taught me on a whim. Until I found out about his side gig hunting bumpies, I thought it was a law enforcement thing. Now I knew differently.

I slid the rake into the keyhole but stopped as the truth crashed over me. Monster hunting hadn't been his side gig. It had been his extra job. That's what he had been up to all the times he claimed he was working overtime and extra jobs. It explained why his paycheck never reflected overtime pay and our bank statement hadn't listed any extra job checks being deposited.

Oh, Jad, why couldn't you have told me what you were doing? But I knew the answer. He had always tried to protect me from the bad in the world. He said that he saw enough bad for both of us, and he wanted me to remain untouched by it. *Damn him!* If I had known there were monsters, maybe I could have protected myself from them.

I was about to give up when the tumblers moved and the

lock clicked. I pushed the door open and entered the small reception area.

Nothing. If there was an alarm, it was the silent kind. I imagined a frantically blinking red light somewhere in the building, possibly accompanied by annoying beeps to notify guards that someone was trying to steal vampire secrets. I locked the door behind me. If anyone showed up, it would gain me a couple of seconds while they unlocked it.

I approached the door marked Grace O'Malley prepared to pick another lock, but its knob turned easily in my hand. Score! I eased it almost closed behind me, leaving about an inch between the door and the frame, hoping it would allow me to hear if someone approached the outer door. My heart pounded loudly and I felt claustrophobic in the small office. I could never do prison. I had to find Bernie's murderer. Although if I were caught burglarizing Grace's office, I might end up stuffed in a dumbwaiter rather than a jail cell.

After debating for half a second, I flipped on the lights. At first glance, everything looked normal. It was your typical office with a large desk in the middle, a small seating area to the left of the desk, and several tasteful wooden filing cabinets to the right. At second glance, something odd jumped out at me. Next to the seating area and pushed up against the wall lay the largest dog bed I had ever seen; either that or Grace took naps on the floor of her office on a large pillow. I was going with dog bed. Thank goodness that beast wasn't left in the office overnight, although my opinion of Grace bumped up a couple of notches. Anyone who brought her dog to work couldn't be all bad, vampire or not.

Now that I was in, I didn't have the foggiest notion where to start looking, or even what I was looking for. I guess I had hoped there would be neon signs flashing the word 'clue' with arrows pointing at objects. Would Bernie's wallet lying on the desk be too much to hope for?

The desk was probably the best place to start. I eased the

smallest rake out of the lockpick kit, in case its drawers were locked. To say that the desktop was untidy would be an understatement. Jumbled papers, numerous pens, and used Post-Its covered every inch. You would think that in several centuries of living Grace would have picked up some organizational skills. I carefully moved the letters, memos, and scrawled notes around, reading only the first line of each for the sake of time. Nothing jumped out at me.

The desk had a pull-out extender on the right side, over a deep drawer that looked like it would hold files. *Pay dirt!* Taped to the extender was a laminated sheet of paper with the names, emails, and phone numbers of the management personnel of Cerny Enterprises and the Dragonfly.

Elated, I slid my phone out of the back pocket of my jeans to take a quick picture, but when I touched the screen, nothing happened. The flashlight must have drained its battery. I scribbled Marek's cellphone number and email address on one of Grace's sticky notes. If I wasn't able to scrape together some real proof against her, at least now I had direct access to Marek.

Next, I tried the center drawer. It slid open effortlessly. I sat in Grace's desk chair—a large leather monstrosity that looked and felt like it belonged more in a throne room than an office—and prepared to dig through the drawer's messy contents. But digging wasn't required. A large personal organizer sat atop the flotsam. Wow, a calendar and an actual hard copy list of phone numbers and emails. Grace was old school. Biting my lip, I opened the book, hoping that she actually used it.

I wanted to yell Eureka! when I flipped through the planner, but I restrained myself. A burglar shouldn't do anything that might draw attention to herself. Its pages were filled with the details of Grace's days.

I found the day I'd gone to the Dragonfly. Had that been only two days ago? The page was filled with appointments, but I didn't recognize any of the names. I held my breath as I turned the page to yesterday's date, then let it out in a sigh. It was a Saturday, so I shouldn't have been surprised that it was totally blank. Had I been hoping that a nine o'clock appointment titled 'Werewolf Ambush' would be penciled in?

A quick check of my watch showed me that I'd been in the office for five minutes. I wanted to take the book with me, but that would be a dead giveaway that someone had been here. Plus, the thing was huge—a red-leather behemoth that would stand out like a sore thumb on my trek back through the lobby. I couldn't chance it.

Working backward from today's date, I scanned each page, still clueless as to what I was looking for. Grace was a meticulous scheduler and note keeper, not to mention extremely busy. The days were filled with appointments and phone calls. She even wrote notes in the margin with details of what had been discussed.

Then I saw it, and everything clicked. The appointment had occurred approximately two weeks ago. Grace had listed herself and one other attendee. That Marek wasn't included backed up my theory that he was in the dark about her schemes. But how did I prove it to him? Debating only briefly, I tore the page from the book and hurriedly folded it into a square small enough to fit in my pocket.

I continued to flip backwards through the book but spotted no other meetings with familiar names; definitely none with the other name I was looking for. But the life of the part owner of an international conglomerate was far more glamorous than that of a would-be small business owner. Every couple of weeks for the last few months, Grace had taken big trips: Ireland, France, and, just a week and a half ago, Argentina. It must be nice to have a company expense account and probably a jet at your disposal. Even if there wasn't a jet, I doubted Grace schlepped around in economy.

Voices drifted in from the hallway. I shoved the planner

back into the desk drawer, tiptoed to the office door, and placed my ear as close to the crack as possible.

"Yes, John, I know we need to talk about the night staffing, but not on Sunday morning. Herself will skin us both if you don't make it home in time for church." Grace's Irish lilt was unmistakable.

A male voice—John, I guessed—replied with a laugh, "You're right about that. My wife is serious about our church-going, but it's not even seven yet. I have time for a quick talk if you do."

What a suck-up!

I looked frantically around her office for a place to hide. The only option was under the desk, and if she came in, I would be trapped. Keys jingled in the hall.

"John, really, I just need to pop into my office for a moment. It's been a long weekend and it is far from over. Can it hold?"

I eased the interior door shut, then turned the deadbolt as quietly as I could. It locked with a click that in my anxious state sounded as loud as a shotgun blast.

"Hold on," Grace commanded, cutting John's brown-nosing off mid-sentence. "Did you hear that?"

Damn that vampire hearing!

I scanned the office again, this time for a way out. The only other exit was a window behind the desk. A second-floor window. I flashbacked to Grace fighting a guy twice her size on the roof of the car last night. That settled it: I would rather jump from the top of a skyscraper than face Grace.

With minimal fumbling, I unlocked the window and shoved the bottom half up. A wrought iron balustrade wrapped around the window, about three feet high and twelve inches out from the wall, with a flower box attached to the top railing. Would an actual balcony have been too much to ask for?

The rattle of the office's doorknob galvanized me. I

climbed through the opening and onto the balustrade. After taking a second to try to fix the drapes into their previous arrangement, I closed the window.

As much as I would have loved to have hung out there hoping that Grace wouldn't notice that her office had been disturbed, my instincts screamed to get as far away as possible. I climbed over the railing, refusing to look down. It was only the second floor, but among my many faults—doormat, unathletic, poor coordination—was a terror of heights. Praying to the gods, I swung over the railing, slid down it and hung from the bottom. I was pretty sure I was out of sight if she just looked out the window, but the dead hang had never been my strong suit. In fact, it was the reason I failed sixth grade gym class.

Below me, a small patch of grass appeared about a thousand feet away. A few feet to the right was a large sycamore tree. Here goes nothing. I let go, trying to drop straight down. The ground rushed up at me, then I felt and heard a snap in my right ankle when I landed. The rest of me hit the ground with a thud. The pain shot through my leg, causing me to gasp and my eyes to water. However, I knew it wouldn't compare to the hurt that Grace would inflict if she caught me. Crawling for all I was worth, I reached the tree and flattened myself against the side away from the window, crossing my fingers that vampires didn't have sycamore X-ray vision.

After a few moments, I couldn't stand it any longer and peeked around the side of the tree to scope out the window. Grace, framed by the curtains, looked out directly at the tree. *Crap, crap, crap!*

I made myself count to ten before I peeked again. The window was empty. Option one was that she hadn't seen me. Option two was that she had and was tearing ass through the hotel to confront me. Either way, I had to get a move on.

When I entered the Dragonfly, I'd had no idea who to talk to next, but Grace's appointment book had taken care of that dilemma. Next on my list was the man she'd met with two weeks ago. The appointment took place right around the time my troubles with Bernie had started. The troubles that led up to my final inspection getting waitlisted.

Grace had met with my wild-card suspect and someone who had been at the Dragonfly the night of my attack: Council Member Austin Crockett.

18

DEATH BY LYCRA

41 Hours
(7:00 a.m. Sunday)

Tentatively, I touched my toes to the ground and waited for the shooting pain to hit. The leg throbbed, but it didn't intensify on contact. Going for broke, I put more weight on the foot. It hurt but was bearable. I had broken it when I hit the ground, but now it felt more like a bad sprain.

In the dim morning light, I could just make out the silhouette of The Madam's turret as it jutted through the heavy mist that shrouded my neighborhood. Normally I would have been enchanted by the sight, but right now it reminded me of every bad B horror movie I had ever seen. The Madam no longer represented safety, but if I could make it to my truck, I should be okay. My broken ankle throbbed with every hop. Crockett might have slipped to number three on my to-do list, with numbers one and two being medical treatment and crutches.

Surprisingly, by the time I limped the to The Madam, the pain in my ankle was barely a twinge. It had to be because of The Change. My body had repaired itself at an astounding rate. If we were unable to stop The Change, I was sure my enjoyment of its perks would come to a screeching halt—or a huge pile of vomit—when it got to the blood-drinking point. But so far, the whole thing kind of rocked.

While I wasn't into the supernatural, a girl would've had to have lived under a rock not to have seen a couple of movies or read a handful of vampire books. In them, only 'bad' people were portrayed as wanting to become vampires while 'good' people were always trying to keep it from happening. But I was starting to think that maybe I wanted to become a vampire. Did that mean I would become an Evil vampire? No matter how great it was to heal a broken bone in less than five minutes, I didn't want to become a vampire if I would be Evil and kill people.

I slid behind the steering wheel of my truck, slammed the door, and hit the lock button for good measure. I was convinced that at any moment Grace would materialize from the fog that enveloped my truck, but I still took a moment to attach my phone to its charging cord. With my ankle miraculously healed, Crockett was back to the top spot on my to-do list, or in this case, my to Speak To list, but I had no idea where to find him. I could try to B&E his office like I did Grace's, but I had a sneaking suspicion that getting in and out of city hall on a Sunday morning would be a lot harder than the Dragonfly.

With some effort, I pulled my large purse/briefcase/lunch box/catchall from underneath the front seat and put it on the passenger side of the truck. I pulled out the box of fliers for The Whine Barrel. No sense in carrying around extra weight when I was on the run. Then I smiled a slow smile. The shiny trifold brochures with pictures of The Madam, dogs, and glasses of wine, reminded me exactly where Crockett would be today and how I could talk to him.

I checked the clock on the truck's dash and groaned. It was barely seven o'clock. It would be hours before he would be there.

It was time to fall back to Plan B, or Plan Bill Martinez, my contractor, since I knew where he would be at sunrise on a Sunday morning. By the time I finished talking to Bill, my phone would be charged enough to call the other people I needed to talk to. Topping my list was Don Williams, to see if I could get him to spill on who had ordered the code inspection.

Pulling out of The Madam's driveway and circling the block, I put my house in the rearview mirror as I headed for White Rock Lake. An avid runner, most Sunday mornings Bill could be found on the ten-mile paved trail that circled the lake. He loved to talk about running, second only to talking about his kids. Sometimes his wife tied with his beloved hobby, but usually she fell a distant third.

I pressed the gas pedal almost to the floor as I rocketed onto the entrance ramp to Woodall Rodgers Freeway. Bill had told me that he always left the lake immediately after his run so that he could attend church with his family. He was very religious, or at least he talked a good Jesus game. We were friends on Facebook and his posts were all about his family, running, and his faith. Mostly the religious posts were scriptures and the Jesus loves you type, but other times they were cringeworthy, equating the liking and sharing of the post as a prayer or a blessing and accusing you of not loving Jesus if you didn't. I don't believe that Jesus measures our love of him by Facebook shares and likes, but maybe that's just me.

Even as strange as Bill was acting yesterday, I couldn't believe that he had murdered Bernie or was sabotaging my business. I might not agree with some of his religious posts, but I believed he was a genuinely good man. Still, there was the chance that by talking to him I would glean something that would help connect the dots between Bernie, Grace, and Council Member Crockett.

A loud beeping momentarily distracted me from the road. My phone had finally gotten enough juice to power up, and notifications flashed on the screen like a strobe light. Driving on the freeway was not a good time to check messages, but Sunday morning traffic was light, so I scanned the alerts. They consisted of missed calls, mostly from Van, and four voicemails. I thumbed the silence button. As a murder suspect currently out on my own recognizance, I shouldn't be talking and driving, right? Van Helsing Anderson would just have to wait.

The parking lot next to White Rock Lake's spillway was filled to overflowing. Bill had told me that loads of people were into this running thing, but since I couldn't fathom putting myself through that much pain just for the fun of it, I'd never believed him. Luckily a car backed out of a spot right in front of me, and I whipped in before any of other cars trolling the lot could beat me to it.

I checked my phone. Van had called again. I sighed and started his voicemails.

"Laramie, I can't believe you left after I told you not to. You understand how serious this is! Call me." He sounded like the situation, or at least his peace of mind, was at DEFCON 3. *Delete.*

"Seriously. This isn't funny. Call me back. Now!" DEFCON 2 . . . or was it DEFCON 4? I never could remember if the levels increased or decreased with the seriousness of the incident. Either way, Van's level had ratcheted up. *Delete.*

"Laramie, Owen here. Bo is good. We stayed up last night watching black-and-white movies and eating popcorn. I swear that diva was a silent film star in another life. She is good here as long as you need her to stay, but please call to dish. Van told me last night that you had been sprung from the big house, but that there were other complications. I want the deets. Oh, and I hope you are okay and all." Just as Owen had intended, I smiled despite my exasperation. He was the biggest gossip I knew and had only been half-kidding when he put wanting to know the details of the situation over expressing concern for my well-being. *Delete.*

"Okay, I give up. I'm past mad. Call me." Van again, but this time he sounded resigned and a little sad. It was the Van voice I had gotten used to hearing since Jad had died. *Double delete.*

I scrolled through the texts, all ten of which were from Van and matched the same pissed-off tone of his first two voicemails.

I relented and texted him a quick, 'I'm fine. Sleuthing. Will call in 15.'

Next, I texted Owen, 'I'm good. Thanks for asking. Give Bo hugs. Will talk later today.' Since Owen had keys to The Madam, I needed to talk with him just to cover all my bases. Plus, he was such a gossip that he might have picked up something during the renovations that I had missed.

I was momentarily blinded when I stepped out of my truck. My eyes were assaulted by Lycra, spandex, and technical fabrics in every shade under the sun, most of which are not found in nature. Running shoes that looked like My Little Pony had pooped on them adorned every foot in sight. In comparison, in my dark clothing I looked like an usher at a funeral. Appropriate, since it would be my funeral if I didn't get Bernie's murder solved.

A loud bang startled me and drew my attention away from all the neon to the far side of the lot. It was only the slamming of a porta potty door after the exit of its latest visitor. The distraction was welcome, though, because it alerted me to Bill's truck parked right next to the, ah, facilities. Nearby was a large tree with a picnic table under it. If it was upwind from the potty, the table would be the perfect place to wait for Bill to finish his run.

Just as I settled myself at the table, my phone buzzed angrily in my pocket. Well, phones can't be angry, but callers can—and if it was who I thought it was, he was too angry to wait the fifteen minutes. I fumbled my phone out of the back pocket of my jeans and Van's handsome face staring up at me confirmed my hunch. I had snapped the picture at the ranch when he had been helping Daddy and my brother Monty with one of the colts. It had been a good day. I doubted that he was relaxed and smiling right now.

My finger hovered over the accept button, then I caught sight of Bill on the far side of his truck. Van would have to wait. I shoved my phone in my pocket and hurried toward Bill.

I had rounded the bed of his truck before I realized he wasn't alone. Almost snuggled up to him and decked out in enough neon to blind me was a woman way too young to be his wife. She could be his daughter, but I didn't think dads and daughters stood that close. At least, not those outside of Arkansas.

I jerked to a halt, embarrassed by my intrusion, but they only had eyes for each other. If I strained, I could almost make out their urgent whispers. I hated to break up this tête-à-tête, but I had a murder to solve.

"Bill." I cleared my throat.

Bill jumped like he had been shot and leapt back to put some space between himself and the chickie. She gasped, but her face lacked the guilty look that covered his. In fact, after the initial surprise, several emotions flitted across her face in quick succession: satisfaction, interest, and finally, suspicion. She closed the gap he'd put between them and laid a possessive hand on his arm; her body language and expression clearly stated MINE.

"Laramie," I said, holding my hand out to her. She hesitated for a moment, clearly shocked. Then, with a flip of her long ponytail and a superior look, she stepped toward me and shook my hand.

"Tiffany," she responded, somehow making it sound like a challenge.

Tiffany? It was just too stereotypical to believe. Midlife crisis much? I struggled to keep my face blank, but Bill's guilty expression convinced me that I might as well have screamed my judgment. He opened and closed his mouth like a fish out of water.

"Laramie, what are you doing here?" he stammered out.

"I want to know why you couldn't be at the inspection yesterday." The direct approach had worked well so far. Why change my tactics?

"Umm . . ." He glanced at Tiffany then back to me. "I told you I got called to another site."

That rat! He purported to be a Christian and a dedicated family man, but in reality, he hadn't hesitated to blow off my inspection to go see his piece on the side. Based on the daggers that Tiffany shot him with her eyes, she didn't care for his answer either.

"Bill! I told you that if you don't start telling people, I will." She focused on me and continued, "Bill was with me. We've been seeing each other for three months and we're in love. He's just staying with his wife for the kids, which is just plumb stupid seeing as they're almost as old as I am. I told him yesterday that I was calling his wife. If she's any type of real woman, she won't want a man who is staying with her out of duty."

I was sure that my eyebrows were raised so high they merged with my hairline. Bill looked like a man caught between a rock and a hard place.

"How did the inspection go?" Bill asked lamely. So that was how we were going to play it?

"Oh, the inspection went fabulously," I replied. "If it had gone any better, I would have ended up in jail. Oh, wait a minute, that's right, I did end up in jail."

"What?" Tiffany gaped at me.

"Tiffany, no disrespect intended, but can Bill and I have a few minutes to talk privately?"

Tiffany must have decided that I wasn't a threat to her relationship. "Sure," she replied. Then she said to Bill, "Twenty-four hours or I'm going to start making all kinds of phone calls."

With that, she got into a sporty red convertible parked a few spaces over from Bill's truck. She gave us a hard look as she drove past.

I looked at Bill and then motioned to the picnic table I had just left. He trudged to it like a man forced to his execution.

After we settled on opposite sides of the table, Bill asked, "What is this about jail?"

I considered throwing out the old detective's line of 'I'm the one asking the questions,' but decided not to be so dramatic. I gave him a quick rundown of the inspection, the body in the dumbwaiter, going to jail, and getting sprung from jail. I left out the vampire and werewolf bits and Grace's office. I didn't want to cop to a B&E in case Bill ever had to testify against me. I don't think the decision to leave out the vamp and were bits requires any explanation.

"Wow," Bill said. "Bernie. Just wow."

If Bill was acting, he deserved an award. After seeing his reaction when I caught him with Tiffany, I didn't think he was that good.

"Okay, I've caught you up. Now spill about yesterday."

Bill breathed deeply and appeared to be collecting his thoughts. "I need to start the story several months ago."

As I nodded, my phone buzzed in my pocket. I ignored it. Van would have to wait.

"I met Tiffany three months ago when she joined our running group. I started out just being friendly, but when she was more than friendly back I was flattered." Bill shook his head sadly. "My wife, Grabela, and I got married when she was eighteen and I was twenty because she was pregnant with our first child, Billy. Twenty-five years together. We love each other, but we'd gotten complacent. Billy's wife gave birth to our first grandchild the week before I met Tiffany. It was exciting, but also scary. Suddenly I was a granddad. An old guy."

"And here was this pretty young thang ready to make it all better," I said. I failed to keep the disgust from my voice, but then, I hadn't tried too hard.

"Believe me, I know it is the oldest cliché in the book."

"So, you want out of your marriage?"

"No," Bill replied emphatically. "When it first started, I was sure that Tiffany was my soulmate, and that I had never really been in love until I met her. It was like she cast a spell over me. But after about a month and a half, I realized that was my little head talking instead of my big head."

I looked at Bill quizzically. He cocked his head to one side, then looked down at his lap and back at me. When understanding struck, I couldn't help but smile at his chagrined look.

"Anyway, I've spent the last month trying to ease out of the relationship, but Tiffany won't let go. She refuses to believe I don't love her and keeps threatening to tell Grabela." Bill wouldn't meet my eyes. "When I called you and told you about the inspection yesterday, I fully intended to be there for it. Then Tiffany started texting me. She had Grabela and Billy's cell phone numbers. She threatened to call them if I didn't go over to her house to talk about our relationship. Honestly, I tried to put her off for an hour so I could do the walkthrough with Don. But she texted that she had called Grabela but got her voicemail and that if I wasn't at her house in fifteen minutes, she would call her back. I'm so sorry that I let you down."

Bill wouldn't hold my gaze. I couldn't tell if he was lying or embarrassed.

"Bill, what I'm going to say will probably piss you off, but the police think I murdered Bernie. So I need to figure out who did, and I don't have time to pussyfoot around. I'm talking to everyone who has access to The Madam."

"Why just people who have access to the house?" asked Bill. "What does that have to do with it?"

"There weren't any signs of a break-in. As much as I hate to think it, the killer is probably someone who has a key to The Madam, and they probably took Bernie inside to frame me for his murder."

I knew the exact moment when he realized what I was implying, because his eyes widened, then narrowed. "I should be offended, but after what you learned about me today, I know I don't have any moral high ground to stand on." He looked at me wryly, hoping, I think, for reassurance to the contrary. Since I agreed with him, I stayed silent.

"I didn't kill Bernie and I can't think of anyone who would want to frame you for his murder. My guess is The Madam was just an opportune location."

"That was my first thought too, but the list of people who want Bernie dead is legion. So I'm going to focus on two main questions: who brought Bernie in to try to stop me opening The Whine Barrel, and who would benefit from it not opening?"

Bill nodded thoughtfully. "When Bernie first showed up, I racked my brain on who would have brought him in. I finally decided that he had gotten bored with his side of town and just wanted to stir up your side. But with his murder in The Madam, I have to agree with you that it looks like the motive is to keep you from opening." He cocked his head at me. "Unless, of course, you did it to get him to ease up."

"Okay Bill," I said irritably, "that offends me, and I do have some moral high ground to stand on. Plus, do you really think I'm that stupid? If I was going to kill him, I wouldn't have done it in my house and left him there to be found."

"Maybe it was a crime of opportunity or passion. No, not that kind of passion," he said when I opened my mouth to vigorously object. "Bernie went back to your house asking for another tour. He pissed you off to your highest level of pisstivity, as only Bernie could. You bashed him over the head. Then, not having a way to get the body out of the house, you stuffed him in the dumbwaiter until you could figure out what to do with him."

"One, are you trying to talk me into jail? Two, Bernie was shot, not bashed over the head, and three, I would have cleaned up the mess before leaving the house, even if I had to leave him in the dumbwaiter." I was pissed that Bill's ability to so easily imagine me as a killer had caused me to blurt out that Bernie had been shot, a fact I had left out when I briefed him. If he had tripped up and mentioned that Bernie had been shot, I would have had my killer.

"He was shot!?" At my nod, he shook his head in disbelief. Was he shocked that Bernie had been shot, or that I already knew the cause of death? Again, I tried to gauge his acting ability and came up short.

"Actually, I believe that you are innocent. I'm just trying to follow the police's line of thought to figure out where they'll look next." Bill paused, deep in thought. "Another thread to pull is the code inspection. Who gave the order? It came out of the blue and at just the right time—or for you, the wrong time."

I was gratified that Bill had followed the same train of thought that I had. At least my process was rational and I wasn't completely out in left field. I decided to lay all my cards on the table. Well, most of them.

"Bill, do you think Marek Cerny or Grace O'Malley could have brought Bernie in to keep me from opening? I've mentioned to you before that Cerny is trying to buy The Madam, right?"

"Yeah, you have. When Cerny wants something he usually goes after it." He shook his head slowly before continuing, "But I can't see either Grace or Marek getting into bed with Bernie. He gave them a little trouble when they were opening the Dragonfly, but they shut him down pretty quick. I only saw him on the property with them once, and they both looked at him like he was something they had stepped in."

"Business makes strange bedfellows, and without The Madam and the lot she sits on, the Dragonfly can't be expanded. When did you see them together, if you don't mind me asking?"

"At the Dragonfly when they were building it. I was the contractor who oversaw the structural part of the build."

"Uh, how was Cerny to deal with?" How had I not known that Bill had built the Dragonfly?

"Mostly I worked with Grace. She was driven and outspoken. She knew what she wanted and wasn't shy about making sure she got it." He leaned across the picnic table and lowered his voice. "I don't talk about other jobs; that's why I never told you that I worked for them. This isn't very professional of me . . . they were pretty good to work for, but I always felt like there was something strange going on there. They kept weird hours. Nothing I could put my finger on, but . . . well . . . for lack of a better term, they gave me the heebie-jeebies."

"The heebie-jeebies?" I asked, eyebrows raised.

Bill nodded but didn't elaborate. He had dished on his former employers as much as he was going to, so I changed my tack.

"What about Council Member Crockett? I can't figure out where he fits in. What do you know about him? Could he be playing both sides?"

"Laramie, Council Member Crockett is only playing one side—his own. Don't trust him. He will support whoever it benefits him to support." Dark storm clouds crossed Bill's face. "You know, I just remembered that he was originally against the Dragonfly opening. I'm not sure what changed his mind, but after a few weeks of holding up permits and such, he was suddenly on board. He even came by the site a few times."

"What about Grace? Was she friendly with him?" I asked, holding my breath.

"Grace was usually the one who walked him around the site when he came to visit. But that doesn't necessarily mean anything, since she was the one overseeing the construction end of the project."

Doesn't mean anything, my ass. She was in this thing up to her fangs. I pushed up from the table and then paused to ask my last question: "Bill, does the name Temple ring any bells for you? Did he ever visit Grace?"

Temple was the other name I'd looked for in Grace's date book—it hadn't been there, but it was worth a shot.

Bill rubbed his chin. "That name doesn't sound familiar."

"Okay Bill, thanks." My shoulders drooped in defeat. I was no closer to finding the killer. My eyes fell on Bill's phone where he had laid it on the picnic table, and I thought of his Facebook posts.

"Bill, have you ever heard of the True Cross?" I asked.

"The True Cross? Like the cross Jesus was crucified on?" Bill's confusion was evident.

"I don't know." An arrow of excitement shot through me. "Does it actually exist?"

"Yeah," Bill said slowly. "Laramie, do you believe in Jesus and that he died on the cross for our sins?"

"Well of course I do," I responded calmly, although I was anything but sure. I needed answers, not an invitation into the fold. "I've just never heard the crucifixion cross referred to by that name. Is it in a museum somewhere?"

"You're not Catholic, are you?" Bill didn't wait for me to answer. "Constantine's mother found the cross in a cave in Jerusalem a few hundred years after Jesus was crucified. Parts of it—relics—are in churches all over the world. Its discovery is marked in September, mainly in the various branches of the Catholic faith, with the Exaltation of the Cross."

My excitement plummeted. What would the Catholic's True Cross have to do with me?

The strains of Darth Vader's ominous theme song filled the air.

I was sure I was losing my mind until Bill pulled out his phone. He read a text and let out an oath under his breath that was not flattering to females. Tiffany.

"Is she threatening you again?"

"Not this time," Bill said, looking up from the phone. "She wanted to let me know that she just saw a story about Bernie's murder and your arrest on the morning news."

"Oh crap!" At the same time, my phone began buzzing again. I looked at it, expecting to see Van's smiling face filling the screen, but it was much, much, worse than that.

The call was from Mama.

19

WELCOME BACK TO THE FORTRESS

40 Hours
(8:00 a.m. Sunday)

I didn't answer the phone. You couldn't pay me enough to open that can of worms. I sped up my goodbyes to Bill, pausing only long enough to ask him to text me Don Williams' cellphone number. I waited until I was in my truck to listen to Mama's voicemail.

"Laramie! What in the hell is going on? Cheyenne just called to tell me you were on the morning news. Something about you murdering somebody in that monstrosity you call a house. She is fit to be tied. She says she will never be able to show her face at the country club again. How could you just let us see it on the news like this? You call me immediately and tell me what you have to say for yourself. People are gonna be calling and we need to have something to tell them."

This was bad—really bad. Mama never cursed. She was mad as a wet hen, but not even a little bit concerned about me. It was typical that she and Cheyenne were only worried about what other people thought. I had gotten the short end of the family stick with those two.

I checked my other messages. Nothing new from Van, but there was a text from Owen saying that he was glad I was okay. Family was supposed to have your back, but so far only Van and Owen had expressed any concern whatsoever for my well-being. I knew my family loved me, even if they didn't express it in the ways I wanted them to—or at all, really. They were there for me in their own way, but I couldn't count on them. And, surprisingly, I didn't want to.

Just as surprisingly, I didn't want to go back and hide in The Madam. Solving Bernie's murder had started out as a necessity, but now I was kind of excited about it. I wanted to solve the mystery and catch a killer. Who was this new Laramie?

The realization of what I was feeling washed over me. It took a near-fatal—or fatal, if Van was to be believed—attack on my life, a murder in my house, and a perp walk to police headquarters in handcuffs, but I finally felt alive. And, despite the throbbing headache that the sun was bringing on, I felt amazing, too. Since Jad died, I had only been going through the motions of living. Now I was ready to take control of my life.

A grin stretched across my face. Today was going to be a good day. I was happy and I wasn't going to ruin it by calling Mama. I tapped Van's name on the phone screen.

"Where the hell are you?"

"Well, hello to you too." I couldn't help but be chipper with the newfound happiness bubbling up inside me.

"Do you know how worried I've been? Laramie, there have been two attempts on your life—by werewolves, no less. My house is impenetrable. You were safe here, but then you had to go traipsing off to do God knows what without even telling me."

"I left a note," I responded, my good humor fading. I had known Van would be mad that I hadn't followed orders, but I hadn't considered that he would also be worried. In fact, after

I left The Compound I had been so focused on solving the murder that I hadn't thought about the werewolves. After a quick scan of the parking lot, I locked my truck's doors. Like locked doors could keep them out. Right.

When Van didn't respond I mumbled, "I'm sorry. I'm headed that way now."

"Please do. Laramie?" he asked right before I ended the call.

"Yes, Van?"

"Please be careful."

———

Van buzzed me through the front gate of The Compound, and he and Yella met me in the parking area behind his wing.

Yella, short for Yellow Dog, was just that: a yellow dog of indiscriminate origins who had been dumped out by some asshole near our ranch in Faith. When she and Van met, it had been love at first sight for them both. They had been inseparable since. Van's love of Yella had created the first hole in the wall I had built to keep him at a distance.

Yella and I normally got along much better than her owner and I did, but today she stopped a few feet from me and sniffed the air cautiously. After a couple of whiffs, she bounded over and shoved her nose in my hand to demand head rubs. I knelt and gave her ear rubs while letting her lick my face a few times for good measure.

"Damn dog." Van tried to sound gruff, but I heard the affection.

When I looked up from giving Yella ear rubs, Van looked haggard and pale, but a small smile threatened to emerge.

"What?" I asked, confused as to what Yella could possibly have done.

"She is *supposed* to be a trained vampire-hunting dog," Van responded. "Her job is to recognize vampires and notify me that there is one close by. And, just for the record, the signal she has been trained to give does not involve rubs and kisses."

"So that means she knows I'm not a vampire yet. Good news, right?"

"Yet," Van said with a tight smile. "Where's my car?"

"Oh God, Van! I'm so sorry! It's in the shed behind The Madam. I completely forgot about it." Van sighed in response and I followed him inside the house.

Although I had experienced the opulent maze of hallways and rooms that he called home last night, I was awed again by the sheer size of his wing of The Compound. It crossed my mind that he was purposely leading me on a confusing route to make it harder for me to fly the coop again. I considered dropping breadcrumbs so I could find my way out. Meanwhile, Yella trotted happily beside us like she didn't have a care in the world. A rich owner who loved her like crazy? Yella had it made, and she knew it.

At the end of possibly the twentieth hallway, Van pushed aside a large, antique and, I'm sure, outrageously expensive tapestry to reveal steel elevator doors. He punched in a number on a keypad beside them. I tried to see the code, but he blocked my view with a slight turn of his body. Where was the trust?

The ride was so smooth that I didn't think we had moved until the elevator doors opened. Then I was convinced that we had been transported to another world, rather than another floor. We stepped out of the elevator into what appeared to be an underground hanger with a small fleet of cars, not one, but two armored trucks, and helicopters of varying shapes and sizes. The smallest helicopter looked barely bigger than a large drone, but based on the seat and controls, it could hold a person. The largest bird was military grade and could carry a company of Army Rangers. What the what? When Van had said centuries of monster fighting, I had imagined a couple of guys with leather briefcases filled with wooden stakes, not a high-tech secret military branch.

"Helicopters?" I asked quietly, not wanting my words to echo in the cavernous space.

"Yep," said Van in a normal voice, obviously not sharing my concerns. "Dad is an enthusiast."

"Your dad flies helicopters?"

"My dad can fly just about anything except a broom, and with a little practice, he could probably fly one of those too."

Curious. I'd always had the impression that Van's father was just a shadowy background figure off doing oil deals somewhere. On the other hand, I'd always thought his mother, Vivian, was a socialite whose only jobs were keeping a tight rein on her family and making everyone else feel inferior. I hadn't pegged her as the reigning matriarch of a monster-hunting dynasty. People will surprise you.

Van blocked my view again at the keypad for a door on the right side of the cavern. The door slid open Yella stationed herself on a small cushioned mat beside it, but Van motioned me inside.

Oh, God! Not her again. And she appeared to have set up residence in a laboratory that would do a military research facility proud.

LaRue, Voodoo Princess extraordinaire, wore a white lab coat and large clear glasses. But neither the slim, black, ankle-length trousers nor the bubblegum pink slingbacks that adorned her feet looked like standard scientist attire. The curls in her hair were perfect, neither frizzy nor limp, and her makeup was exquisite. I felt grubby in comparison.

LaRue pinned me with a stare through the lab glasses and said caustically, "The prodigal has returned."

"Are we ready?" Van asked her.

"Just waiting on her highness to grace us with her presence." LaRue turned to check a bubbling concoction in a glass beaker over a Bunsen burner on the counter behind her.

"Are you this big of a bitch to everyone or is it just me?" Even as I heard the words coming out of my mouth, I couldn't believe I was saying them. I don't do confrontation.

"It's just you," LaRue responded, unperturbed.

"What did I ever do to you?" I asked indignantly.

"Ladies, please," Van said, but LaRue—who did do confrontation—talked over him.

"Oh, Jad, I'm so helpless and shy, please don't leave me. Oh, Van, I'm so hurt and wounded, please help me. Vampires and werewolves? Oh my, whatever will I do? Please, please, save me because I can't help myself when there are big strong men around to take care of me," LaRue said in a high-pitched voice. Then she continued in her regular voice, "I hate helpless women who manipulate men to stay with them, and you are at the top of my list."

During her rant, LaRue's complexion had darkened with anger, but then tears had filled her eyes. I knew they were angry tears rather than sad, but they still broke me. I can't stand to see anyone cry. Worse still, her anger spent, LaRue had shrunk into herself.

"Oh, honey." I started around the counter that separated us, my arms outstretched, wanting to be mad about the horrible things she said to me but unable to when faced with her sadness.

"Oh, damn it! Stop!" she yelled when she realized I was trying to hug her. "Have some self-respect."

I halted mid-stride. Admittedly, the hug had been a bad idea, but processing something she had said during the rant was what stopped me.

"Why would you say I manipulated Jad into staying with me?"

Van and LaRue exchanged looks, then LaRue turned back to the bubbling beaker.

"Answer me," I ordered, finally red hot, steaming mad. A red haze tinged my view of LaRue, the counter that separated us, and the surrounding lab. That she hadn't even turned to face me incensed me further. I launched myself at her, but a hard body slammed into me midair and we crashed into the far wall of the lab. Unscathed, I struggled to gain my feet. I was still consumed by the desire to rip LaRue limb from limb, but the body kept me pinned to the floor.

"Laramie, calm down! Laramie!"

I quit struggling when Van's voice broke through my anger. Slowly, very slowly, the red haze lightened to a cotton candy pink. The laboratory came back into focus and I realized the body belonged to Van.

"You good?" he asked, his face close to mine. He lay on top of me, restraining my arms against my sides.

"Yes," I replied hoarsely, not sure if I meant my anger level or how good his body felt pressed against mine.

A loud beeping distracted me from Van. The door slid open and a man dressed like a cast extra for *Walker, Texas Ranger* stepped through it. He had sauntered a good ten feet into the lab before coming to an abrupt halt upon taking in the tableau.

"Uh, Van, you need some help there?" The cowboy smirked broadly.

"No," Van replied, practically leaping to his feet. He held out a hand to help me up and I checked for soreness as I stood. Nothing. Not even a twinge in my broken, now not-so-broken ankle. I made a show of brushing myself off. There wasn't a speck of dust in the lab, but it gave me time to compose myself.

Van turned furiously on LaRue.

"What's wrong with you? You know going into a rage like that could speed up The Change. If you can't handle this, then you need to leave. We'll get someone else to help us figure this out."

I watched LaRue surreptitiously. Hurt pride warred with regret, and she clenched and unclenched her fists as she faced off against Van. For several moments Van's harsh breathing was the only sound in the lab.

Finally, LaRue said, "As much as I would like to walk away from this hot mess, I can't. There's no one else you can get here in time."

Van stared at her, waiting.

LaRue rolled her eyes at him. "Fine! I'll do my best to behave. This is hard for me and it hurts that you're taking her side. It brings it all back. But I know it's what he would have wanted, so I'll do it for him."

Van wrapped LaRue into a tight embrace and she melted into it. I was envious. The full body contact on the floor had been nice, but that was to keep me from killing LaRue, so it didn't really count.

I fiddled with the front of my shirt, uncomfortable with the swirl of emotions inside me. The jealousy and possessiveness I felt toward Van around LaRue had to be products of the same chemical reactions from The Change that had caused the rage. Of course, I hadn't made it to the age of thirty without getting furious more than a few times. But I'd never physically attacked someone in anger, much less launched myself through the air at them. I told myself that the sudden heat I felt whenever Van and I touched was also a side effect. Not that it mattered. Even if I had feelings like that for him, he didn't see me that way.

Meanwhile, the new guy had moved his smirk from Van to me. I had the awful feeling that he knew exactly how I felt about Van hugging LaRue and my cheeks warmed with embarrassment. Could vampires blush? If they couldn't, put another check in the pro column for The Change.

"Wade Stephens." He stepped toward me with his hand outstretched. He was a couple of inches shorter than Van, with sandy brown hair and brown eyes. He wore a long-sleeved collared shirt tucked into jeans that covered cowboy boots. He epitomized nondescript, except for the big-ass belt buckle he wore on his western-styled leather belt. The belt buckle, complete with a raised outline of the state of Texas in the middle of it, would give a good-sized salad plate a run for its money. Something about him—his eyes, maybe—brought to mind a bloodhound: a little droopy, but still attentive.

"Laramie Thompson," I responded, shaking his hand firmly. I couldn't help but think that with all the craziness going on, the normal niceties, instead of feeling out of place, somehow put everything back on an even keel.

"Wade is our bloodhound," said Van by way of introduction.

His eyes had reminded me of one.

"Um, I'm new to all this so I'm not sure if it's polite to ask, but, how does one become a bloodhound? Were you bitten by one?"

All three looked at me blankly for a moment, then Van started laughing. A little hysterically, I might add. Wade and then LaRue joined in. At first, I smiled a little bit and went along with it. When the laughter continued to the point that Van was wiping tears from his eyes, I started getting a little peeved.

"What's so funny?" I asked primly.

Van wiped his eyes one more time and then responded, "Wade is our investigator. He isn't an actual bloodhound. He's an excellent tracker, so we call him that."

"So, you track bumpies?" I asked.

They looked at me quizzically.

Once again I felt a blush crossing my cheeks. "Um, I'm just not comfortable with the term monsters. It sounds so comic book, so I thought I would call all the things bumpies. You know, short for things that go bump in the night."

"Okay . . ." Van drew out the word in a manner that let me know he thought I'd finally lost it. "Wade tracks people, property, monsters—uh, bumpies—and just about anything else you can imagine. If we need it found, he finds it."

"Oh?" was all I could think to say.

"Wade is trying to track down Marek for us. We need him present and accounted for before we can do the procedure to reverse The Change." Van turned to Wade. "Any luck?"

"He went MIA last night after following you here. I haven't been able to pinpoint exactly where he is today. Mainly because he appears to be doing some tracking himself, and is bouncing around like a pinball. Grace has been helping from the hotel. They have a million feelers out."

"What is he tracking?" Van asked, concern etched on his face.

"The signs suggest he has several irons in the fire on that front." Wade picked up a cup from the counter, held it to his mouth and spit in it. Snuff. Ugh. I had been so preoccupied with my anger at LaRue, I hadn't noticed the cup or the nasty stuff in his mouth. But something gave me the impression it was more of an accessory for his aw-shucks country boy image than a habit.

"He's hunting the werewolves that attacked your girl," he said, waving the spit cup in my direction. "And he's trying to track down the special project we've been working on."

Van reared back like he had been slapped and LaRue sat heavily on a stool next to the bubbling concoction. I might have been in the dark about the "special project," but she obviously wasn't.

"Has he found h . . ." Van trailed off with a sideways glance at me and then continued, "anything?"

"Nope. He hasn't had any more luck than we've had. But, of course, he just started about" —Wade checked his watch —"thirty-four hours ago, so he has some catching up to do."

Van nodded and, while I may be slow, even I understood the significance of the thirty-four hours. The special project was somehow tied to me.

"Look, at some point you have to start sharing information," I said. "If I'd known about . . . bumpies, maybe I wouldn't have been attacked, or at least I could have defended myself. As it is, I'm turning into a vampire as we speak and you're still hiding things from me."

"It's ready," LaRue said, looking intently at the bubbling contents of the beaker over the Bunsen. "If we're going to do this, we need to do it now."

"You're right." Van nodded at me. "There are things that we've been keeping from you and you deserve to be in the know. That said, we need to table the talk for a little longer while we do this."

"At least tell me what this is," I said petulantly. "I don't even know what the witch has been brewing up." So much for our truce.

"Voodoo priestess," corrected LaRue between clenched teeth, "and this is a ritual that will show us your true self. It should indicate whether you will be a Good or an Evil vampire after The Change. Now," she said, holding up a small pair of scissors, "I need a lock of your hair."

I held out my hand for the scissors. No way in hell was I letting her attack my hair. I didn't want to be scalped.

"What does it matter what I'll turn into? We're going to stop The Change before it happens, right?" I asked, snipping a small lock from where I hoped a gap would be the least conspicuous. I was met with silence.

"Right?" I prompted again, feeling a sinking sensation in the pit of my stomach.

"Laramie, to reverse The Change we need the blood of the vampire who turned you. That means we need Marek to agree to give us his blood. The process is similar to making anti-venom for a snake bite. The venom from the snake is needed before the anti-venom can be made," Van said.

"If we are making an anti-venom, wouldn't we need his venom instead of his blood?" I asked.

"With vampires, everything comes back to blood," Van answered.

"Everything always comes back to blood," LaRue said. "Life, death, the undead and voodoo. It always comes back to blood."

"Vampire blood will heal you of most injuries unless you are too close to death for it to be pumped through your system," Van said. "So, if we put the blood of the vampire who venomed you into your system—"

"Boosted with voodoo to increase its potency," LaRue interjected.

"It should cleanse the venom from your body and heal any cells that have started changing," Van finished.

"So, we call Marek and ask him to give us some of his blood," I said as I dug around for my cellphone and the sticky note in my black hole of a purse. I didn't completely understand the whole 'blood cancels out venom' thing, but they had convinced me they knew what they were talking about. "He seems like a reasonable guy. I'll call him and explain the situation. I bet he'll help us out."

"Laramie, Marek isn't a reasonable guy. He is a somewhat reasonable vampire, but still a vampire, and he won't give us his blood." Van said.

"Why not?" I demanded. "If he's really so against having other vampires running around, why wouldn't he help us?"

"If we get his blood, we can also figure out a way to kill him," replied Van.

"I don't understand. What does his blood have to do with it?" I heard the panic in my voice. This was no longer fun and games and fast healing. I'd been failing at being a regular human, and I'd had thirty years of practice at that. I couldn't start all over again as something else at ground zero, not understanding any of the rules. I didn't want to become a vampire, no matter what the perks. It would be too hard.

"Y'all, I'm not kidding, the window is closing; we have to do this right now!" With that, LaRue snatched the lock of hair from my hand. "Laramie, stand next to me. I'll need your blood during the ceremony."

LaRue ignored my gasp. My eyes met Van's; he nodded and gave me what was supposed to be a reassuring look. It didn't work. I unexpectedly felt a kinship with Marek over the whole blood thing. LaRue might not be able to kill me with it, but I still didn't want to give her any of mine.

LaRue fiddled with her phone and drumbeats thumped from its speaker. She motioned impatiently for me to stand on her right side. As I stepped closer I noticed several small jars, a gourd, a black-handled knife, a white stick about eight inches long and a silver hat pin—just like my grandmother used to keep on her dresser—all crowded together on a small woven mat next to the Bunsen burner. After some mumbling and waving my lock of hair around in the air a few times in a clockwise motion, she dropped it into the beaker.

LaRue continued to murmur and sway in time to the drumbeat as she used the end of the white stick to push the hair beneath the surface of the muddy brown, bubbling liquid. Counting each rotation, she stirred the concoction clockwise. At the fifth stir, she pulled the stick out of the goo and, after more mumbling, snapped it in half. When she laid the two pieces on the counter I saw that it wasn't a stick at all, but a bone. I didn't want to think about where, or what, it had come from.

LaRue grasped my left hand and held it over the bubbling potion, palm down. The words she murmured sounded foreign, but I couldn't place the language. The steam that emanated from the mixture warmed my hand uncomfortably, but before I could snatch it away she lifted a small jar from the mat. She tipped it, allowing a single drop of oil to land on the back of my hand. LaRue returned the jar to the mat and I jerked when her hand hovered over the knife. I hadn't trusted her with a minute pair of scissors to cut my hair, and I sure didn't trust her with a knife.

Instead of the knife, LaRue selected the silver hat pin. She rested her left hand over mine for a moment before gripping my index finger. Using the pin in her right hand she lanced the pad of my finger and squeezed it until a large, bright red bead of blood dropped into the bubbling potion. She pushed my hand away from the potion but didn't address me.

"What now?" I asked, using my thumb to apply pressure to my lanced finger.

"We wait," answered LaRue shortly, crossing her arms. Van elbowed her and she sighed. "If the potion turns blue it means that you have a pure soul and will most likely be a Good vampire. If it turns black, you have a dark soul and, well, let's just say that you as a vampire won't be all sunshine and kittens."

"How long?" Wade asked, voicing the question in my head.

"I'm not sure," replied LaRue. After starting a timer on her watch, she looked up at us with a slightly evil grin. "Now might be a good time to give Laramie a little history lesson so she has a better understanding of the stakes. Pun intended."

20

VOODOO HOODOO

**38 Hours
(10:00 a.m. Sunday)**

"Let me try to start at the beginning and give you some of the basic groundwork," Van said, leaning against a counter so he could face me while keeping an eye on the swirling gunk in the beaker.

Like Van, Wade leaned against a counter, crossing his cowboy boots at the ankles, his arms across his chest, and his cup in his right hand, in easy spitting distance. I'd seen my brother, Monty, assume the same position many times, but he always leaned against a fence rail rather than a counter in a high-tech lab. Wade didn't look out of place, though. LaRue sat on a high stool near the beaker. To ensure some distance between us, I moved to sit on a different stool and leaned against the wall to get comfortable. With everyone settled, Van started the history lesson.

"Vampires and werewolves go back for centuries. Although there are a lot of theories, we don't know exactly how or when either condition started. Both species have strong footholds in folklore by different names and various descriptions in almost every culture. There are numerous theories, but if we go down that rabbit hole we will be here all day. So, it is more expedient to stick to the recent, need-to-know information."

"Need to know? You make it sound like the information is classified," I said.

"A lot of it is," Van replied without blinking an eye. "Let's start with vampires, since I think they are the most relevant to your situation. While vampires go back centuries in myths and legends, the Van Helsings were first mentioned by name in Bram Stoker's novel *Dracula* in the late 1800s. The truth is, our family has been hunting them for almost as long as they've existed."

I considered making a *Buffy the Vampire Slayer* joke, but I didn't think Van or LaRue would appreciate it. Wade might be another story, but I figured I should wait to get to know him a little better before introducing him to my particular brand of humor. Jad had always classified it as "lame."

"Our family has many branches and most of them are in the family business, so to speak. Or The Organization, as we refer to it. My mother is a direct descendant of Dr. Abraham Van Helsing of *Dracula* fame. She considered keeping the Van Helsing name when she married Dad, but ultimately she took his name to keep Bunny and me a little more incognito until we were old enough to fend for ourselves."

"Vivian and Bunny are also vampire hunters?" I asked weakly. Van's mother and sister, tall striking blondes who shared his Wedgwood-blue eyes, were socialites through and through. Neither looked as if they had ever so much as chipped a fingernail, much less staked a vampire.

"So, what, they carry around wooden stakes in their Hermes handbags?" I asked, my disbelief in my voice.

"As a matter of fact they do, along with other tools of the trade." Anticipating my next question, Van held up his hand to stop me. "We'll get to that in a minute. Quit interrupting me so I can tell you this in a way that makes sense."

"Okay," I agreed grudgingly.

"So, my family has been hunting Evil werewolves and vampires for centuries, as well as random Dualistics when they go rogue," said Van, raising his hand again to stop my question. "Like we discussed last night, not all vampires and werewolves are bad. A lot were, but that changed in the 1940s."

LaRue harrumphed from her stool.

"Anyway," Van said, mostly ignoring her, "Vampires and werewolves rocked along for centuries, with our family hunting down the particularly bad ones. Like any family, we had some bad apples. Ones who wanted to kill all the creatures—Good, Evil, or Dualistic. Because of this, even the Good ones don't like or trust us. When the sups, short for supernaturals, and the Van Helsings need to band together we do, but it is a very uneasy truce. One of those alliances happened in the late 1930s, when a truly evil man came to power, and the world divided."

"Hitler," I said.

"Correct. Like most conflicts, everyone who followed him wasn't truly evil, and everyone against him wasn't truly good. However, the factions of the underworld broke down along those lines. Yes, we do call the world of the vampires and werewolves the underworld, just like in the movies. It isn't an entirely different world like, say, the Hobbits' Middle Earth. But, because the majority of our world doesn't know they exist, vamps and weres move around, kind of under our world."

I nodded slowly, determined to circle back around to the Hobbit reference later.

"Vamps and weres can live for centuries and normally take humans' world-conquering tendencies with a grain of salt. But the Good vampires and werewolves recognized true evil and a threat to the entire world in the Nazis. The Evil and Dualistic vampires and werewolves saw opportunity. Hitler leveraged it. He promised if they fought on his side, he would give them free rein after the war. They'd be able to live in the open and kill and feed indiscriminately without repercussions."

"So, Hitler knew about the vampires and werewolves? Who convinced him?" I asked, wondering how that conversation had gone down.

"We aren't sure how it happened. We think one of the factions approached him and were, obviously, able to convince him. What we do know is that he was very superstitious and believed in the supernatural.

"We saw the writing on the wall," Van continued, "and one of those uneasy truces that I mentioned earlier happened. The Van Helsings, the majority of them anyway, and the Good vamps and weres banded together and offered our services to the Allied forces."

"Was your family involved too?" I asked LaRue. She had been quiet while Van talked.

"No. We aren't joiners. We normally work on our own, but I've been acting as a consultant for a few years now. And I'm going to move this along. If I leave it up to Van, we'll be here all day," she added, with an eye roll at Van. "The vamps and weres were nearly unstoppable on both sides. The only thing holding them back was being unable to fight during the day. Just like the legends, they are both almost impossible to kill. But they told their respective sides how to contain and kill the enemy."

"Silver," LaRue said before I could ask. "Regular cages can hold weres in human form, but once they change into their wolf it takes silver, either bullets or chains, to subdue them long enough to get them into a cage. As for vamps, fire, a wooden stake or a silver bullet in the heart, and decapitation are about the only things that work. Sunlight used to kill them before Hitler got ahold of them, but I'm getting ahead of myself."

"It isn't easy to condense, is it?" Van asked LaRue before he picked up the thread of the story. "Both sides provided names and descriptions of their sup counterparts. The Axis and Allied forces conducted massive vampire and werewolf hunts. So, the killing of vamps and weres started in earnest. By the Allies, anyway. Hitler was at the height of his power and had his mad scientists working on ways to create a super race. The majority of the Good sups were in Europe with express orders to take out Hitler's top commanders and Hitler himself, if possible. The bulk of the Good sups were captured and experimented on. Hitler wanted to recreate their species and make them even harder to kill. Many members of my family also met the same fate."

"How many?" I asked.

"Around twenty humans from the Van Helsing line were captured by the Nazis. Only five survived the war, my grand-father being one of them. Vampires and werewolves? A mix of approximately fifty were captured by the Nazi forces throughout the course of the war. Another sixty to seventy were killed outright by the Axis forces when they couldn't be captured. About two hundred and fifty vampires and were-wolves were killed by the Allied forces. I know. It doesn't sound like a lot. One of the ways the legends get it wrong is about how many there are. Vampires don't create many others, and the ones they create usually don't survive long. Even the Good vampires aren't a maternal lot. The Evil ones, like bad parents, don't take care of the ones they make. So they usually died young, either by walking into the sunlight because they weren't told it would kill them or because they started killing people willy-nilly and my family had to get involved."

"I'm confused. Does sunlight kill them or not?"

"Most of the vampires died during the experiments," LaRue said. "Some were put into direct sunlight to see how long it would take them to die. Others were staked with different types of wood to see which worked the best. The werewolves also took a big hit. They were put in cages together during full moons to fight, fed poisoned meat to see how it would affect them, shot multiple times with regular bullets to see how wounds and blood loss affected them. The werewolves, vampires, and Van Helsings were injected with various drugs and concoctions to see if their powers could be improved and their weaknesses overcome. The ones who survived were still being held in underground bunkers when the war ended. Allied forces freed them, having no idea what they were letting loose on the world."

"LaRue, don't be so dramatic," Van admonished. "The werewolves and vampires who fought for the Allies were war heroes."

LaRue rolled her eyes at him and sighed loudly to let us all know what she thought about that. She needn't have bothered. Her feelings had already come through loud and clear.

"Really," Van said pointedly to me. "The Allies tried to give them war medals. Of course, most refused to attend the ceremonies. They were convinced it was a trick to lure them to one place then kill them. But the takeaway from this is that they were all physically changed by the experiments. The vampires who were experimented on can now tolerate sunlight. It will make them nauseous, dizzy, and give them throbbing headaches, similar to a hangover, but they can survive it."

"The weres who survived captivity really came out of this ahead of the curve. They no longer automatically change into werewolf form when the moon is full. They can turn into a werewolf at night anytime during the rest of the month, although it is easier during a full moon. In other words, they can control The Change. For the most part, they can live normal lives if they want to."

"Most don't," LaRue interjected. "They stick with their packs and with their wolfie ways."

Van and LaRue both fell silent at that.

"Question time?" I asked.

"Question time," Van confirmed.

"You said that you didn't know Marek could make another vampire? Why wouldn't he be able to?" I asked.

"We believe that one of the benefits of the experiments—or drawbacks, depending on which side you are on—is that they were effectively sterilized. Their bites, anyway. Weres are still able to have children in the traditional sense who are werewolves, but being bitten will no longer cause a person without werewolf genetics to become one. Vampires have never been able to give birth and, since the war, their venom hasn't been able to bring about The Change," explained Van.

"Until now," LaRue said quietly.

We all fell silent for a few moments, but Van could tell I was on information overload.

"The condensed version," he added, "is that the vampires who were experimented on, the Good vampires, were left with the ability to withstand sunlight, but they lost the ability to create other vampires. Because the Evil vampires were not experimented on, in theory sunlight is still deadly to them and they can still create other vampires. I say in theory, because it is our belief that none of the Evils survived the war."

"For Marek to have been able to create you, the effects caused by the experimentation must be wearing off," LaRue added.

"Why me?" It was the main question that had been going around and around in my head since the attack. Why was I attacked by werewolves, why had Marek brought me back to life, and why the heck was there a dead body in my dumb-waiter? The events had to be connected, but for the life of me I couldn't figure out how.

"Lar, don't you think I've been wracking my brain trying to figure that out?" The anguish in Van's tone was unmistakable.

"So, back to Marek. Why wouldn't he just give me his blood so we can stop this?"

"Nazi scientists figured out a process for mixing compounds into the vampires' blood so that later, the vampires could be injected with a substance created from that compound and it would kill them. Each vampire was injected with a different compound. Probably the plan was that only the Nazis would know what compound would kill which vampire, so they could threaten them with death if the vamps didn't play nice. They didn't want there to be just one compound that someone could use to kill all their vampires. When the Allied forces reached the facility, the scientists burned the records that documented which compound was linked with which vampire." Van paused and seemed to be groping for the right thing to say.

"Marek has shown quite a will to survive," Wade interjected. "Vampires are hard to kill, but it can be done. Very few make it to the age Marek has. He isn't going to willingly put a weapon that can kill him in our hands. If we have his blood, we can test it for the compound, thereby knowing how to kill him. Marek has been steadily opposed for at least two centuries to making more vampires, and, frankly, I'm shocked he venomed you, no matter what the circumstances. So he must have a pretty compelling reason to save you. I have a few theories on that."

"No!" Van and LaRue said simultaneously and then exchanged guilty looks.

That pissed me off more than I can tell you. It didn't take a rocket scientist to know that they were still hiding something from me. A very big something that had the two of them completely freaked out, and it was time I got to the bottom of it.

"The potion," gasped LaRue.

ALL THE PRETTY COLORS

37 Hours
(11:00 a.m. Sunday)

"Any time now," LaRue repeated for the third time in as many minutes.

The mist that had billowed from the top of the beaker had halted our conversation as effectively as a beer keg arriving at a frat party. We had crowded around it, only to watch the muddy brown mixture continue to swirl counterclockwise in its glass prison without any further theatrics.

We hoped the mixture would change to blue. If we couldn't stop The Change, then at least that meant I would be a Good vampire. By we, I mean Van, Wade, and me. I thought LaRue would be happy for it to turn black so she would have the perfect excuse to kill me outright.

"Did you leave anything out?" Van asked LaRue in an accusing tone.

"No!" she responded sharply.

"It's okay, LaRue. We only know about the test from books and handed-down stories. Maybe it doesn't even work," Van said quickly, obviously trying to smooth over his misstep.

As if to prove him wrong, tendrils of azure blue started winding their way through the mixture. I felt a huge weight lift from my shoulders. Van shouted, "It's blue, it's blue!"

Wade leaned against a counter and let out the breath he had been holding in a loud gust. I even saw a ghost of a smile on LaRue's face.

Van grinned at me like a kid on Christmas morning and I grinned goofily back. I thought a hug might be in order, but LaRue's gasp drew my attention back to the potion. Her nose almost touched the beaker as she studied its contents. The swirls of color had darkened from beautiful blue to beastly black. I sat heavily on a stool. Van leaned over the opposite side of the counter from LaRue and stared at the mixture as the brown turned to midnight.

"No, no, no, no," he kept repeating.

The potion, which had been swirling counterclockwise, stopped. Then, as it slowly started swirling clockwise, another color became visible, causing Wade and I to crowd around the beaker with LaRue and Van. Vibrant red streaks the hue of fresh blood crept through the mixture, intertwining with and choking out the black until it was mostly crimson with thin tendrils of black. Surprisingly, another swirl of blue broke boldly through the red and black.

The swirling slowed and then halted completely. It was a beautiful mix of red, black and blue tendrils, with red being the predominant color. No one spoke for a full minute. Finally, I broke the silence.

"What does that mean?" Wade asked.

"Maybe it means she will be Dualistic? I don't know for sure," responded LaRue uncertainly. "I'm going to have to read back through the ritual book and do some research. I can't recall anything about the mixture turning red, much less a mix of black and blue."

"It means we are back to square one!" Van shouted. "Damn it!"

He turned and in one vicious movement, swept everything off the counter behind him. Cursing words that would make my father blush, he gave a lab stool a hard kick that sent it crashing through the glass doors of the cabinets that lined one wall. The glass shattered and shards rained onto the laboratory floor.

Yella barked frantically in the hallway. She threw herself against the door repeatedly, trying to get to Van. She might not go into attack mode at the site of my vampire larva self, but when she thought Van was in trouble, she pulled out all the stops.

Yella's distress halted Van's destruction of the lab. He strode to the door, keyed in the code, and stepped outside, letting it close behind him. Wade and LaRue looked as shaken as I felt.

"Have either of you ever seen him act like that?" I asked.

"Only once," Wade responded with a look at LaRue.

"What caused it that time?"

Wade didn't answer, but he continued to stare at LaRue. I couldn't tell if he was waiting for her to speak or silently asking for permission to tell me himself.

"Jad's death," she finally answered without looking at either of us.

Twenty minutes later I had cleaned up the glass, mainly so I had something to do. LaRue was deeply engrossed in research on her computer. Not that I had ever given it much thought, but I guess I expected voodoo research to involve dusty, centuries-old books with notes and rituals handwritten on their pages. When I had asked, she looked up from the computer screen and told me huffily that it had been scanned and saved to a drive. Voodoo and technology, who would have thought?

Wade had alternated between texting and making phone calls. He kept his voice low, but my hearing was improving. I hadn't had any trouble eavesdropping on both sides of his conversations. He had mostly worked on tracking Marek. Two cryptic calls had to do with the 'mystery project' but they had consisted of checking in with people and getting negative responses about progress. Still, I had a feeling that I might know what it was.

The door to the lab opened and Van returned. His face was still red, but he seemed to have regained his control. LaRue and Wade raised their eyes from their devices and looked at him expectantly, but Van spoke directly to me.

"Laramie, we will figure this thing out."

It was the opening I had been waiting for. "Van, who is Temple and why does he think I'm connected to the True Cross?" I glanced around the room to check the impact of my words. LaRue dropped her eyes back to her computer, Wade looked perplexed, and Van shook his head.

"You mentioned the reference to Temple and the True Cross last night. They are both old legends—urban myths, if you will."

"Van! A word." LaRue's tone brooked no argument.

When they moved to the opposite side of the lab, I glanced at Wade and he busied himself with his spit cup. I had no trouble hearing their conversation.

"Tell her," LaRue ordered

"I don't want to hurt her," Van whispered.

"She needs to know," LaRue responded softly.

"What do I need to know?" I asked. My voice sounded harsh to my ears, but I didn't care. I was tired of being kept in the dark. Van sighed and returned to stand in front of me.

"There is a rumor that an Evil vampire named Temple survived the war and escaped to South America. A lot of the Nazis settled in Argentina, but The Organization has never found a trace of him. In fact, the very few Evils who were rumored to have avoided being killed by the Allies have been untraceable since the war. That is why I said earlier that it is our belief that no Evils survived.

"The True Cross refers to the cross Jesus was crucified on. Its wood is purported to have healing powers. And it is the supernaturals' version of the Holy Grail. They believe that it has the power to turn vampires and werewolves into mortals."

"What does this have to do with me?"

"In the year before Jad's death he became fixated on the True Cross. He researched it extensively in the Van Helsing archives and even traveled to a couple of churches that were reported to have pieces of it."

"And?" I asked. My breathing felt forced, and I knew that the worst was yet to come.

"Fakes. But the main thing . . ." Van paused for a breath. "I had forgotten about Jad's obsession until you mentioned the cross last night. Now I'm wondering if his inquiries didn't put him on someone's radar. Someone who may now believe that you know something about the cross."

I sat on one of the stools as the lab dimmed. This time, I might actually faint.

"You think he was murdered by vampires." It was a statement, not a question.

"I've believed for a while that he was murdered, but I didn't know why. I hadn't connected his interest in the cross with his death. Even if his murder was over the cross, it doesn't mean vampires are responsible. There humans who want it, and some will kill to keep it from being found."

"Why would humans want it?"

"Oh, use your head!" LaRue interjected. "If the legends are true, it can heal any sickness, cure any disease. Imagine the power and wealth it would bring to whoever possessed it. Wars would be fought for it. It is more valuable to humans than to the supernaturals. If it does exist, it is better for the human race that it never be found."

"Really?" I asked. "I think that as a race we are better than that. It could be used for good. The countries of the world could work together and share it. Why would it have to be fought over?" Even as I said the words, I knew that I was wrong. Jad may have been murdered just because he was looking for it. What would happen to the world if something that powerful was found?

Van and Wade exchanged looks. LaRue coughed and it sounded suspiciously like "Pollyanna."

Van was the first to break the silence. "Debating the existence of a legend is getting us nowhere. I lost Jad. I'm not going to lose you too." He looked from LaRue to Wade and continued, "From this moment on, we put all of our resources into finding Marek. We do whatever it takes."

"What are we going to do when we find him?" LaRue asked. "We've already established that he isn't going to happily hand over a pint of his blood."

"Tranquilize him. Then bind him with silver chains and do the ritual with his blood to stop The Change."

"A Van Helsing attacking and restraining a vampire?" LaRue asked incredulously. "That will cause a war between the supernaturals and The Organization. Not that the sups care about Marek, except for Grace, but the others will rise up on principle."

"There has been an unspoken truce since World War Two," Wade added. "Are you really going to throw that away?"

"I don't see another way," replied Van. LaRue opened her mouth, but Van pointed at her and said forcefully, "Don't. There are so few supernaturals left, and so many of us, it would be more of a skirmish than a war. If it comes to it, we can win."

LaRue raised her hands' palms up, but remained silent.

Wade spit a stream of brown into his cup. "Van, Marek's in the wind. I've been on the phone for the last twenty minutes checking in with all my contacts and we aren't any closer."

Van looked discouraged, but LaRue seemed relieved. If we couldn't find Marek, she would get her way by default.

Wade let loose another stream of snuff-laden spit into his cup, but his gaze stayed fixed on Van, his face not giving anything away.

"Look," I said timidly, "although there have been some pretty amazing things happen to me today and the eternal life thing doesn't sound so bad . . . I faint at the sight of blood. And I've always assumed I would have children one day. But," I walked over to Van and stood directly in front of him, "I really, really, really don't want to be the cause of a war. Let's call Marek. If he won't give us the blood, then maybe he has another idea. He told me that he was working on fixing the problem. Maybe he knows a way that you don't."

"I've left message after message for him and nothing. Call him," Wade said, shaking his head.

I've always been the type that no matter how many people are standing outside a locked door, I have to try the knob myself. So I took out my cellphone and the scrap of paper with Marek's number. I tapped it into my phone and, before I lost my nerve, hit the send button. It rang once, twice, and then a third time. I was attempting to compose my scrambled thoughts, so I could leave a semi-coherent message, when the call went to voicemail.

"Marek." I waited for the message to continue, but was met only with silence.

"Laramie, are you there?"

"Uh," I said, my thoughts re-scrambled by Marek answering the phone in person. "How did you know it was me?"

"I saved your number when Grace and I started trying to talk to you about your property," he stated. "I'm glad you called. I have been meaning to reach out to you but, after the events of last night, I wasn't sure you would answer."

Apparently I wasn't the only one had who thought the call would go straight to voicemail. The others looked dumbfounded, especially Wade. Van gave me the universal sign to keep talking and mouthed "speaker." At my blank look, he pointed at the phone. Finally understanding, I hit the speaker button.

I was so off-kilter, I responded honestly to Marek's comment. "I'm not sure I would have answered either. Last night felt more like a kidnapping than a rescue. I appreciate the lawyer and all, but I got the feeling it was more for your benefit than mine." My statement was met by silence, so I continued, "But things have happened that I can't explain. I'm hoping you can."

"This is why I asked you to wait in the hotel room, and why I was trying to explain things to you last night." He sounded peeved, then sighed. "We have to talk, and it is better done in person than over the phone."

Van looked ecstatic. Wade and LaRue still looked shell-shocked.

"I agree. Where and when do you want to meet?"

"Are you still with Van Helsing?" asked Marek. "I'm in the middle of something. I will send Grace to pick you up."

Van frantically shook his head and mouthed "The Madam." After glancing at his watch, he looked at LaRue and held up seven fingers. She considered it, then nodded, and Van held up the seven fingers at me.

"Laramie? Are you there?" Marek sounded amused.

He knew exactly what was going on, or at least that we were up to something. It rattled me.

"I don't trust Grace," I blurted, then inwardly cursed myself.

"You don't trust Grace?" he asked, more incredulous than amused this time. "Well, I can't retrieve you now. I am attempting to fix this debacle. You are going have to trust her."

"No," I responded. "I also have things to discuss with you in person, without Grace. Could you meet me at The Madam tonight at seven o'clock?"

The silence stretched out for what felt like an eternity.

"Eleven o'clock would be the earliest I could arrive, but it will probably be closer to midnight," Marek finally answered. He paused for a beat. "I cannot stress this enough. You are in extreme danger. Whatever you think you know about what is going on is completely off the mark. Do not go home until eleven. Once inside, don't unlock the door for anyone except Grace or myself. Yes, I know what you said, but you can trust her."

"I'll see you when you get there," I said, ignoring the rest of his message. I had every intention of getting to The Madam way before eleven o'clock, but he didn't need to know that.

Faint cursing in a language I couldn't identify sounded from the phone's speaker before Marek said tersely, "Van, take care of her. Keep her from doing anything stupid." The call disconnected.

"So he was on to us the whole time," said LaRue. When no one responded she added, "I kinda like his style. If he wasn't a vamp, he would be my kind of guy."

I was kind of starting to like him too, in spite of his auto-cratic ways and possibly having murdered someone in my house. "We can't hurt him. Tonight I'll explain our plan and ask him to help us. No drugging and no binding with silver," I said, pointing at Van.

"Explain what you meant about not trusting Grace," he said. Apparently I wasn't the only one who ignored what didn't match my agenda. Note to self—drive home the 'no drugging, no binding' point later. I refused to let Van start a bumpy/Van Helsing war over me.

"Okay," I responded, "but I need to sit down."

The fact that I was exhausted had crept up on me. I hadn't slept in twenty-four hours and the only thing I'd had food-wise was the wine with Tom in the early morning hours. If you count wine as food, which I do. My headache was still a low throb, but that was better than the pounding bass it had been.

"So, remember when you told me to stay in the house and I left?" I asked with a smile, hoping to lighten the mood. Van's small, grim nod let me know it hadn't worked.

"Well, I couldn't sleep, so I decided to go over everything that's happened since Friday night."

"Let me guess," Van said, a ghost of a smile finally visible. "You made a list."

My list-making habits were legendary. I was surprised by the attempt at humor, but also encouraged. Maybe he had started to bounce back from his earlier shock.

"Yes, actually, I made several," I said, returning his smile. "I knew you would be working on the vampire/werewolf component in all of this, so I focused on solving Bernie's murder."

"I could argue the safety of that," Van said wryly, "but you would just ignore me, so tell me what you found out."

"Not much," I conceded. I quickly explained my decision to focus on who had a motive to torpedo my business rather than everyone who wanted the satisfaction of murdering Bernie. They all nodded, giving me the point.

"Next I considered who had access to The Madam. The police didn't find any evidence of forced entry."

"So, someone with a key," said Wade.

"Or another way in. Okay, so don't laugh when I ask this. Remember, I'm new to this vampire and werewolf stuff," I warned them. My face warmed at the memory of the hysterical laughter at my bloodhound question. "Can vampires turn into fog or bats or basically anything that would allow them to get small enough to enter The Madam without forcing a door or a window?"

They exchanged looks while I waited impatiently for an answer. Ultimately, Van decided to field the question for the team.

"Some can and some can't. It depends on a lot of things, like who sired them, how old they are, and how recently they have fed and on what."

Ick.

"What about Marek or Grace?" I asked. "Does either have the ability?"

Again, with the looks between them! Again, Van answered for the group.

"We aren't sure. They're both old enough and powerful enough. I suspect they have the ability, but it would also depend on whether or not you have invited either of them into The Madam."

"Crap," I said. I had been sure it was Grace. "So, they really do have to be invited in before they can enter a place?"

Van nodded, but LaRue jumped in. "It depends on the place. Well, the type of place." At my look of confusion, she added, "Generally homes are the only place they have to be invited into. Businesses, vacant buildings, warehouses—basically any building that isn't a current residence—they can enter without an invitation."

"But The Madam is Laramie's home," Van reminded her in his 'I'm talking to a five-year-old' voice that I thought he reserved solely for me.

"But," LaRue said, mimicking his voice, "Laramie is turning it into a business, which negates the home part. It is open to the public, so the invitation isn't needed."

"But," Wade said, getting into the spirit, "it hasn't opened, so it isn't operating as a business yet."

They fell silent.

Well, that was clear as mud.

"But I think I found her hair in the dumbwaiter shaft." I dug in my bag for the envelope containing the hair I'd found at The Madam.

They looked skeptical, but crowded around nonetheless. I

handed the envelope to Van. A stunned silence followed when he removed the long red hairs.

"LaRue, can you run tests on this?" Van asked.

"Definitely," LaRue answered.

"This is big, Laramie. Great work." Van said. I felt warm and tingly under his gaze, but he had to ruin it by continuing, "Unfortunately, it won't prove that she murdered Bernie, just that she gained entry into your house. Also, this whole scenario doesn't seem like Grace's style."

"I have to agree with you there," Wade said. "Do you have anything else for us?"

With my supernatural list exhausted, I moved on to my human suspects who possessed keys to The Madam.

"Well, my money is on Van," Wade drawled with a smile after I listed them. I smiled back at him. His humor made me feel safe and normal, two things that had been sorely lacking for the last thirty-six hours.

"Why do you have a key to her house?" It may have been phrased as a question, but LaRue made it an accusation. She sounded jealous.

"From when I used to hang out there with Jad," Van said simply. When LaRue continued to stare at him, he added, "It was always more fun there than here."

After a last hard look at Van, LaRue turned back to me. I could tell she was working up to a snarky remark, but I was saved by the bell. Literally. Van pulled his ringing cell phone from his pocket.

"Oh crap!" he exclaimed when he saw who the caller was.

I was immediately on alert. Had Marek reached directly out to him? Was it the police department looking for me?

"Who is it?" I wasn't sure I wanted to know the answer. It turned out I didn't.

He looked at me with dread.

"Your mother."

THE SUN IS NOT MY FRIEND

**36 Hours
(Noon Sunday)**

Van, being a much better person than I was, answered the call instead of sending it to voicemail. With all the excitement we had forgotten my belated birthday party, rescheduled for that afternoon. Mama clued in on that fact when she asked him to pick up my birthday cake from the Walmart in Faith and he innocently admitted he was still in Dallas.

Rookie mistake. Never, ever, admit to Mama that you aren't already on your way. Her conniption fit was one for the books.

I signaled like a maniac, trying to get Van to tell her he couldn't go. That would make it easier for me to get out of the party. I mean, hello, way bigger fish to fry than spending the day getting the third degree about my arrest. But he ignored my frantic gesturing and agreed to all of Mama's demands. After he disconnected, he effectively silenced my protests by simply stating that I needed to see my family today. He left unsaid that if we couldn't stop The Change, I might never be able to see them again.

Van was hell-bent that I should ride to Faith with him, but I sidestepped that by saying I had to pick up Bo. We were already late, and he still had to get the cake. I was surprised when my plan worked.

Soon I was alone in my truck, driving from his house into downtown Dallas. Van had made me promise that my only stop would be to pick up Bo and then I would drive straight to Faith. Do not pass go. Do not collect two hundred dollars. Van's efforts to rope Wade or LaRue into riding with me had been met with protests all around. Wade had reminded him of all the sleuthing that needed doing, while LaRue had just given him her 'Hell would freeze over first' look.

Wade had promised to run computer checks on everyone on my list. While he personally wouldn't have time to do it, he had said he had 'people' who could. It must be nice to have people. Maybe when I got The Whine Barrel open, I would have people. He had even said that he thought Bill's girlfriend Tiffany would be worth checking out. When I told him that I didn't know her last name he had just smiled a sly smile and said, "Leave it to me."

I smirked to myself as I maneuvered the streets directly north of downtown. I had some sleuthing to do, myself. Or, at the very least, mark another item off my Who Killed Bernie to-do list. I needed to collect Bo from Owen, but who said I couldn't kill two birds with one stone?

Earlier, the fliers in my truck had reminded me that Owen and I were scheduled to be at the Klyde Warren Park this afternoon participating in the Local Showcase Festival. Even though The Whine Barrel wasn't open yet, the event would be excellent publicity for it. Owen had gone early to set up the booth and could handle the event by himself.

I parked in a downtown lot and rummaged in my purse for my vendor pass. Pay dirt! I would still go to the park, but I had another agenda now. One of my suspects was scheduled to address the crowd and I hoped my vendor pass would get me backstage access.

After Van's meltdown about me leaving The Compound I had decided not to tell him about my run-in with Tom Harner in The Madam. It would have just gotten him all worked up. There would be time enough to tell Van later, and I didn't want him handcuffing me to his wrist. I had also failed to mention my little visit to Grace's office. That would have brought on a fit to end all fits. However, I had meant to tell Van that Crockett had been at the Dragonfly the night I was attacked, and mention his involvement with the code inspection issues. There had to be some kind of connection there. But due to the panic induced by Mama's call, I had forgotten. One more thing to add to the to-do list.

As I walked to the park I checked my phone. There were voicemails from Mama, with the calls showing to be from her home phone number. I had texted her from Van's that I would be at the party, but that I might be late. She hadn't responded. She hated texts and rarely even checked her cell phone. To my way of thinking, I was covered. It wasn't my fault she didn't check her texts. That I didn't apply that same logic to my refusals to check her voicemails was neither here nor there.

I had a text message from an unknown number and tentatively opened it. Please don't let it be a reporter texting about my arrest, I thought.

'Laramie—This is your attorney, Healy. Police have released your house. The cleaning crew can be in this afternoon. Let me know.'

Wow! Talk about service. I texted back.

'On a Sunday?'

His reply was immediate.

'Yes.'

Not only was he a savior, he was an amazingly speedy texter. The park was only a few minutes from The Madam.

After talking to my suspect, I could drop by to hide a key for the cleaners.

'Thanks! You're a miracle worker. Give me 45 mins & I'll hide a key under the front steps.'

'Don't bother. They can get in.'

My stomach sank all the way to my toes. If it was that easy to get into The Madam, was I barking up the wrong tree focusing on suspects who had access to the house? Then I gave myself a mental shake. I was about to talk to a suspect who didn't have access, so I was covering all the bases.

My headache returned with a vengeance during the block-and-a-half walk from the lot to the park. Although the day was cloudy, the weak sunshine felt like a megawatt spotlight focused directly on me. In fact, I was positive my skin was melting. I dug my dollar store sunglasses out of my purse. They helped a little, but I needed to find some shade, pronto.

As I entered the park, I was underwhelmed, as usual, by the project that was trying to link downtown Dallas with uptown. It stretched over a freeway that bordered the north side of downtown. From a distance, say from the fortieth floor of one of the skyscrapers that towered over it, the large block looked like a green oasis in the middle of the tons of concrete. But when viewing it from ground zero, so to speak, it was not as enchanting. Up close, the difficulties of growing grass in the brutal Texas sun in an area with zero shade became apparent. The grass, though a dazzling shade of green, was brittle underfoot. My guess was that it needed more color applications to stay emerald green than a rodeo queen did to stay platinum blonde. As with most Dallas projects, the park looked like it was trying a little too hard, and failing.

I reached the first row of booths and paused to get my bearings. The vendors were divided into sections: arts and crafts, produce, restaurants, hotels, and retail. Because a business that combined a wine bar, dog park, pet boutique, and a future bed and breakfast didn't fall neatly into any of those categories, The Whine Barrel had been assigned a booth bordering the restaurants and retail sections.

Although the festival had just started, people were already filling the park. When I found it, The Whine Barrel's booth was open and ready for visitors. Owen stood behind the counter with fliers stacked in front of him and large promotional posters on easels behind him. Bo sat beside the booth, reigning over it like the queen she believed she was.

While there was no hiding the fact that American Staffordshire terrier, or pit bull, made up the largest part of the audacious mix of breeds that was Bodacious, I tried my best to make her look as non-threatening as possible with bright, frilly accessories. Today she wore her bright pink harness and lead. I noticed that her toenails had been painted in a matching shade—Owen's work—and a large set of plastic pearls hung around her chubby neck. She was being rubbed and petted by almost every person who passed the booth. There would be no living with her after today.

"Hey darlin'," I called.

"Hey yourself," Owen responded, a broad smile stretched across his thin face because he knew I had been talking to Bo.

Bo, on the other hand, immediately leapt to her feet, on guard. Now that I knew about The Change, I realized that she was responding to the vampire. It saddened me that Yella didn't see me as a threat, but my own Bodacious did. But I guessed Yella had more experience with the bloodsuckers, while I was the first one (kind of) that Bo had (hopefully) ever met.

I gave her big block head a rub. At that, her tongue lolled out of her mouth and she gave me her huge pittie grin. I smiled back at her, all my worries—for the moment, at least—forgotten. I dare you not to return it when a pittie smiles at you. I double dog dare you.

"So," said Owen, leaning over the booth's counter to eye me up and down, "I feel like I should ask you how you are doing and are you okay in a really sympathetic voice before I order you to tell me everything, but I don't know if I could pull it off." He smiled at me mischievously.

Owen, like Bo, with a wink and a smile was somehow able to make my problems seem completely surmountable. Throw in a margarita and we could solve the world's problems.

"Owen, it would take too long to catch you up on all the gossip and you wouldn't believe ninety percent of it."

"Well, I would love for you to try me. At least then I would have the full story, however crazy it might be."

"Well, I have crazy for you, but I have to keep it short." I moved into the booth's shadow and launched into the story. Once again, I just covered the basics of getting sprung from jail and trying to figure out who the killer was. As with Tom and Bill, I left out the supernatural stuff and my B&E of Grace's office.

I'd gotten much better at telling the story, or at least faster. I conveyed the bones of it to Owen in about three minutes. He was speechless. Literally. He just stood there for about twenty seconds, his hand covering his open mouth. I let him soak it all in.

"I have a few questions and comments."

"I would be simply shocked if you didn't. Shoot," I said, then cringed at my word choice. I had also left out the part about Bernie being shot. I didn't know if the police had told Owen that in addition to being stuffed in a dumbwaiter, Bernie had a bullet hole in him, nor did I know what had been reported on the news. I wanted to see if he would mention it first. Owen had been an ardent supporter of The Whine Barrel concept from the beginning, so he was low on my suspect list. Still, a girl could never be too careful.

"Actually, before I start with the questions and comments, I need to make a statement. Please don't take this the wrong way, and I don't mean to be disrespectful to our dearly departed, but you look like death warmed over. Why don't you step into the booth and I will pour you a cup of liquid rejuvenator?" He made a sweeping motion with his arm that would have made Vanna White proud.

I stepped into the booth for a closer look. A small cooler on the floor was mostly hidden by boxes containing fliers. The tops of several wine bottles, corks loosely pushed into their openings, poked through the ice that filled it.

"Owen! You know we don't have our license yet. We can't serve wine here."

"I know, I know. Don't get your panties in a wad. These are just here for us, special friends, and any influential people who may stop by." Owen winked at me. "Don said he's bringing his wife and Buck to the festival. I want to give our friendly neighborhood code inspector a sample of our wares." He gave a slight bump of his hips that made me think he would happily give Don a sample of more than our wine wares.

Shaking my head, I moved further into the booth as Owen pulled a bottle of Nude Dude from the cooler. That solved the mystery of the wine missing from the storage room at The Madam. With the booth blocking the sun, blessed relief washed over me. The vise that had been ratcheting tighter around my head eased a notch. Only a notch, but I'd take it. Owen filled a red Solo cup with a straw-colored sauvignon blanc. Maybe I'd become a savage, but I didn't take even a nanosecond to mourn the fact that I was drinking from plastic. I downed half the liquid in one gulp, took a breath, and downed the other half. I held out the cup for a refill.

"Thirsty much?" Owen asked incredulously. He'd never seen me gulp wine before.

His judgment didn't faze me. For the first time in over thirty-six hours, I felt halfway to human. The wine warmed my throat and my stomach. The vise loosened another notch. Maybe the answer to managing the stresses of life was to keep a slight buzz going.

My buzz fizzled when Owen started in with his questions, ticking them off on his fingers as he asked them.

"One, did you get laid on your birthday? Two, I understand that Bernie was found dead in your home, but why would that give the police enough cause to arrest you? I have to say that I think you are leaving something out there. Three, did you sleep with Cerny—and by sleep, I don't mean sleep— on your birthday and is that why he hired you a lawyer? And, finally, four, where does Van fit into all this?"

It was my turn to be struck speechless. I hadn't told Owen I was trying to get laid on my birthday, only that I was going out to celebrate and needed him to keep Bo. I had told him some lame story about staying overnight at the Dragonfly to check out the competition. So I could follow his logic from there to sleeping with Cerny, because I stayed at his hotel and he got me a lawyer. Even business moguls don't just hire attorneys for people they barely know, much less the owners of businesses they are trying to buy out. The question regarding the evidence the police had was also very astute.

I tended to underestimate Owen due to his frivolous and sarcastic approach to life. It had occurred to me before that it was a well-put-together act and that there was a lot more going on under the surface than I gave him credit for. But I had been occupied with my own life and problems and had been too lazy, or shallow, to dig deeper. Maybe he had an ulterior motive for wanting The Whine Barrel not to open. Or Bernie dead. I was forced to accept that Owen was a more viable suspect than I wanted him to be.

"One and three, I did not get laid on my birthday, by Cerny or anyone else, for that matter," I said, playing his game. "Two, there was evidence in the house that might link me to Bernie's death and four, you know Van just feels obliged to look after me because of Jad."

"Oh, don't play coy with me. Van, for all his yummy sophisticated bad-boy image, goes all gooey-eyed whenever he is around you. If you were in trouble, he wouldn't be far behind, and obligation doesn't play into it. You should have seen him after the police dragged you out of The Madam. He was trying to call in every favor he could to get you out. The attorney that his family keeps on retainer was out of town and he thought you were going to have to sit in the hoosegow until he could find someone else worthy enough to take your case. I swear, I thought any minute he was going to whip a white stallion out of his ass and go charging off to save you."

I couldn't help but snort with laughter at the mental image that produced.

"Bernie's dead body in your house links you to his murder. Him trying to keep you from opening your business gave you motive to whack his ass. But I've seen a cop show or two in my time. Those things are circumstantial. The police might request that you come down to the station and answer some questions, but they wouldn't put you in cuffs and parade you around for the media unless they had something else. So spill it."

My bullshit radar was pinging louder than Mama and Cheyenne's submarine dive ringtone. Did Owen really know how murder investigations worked from police shows, or was he aware that Bernie had been shot? Owen, along with Tom, was also one of the few people who knew I still had Jad's gun and that I kept it at The Madam. He'd told me not long after he started designing The Whine Barrel's web page that I needed to be careful living there alone. I told him that I had the gun and knew how to use it. Without hesitating, he responded that just because I knew how to shoot it didn't mean I could. He was right about that. I really didn't know if I could fire the pistol at a human being if my life depended on it. But I had a decision to make now.

After a few seconds of us staring at each other, I buckled. "Bernie was shot and then stuffed into the dumbwaiter."

Owen gasped and covered his mouth with his hand for the

second time that day. A real gasp, or more of his drama? I couldn't tell.

"Was he shot with your gun?"

"No. When the police do the ballistics they will see it wasn't my gun, but they felt like it was enough of a link to haul me in to headquarters yesterday." I left out the shredded, bloody dress. That would have taken us down a bumpy route, pun intended, and I knew that the blood on my clothes wasn't related to the murder. Now I wanted to see if I could turn the tables on Owen.

"Was he shot with your gun?" I asked bluntly. Owen had admitted to having a pistol after I told him I had Jad's. I held my breath. Like asking Tom for his key to The Madam, this could be a jump-the-shark moment in our relationship.

Owen stared at me for several seconds. I broke into a sweat, although I wasn't sure if it was nervousness about his reaction or if I was still feeling the effects of the sun. Then he threw back his head and laughed like there was no tomorrow.

"Oh, you had me going there for a moment," he finally managed. He caught my eye, then sucked in a sharp breath. "Wait, are you serious?"

I nodded, albeit sheepishly.

"You don't really . . . I mean, me . . . what the hell?" And we were back to staring at each other. He rubbed his chin, thoughtfully. "Although you know, I'm kind of flattered actually." The frivolous, living-life-by-the-seat-of-my-pants look fell from his face and his copper eyes hardened.

"I hated him and wanted him dead," he said. "When I got home yesterday, I opened a bottle of champagne." I gasped at that. Owen waved his hand. "Well, sparkling wine. You know with what you pay me I can't afford champagne."

"My reaction was to the fact that you celebrated me going to jail, not what you drank," I replied, not a little miffed.

"I didn't celebrate you going to jail. I toasted his demise. I have my reasons for hating Bernie and wishing him dead. And for the record, I don't think you did it. God knows I wanted to kill him, but I didn't." He leaned against the back of the booth and crossed his ankles. I moved further into the booth to try to get just a smidge of shade.

"I know why I wanted him gone. Although I didn't do it," I added quickly. "But why did you want him dead?"

"I can't go into detail here, because I don't want to cry in public." Owen had redonned his frivolous manner and said it with a dramatic fanning of his face, as though he was trying to hold back tears. "Let me just say that Bernie caused the downfall of someone very close to me. I wanted him dead but, when push came to shove, I couldn't do it. But I won't pretend to feel sorry that he is gone." Owen smiled mischievously. "Unless the police are asking. Then I am very sorry and will cry huge crocodile tears while they question me."

I smiled in spite of myself. Despite the drama, I believed him. "I wish I had thought to cry huge crocodile tears when they questioned me. Maybe then I wouldn't have been taken to the station." We grinned at each other for a few seconds before Owen sobered again.

"Really, are you their only suspect?"

"I believe so," I replied grimly. "But I'm determined to find some other suspects for them."

"Hence the probing questions?"

"And you nailed it in one."

Owen was quiet for a few moments, obviously deep in thought. "So, half the city wanted Bernie dead for one reason or another. The other half would dance gleefully on his grave, because even if they didn't have a reason for murdering him, they recognized him for the self-aggrandizing, opportunistic slug that he was."

I shrugged and motioned for him to continue.

"It would be almost impossible to narrow down who has a motive for killing Bernie. You have to combine who has the means—and by that I mean who can get Bernie into your house and shoot him—and who has a motive not only to do away with Bernie but to cause you trouble in the process."

"Owen, are you sure you weren't a detective in a former life?"

He grinned at me again—very cockily, I might add. "While you haven't accused me in so many words, your questions are very pointed. Let me try to put your mind at rest. To recap, I wanted Bernie dead. I do have a gun. And I don't suppose it has slipped your mind that I have a key to The Madam. But I want The Whine Barrel to open. I need it to open. The website will give my design business much needed exposure. The job you've offered me conducting wine tastings and working in the boutique will help supplement my web design income. Finally, I hope to be able to move into The Madam at some point, as I am miserably lonely in my garage apartment."

I looked at him questioningly.

"I intended to hit you up about that last part when the business opened. In addition to your and Bo's lovely company, I would like a dog of my own and my landlord refuses to let me have one. I know you plan on turning the upstairs into a bed and breakfast at some point. Until then, I'm hoping you'll rent me a room and let me have a dog."

Now it was my turn to stare at him for a few moments. His face was guileless, but his eyes were sharp. My faith in him mattered more than he wanted to let on. Finally, I reached out my hand. "You've got a deal. Providing I beat this rap and don't have to put The Whine Barrel up as collateral to pay my legal fees." We solemnly shook on it.

"Thanks, roomie! Now, that brings us back around to why Cerny hired a shark for you."

Owen was like a dog with a bone. "I don't know. I think he's up to his neck in this." I paused for a moment, weighing whether I should say more. What could it hurt? "I'm meeting him tonight at The Madam. I tried to talk to him earlier, but he says he's tied up until late tonight. He can't even come by until after eleven. I'm hoping I can get some answers out of him."

"Meeting him!" Owen screeched. "Tell me you aren't meeting him by yourself."

"Van is going to be there with me." At Owen's concerned look I asked, "What?"

"Um, I really like Van and he is obviously crazy about you. But, and I can't pin down why, I feel like there is more there than meets the eye," he said hesitantly.

That was the pot calling the kettle black.

A burning sensation drew my gaze from Owen. At some point during our discussion, a shaft of sunlight had pierced my piece of shade in the booth and seared my left hand a bright pink. Luckily, the long-sleeved tee I wore protected the rest of my arm from the same fate.

"Crap!" I exclaimed, not about the sunburn but about the time showing on my watch. "I have to get over to the main stage. I want to talk to Crockett before he starts his speech." I headed out of the booth at a fast walk, giving Bo a quick rub on the head as I passed her.

"Be careful," Owen called after me. "Don't trust that guy an inch."

I turned, but kept walking backward away from the booth. "Why, do you know something?"

"Yeah, I do."

I stopped. Maybe this was the big break I'd been hoping for. "What?" I asked hopefully.

"He's a politician. Everybody knows those guys can't be trusted." Then he flashed his trademark Owen grin.

I shook my head and grinned back. Determinedly, I turned and started toward the main stage. I was a woman, er, vampire larvae, on a mission.

23

EVERYONE IS A SUSPECT

35.5 Hours
(12:30 p.m. Sunday)

Workers fiddled with sound equipment as I approached the park's main stage. Several bands were scheduled to perform throughout the day but if I remembered correctly, Council Member Crockett would be kicking off the festivities. People were already jockeying for space directly in front of the stage. A sign listed the speakers and acts for the day. Score! Crockett was first up, and he'd be starting in fifteen minutes.

I had to find Crockett before he started talking as, like most politicians, he could get longwinded when he had an audience. I didn't have the time or inclination to be stuck for the entirety of his speech. There was a large white tent directly behind the stage. The electrical cords snaking under its sides and the sound of swamp coolers running inside the structure made it a good bet that it was where the VIPs were hanging out.

But how to get in? The tent's entrance was guarded by a woman holding a clipboard and wearing a navy uniform with patch that said Parker Security. I was pretty sure that my vendor credentials wouldn't pass muster for the VIP area, so I sauntered past her and turned the corner. Maybe there was another opening that wasn't being monitored as closely.

Then, pay dirt! Crockett stood behind the tent with his back to me. I started toward him but halted when he raised his voice. He was in a heated conversation with two, large, burly guys who looked more like dock workers than festival goers. I could make out Crockett's angry tone but not his words. Turning slightly, I pretended to inspect the tent's ropes, watching the group out of the corner of my eye. Based on Crockett's arm waving, maybe they hadn't set the tent up to his standards. He had a reputation for being hands on, but I would have thought the festival coordinators would handle this type of thing.

A group of attendees passed between us and I briefly lost sight of Crockett. When the group had passed, he was gone. Both he and the workers had just vanished into thin air. *Dang it!*

I hurried toward where they had been standing and then spun in a quick circle, trying to see where they had disappeared to. There was no sign of them, but my gaze fell on a small gap where two sections of the tent met. Crockett must have stepped inside.

I slipped through the opening. Although empty of people, the tent was filled with all the things a festival VIP tent should have: musical instruments, power lines zigzagging across the ground, and a large food table covered in all types of offerings.

I hadn't eaten in over thirty-six hours but the aromas that wafted off the cheeses at one end of the table were repugnant. I swallowed hard to push down the bile that rose in my throat. I wasn't sure if the smell had caused the nausea, or if it came from the thought that if The Change occurred, I might never be able to eat cheese again. Was life without cheese even worth living?

Murmurs sounded outside the tent's main entrance. Hopefully Crockett would come in and I could get this over with. Then I recognized one of the voices and frantically looked around for a place to hide. I dove underneath my only option —the smelly cheese end of the food table—and sent a quick thank you to the gods for the tablecloth that brushed the dusty ground. I was trying to still the sway of its fabric when the owners of the voices entered the tent.

"Austin, you promised Marek that you would sort this." Grace's strident words carried clearly.

"Well, he can consider the problem fixed," Crockett responded, fairly snippy himself.

"That wasn't exactly what Marek had in mind and you know it."

"Yeah, well if Marek wanted it handled differently, he should have taken care of the problem himself."

"It was your problem," Grace said. "You created it, you encouraged it, and now what you call 'fixing it' has made the situation worse."

"Hey, hey, hey," said Crockett soothingly, "I don't know where this attitude is coming from. The threat has been dealt with, and all without either of you getting your hands dirty. Plus, I think you are focusing on the wrong problem. We have much bigger issues to deal with."

"I can't argue with you there," responded Grace. "Marek is trying to track him down. As for the weres, do you have any idea why they are after her?"

I swallowed my gasp before it made it past my lips. Crockett had all but admitted to killing Bernie, and that Grace and Marek knew about it was shocking enough. But now, they had to be talking about me.

"Now Grace, you know as well as I do that all this started when Temple changed him. He thought it would be a lark and a way to send the Van Helsings, not to mention the rest of us, a message. Who knew he would go rogue? I think the weres were trying to lure him out."

"He doesn't seem to be able to stay away from her," Grace said. "And he is too much of a wild card to let him roam around unchecked. We must either bring him in or eliminate him. Then we are going to have to deal with her. If the weres don't get her first. We tried to bring her in, for her own protection, but the weres attacked us and she did a runner. Anderson has her holed up in the Van Helsing compound, but that won't last forever. That said, we can't allow the weres to attack on our turf without consequences. I don't want to start a vamp-were war—God knows there are too few of us left as it is—but if this doesn't come to an end soon, we aren't going to have a choice. Not to mention what could happen once the Van Helsings put it all together. We could end up with them hunting us again."

"Yeah," said Crockett. He didn't sound too broken up about it—any of it.

"Yeah?" asked Grace, testily.

"Look, Grace, no one wants a war, but you have to admit, we could all profit from one. Hold on, just hear me out. I disagree with you. I think we could do with a few less Van Helsings and weres. Just think if we could get them to turn on each other. There are also a few of our kind who have outlived their purpose. Some who make it really hard on the rest of us to live normal lives and fit in with society. It would benefit us all if they were taken out. As a matter of fact, I don't mind helping y'all out with the girl. I'm sure there is a way to get her away from Anderson."

Oh my God! Crockett was a vamp? Why hadn't Van told me that? I was stuck in a deserted tent with two vampires who were convinced, for some reason, that I was a problem. The good news was that they thought I was in The Compound with Van. The bad news was that I wasn't.

"Taken out like Bernie was, you mean? You're the one

who allowed a non-sup to find out about you and then black-mail you with that knowledge. If you're saying it's okay to take out those of us who make it harder on the rest, I'll be more than willing to start with you," Grace said. "And don't go anywhere near Laramie Thompson. Marek is determined to take care of that problem personally. Consider yourself warned that if you've a mind to 'fix it' yourself, you'll have Marek to answer to. And as far as Anderson is concerned, getting her away from him will be fair easy when she finds out what he's been hiding from her."

Under the table, I had shrunken back as far as possible from the voices. I had to get out of there. Luckily, the table was against one wall of the tent. A sliver of light shone between the bottom of the tent and the ground. Hopefully, I could lift the heavy plastic enough to roll under it.

I carefully eased up the bottom of the tent. The rustling noise let me know it wasn't careful enough.

"Quiet!" Grace said, interrupting Crockett, who had gone back to expounding the merits of a supernatural war. "Did you hear that?"

"Hear what?"

Footsteps approached the table and stopped in front of the cheeses. In other words, right in front of my hiding place. I held my breath.

"I don't hear anything."

"I don't hear anything either," said Grace, "but I do smell something."

"All I smell is cheese," Crockett said. "They stink."

I heard him moving away from the table.

My chest was on fire from lack of oxygen. Any moment I'd have to take a huge gasping breath, and then the jig would be up. I clenched my mouth shut, determined to hold on a little longer. Black spots danced in front of me. Finally, I heard Grace move away from the table.

"The smell I'm talking about is the wet-dog stench coming

off you," Grace said. "Have you been hanging out with weres?"

"Now . . . Grace!" Crockett's soothing words ended with him practically screaming her name. A loud crash was followed by the thud of, I think, flesh striking flesh. They were fighting!

I pulled up the bottom of the tent, no longer concerned about being quiet, and rolled out into the scorching sunlight.

24

DON'T YOU DARE HURT MY DOG

**35 Hours
(1:00 p.m. Sunday)**

I sprang to my feet, took a moment to orient myself, and then sprinted toward The Whine Barrel's booth. I'd grab Bo on the way to my truck. Festivalgoers stared as I wove around small groups of people, but I didn't care. Putting as much space as possible between me and the fighting vamps was priority numero uno.

After what felt like an eternity, I reached the row The Whine Barrel's booth was on and turned down it without slowing. It was less crowded here and I could see my booth about one hundred feet away. But the sight that greeted me caused me to falter.

Tom Harner was standing in front of the booth, talking to Owen. He wasn't what caused me to hesitate, though; he was just a creepy bonus. Directly behind Tom, with their gazes locked on me, were the two burly workers Crockett had been talking to by the tent. I had been so focused on the council member I hadn't paid them any attention. Now I realized that they looked suspiciously similar to the guys who'd ambushed us in Deep Ellum—minus the wolf heads. Not only that, but I was sure one of them had been Mr. Big, Hairy and Stinky, the guy who had kept bumping me at The Perch.

I jerked to a halt, uncertain of what to do. It galvanized them into action, and they ran toward me. I spun around and headed back in the direction I had come from. Fighting vamps, or fighting weres? Talk about a rock and a hard place.

Down a row to my right, I saw a large crowd of people in front of a booth that sold frozen margaritas. We Texans do love our margaritas. I veered right and dove through the crowd, then darted between two booths. My first priority was to lose the weres. My second was to make it to the relative safety of my truck. I say relative because Grace's car hadn't provided a whole lot of protection last night. But as they say, any port in the storm. Bo would be safer with Owen.

My route would not be an easy one. The weres were between me and the parking lot. I could try to make it back to The Madam and pick up Van's car, but I stood the chance of running into the fighting vamps. I would rather take my chances with the werewolves than with Grace.

Decision made, I turned back down a row of booths that paralleled The Whine Barrel's row. I was moving much faster than my normal speed, but it was nothing compared to last night in Deep Ellum. The sunlight was slowing me down. I hoped it had the same effect on the weres, not to mention Grace and Crockett if they ended up in the mix.

I was almost even with the booth behind The Whine Barrel's when I heard a shout. A quick look over my shoulder confirmed that I had been spotted by one of the weres.

When I passed the opening between The Whine Barrel's booth and the one next to it, I caught the barest glimpse of Bo staring in my direction.

Three steps later, something hit me hard from behind, knocking me to the ground. The pressure on my back triggered memories from Friday night outside the Dragonfly: the weight on me, the sounds of growling, and the feeling of teeth and claws tearing into my back and neck. The flashback paralyzed me, and I couldn't fight back. Then the weight was gone.

I rolled over and leapt to my feet. What I saw shocked me almost as much as the memories had. Bo, who was deathly afraid of the feral kittens that lived in our shed, had latched her jaws onto a werewolf's neck and was holding on for dear life. He was fighting to get her off, but so far she was managing to hang on. That spurred me to action.

I launched myself at them, more like a tiger than a human. Seconds before I hit him, the were pulled Bo free and threw her, hard, against the booth next to him. She yelped once when she hit the side of the booth, then fell to the ground and lay there, not moving.

As I collided with the were, the same red haze I'd experienced in the lab descended. Then I was sitting on his chest, squeezing a death grip on his neck with my left hand as I repeatedly punched his face with my right fist. Blood poured from a gaping wound on his throat. Feeling as if I were watching the scene from a distance, I saw the blood covering the hand clenched on his throat. I hoped the bastard would bleed out. But if not, I was determined to kill him.

You can mess with me all you want, but don't you dare hurt my dog.

I had made a tactical error, though, in my rage. I had forgotten about the second werewolf. A hairy arm swung over my left shoulder, the elbow crooked, and the giant hand disappeared over my right shoulder. The chokehold cut off my air supply. The were was determined to pull me off his buddy, and I was equally intent that it wouldn't happen until I finished him off.

My rage kept me from feeling the effects of the choking, but my body could only operate for so long without air. The red haze that clouded my vision dissipated and was replaced, for the second time that day, with dancing black spots. I noticed, almost absently, that the world around me had turned gray and was receding.

Calls of "Help her!" "Get him off her!" "Get the police!" sounded faintly, as if from a distance. There was also a lot of just good old screaming. I didn't think it was coming from me. You need air to scream.

The chokehold released. I fell limply to the ground, but the world rushed back at me as air filled my lungs. I gazed around dumbly, trying to determine which direction the next attack would come from. A ray of hope shot through me when I took in the tableau.

Grace O'Malley, red mane swirling around her, pirouetted in midair before delivering a vicious kick—with a foot clad in a gorgeous leather boot, I might add—to one were's face. Oh, what I wouldn't give to have just an ounce of her style. The were's head snapped back from the impact of the kick and a gash appeared on his cheek from the toe of the boot but miraculously, he remained standing. Grace, like the night before, laughed like it was the most fun she'd had in months. Centuries, maybe.

"Run!" Grace yelled at me when she saw me watching her. Then she punched the were, first with her right fist and then with her left. Rocky Balboa had nothing on her.

I was still woozy, but I didn't have to be told twice. Relief flooded through me when I saw Bo standing next to the bloody were, who lay unmoving on the ground. Bo looked as woozy as I felt, but she didn't seem to be in pain. I scooped her into my arms and ran.

25

TRUST ISSUES

34.75 Hours
(1:15 p.m. Sunday)

As I eased Bo onto the back seat of the truck, she slid her huge pink pittie tongue across my cheek. My girl believed in the power of kisses and gave them without reserve to me and everyone else she met. But this was the first time she had kissed me since the attack on Friday night.

I glanced around quickly to make sure I hadn't been followed. I didn't see anyone. Even though I knew we needed to keep moving, I took a second to place my forehead against hers and wrapped my arms around her.

"It's you and me against the world, baby girl." I've touched foreheads with her while saying those words at least once a week since Jad died. Some weeks, the really hard ones, it happened a whole lot more than once. The statement had never felt truer than it did today.

In that moment back at the booth, when I'd seen her thrown through the air, my entire world narrowed down to what was important to me. The Madam was just a house. The dream of The Whine Barrel was just that, a dream. All of the money I'd poured into it I could live without. Bo was the only thing not replaceable. And if I became a full-fledged vampire after tomorrow night? Well, I would be better able to protect her from the people who seemed determined to get rid of us.

Bo would be able to adapt to The Change if it happened. Yes, we would be fine—just the two of us.

I took a moment to wipe the were's blood off me with some wet wipes I kept in the glove compartment. If I got stopped by the police, I didn't think it was a good idea to be covered in blood. Bo got a wipe-down to remove the bloody swipes my fingers had left in her white fur when I carried her. Her snout was also decidedly pink, probably from her throat lock on were number one. After I gave that a good rubdown, I stuffed the soiled wet wipes under the back seat. The evidence was still there, but at least it wouldn't be as immediately visible as bloody hands gripping a steering wheel.

With both of us looking a little more presentable, I drove out of the parking lot. The shortest route to the freeway involved jumping a few curbs, which I did without hesitation. Thank God for trucks. I didn't feel safe until we were traveling eastbound on I-30, headed away from downtown.

At least Bo didn't seem to be suffering any ill effects from her run-in with the weres. She was back to her regular joy-riding self, running back and forth across the rear seat to look out the windows on either side.

I decided the situation warranted the breaking of my hard and fast 'no texting and driving' rule. Owen would be beside himself worrying about me and Bo, although not necessarily in that order.

'We R safe. Bo fine. Talk soon.'

It took a few minutes, but his longer and better typed out response pinged into my phone.

'Thank God! Give Bo extra treats. She saved you, but you came back fierce. That redhead? Wowza!'

I cringed. He'd seen the whole thing, and that put me on

the hook for more questions. Based on his remark about Grace, she had come out of the fight alright. I didn't know how to feel about that. On one hand, after overhearing her talk with Crockett, I knew that she and Marek had a personal agenda for me that didn't involve my safety. On the other hand, she had saved me twice from the weres. Was it a case of live to die another day?

Crockett had been talking to the weres behind the tent when I first saw him. I bet he had told them where to find The Whine Barrel booth. He knew if I showed up at the festival I would stop by it. If they, or Crockett, were still at the festival, Owen could be in danger.

I quickly typed,

'Leave festival NOW. Not safe. Lay low.'

I glanced anxiously back and forth between the road and the phone screen until he responded.

'In truck. Headed home. C U tonight.'

Relief washed over me. I couldn't live with myself if I got Owen hurt. But what did he mean about tonight?

'?????'

'Don't trust Van R Marek. C U 10:30.'

He couldn't be there! Van and LaRue were going to ambush Marek. After overhearing Grace tell Crockett that Marek wanted to "deal" with me personally, I was over any squeamishness I had about binding him. We needed answers, and it might be the only way to get the real story.

I couldn't allow Owen to get any deeper into this. If he didn't end up being killed in the crossfire, his sanity would be in question afterward. Although, he seemed to have handled seeing Grace and I beat up a couple of weres without batting an eyelash. Even though he didn't know what they were, it still couldn't have been a pretty scene. I texted back,

'No.'

There was no response. When I got to Faith, I would call Owen and reiterate my stance.

First, I had found out that Van had a much larger back-story than I could ever have imagined, and now, that Owen was made of much stronger stuff than I had given him credit for. It made me wonder who else in my life I had been under-estimating. The answer to that question came pretty quickly: myself. I had been underestimating myself for . . . well, for my entire life. That stopped now.

I settled back for the rest of the drive to Faith. I had some serious thinking to do.

My eerie calm after the events at the park dissolved less than ten minutes into the trip, leaving me with hands that shook so badly I could barely grip the steering wheel. Initially, I panicked that The Change was happening early, but when fangs didn't pop out I figured that it was a reaction to the adrenaline dump during the fight with the weres.

Before Friday I had never been in a physical fight in my life. I had even kept the verbal fights to a minimum, as I hated confrontation. Since then, I had been attacked three times by werewolves and my neighbor had brandished a crowbar at me. Heck, I had even attacked another person—although I would argue that LaRue had it coming. My life had suddenly become one big WWF match.

As I passed the Faith Walmart, I smiled at the thought of Van in there trying to pick up my birthday cake. The store was a nightmare any day of the week, but right after church on a Sunday? Van had become fairly well known in Faith over the years and he hadn't acquired the skills necessary to navigate Walmart while avoiding the people who recognized him. Those skills took nearly a lifetime of growing up in a small town to hone. He might still be in there, held hostage by the Sunday socializing that was practically a requirement.

My smile faded when I thought of everything I needed to

tell Van. For nearly an hour my thoughts had been zinging around my head like fireflies on a summer evening as I tried to process what I had overheard at the festival. Crockett was a vampire. He had all but admitted to killing Bernie, and he was in league with the weres. It sounded like Grace and Marek were up to date on the Bernie part of it, but when Grace realized Crockett was in cahoots with the furries she'd attacked him, so that must have been new information to her.

The talk about someone going rogue after Temple changed him to send a message to the Van Helsings convinced me that Temple was real, not an urban legend like Van believed. And if he had sent a message to the Van Helsings, they had missed it.

Then—the biggest shocker of the day—they all seemed to be after me. Why? And who would I be able to draw out?

There was one bright spot in everything I had overheard. We could start focusing on gathering evidence against Crockett and getting me off the hook, now that we knew he was the killer. But I still didn't know why he had killed Bernie. I kept getting bits and pieces of the story, but they didn't add up.

I needed to tell Van all of this before I got to the ranch. We couldn't talk about it in front of my family. I had my cell-phone in my hand and was scrolling for Van's number when I remembered something else Grace had said.

"And as far as the golden boy is concerned, getting her away from him won't be so hard when she finds out what he's been hiding from her."

Marek had told me not to trust Van because he had an agenda, and now this from Grace. I hadn't known anything about the supernatural world when they had picked me up from police headquarters. Maybe she thought Van was still hiding it from me. I might discount Grace and Marek's comments about him as vampire mistrust for a Van Helsing, but I had known in the lab that Van, LaRue, and Wade were hiding something from me.

I slowly put the phone back on the seat beside me. Until this weekend, I hadn't liked Van very much, but I would have trusted him with my life. Now I found myself liking him, maybe a little too much, but I couldn't trust him.

I couldn't trust anyone.

26

FAMILY - THE GREAT EQUALIZER

**33.5 Hours
(2:30 p.m. Sunday)**

M y truck bumped down the narrow driveway of my
family's home before I was ready to be there. Harper
Ranch was small potatoes compared to Thompson Ranch,
which belonged to my in-laws. But what we lacked in acreage,
we made up for in know-how. No kidding.

My parents had been rodeo stars in their youth. Mama
had been a national barrel racing champion several years
running and Daddy a bull riding champion. They'd combined
that knowledge to breed rodeo bulls and champion barrel
racing horses. A few years back they expanded into cutting
horses.

As the driveway widened into a large parking area, the
small house I grew up in came into view. It was dwarfed by
the metal-roofed arena behind it. I parked on the dusty patch
of land that surrounded the house. Its dirt was packed hard
from the numerous trucks, tractors, and livestock trailers scat-
tered around the property at any given time of the day, but

most frequently around mealtimes. Today's trucks were Mom's, Dad's, Monty's and Van's. Either I hadn't given him enough credit, or I was later than I thought.

A quick glance at my phone had me cursing. It was nearly two-thirty. Mama was going to skin me alive. Still, I took a moment to look over the house, the arena, and the hodge-podge of pens and outbuildings that dotted the landscape around it. The red brick 1960s ranch house had no redeeming architectural features. Its only real qualities being that it had sheltered a family of five and would always be home.

Hardly a week went by that one of our bulls or horses wasn't shown to a potential buyer in the large arena behind the house. It also served as a school ground of sorts for young rodeo hopefuls who came from all over to be trained. Even though I had decided to take a different path, I was proud of what my family had accomplished here.

A sharp yip drew my attention to the side yard, where Yella played with the ranch dogs, Willie and Waylon. All three tussled over something that I hoped wasn't the remains of a dead animal they'd found somewhere on the ranch. Yella gave a happy bark when she saw my truck and trotted over to meet us. Despite the tension between their owners, Bo and Yella were like sisters. Sisters who actually liked each other. Something I knew nothing about.

I could tell you that faced with the possibility of never coming home again, I saw the place with a combination of fresh eyes and nostalgia. I could but I wouldn't, because it would be a lie. The thought of spending the next few hours with Mama and Cheyenne made me consider driving right back down the driveway and not stopping until I pulled up in front of The Madam. I didn't have it in me to fight with them today, but I knew I needed to spend time with my family. It was the right thing to do.

Bo launched herself off the back seat as soon as I opened

the door and, without a backward glance, tore off to play with the ranch dogs and Yella. She wasn't suffering any ill effects from the fight at the festival. In fact, if I didn't know better, I would think she couldn't wait to tell Yella all about it.

Bo and Yella met about twenty feet from the truck, touched snouts, and then proceeded to the butt-sniffing part of the welcome process. Yella threw a quick, slightly nervous look back over her shoulder as she and Bo trotted over to where Willie and Waylon were engaged in a tug of war with what looked suspiciously like a strip of animal fur. Had Yella recognized the smell of werewolves? I shuddered. Not from the thought of the weres, but over the dogs' choice of toy. Bo would need a bath and her teeth brushed tonight.

"Hey!" I called out when I entered the house.

"In here," Mama yelled.

When I entered the kitchen I was greeted by the view of Mama's skinny behind, clad in denim. Her head was almost completely in the oven, checking what appeared to be a chicken broccoli casserole. My heart sank.

"Well, it's about time. Start setting the table for the party," she ordered after a brief glance back at me. Then she turned and gave me her full attention.

"What the heck happened to you?" she demanded.

I looked at her questioningly, trying to buy time. After the excitement at the festival, I had completely forgotten that Mama would grill me about my arrest. I opened and closed my mouth several times, not knowing where to start.

"Your hair hasn't seen a brush today. You're not wearing a lick of makeup and," she moved in closer to stare at my neck, "is that a hickey?"

Mama stared at me, hands on hips, and waited for an explanation for my failings.

I clenched my hands behind my back to keep them from covering my "hickey" or straying to my hair to check how badly it was tangled from the throwdown with the weres. I must have lost my scarf during said throwdown. It hadn't crossed my mind to run a comb through my hair before getting out of the truck, or even check my appearance in the rearview mirror. I'll never learn.

"I had a late night," I said lamely. Deciding that offense was the best defense, I asked, "Where is everybody? The house is silent as a tomb."

Mama eyed me. I swear she had been a general in a former life, reincarnated into a rodeo beauty queen in this one. The two inches she had on me allowed her to look haughtily down her perfect nose at me. A nose set on a face that should have been showing its middle age, if for no other reason than all the years spent riding horses in the sun, but wasn't. Because Mama looked so youthful we could have been mistaken for sisters, but it never happened. We looked nothing alike. Her blond hair—not natural, but you couldn't tell by looking at it—was short, pert, and expertly styled, even on a Sunday afternoon at the ranch. The blue jeans and burnt orange button up shirt should have looked casual. On Mama, nothing looked casual. When she cocked her head to one side, I knew she was mentally circling me, probing for the weak spot to attack. That look made me long to be back with Grace and the werewolves.

"Your dad, Monty, and Van are in the arena working a new horse. Cheyenne is on her way with the girls. You go to my room right now, fix your hair and makeup. Find a scarf to cover up that thing on your neck." She had decided to let my explanation go unchallenged while still keeping the upper hand. "Van drove all the way out here, picked up your cake, and gave us a brief accounting of your, uh, situation. I don't intend for him to see you like this."

What had Van told them? He must have left out some pretty large chunks if Mama didn't know he had already seen this disheveled version of me.

"Don't just stand there!" Mama ordered in a tone that Hitler would have envied. "Get moving. And don't forget that table isn't going to set itself. I want to be ready to sit down as soon as Cheyenne gets here."

I trudged down the hallway to Mama and Daddy's room. As usual, everything revolved around Cheyenne. Three years younger than me and the proverbial baby of the family, she was the one Mama pinned all her rodeo queen fantasies on after I let her down. I loved being on a horse, but I didn't like the speed. Above all, I hated that all eyes were on me. By my early teens, Mama finally admitted that I didn't have what it took. I have been a constant source of disappointment to her ever since.

My brother Monty, two years older than me, had been a passable bull rider. He had gone pro and even made a little money at it, but he had never been the champion that Daddy was. That was okay, though. He was going to run the ranch one day. All he needed was a little rodeo cred to show purchasers and students that he knew what he was talking about.

Mama's closet ran the gamut from working clothes for the ranch to sequin- and rhinestone-studded cowgirl outfits for the local rodeo appearances she still made. I rummaged until I found a scarf I didn't think she would miss. I restrained my hair, powdered my face from a makeup collection more extensive than her wardrobe, and swiped my lashes with mascara. I wouldn't win any beauty pageants, but it was an improvement.

When I returned to the kitchen, Mama looked me up and down. She shook her head and turned back to the stove. So much for unconditional love and support.

I entered the dining room just in time to see Monty and Van finish setting the table. I stopped in the doorway for a moment, struck by how handsome they both were. Even though Monty was my brother, I could still see that he was quite the looker in that quiet cowboy way that he now had.

He'd had the typical bull rider swagger up until about a year ago, when his wife, Daisy, left him and took their two little boys back to Montana. Her leaving had been a huge hit to his confidence and it just about killed him to see the boys only a few weeks out of the year.

As sad as I was for him, the whole experience had made him more likable. Up until it happened he had been the male version of Cheyenne. Afterward, he finally understood that life could knock you down. He had been nicer to me since.

Monty and Jad, being the same age in a small town, had grown up together. When Jad died, Monty and Van had drifted together. When Van was off-duty from the police department he could often be found at the ranch, helping with the horses and cattle. I knew he also still spent time at my former in-laws' ranch, helping out where he could, basically being a surrogate son to the Thompsons.

"Happy belated birthday Lar," Van said.

My eyes misted when I realized that I had gone my entire birthday without anyone wishing me a happy one. Monty nodded at me and smiled. That meant almost as much, but leave it to Van to be the one to remember to finally say it. That he called me Lar added to the sentiment. Only Monty and Jad had ever called me Lar until recently. I wasn't sure exactly when it started, but Van sometimes used it now.

A calm conviction filled me. I could trust Van. He might be hiding something, but I was certain that he was hiding it from the old Laramie. The Laramie who'd shrunk from conflict and hidden from hard truths. Well, I'd changed. I would tell him about the festival and everything I had over- heard as soon as possible. That would convince him that this Laramie was someone who didn't need the world sugar- coated. This Lar was someone worthy of him and his trust.

"Van, can we step outside and talk?" I asked. I didn't want to wait another second before catching him up to speed.

Van was nodding in agreement when Cheyenne, with daughters Amber and Avery in tow, walked into the room and said as way of greeting, "Are we ready to eat? I've got a thing at the country club this afternoon and I can't be late."

It really was all about Cheyenne. She had been on a trajectory to become a National Champion Barrel Racer. Then, at nineteen, she announced that she was pregnant and that she and the father were getting married. She presented Bradley Jordan, heir apparent to the Faith Ford dealership, as the father. Knowing how close she had been to several cowboys on the circuit, I'd always had my doubts about Amber, her oldest, being a true Jordan.

After marrying Bradley, Cheyenne had found out that being wealthy and married to the heir of one of the founding members of the Faith Country Club was an easier way of gaining attention than riding a horse every day. She had announced her retirement from the barrels and hadn't looked back.

As much as you think Mama would have held quitting rodeoing against her, Cheyenne providing her with grandchildren turned it all around. Maybe Mama just couldn't stay mad at her favorite. Whatever the situation, they were closer than ever.

While I stood there glowering at the back of Cheyenne's two-hundred-dollars-a-visit blond head, she seated Amber and Avery at the table and Mama called Daddy in from the living room. I resolved to talk to Van as soon as the meal was over.

Cheyenne was a carbon copy of Mama, right down to the perfect skin and haughty attitude, but Monty even more closely resembled Daddy. Their sandy blond hair, when not covered up by either a cowboy or baseball hat, had the same endearing cowlick in front. In contrast to Mama's smooth, white skin, Daddy's was tanned and creased from his time in the sun. His constant uniform of Wranglers, white shirts and cowboy boots only changed from slouchy and worn to crisply starched and pristine, depending on whether he was working on the ranch or going out somewhere with Mama. Monty could look at Daddy and see his future self, and his future looked good.

I, on the other hand, was a conglomeration of both my parents' features while at the same time not looking particularly like either one. My green eyes came from Daddy, and, judging from her roots, my brown hair from Mama.

When we were finally all seated around the dining table, there was an expectant moment of silence where Mama just looked at me.

"Aren't you going to say thank you to me for your party and fixing your favorite dish?" asked Mama, who needed to be the center of attention almost as badly as Cheyenne did.

I've learned over the years that it is better to just go along with Mama, but I couldn't let that pass.

"Thank you for fixing Monty's favorite dish," I replied sweetly.

"It's not his favorite, it's yours," she replied.

"I think I would know what my favorite dish is," I retorted.

"Now girls," Daddy interrupted, thrown into the role of peacekeeper as usual. "Laramie, tell your mother thank you for this birthday dinner and Josie, for God's sake, tell your daughter happy birthday and get off her back for just this one day."

"Mom," interjected Monty, saving both Mama and me from having to give in to the other one, "Lar's right. Her favorite dish is steak fajitas. Chicken broccoli casserole is mine."

Mama pretended not to hear. Daddy, having made his best effort, shrugged and dug into the mound on his plate. I normally liked the dish all right, but today nausea rose like a wave in my stomach and rolled up my esophagus. Since Mama would hit the roof if I didn't eat anything, I forced a few mouthfuls down. Then, despite my best efforts, the casserole started its voyage back up.

The run to the hall bathroom seemed endless. Afterward, I washed my face, taking off the layer of powder I had put on barely thirty minutes before. Not bothering to reapply it, I rinsed out my mouth and returned to the table.

"Did you have too much fun last night, sis?" Monty suggested with a twinkle in his eye.

"Or do you have a boyfriend you haven't told us about?" Mama asked with a sideways glance at Cheyenne, who had stayed in a near-constant state of morning sickness during each of her pregnancies.

For once, Cheyenne didn't chime in. Her silence was probably due more to her desire to get to the country club than any consideration of my feelings.

"Guys, me. Police. Last night. No fun at all," I said indignantly, and then blanched. The last thing in the world I wanted to do was to open that conversational can of worms. Thankfully, no one took the bait. After a few quick glances at Van, everyone at the table stared guiltily down at their plates. I didn't know what he had said to them before I arrived, but whatever it was, I owed him.

Lunch was downhill from there, and not just conversation-wise. I dared not eat another bite. The cake was chocolate with white buttercream frosting—Cheyenne's favorite. I took a piece, but pushed it around on my plate and mashed it with my fork until it looked like I had eaten about half of it. No one paid any attention to me except for Van. He spent the whole meal watching my every move like I was a bug on a pin.

Monty helped me clean up the lunch dishes after Mama had declared herself "beat" from cooking all morning and Cheyenne left for her shindig at the Faith Country Club. Daddy was never expected to help out in the kitchen and commandeered Van to go into the living room with him. He needed help with the new television's remote control and knew Van could figure out just about anything.

"You know we love you," Monty said quietly as he dried a plate. "Even Mama. Although, admittedly, she has a funny way of showing it."

"I know. It's just that the last few years have been really hard and, although I shouldn't, I was just hoping today would be a little different," I responded. If we couldn't stop The Change, I didn't know if I would see my family again, or under what circumstances.

"I know," Monty said, "I miss him too."

Jad Christopher Thompson had been Monty's friend before he had been my boyfriend and then husband. They had been inseparable until the year they turned sixteen and Jad suddenly noticed me as a girl instead of his best friend's pest of a little sister.

The way Monty tells the story, they were in the locker room one day after football practice. It was their junior year and I was an awkward freshman who had just started to fill out. One of the other players, a senior, made a sexual innuendo about me, trying to get a rise out of Monty. It was Jad, however, who punched him.

Jad had been suspended from school for one day and had to sit out a football game. But the way he told the story, it was worth it because it had made him really look at me for the first time.

Monty put his arm around my shoulders and pulled me close. I rested my head against him, enjoying the comfort, and tried to silence the inner voice that told me I was a fraud. Besides Jad and me, there was only one other person who knew how bad things had gotten between us before Jad died, and that person wasn't Monty. That person was in the living room showing Dad how to work the remote, and he didn't even know about Jad's last day.

"You ready to go look at that bull?" Monty said over my head.

Speak of the devil. Van had wandered into the kitchen and was leaning against the door frame, watching us. He wore the slightly worried expression he always got whenever his gaze fell on me, even before I was venomed by a vampire. He looked like he wanted to say something but held it in check. After one last searching look at me, he followed Monty out the back door toward the arena. I knew I should follow them and catch him up to speed, but I also knew that it would put an end to the day. Monty had seemed somehow vulnerable just now. It wouldn't hurt to let him have a little friend time with Van.

I leaned against a kitchen cabinet, dreading what was to come. Bamboo stakes under my fingernails were preferable to spending a few hours alone with my parents. When I finally felt like I had braced myself for what was ahead, I stepped into the living room only to see that something was finally going my way today. Daddy was asleep in his easy chair, Mama napped on the couch, and the television blared. I knew I would pay for it later, but I figured it was time to get while the getting was good.

I quietly grabbed my purse and jacket, then, holding my keys so they wouldn't jingle, I headed out the back door toward the arena. Friend time or not, I needed to talk to Van before I left.

———

Bo was lazing in the sun with the other dogs, but jumped up excitedly when she saw I was headed to the arena. Her enthusiasm wasn't due to her all-consuming love for me. She thought I was going to visit my horse, Deadwood. Visits with him involved treats and, being a messy eater, he dropped bits of them on the ground. Bo wasn't a picky eater and would quickly steal the pieces he dropped. With Bo, it was all about her stomach.

I should visit Deadwood and check on his leg while I was here. It had been about a month since he had tossed me in a back pasture after something had spooked him—I never figured out what. I had been sore for several days after the accident, but my pride had been my main injury. Deadwood hadn't been so lucky. He had cut his right front leg and had needed stitches.

"Lar!" Monty's call interrupted my thoughts. He was leaning against the fence at the main arena and waved me over. I scanned the area and saw Van by one of the smaller pens, looking at a bull Monty hoped to have ready for next year's rodeo season.

As I joined Monty, I noticed the sun was low in the sky. I checked the time and was surprised to see that it was after five o'clock. It would be getting dark in another hour or so. The wind had picked up and the trees in a small grove on the other side of the arena swayed and creaked in an eerie fashion. Most of the land around the ranch had been cleared to act as grazing pasture, but Daddy had left a couple of acres of woods and thick brush as a windbreak for the outbuildings. I had always found the woods a little spooky and dark. Even now, I shuddered at the fanciful thought that someone could be in there watching me and I would never know.

"You headed out?"

"Yeah, they're both asleep and I figured it was a good time to beat a hasty retreat."

"I can't say that I blame you," Monty replied, a slight smile creasing his face.

"I don't know how you can stand to live with them again," I said and then flinched when I saw that I had wiped the smile off his face with my careless remark.

"It's hard," Monty agreed, "but it's something I need to do to be able to provide for Daisy and the boys."

I stared uncomfortably across the arena into the trees, not knowing what to say. Jad had died, not left. I couldn't imagine how being left would feel.

"You know, until it happened, Daisy leaving with the boys? I didn't know how it felt to live your life constantly trying to ignore the pain of loss. Now I realize how quickly an offhand remark can bring that hurt to the surface."

"Oh, Monty," I said, turning to look at him. "I'm so sorry. I didn't mean to bring it all back."

"No, I'm trying to apologize. I didn't mean to bring up Jad today. I'm sorry I made you sad."

I was at a loss. The old Monty would never have realized how much talking about Jad hurt, much less have apologized for bringing him up.

"Monty, you have nothing to apologize for. I was the one who brought him up by talking about how hard the last few years have been for me."

"Were you?" Monty said, scratching his jaw thoughtfully. "It's just that I seem to be thinking of him all the time lately." He looked over at the trees across the arena from us, dark and forbidding in the late afternoon light.

"I do too. I actually . . ." I trailed off.

"What?" Monty asked after a long silence.

I had been going to say that I'd imagined Jad standing over me after I was attacked, but I couldn't tell Monty that without opening a huge can of worms. But there was something safer that I could tell him. "Well, uh, the officers that pulled up at The Madam yesterday . . . I actually thought for a second that one of them was Jad. I nearly fainted when I saw him."

"Really?" Monty asked, sounding relieved. "Sometimes I think I see him over there in the trees at night, just watching the house. Silly, right?"

I could only stare at him as pieces started clicking together. Suddenly I knew with horrible certainty just what, or whom,

Van had been hiding from me. I looked past Monty to where Van leaned against the pen, watching us. He must have seen something on my face, and he started toward us.

Through numb lips, I managed, "It's not silly at all. We both loved him; it's only natural that we would still imagine him sometimes. Excuse me, I need to talk to Van."

Without waiting for a response, I strode along the fence and intercepted Van.

"Is Jad still alive?" I asked.

"What?" Van responded, the color draining from his face.

"It's what all the secrecy is about, isn't it? You, LaRue, and Wade know Jad is out there somewhere and you're keeping it from me."

"No," Van said, but his obvious struggle for composure didn't convince me.

"No he isn't alive? Or no that isn't what the secrecy is about? I want answers, Van, because you are still keeping things from me and they all center around Jad."

"Yes, that is what the secrecy is about, but no, we don't think Jad is out there somewhere." I tried to break in, but he continued, "Yes, we have been looking, but we haven't found any trace of him."

"Why? Why have you been looking?"

"In our line of work, when a body disappears you can never be too careful."

Uh, uh, not good enough, buddy. Tendrils of dread stretched through me. I imagined them swirling around inside my body like the tendrils of color in the potion. I knew. I just knew, dammit.

"Is that the only reason?" I asked. My heart felt like it was slowly being encased in ice.

"No. Reports of vampire-type incidents started turning up not long after Jad died."

"Vampire incidents?"

"Bodies with blood drained from them. We have . . . I

guess you could call them tripwires . . . set up all around the world, that alert us about incidents that could involve supernatural beings."

"So this could be Jad?" My voice was steady, but inside I was reeling.

"No!" Van said a little too loudly, then glanced over my shoulder to see if Monty had heard. I didn't take my eyes off his face, trying to read the truth there and decipher it from all the lies he had been telling me since the first day we met.

"No. We have no proof that it is Jad, and nothing to lead us to believe it could be. Like the rumor about Temple, there have been whispers about other vampires who survived the war, but we've never been able to find them. If they lived, they've kept low profiles." Van turned thoughtful. "It's troubling that one turned up right around the time Jad died. His death looked like an accident, but I don't buy it. Your attack, with the message about the True Cross? That's the first clue we've had about why Jad might have been targeted. Something in his search has brought one of the vampires out of hiding."

"Or," I said woodenly, remembering Crockett's comment about Temple changing someone on a lark, "maybe one of the under-the-radar vampires changed him, and Jad is the vampire you are getting reports about."

"Oh Lar, I would ride through Hell and half of Texas to bring Jad back to you if I could," Van said, the sympathy on his face almost crushing me. "But I can't. Jad's gone, honey, and even if he wasn't, you wouldn't want him as a vampire. They are just things, little better than snakes or rabid dogs."

I realized three truths then. The first was that Van believed that I still loved Jad. I hadn't loved Jad in years. As a matter of fact, I hadn't loved him in more years than he had been dead.

The second truth was that the person I wanted Van to ride through Hell and half of Texas for was me. Not to bring me Jad, but just to be with me, because I was his whole world.

The third truth was that if we didn't stop The Change, I could never be that person for Van.

Make that four truths, because I saw clearly now that despite the secrets he had kept, without Van to share at least some of it with, living for eternity would really suck.

27

MEMORY LANE

**30 Hours
(6:00 p.m. Sunday)**

I had walked away from Van at the arena and he had let me. Maybe we were both coming to grips with the enormity of what faced us. Vamps and weres were hunting for me, so a side trip down memory lane shouldn't have been in the cards. Despite the overwhelming logic of heading straight back to The Madam, I drove toward the Thompson's ranch. The last two days had been horrible, and while I knew from past experience that this little jaunt would make me feel even worse, I couldn't help myself.

As I approached my in-laws' property, I saw the familiar driveway at the main entrance. Yards of black wrought iron loomed over the opening, stretched between the pillars flanking either side. In the middle the letters T and R, for Thompson Ranch, were intertwined in fancy scrollwork. They were large enough to crush a vehicle if the welding gave way.

I passed below the monstrosity without slowing. About a mile down the driveway, I turned onto a smaller dirt drive that was almost completely overgrown. Most people drove right by it, never knowing it was there. Not me, though. It had been my driveway for the six years I was married to Jad.

I carefully maneuvered my truck along the rutted dirt track. I didn't need a broken axle adding to the misery that had become my birthday weekend. After about a quarter of a mile, there was a slight opening and I parked in front of a small, abandoned, wood-clad farmhouse.

It had been the foreman's house for the Thompson Ranch since the 1960s and was vacant for at least ten years before Jad and I moved in. No one had lived in it since Jad's death. The white paint we'd painstakingly applied sometime during our first year there was dingy and peeling. The front porch sagged, and more than a few boards had started to rot. It always saddened me to see that the house, once filled with love, hope, and dreams, had come to this.

I let the truck idle while I weighed whether or not I wanted to look in the windows or walk to the spot where Jad had died. Bo whined and pushed her head over the back of my seat. It reminded me of sitting beside the tractor, holding her and crying while I waited for help. Help that hadn't been able to save Jad, only manage a bad situation. Or so I'd thought at the time. Now I wondered.

If Jad had been bitten and injected with the venom, had he just been in the dead-to-the-world sleep that I'd been in for twelve hours after I was bitten?

I couldn't think about that, so instead, I remembered.

Jad had gone to the University of Texas at Austin on a baseball scholarship after he graduated high school. When I graduated from Faith High two years later, he begged me to join him. I hadn't. There were plenty of excuses not to go, with the biggest being that I was secretly scared to leave home. Better the devils you know . . . .

So I went to the community college in Faith for two years, then finished up my degree with a double major in marketing and business at Texas A&M in Commerce, a university located about forty-five minutes from Faith. Jad offered to transfer there so we could be together. In one of my few shows of backbone, I threatened to end things with him if he did. I had been determined not to hold him back, and that included refusing to let him hold himself back.

When things were really bad, usually in the middle of the night when a person is most likely to question their decisions, I wondered if I had allowed him to come back from Austin, would things have been different? But I was pretty sure it wouldn't have changed anything. Within a week of being at UT Jad had met Van. And that was the beginning of the end. An end that was nearly twelve years in the making, but I still linked it all back to Van.

Bo whined again, pulling me back to the present. I got out of the truck and opened the door to let her out. Bo stood on the rear bench seat with her nose stretched out, sniffing the air. She whined at me again.

"Whatever, Bo. Suit yourself," I told her and turned to walk to the house.

By the time I placed my foot on the first step leading to the porch, Bo was hugging my side. She had accepted long before I did that Jad was gone and the house was a part of our past. She usually exuded boredom on our visits, but today she seemed more leery than bored. My going through The Change had really done a number on her. Just when I thought she was adjusting, she started acting wary again. At least her wariness seemed to be focused on our surroundings and not on me.

Jad and I had managed to maintain our long-distance relationship while he was in Austin, but it had been hard. After he met Van there seemed to be a never-ending stream of frat parties and road trips. He broke a lot of weekend plans last minute and I didn't make many trips to Austin. I wasn't comfortable around his new friends. Everyone seemed to have more money, better looks and so much more confidence than I had. I was pretty sure there had been other girls for Jad.

There had never been anyone else for me. Jad had been all I wanted. I couldn't believe that he'd wanted me and had been determined not to screw it up.

The boards creaked when I stepped onto the porch but held my weight as I crossed it to peer into a window. I wiped the dirt off the glass and braced myself for the onslaught of memories. Then I leaned close to gaze through the smeared pane. But instead of my living room, I saw only brown plywood. It had been put up on the inside of the house instead of the outside. I stepped over a rotten board and tried the front door. It was locked.

Strange. Not that it was locked, but that the doorknob and lock were new. I walked around the entire house. All the windows had been boarded up on the inside and there was a new lock on the rear door, too.

Maybe it was better that I couldn't go in and see the rotting, dust-covered furniture. I could close my eyes and see it exactly as it was the day Jad died, and that hurt bad enough.

When Jad graduated from university and came back to Faith he had been restless working on the ranch. Out of the blue, he and Van wanted to be police officers. I had been against it, but Jad argued that it was their chance to give something back—to protect others and get some excitement in the bargain.

I finally agreed, mainly because I didn't think police work would stick as a career for either of them, especially Van. He had never acted like he thought the rules applied to him and had bounced from one spot of trouble to the next. They had been small infractions, mostly—missing curfew for the baseball team or skipping morning classes—but the type of thing that showed a problem with authority and rules.

Jad hadn't wavered on marrying me. We had talked about it and planned it almost from our first date. We were perfect for each other. Or we had been, when we were both living in Faith and playing grownup. But 'a promise is a promise' was Jad's motto, and while it wasn't very romantic, I hadn't been able to see that he was marrying me out of obligation. I hadn't wanted to see it.

We had planned to wait until I graduated from college, but when he was hired by the police department he didn't want to wait. Neither did I. I could feel that we were drifting apart and was sure that once we were married, things would be fine.

So a judge friend of Hattie's married us at The Madam with Van and Jad's aunt as our only witnesses. We didn't even tell our parents until the following weekend. Mama had been fit to be tied. I never believed that Mama cared that I got married without her. She'd just missed out on a day when she could get all gussied up and be the center of attention.

Looking back, it was sad that my life had been so wrapped up in Jad from the time I was sixteen that I hadn't even had a girlfriend I could have asked to act as my witness. Come to think of it, I still didn't. And none of the women I'd met recently—Tiffany, Grace, or LaRue—seemed particularly likely to be the 'get drunk and braid each other's hair' best friend that I had always secretly hoped to have.

When Jad and I got married, I wanted to remain in Faith. I had a year left of college and I hadn't wanted to give up my job at the town's only wine bar. The bar I had hoped to someday own. If I was being honest with myself, that was just an excuse. I had been too scared to move to Dallas; too afraid to try to start a new life, even with Jad at my side.

No surprise to anyone except Jad and me, marriage turned out to be a lot harder than we thought it would be. For the first few years we really didn't notice. I was busy with university and he was learning how to be a police officer. I graduated and began working full time at the wine bar, first as an assistant manager and then as manager. Eventually we realized just how little we had in common. We limped along for several more years, neither of us wanting to admit we had made a mistake.

Jad spent several nights a week at The Madam, with Hattie. He had been working a lot of hours with the police department and doing extra duty jobs. It made sense for him to stay in Dallas rather than making the commute from Faith every day.

Based on the hours he claimed to be working, it seemed we should have had a lot more money, but there had always been excuses—the truck needed new tires, or gas prices were up.

I'm not sure when I became convinced that he had a girl-friend in Dallas, but I became obsessed with the idea. I began hounding him to account for every minute of his time and to show me where the money was going, or prove it was even coming in at all. The situation had come to a head the summer of the seventh year we were married, right at the height of hay season.

Now, turning away from the old house, I looked out over the pasture. I crossed the driveway and stopped in front of the rusty barbed wire fence that separated the yard from the field. Did I want to walk out to the spot?

"What do you think, girl? Do you want to go for a walk?" Bo had followed me to the fence. She glanced up at me hope-fully at the word walk, but immediately settled her gaze back on the house. There must be possums or, God forbid, skunks living under the front porch. She had barely taken her eyes off the old building. I turned my gaze back to the fields and toward the spot. It wasn't visible from here, but I knew exactly where it was.

Jad worked evenings at the police department and his shift usually ended at eleven at night. On the nights he came straight home, which had become fewer and fewer as our marriage progressed, he arrived just after midnight. If he was going to be any later, he would call.

The night he died, I'd gotten off at the wine bar at eleven and gone home. As I didn't have to be at work the next day, I figured I would wait up for Jad and we could have some time together. I even put on my sexiest underwear just in case, although it had been a long time for us in that department, too.

When Jad hadn't arrived by 12:30 I became worried. Despite numerous calls, he hadn't answered his phone or returned my messages. Since the police department would have contacted me if he'd been injured at work, I knew whatever he was up to wasn't job-related. I stayed up all that night waiting for him to come home.

About an hour after sunup, Jad's truck had pulled into the yard, but he hadn't wanted to talk. "Don't start. I've had a long night and I have to get to work on the hay. I know we have a lot to settle, and I swear that it will happen today. Just let me get the hay in first."

I still don't know why I agreed. I think I'd just been trying to put off the inevitable. He walked back out the door without a kiss or even a hug. It's not like I would have let him touch me, but when I think back on it, I wish he had at least tried.

After the sound of the tractor faded, I had walked to our bedroom and filled a suitcase with my clothes. From Jad's face it was obvious he was done, and I couldn't take anymore either. I had known our marriage was going to end. I just hadn't realized then that I had the 'how' part of it wrong.

A low whine brought me back to the present. Bo was still staring at the house, trembling at whatever scent she smelled. I took pity on her and on myself. When I opened the door to the truck she almost flew into the front seat. I sat behind the steering wheel and lifted my hands, our unspoken symbol that my lap was open and she was welcome. She laid her big, block head on my leg and lifted soulful eyes to me. Then she rolled over on her side so that I could rub her pink, speckled tummy. She could always tell when I was upset, and she knew how to make me feel better.

Packing my clothes had helped wear down my mad, and after being up all night I had been exhausted. I had drifted to sleep on the sofa and the next time I woke up it was midafternoon. Jad hadn't come home for lunch. He had wanted to avoid a confrontation, and it was easy enough for him to eat with his parents. Several times I had to fight the urge to put the suitcase in the car and drive away, but eleven years together, with seven of them married, deserved a face to face.

When he hadn't returned by late afternoon, I called his mother. They hadn't seen him at all that day. I stood in the living room of the house, holding a phone that had suddenly become very heavy. The tractor would have woken me up if he had returned. He was still out in that pasture somewhere. Jad's mother had known from my silence that there was a problem and she put Jad's father on the phone. All I said was, "Start a search."

I was the one who found him. I had followed the indents the tractor tires left in the grass to the edge of a dam that created a small pond in the pasture for the livestock. From there, it looked like a tire must have slipped off the edge and the tractor rolled. The machine lay on its side with Jad's body under it.

A paw pushed my arm and brought me back to the present. In my reverie, I had quit rubbing Bo. She pawed my arm again to let me know that was unacceptable.

"You are so needy."

Bo answered by pawing my arm again. With one last rub of her tummy, I said, "Enough of memory lane for today. Let's head back to Big D."

I didn't have the energy to relive the nightmare days after Jad's death, or consider the implications of his body disappearing before the autopsy, now that I knew all the possibilities.

THEN THERE WERE NONE

**28 Hours
(8:00 p.m. Sunday)**

On the drive back to Dallas, I attempted to bury the memories and focus on the present. My whole future depended on how the next few hours would play out and I needed to be at the top of my game. Did I have game? I hoped that at least for tonight I did. The way Grace had talked so cavalierly to Crockett about her and Marek taking care of me had scared me.

Van needed to know what I'd overheard Grace and Crockett say about Temple, but I didn't want to talk to him right now. He had hidden so much from me. Hell, he hadn't even told me about Crockett being a vampire. The only person left in my life who I felt like I could trust was, surprisingly enough, Owen—and what help would he be dealing with vampires?

The ringing of my cellphone pulled my eyes from the road to where it lay on my truck's dashboard. Wade Stephens' name and number flashed on its screen. *Dang it!* I had forgotten about the private investigator. I should have let him know that he could cancel the dig for dirt on my list of suspects. So much for my 'the killer must have had a key' theory.

But now that I knew Crockett was Bernie's killer, I was going to need help proving it. I fumbled for the phone. "Wade!"

"Laramie! Are you okay?"

"Yes, I'm fine," I said. "Sorry, I just couldn't get to the phone."

"Okay . . ." He chuckled, obviously convinced I was a crazy person.

I needed to pull off the freeway for this conversation. I told Wade to hang on and took the next exit. I pulled into the first parking lot I came to and positioned my truck so I could see anyone else who exited the freeway or pulled into the lot. I was learning. My self-preservation instincts had finally started to kick in.

"Hey—"

"I think I've found some information you'll be interested in," Wade said.

"I overheard a conversation between Council Member Austin Crockett and Grace," I interjected. "Did you know Crockett's a vampire? Well, he admitted that he "took care" of Bernie. They didn't discuss specifics, but it looks like I was way off base on my theory that someone who had a key to The Madam had to be the killer."

Wade was quiet for a moment. "Well . . ."

"Well, what?"

"Well," said Wade, "I dug up some stuff and there are a couple of people I wouldn't discount right away. Yes, I know Crockett is a vampire, but he could have had some help, right?"

"Crockett is working with the werewolves," I said tartly. "Why would he need human help?"

"Hey, hey, hey, don't discount us humans too soon. We can

still be fairly deadly. Plus, we have our own motivations and we are easily manipulated by the sups. But why do you think that Crockett is with the weres?"

Manipulated? Sounded like Wade had a story of his own.

I relayed what I had seen and heard at the festival. I also told Wade about how Temple's name kept popping up.

"Wow, that is a whole lot of information to take in."

"Yeah. What about Temple? Have you run across anything on him?"

"Honestly, I haven't had a chance to pull that thread since we talked earlier. I'll do some digging on him. I wish I'd known sooner that Crockett was involved in this. I'll check his phone calls and his movements for the last few weeks. I still think you should hear this other information I found, because there is a link with Crockett."

"Wow! Okay," I agreed. "But one more thing on the Grace front. When you mentioned checking Crockett's movements it reminded me of something I saw in her day planner. She was in Argentina a couple of weeks ago. Isn't that where a lot of the Nazis hid out after the war? I know Van said they hadn't been able to find any sign of Temple there, but it seems like an awfully big coincidence to me."

"Yeah, it does," Wade said thoughtfully. "How did you see Grace's planner?"

Drat! "Uh, not important," I said, hurriedly. "Now, tell me about Crockett."

"Alright, keep your secrets. I'll start with the people who basically came up clear and work my way to the possible baddies," said Wade.

"Fine," I responded impatiently. "It's your show."

"And don't you forget it." With that, he got serious. "So, in addition to the names you gave me, I told you I was also going to look into Tiffany because we know she has an ax to grind. I also checked Bill's wife, just in case she found out about his piece on the side and wanted to cause him some trouble."

"Uh huh," I said, in a way I hoped he understood meant he should move this along.

"Van, I didn't even look into. He is a no-go for wanting to hurt you in any way."

I wasn't sure that I agreed with Wade's assessment after the things I had learned today, but I didn't interrupt.

"Okay, so Bill's wife. I doubt that she is in the dark as much as Bill thinks she is, but I can't find anything linking her to your house around the time of the murder. Tiffany?" he went on, "Now that girl is into some crazy shit. Bill will be lucky to get out of that relationship with his skin intact, much less his marriage." Wade paused for effect, then continued. "But she is constantly on her phone and it didn't light up any towers near your house. If, when all this is over, you want to help Bill out, I think we can easily prove that she has a thing or three on the side her own self."

I couldn't help but laugh. As much as Bill deserved to twist a little over what he had done to his wife, I wanted to see the tables turned on Tiffany.

"Now we're getting to the good stuff. Tom Harner."

I sat up a little straighter. If anyone from my list was involved with Crockett, my money was on Tom.

"Tom's cell had multiple calls to Bernie and to Crockett. Since Crockett is a vampire, and has always been a shady SOB, I figured that was a link. I didn't realize how closely he was involved until now. Tom has made several offers to buy The Madam, right?"

"Yes." None of this was surprising. Tom had claimed that he was running interference with Bernie and had asked Crockett to help smooth things over with him. Of course there would be calls between them.

"Tom is not only flat broke, but he is also so far in debt he is in danger of losing everything," Wade said smugly.

I blinked. "I thought Tom was a successful author? Also,

the house was left to him by his mother. He should own that free and clear."

"Harner's first book was fairly successful but his others have bombed. He mortgaged the house a couple of years ago, right before his second book came out. I guess he has been paying the minimums on his credit cards with the cash he got from the mortgage, but it looks like he can only keep up the juggling game a few more months."

"So what was he planning to use to buy The Madam if he's so broke?"

"That, I don't know. He obviously has some kind of plan. My guess is that he thinks he can make some fast money on it. Maybe sell it on to Cerny for his hotel empire expansion?"

I thought for a moment. "I wonder if Cerny has made him an offer on his house?"

"Could be," Wade said thoughtfully. "Although I don't see Cerny buying Harner's land unless he has yours. It would be useless to him if you hold out."

"Good point. And Harner put in an offer months before Marek did," I said.

"Marek?" The teasing in Wade's voice was evident.

I blushed and was glad that the only one to see it was Bo.

"Didn't you only get the house recently?" asked Wade.

"About a year ago, when my husband's great aunt died and left it to me. Tom made the first offer for The Madam after the burial. If Marek," I refused to back down now and let Wade know he'd made a point, "made an offer to Hattie, she never mentioned it to me."

"It's another string to pull and see what unravels."

"It is. Wade, thank you so much for this. It has given me a lot to think about."

I was about to say goodbye and end the call when Wade cut me off. "Hold on darlin'. I saved the best for last."

"But there isn't anyone else."

"*Au contraire, ma petite*," Wade said in a West Texas drawl that made the French words laughable. "We haven't discussed your best buddy Owen yet."

My stomach sank all the way to the truck's floorboard.

"Tell me."

"Owen has the biggest dog in this fight," Wade said soberly.

"But what did I ever do to Owen?" I was genuinely confused.

"It isn't what you did to Owen," Wade answered. "It's what Bernie did. It was so big and bad that if Owen killed Bernie, you're just collateral damage."

"Tell me," I repeated. I wanted to lean forward and rest my head on the steering wheel, but I had to keep watch for approaching cars. And werewolves. And vampires.

"Owen had a twin sister named Oralee. She opened a business in East Dallas a couple of years ago. She put her life savings into a small, specialty coffee store on a street filled with bars. The sister tried to play Bernie's game and hired him to do marketing and social media for The Bewitched Bean. That was the name of her shop. Anyway, she was operating on a shoestring. It looks like she might have been able to keep her head above water, but your friend Bernie started a concerted attack on her shop once she could no longer keep him on the payroll. He spread rumors that she was bootlegging alcohol out the back door and selling drugs from underneath the counter. There wasn't a shred of evidence, but somehow Crockett ended up on board and they shut her down."

"Wait a minute. What was the name of the shop?" I asked.

"Caught that, did ya? Yeah, in addition to coffee it catered to the paranormal crowd. You know, Wiccans, crystal huggers and the like. She also carried books about all kinds of interesting subjects."

"Vampires and werewolves?"

"Could have been. We don't know for sure—just that they probably weren't your normal romances and mysteries."

"Where is she now?" I asked, but I had a bad feeling that I already knew.

"Oralee killed herself a little over a year and a half ago, just after the shop was closed. After the funeral, Owen attacked Bernie on the street in front of Bernie's house. Gave him a black eye and a broken rib. He also told Bernie that he would be back, and that he should be very afraid."

The nausea that had been my constant companion today had returned, but I didn't think it had anything to do with The Change this time. I had seen how loyal Owen could be to his friends. He had stuck by me the last year and been a constant support, and I was only his employer. What lengths would he go to for his sister? And was he somehow involved in the supernatural world?

"Laramie? Laramie!"

I heard Wade calling me. I told him my thoughts and added that I couldn't believe that Owen would set me up.

"Laramie, you are looking at this like he planned it. Maybe it was just a crime of opportunity. He caught Bernie snooping around the house and killed him. He intended to get the body out and then the code inspection happened."

The image of Owen pouring me a glass of wine at the festival came unbidden to my mind, along with the missing stock from The Madam's storage room. Owen had been in the house sometime during the last few days to pick up the wine and promotional items for our booth. Had Bernie dropped by while Owen was there?

"But that brings us back to Crockett, who said he "took care" of Bernie. So, if Owen was the one who actually killed Bernie, then he was working with Crockett. Working against me."

"Well, when you put it like that . . ." Wade let his words trail off.

I noticed the time on my truck's dashboard clock. "Wade," I said hurriedly, "I've got to get going. Thank you so much for the information."

"No problem. Do you want me to pass it along to Van?"

"Nope, I'll update him when I see him. We're supposed to meet up in a little while. Uh, Wade . . . Never mind. One of us will touch base with you later."

"Okay, talk soon." With that, Wade hung up.

I leaned my head against the back of my seat with a sigh. There was no one I could trust. That pause at the end of the conversation? I had been trying to figure out a way to ask Wade about Jad, then decided against it. He wouldn't even check into Van. Would he tell me anything about the search for Jad? Doubtful. I was truly alone in this thing.

I put the truck in gear and headed out of the parking lot toward the freeway. I had an appointment with a vampire.

29

LET'S GET THIS PARTY STARTED

**26.5 Hours
(9:30 p.m. Sunday)**

I left my truck parked in my normal spot behind the house. Bo ran around her kingdom, sniffing everywhere, acting as if she had been gone a week instead of a day. Well, I guess in dog days . . .

While Bo christened her yard, I gazed up at The Madam. Even from the back and at night, she was breathtaking. With the light from the waning full moon illuminating her, she looked like a dignified lady just waiting to be asked to dance. She had endured for so long. It was self-centered to believe that The Madam needed me to survive. She could do quite well without me, if it came to that. I had realized today that as long as Bo and I had each other, we would be fine. But The Madam had come to mean so much to me and my dreams were wrapped up tightly in the old lady. She was our home and our future. As with Bo, I would do anything necessary, fight any foe, to keep The Madam safe.

With one last look at Bo sniffing around the yard, I headed

inside. She would come in through her dog door when she was ready. I would have to make sure she was upstairs before all the fun started. She had almost held her own with the weres, but I didn't want her thinking she could mix it up with vampires.

I set my purse down on the kitchen island and tentatively sniffed the air. Glory be! The spoiled steak smell was gone!

I hurried out of the kitchen, crossed the saloon, and bounded up the stairs two at a time. I sniffed again when I reached the third-floor crime scene. Nothing but clean and fresh assailed my nostrils. I looked closely at the floor and walls, but couldn't see the slightest evidence of stains. The hole left by the bullet had been plastered over and the paint touched up. I lightly touched the tip of my finger to an area that looked a little shiny. A small amount of color came away on my finger.

Note to self—send The Shark a thank-you case of wine. It was nothing short of amazing. If my construction crew had worked this fast The Madam would have been open for business months ago.

A creaking noise shattered my sense of awe over the cleanup. Serious déjà vu, y'all. Old houses creak a lot, I told myself. I was just being paranoid because the last time it creaked, someone had been inside. At least this time I knew it couldn't be Tom. I had his key.

I heard another creak from downstairs. Maybe I wasn't being paranoid.

Then I remembered that my keys were in my purse on the kitchen island, along with my cellphone. Stupid! So much for my self-preservation instincts kicking in. I knew from my run-in with Tom this morning that there wasn't anything nearby I could use as a weapon. If I could get to my bedroom I could . . . what? Stab the intruder with my mascara wand? I didn't even have a working phone line in The Madam. The phone number for The Whine Barrel was scheduled to be turned on later this week.

I hoped as many people showed up to The Madam when she finally opened for business as had shown up uninvited over the last few days. Another creak, this time from the main staircase, had me turning for the back stairs.

Bo! She should have been barking at the intruder by now. Fear fueled my headlong rush down the back stairs, noise be damned. My only thought was to get to her. But I hesitated by the back door. I couldn't get either of us away from here without my truck keys and cellphone.

I hurried into the kitchen. I had almost reached my purse on the island when the industrial lights were switched on. Instinctively, I crouched to meet the threat and a low growl rumbled in my throat. I don't know who was more shocked, Tom Harner or me.

"Ah, Laramie?" Tom asked.

He was just visible through the red haze that had descended over the kitchen. Was this going to happen every time I got mad or felt threatened? But I was getting better at regaining control of myself. The red had already receded to a pink mist, and I slowly rose from my crouch.

"Whoa! What just happened?" Tom exclaimed.

"What I would like to know is what are you doing in my house? Again."

"Uh . . ." As Tom struggled for a response, he slid his left hand into the pocket of his jacket. The garment hung a little lower on the side his hand was in. Just like Jad's coat used to hang when he had his gun in his pocket.

I slid my eyes to my purse on the island. Could I grab it and get outside before he shot me? With my new speed and strength I was sure I could make it if there wasn't a gun in his pocket, but I didn't think I was faster than a speeding bullet. Yet.

Tom smiled. It was a particularly nasty smile. He moved forward and leaned against the island, right next to my purse. He didn't remove his hand from his pocket. He had gotten over his shock at my reaction and seemed to feel he was back in control. I guessed the steel courage in his pocket didn't hurt.

"So, Laramie, what did Bernie look like when they pulled him out of the dumbwaiter?"

"What?" I was dumbfounded by his callousness.

"You know, I hated that fat little weasel." He was almost unrecognizable, his once handsome face contorted by anger and hate. "Have you ever heard the parable of the scorpion and the frog?"

I nodded. When he stared at me expectantly I said, "The scorpion needed the frog to carry him across the river. The scorpion stung the frog halfway across, causing them both to drown. When the frog asked him why he would cause them both to die, the scorpion responded that he couldn't help himself. It was his nature."

I jumped at the bark of laughter from Tom.

"Bernie, although I called him a weasel, was actually a scorpion. He couldn't help but sting people; it was just his nature. Until he stung the wrong person, that is."

"And who was the wrong person, Tom?"

"Laramie, I'm pretty sure you already know the answer to that." An evil grin spread across his face.

"Crockett or Grace?" I asked, testing the waters.

"Grace?" he asked, confused. My question had thrown him off course.

At that moment, I heard the best and worst sound in the world. Bo's dog flap slapped open and then closed. The tapping of her pink-painted toenails on the hardwood floor echoed in the stillness. It was the best sound because I knew she was okay. It was the worst sound because I knew if I didn't do something soon, she wouldn't be that way for long.

The tapping stopped when she entered the kitchen. A low growl rumbled through the room. This time, surprise, surprise, it wasn't from me. My gaze swiveled to Bo. The fur on her back stood so high she looked like she had a Mohawk. Her pink lips were raised above her teeth and an impressive amount of ivory showed.

The hair stood up on the back of MY neck and she wasn't even focused on me. She only had eyes for Tom. I glanced at him in time to see the fear flash in his eyes. Before I could savor the spurt of triumph, I saw the black object in his hand.

Yep, that had been a gun in his jacket. Unfortunately, it was no longer in his pocket. Tom pointed it straight at Bo. She moved slowly around the kitchen island until she had a clear pathway to him. Conversely, his bullet had a clear pathway to her.

"You better call off that bitch. I would never want to hurt a dog, even that one, but I will if I have to."

"You would kill a person, but you draw the line at a dog?" I asked with a sneer in my voice. Although to be fair, Bernie had been a miserable excuse for a human being. I would choose a dog over him any day.

"We've already established that Bernie wasn't much of a human being," Tom said, mirroring my thoughts.

Bo growled low and took another slow step forward, almost as if she was stalking Tom.

"Call her off!" he screamed.

"Bo," I said, my voice barely above a whisper. I didn't want to startle her.

Bo responded with another low growl and a step toward Tom.

Tom's finger was on the trigger, his hand shaking so hard I was sure he would pull it any second. I knew what I had to do. I bunched my muscles to propel me into a leap, while I judged where I needed to land to place myself between Tom and Bo.

Hopefully, I had become a little bullet resistant over the last forty-eight hours. If not . . . I would cross that bridge when I got to it. Anything for Bo. Wasn't she doing the same for me right now?

"Yoo-hoo!" someone called out from the front of The Madam.

30

JUST A BIG OLD HOOTENANNY

**26 Hours
(10:00 p.m. Sunday)**

"Yoo-hoo!!" came a second time.

Bo, Tom, and I stood frozen. Then Tom scurried behind the swinging door that separated the kitchen from the bar, concealing himself from whoever was about to walk into the kitchen. Bo took his movement as her cue and lunged.

"No!" I screamed, but it was too late. Bo was already in motion. I waited for the gunshot. In an instant, Bo was past Tom and into the bar, the door swinging wildly in her wake. Tom and I shared a surprised look. She had moved so fast, he hadn't even thought to pull the trigger.

"There's my girl," I heard Owen cooing. I had a sudden flashback of seeing Tom at the booth talking to Owen right before the weres caught up to me. Was Owen here to help Tom "take care" of me?

"Go out there and get rid of him. You even hint about me being here and I will shoot all three of you."

That answered that question.

Tom pointed the gun at me, since Bo had fled the room

for greener pastures and belly rubs. He motioned with it for me to walk past him and out into the bar. I glanced at my purse, but Tom shook his head and raised the gun a fraction.

I walked slowly across the kitchen toward him. With my improved speed and reflexes, I could probably wrestle the gun away from him. But I couldn't chance a wild shot hitting Owen or Bo. No, my best bet was to convince Owen to go home and take Bo with him.

"Hey," I said as I pushed through the swinging door. The sight of Bo lying on her back, belly up, had me shaking my head. She had come through in a pinch with the weres earlier today and she'd faced down Tom, but at the first opportunity for tummy rubs from Owen she'd deserted me.

Owen looked up from his crouch and grinned in response. Those two were such a pair. If all our planning went to shit tonight and I didn't make it through, at least Bo would be well taken care of. Tears pricked my eyes.

"What's wrong?" Owen stopped rubbing Bo and stood, concern on his face.

"Nothing's wrong. Not a thing in the world. Life is peachy," I blathered, trying to rearrange my features into a happy expression. From the look on Owen's face, he wasn't buying it. I frowned and said, "That wasn't convincing, was it? I mean, I'm trying to be upbeat, but with the murder, the arrest, and everything else, it's hard."

"Not to mention you getting attacked by some big, burly guys at the festival today," Owen deadpanned. He crossed his arms and arched one eyebrow. When I didn't immediately respond, he twirled his finger at me to spill the beans.

"Ah . . . ," I hedged, trying to give my brain time to catch up with the conversation. "Not that I'm not happy to see you, but what are you doing here?"

"Evasion," Owen responded. "Nice tactic, but it isn't going to work on me. I told you at the festival I would be coming by tonight as backup for your meeting with Marek.

My guess is that he had something to do with the attack. Do you think he will show tonight after that stunt this afternoon?"

"Well, you never cease to amaze me," was all I could choke out. I had forgotten that Owen had been adamant about joining me for the meeting with Marek.

Today had been a day of revelations, each one convincing me that someone different was my main suspect. I had a lot of possibilities, with all of them having a solid motive or opportunity. Heck, two of them had even taken credit for Bernie's death and made it clear that they wanted me to be next on the list. I still had no idea who I could trust.

Bo stared up at Owen with a strong case of hero worship. I made a snap decision. I didn't think Owen had killed Bernie or was involved in a vampire/werewolf/creepy neighbor plot. The person who could give me answers and was in a talkative mood was in my kitchen, so I needed to get Bo and Owen out of there, ASAP.

"I appreciate you wanting to help me with Marek, but I can handle it. Could you take Bo for the night? I know you've had her a lot lately but, pretty please, one more night?"

"Nope." Owen smiled guilelessly at me.

"No, you won't take Bo for the night?"

"No, I'm not going anywhere." Owen's face hardened as he talked. "You're obviously in trouble and I'm not leaving you here alone to deal with it. I know you don't like asking for help, so consider it me insisting instead of you asking."

He was not going to cooperate.

"Okay, well could you do me a quick favor and take Bo out front for a couple of minutes to do business? I just got here, and I need to straighten out some stuff in the kitchen." At Owen's suspicious glance I finished lamely, "I don't want her out back. I'm not sure I latched the back gate securely."

"Okay, but don't even think about trying to lock us out in an attempt to make me leave. Remember, I have a key to every lock on this house. That makes me a suspect," he finished with a villain's grin and a twirl of a non-existent waxed mustache.

Not anymore you aren't, I thought, but only nodded in response and forced a weak smile. I stood like a statue until he walked out the front door with Bo prancing ahead of him, eager to smell all the smells. When they were safely out, I turned purposefully and strode toward the kitchen.

I gave the door a heave as I went through, hoping it would swing back with enough force to knock the gun from Tom's hand. It banged against the wall stopper and swung back into me. I gave it another shove as I walked through. The room was empty.

31

THE GIG IS UP

**25.5 Hours
(10:30 p.m. Sunday)**

I raced to the island and grabbed my purse. I needed to get out of the house. But which way to go? My truck was out back, but Owen and Bo were out front. Tom? I wasn't sure where he was, but I'd bet that he hadn't given up that easily. I spun around the room, looking for a weapon. I reached the knife drawer in two strides and rummaged through it until my fingers landed on the longest knife. I pulled it free from the others.

Jad's mantra about never bringing a knife to a gunfight flashed through my mind, but since the police still had his gun, a knife was my only option. I would have preferred something longer, like a fire iron or a baseball bat that I could swing and smash, but as I didn't have one of those lying around, the knife would have to do. Note to self—hide a baseball bat in the kitchen.

I hurried to the door that led into the saloon. If I could make it across the room and out the front door, Bo and I could leave with Owen in his car. But just short of the door, I stopped. What if Tom had heard Owen leave the house and was waiting to jump out at me like some freak show clown?

Moving forward was better than standing still. If I lived through this thing, that might be my new life mantra. I shoved the door, hard. It swung open a few inches before stopping with a thud and an "oomph!"

I shoved it again, ready for a showdown. This time it swung open easily and I charged through.

Instead of Tom, Owen stood directly in front of me with Marek Cerny right behind him. With a burst of inhuman speed, Marek whipped around Owen and blocked him from the knife that led my charge. I stopped my forward motion with barely an inch to spare between Marek's chest and the knife's tip.

Bo, who stood directly behind them, barked one sharp woof at me. She and I really needed to have a sit-down about whose side she was on.

"Uhhh," was all Owen could get out. His eyes were wide and focused on the knife and he was rubbing his chest where the door had caught him.

"How did you get in?" I demanded of Marek, too stunned and relieved to say much else. You know what I wasn't too stunned to do? Register how amazing Marek looked, that's what. His jeans, turtleneck and boots fit him as perfectly as the suits he had worn on our two previous meetings. They were all black, which seemed to be his theme. If black made me look that special combination of sexy and deadly I would never wear any other color either.

"I invited him," Owen responded.

"You really should keep your friends more up to date," Marek chastised. Ah, yeah, that was the understatement of the century—or centuries, where Marek was concerned. At my lack of response, he continued, "You should tell him. He is in this deeper than you think. You are only putting him in further danger by excluding him."

I wasn't sure what Marek meant when he said that Owen was in this deeper than I thought. But I knew from experience, gained firsthand over the last forty-eight hours, that being unaware of the scary things around us doesn't keep us safe. And Marek's chastising worked in another way. I had to face up to the fact that I hadn't been as forthright about sharing information with everyone around me as I could have been. I hadn't told Van about the conversation I'd overheard between Crockett and Grace. I had let my trust issues, resentment of Van—and, yes, my hurt feelings—cause me to act like a five year old. At any time during the drive back from Faith I could have called Van and told him all of it, but I had let pride hold me back.

Where had that gotten me? Standing in my house with my beloved Bo and Owen—the closest thing I had to a friend in the world—with a vampire who was supposed to be "taking care" of me and a murderer lurking around, that's where. Apparently that was what it took to finally make me admit that I needed a major overhaul on how I was dealing with the train wreck my life had become.

"Marek, along those lines, I think that Tom Harner is somewhere in this house. He was here earlier with a gun and all but admitted to Bernie's murder. He disappeared after Owen showed up."

"I'll search the house. Why don't you use that time to get Owen up to speed?"

I nodded, but Marek had already turned his back and was sniffing the air. He walked away from us and through the swinging door into the kitchen.

I looked at Owen then around the room, suddenly awkward.

"Why don't we sit down?" Owen motioned toward one of the tables that dotted the room.

We moved to the table and sat down in chairs facing each other. It was the same table I had sat at while the police had searched my house and questioned me. Had that been only yesterday?

A silence descended as I tried to figure out where to start, then was broken by a loud, put-upon groan by Bo as she flopped down underneath the table. She had been outside twice and hadn't received a single treat for her efforts. She was not happy with this sorry state of affairs. Welcome to my world, sister.

"Let me tell you about bumpies," I said to Owen with a grim smile.

IS THAT A GUN IN YOUR POCKET OR ARE YOU JUST HAPPY TO SEE ME?

**25 Hours
(11:00 p.m. Sunday)**

My talk with Owen went a lot better, not to mention faster, than Van and LaRue's talk with me had. I kept it short and sweet, telling him only that what we thought were mythical creatures like vampires and werewolves actually existed, but that I didn't know the specifics about what their powers were. It helped that he didn't bombard me with questions. In fact, he commented only once, a slightly incredulous, "you don't say" when I said that I thought the creatures were involved in Bernie's murder.

When I finally petered to a stop, convinced that Owen was either in shock or going to have me committed, I still hadn't shared my part in it. I thought that talking about the werewolf attack, the Van Helsings, or naming any of the vampires we knew would send him over the edge. He remained silent for a few moments, looking thoughtful. When he finally spoke, I was completely unprepared for what he had to say.

"Well, thank God. I thought I was going crazy."

It was my turn to be speechless.

"Some things, bad things, happened in my life a while back. I started doing some digging and nothing I found added up. Until now."

"The house is clear. His stench lingers on every floor, but he isn't here now." Marek had descended the grand staircase silently and crossed the room to stand by our table.

"Do we know any vampires?" Owen asked, with a pointed look at Marek.

When my eyes met Marek's dark gaze, he only shrugged. So, I outed Marek and Crockett. The Crockett reference elicited a "No shit!?" from Owen. I figured if we were playing twenty questions, I should get my turn. I placed my hand over the grip of the knife, but didn't pick it up.

"Marek, I overheard Grace and Crockett at the festival today talking about me. It seems that you and Grace are working with Crockett and he is working with the werewolves. Why are you plotting to take my business and frame me for murder?" I said the first part to clue Owen in on where things stood with Marek. The question was all for me.

Marek's lips tightened. "We aren't plotting to take your business or frame you for murder. You are obviously someone who sees only the bad. You failed to mention the good we have done for you—bringing you back into the hotel after the werewolves attacked you, hiring a lawyer to get you out of jail, and doing our best to protect you from the weres in Deep Ellum and at the festival. Maybe too much time around Anderson has warped how you see the world."

Owen's chair scraped back from the table and he put his head between his legs. I could hear him drawing great breaths of air but when I rose to go to him, he held up a hand to stop me. After a few more breaths he sat upright. His brown hair stood on end and his pale face was clammy with sweat.

"I'm okay," he said. "It just hit me all at once. What does Van have to do with this?"

I gathered myself to try to explain the Van Helsing

connection, but Owen wasn't looking at me. His eyes were focused on Marek. More aptly, a point behind Marek.

My fingers closed around the knife's grip as I stood, whirling to meet the threat. Marek's eyes met mine but before he could turn, there was a streak of silver and a dart embedded itself in his neck. Marek spun and leapt through the air toward the threat. Van stood at the kitchen door. The dart gun in his hand jerked twice and two more darts lodged in Marek's chest. He crashed to the floor barely a foot short of his mark. Van threw a handful of silver glitter over his still form. When it landed I saw that it wasn't glitter but a net woven of finely crafted silver chains that covered him from head to toe. Although Marek appeared comatose from whatever had been in the darts, his fingers twitched where the silver touched his bare skin.

"What the hell, Van!" I yelled, starting toward Marek to help him.

"Drop it!" a voice yelled and I saw the large silver barrel of a gun pointed at me just over Van's left shoulder. Crap! Tom must have followed Van in. I tightened my grip on the knife, ready to do whatever was necessary to protect my friends. Except . . . the barrel of Tom's gun was black and this one was silver.

"LaRue! Put the gun down," Van barked at her as he pushed the gun's barrel toward the floor. Owen had the wherewithal to step out of the line of fire, dragging Bo with him and shielding her with his body. LaRue merely swung the barrel out from under Van's hand and raised it level with my chest.

"Van, she's turned early and is Evil. She is going to kill us. Just look at her!" LaRue's voice had a pitch of hysteria that scared me more than the gun she was holding.

Fear turned my fingers to Jell-O, and my knife clattered to the floor as I reached for the sky.

"I haven't turned," I said. "And I'm not bad. Tom Harner

was here with a gun. He threatened me and hid in the kitchen when Owen arrived. He also kind of admitted to Bernie's murder."

"LaRue, put the gun away!" Van ordered.

LaRue sniffed and put the gun into a big, black Michael Kors purse. How many designer bags did she own?

"Can you blame me? I mean, look at her. Have you even looked in a mirror today?" That last part was directed to me.

"I've been a little busy trying to solve a murder, staying ahead of weres who have it in for me, and fending off a vengeful neighbor. I'm sorry that I've been just a tad too occupied to put on my Prada."

LaRue rolled her eyes. "Like you have Prada."

"Ahem." Owen, still crouched with Bo, cleared his throat. "Turned? Bad? What is going on here? Plus, is someone going to introduce me to this simply ravishing pistol-packing mama?"

I looked helplessly at Van and LaRue. Finally, LaRue crossed the saloon with her hand outstretched.

"LaRue Landry. I'm friends with Van. As for the rest of it, the less you know, the better off you are."

The soft lighting in the room glinted off the highlights in LaRue's cinnamon colored hair and made her caramel skin glow. In her black leather skinny pants—designer, I was sure—high heels, and form-fitting black top she looked like she had stepped out of a *Cosmo* photo shoot. Voodoo Princess chic? When I looked down at the mismatched outfit I'd borrowed from Mama I could see the tangled ends of my hair that had come loose from the ponytail. It hung in disarray around my shoulders and reminded me that my last shower had been at least thirty-six hours ago at the Dragonfly. Murder, vampires, and werewolves were hell on a girl's beauty regimen.

"Um, okay," replied Owen weakly in an attempt to rally. It galvanized me into action. Well, that and LaRue's recovery.

No way was I going to let that bitch show me up, Prada or not.

"Yeah, well, that ship has already sailed. I had to tell Owen that vampires and werewolves exist." I hoped that LaRue and Van would pick up on my unspoken message about what I hadn't told him.

"Owen," I said, in my best 'I am your boss, and this is an order' voice, "I can't let you get involved any deeper in this. Van and LaRue are here to help me with the, ah, meeting with Marek." I tried not to let my eyes wander to Marek's prostrate body. "I need you to . . . I will explain more tomorrow."

I pushed Owen bodily toward the front door. When we reached it, I noticed Yella standing guard at the bottom of the grand staircase. She must have entered the kitchen with Van but had taken the route through my office and the gift shop to get there. She watched our approach and, I swear, smiled at me. As if through telepathy, Bo noticed her at the same time, ran to her and began the welcome sniffing ritual. Yella nudged Bo with her head in greeting but maintained her on-guard stance.

I glanced at Van with a raised eyebrow.

"I wanted the main exits covered," he responded without shame. "LaRue and I will start setting up in there," he motioned toward the doors leading into the gift shop, "while you say goodbye to Owen and Bo."

Van looked exhausted. He was wearing the same clothes from my 'party' at the ranch, with the addition of a coat that looked way too heavy for early October in Texas. Typical Van; although he looked tired, he could have just stepped out of an urban casual layout in *GQ*. Figures. Everyone in the room looked better than I did. Even the guys. Especially the guys.

Van motioned at Yella to sit beside Marek. He and LaRue walked through the double French doors that led into the shop, leaving one door slightly ajar, probably so they could hear what was going on in the saloon.

Marek seemed reasonable to me. After all, he had helped me by searching the house for Tom and telling me to talk to Owen. I was convinced we could talk this out with him and come to some sort of agreement, although I had to admit that drugging him had probably set the negotiations back a bit.

Owen had been mostly silent since Van tranquilized Marek, but I could tell he was working up to say something. I decided to beat him to the punch. "I'm okay. Really. The best way you can help me right now is to take Bo and stay safe until I show up for her. I promise I will explain as much as I can."

Once he and Bo were safely out of the house, we could get on with it. If Marek agreed to give us some of his blood to do the ritual, then The Change might be stopped in the next few hours. Then we could focus on finding evidence that Crockett and Tom killed Bernie and prove my innocence. Within twenty-four hours my life could be back to normal. That's what I wanted, right?

Owen nodded and I started walking them out. But when I went to open The Madam's front door, Yella let out a low growl that made the hair on the back of my neck stand up. When I glanced back, Owen was standing in the open doorway of the gift shop. Bo was still next to me, gazing at the door with her head cocked. I couldn't help but be reassured by her presence. Then a loud thump made me jump a mile high. After a pause, there was another thump. Someone, or something, was out there.

"No!" Owen hissed as I reached for the doorknob.

I turned the knob slowly until I heard the click of the tongue leaving the hasp. The door creaked when I pulled it open, just a few inches, and peered out. As my eyes slowly adjusted to the total darkness, I began to make out the shapes of the pillars and porch railings. Then I could see . . .

Nothing. I still saw nothing. I opened the door wider and scanned the porch. The sound of panting reached me and I looked down. Dark eyes stared up at me from a huddled bulk. I took a quick step back from the door and light spilled from inside The Madam, revealing that the bulk was covered in fur. Werewolf!

Before I could shove the door closed, a blur of black and brown fur streaked through the opening, rocketing past me and into the saloon.

Yella lunged at it with a growl.

The furry mountain wasn't a werewolf—it was an enormous German Shepherd, at least twice Yella's size. The dog skidded to a stop and threw himself on his back with his stomach up toward her in the most submissive pose something that big could achieve. Yella stopped her advance but circled him on stiff legs, sniffing him all over. Bo enthusiastically joined the greeting party. After giving him the once-over, she nudged him with her nose, dropped her head and kept her butt high in the air, the universal 'let's play' in doggie body language.

The big guy opened his mouth in a wide upside-down grin and his tongue lolled out. Even Yella couldn't resist his charm and sat back on her haunches. He rolled to his feet and bumped noses with Bo. He ambled over to Marek and lay down by his side with a soft whine.

"Marek's dog," Van explained unnecessarily from the doorway.

"Worthless," Marek mumbled. The shepherd's ears pricked up and he gave Marek's face an enthusiastic lick. "Blah . . ." was all we could make out of whatever Marek was trying to say when the huge tongue went into his mouth. Marek's eyes closed. Worthless—I didn't know if that was his name, but it was forevermore how I would think of him—plunked his head on his master's chest, turned large soulful eyes on us and breathed out a huge sigh.

"Laramie, we need to talk. In the kitchen, now!" Van turned toward the kitchen without even checking to see if I was following him.

He'd never used that tone on me before. Over the years he'd had spoken to me in bored and condescending tones when Jad was alive, and pitying and careful tones since his death. Forceful Van was sexy.

"No, Van," LaRue said. She and Owen stood in the doorway of the gift shop. "We are all in this together. No secrets. Whatever you have to discuss, we all need to hear."

Van whirled to face her. "Really, LaRue? No more secrets? Are you ready to apply that rule to yourself, right here, right now?"

LaRue and Van faced each other across the room. Van was the angriest I had ever seen him. LaRue looked . . . sad. With a slight shake of her head, she took Owen's arm and led him back into the gift shop. Owen shot me a questioning look over his shoulder but went with her. LaRue closed the double French doors behind them, giving us privacy in the saloon.

"Do you have a death wish?" Van asked. "I can't save you if you keep tearing off on your own, confronting vampires and werewolves, and opening doors in the middle of the night when all manner of creatures want you dead. For God's sake, haven't you ever watched a horror movie?"

Confronting vampires? He somehow knew about Crockett. He was right, at least about opening the door, but I had a bone to pick about the Crockett situation.

"Why didn't you tell me Crockett was a vampire?" I asked. "I might not have been so quick to confront him if I had known."

"Why didn't you tell me about the conversation you overheard between Crockett and Grace? You knew that was important and yet, you didn't tell me? I had to hear it from Wade."

"I couldn't tell you in front of the family. I followed you

outside to tell you and you dropped the bomb on me about Jad. When did you talk to Wade?

"Just now. He texted to see what I wanted him to do next. He said you had been going to tell me." Van paused, glanced toward the closed doors of the gift shop and then lowered his voice. "He also told me about Owen's past. I don't think he should be here."

"I do." Despite Owen's layers, his pushy nature and his past, I trusted him to be on my side and I needed him there.

"Fine," Van said through gritted teeth. "Is there anything else that you haven't told me?"

"Uh . . ." I said.

"Laramie, what?"

"When Crockett and Grace were talking, they mentioned Temple. He is obviously real. Do you know anything else about him?"

"I don't. But . . . when Jad was looking for the True Cross, he thought there might be a connection to Crockett. Jad had been keeping tabs on him for several months before he died. Afterward, I started looking into Crockett, but I couldn't link him to anything."

"You didn't think to mention any of this when Crockett got the code inspection held up for The Whine Barrel?" I yelled. "Or when you told me about Jad's obsession with the True Cross?"

"YOU never told me he was involved," Van yelled back. "You only told me that Bernie and Tom had caused you issues after you found Bernie in your dumbwaiter. You never mentioned Crockett. I didn't mention him earlier because you were on information overload and I didn't know you even knew the guy."

We stared angrily at each other. We both had a lot to answer for in the not-sharing category. But my not-sharing only covered the last few weeks, whereas his not-sharing covered a decade. I wasn't going to take responsibility for this, but I couldn't hold his stare any longer.

When I looked down, my gaze fell on Marek's still body. Worthless, lying next to him with his head on his chest, returned my gaze steadily.

"Speaking of Marek," I said tentatively. "I don't feel right about this. We shouldn't take his blood without his consent."

"Laramie, he is in it up to his ears. We have to do this, and we have to do it before any more time passes. Lar," he added, lowering his voice to a whisper. "Do you really want to spend eternity as a vampire?"

33

AND THEN THERE WAS BLOOD

**24.5 Hours
(11:30 p.m. Sunday)**

Van, with Owen's help, dragged Marek into the gift shop. I followed them inside, not feeling quite right about what was going on, but not knowing how to stop it. I was shocked by what I saw.

The gift shop's walls were lined with shelves and display cases were strategically placed around the room, along with unopened boxes of wine and pet accessories. New to the room were two wooden chairs from the storage room, set side by side facing the large bay window overlooking the front porch. A small table sat between them.

My shock came from the sight of a small cast iron cauldron atop the table. LaRue had an assortment of what looked like herbs and twigs—hopefully twigs and not bones, I thought with a shudder—lying in a circle around the cauldron. She chanted and occasionally threw pinches of the different substances into it. A cloth had been thrown over boxes stacked along one wall to form an altar, and assorted candles burned on it. What was this, have candles and cauldron, will travel? I had no idea those things were so portable.

While I took in the scene and the Voodoo Princess at work, Van and Owen heaved Marek into one of the chairs and secured him to it using silver chains. Worthless, Yella, and Bo had followed us into the room and sat in a row by the door that led back into the saloon. Maybe it was my guilty conscience, but I was sure I read censure in their gazes.

I would love to tell you that I stood up to Van for what I knew was right. That I refused to take part in a voodoo ceremony that stole blood from a man, er, vampire, when he was unconscious and unable to defend himself from the assault.

But I can't tell you that, because I didn't.

It took Van a piteously short amount of time to convince me to go along with his plan. I knew that taking someone's blood was wrong. But, despite liking Marek and wanting to believe him when he said he wanted to help me, there was just too much evidence that he had somehow, even peripherally, been involved in my attack. And hadn't he injected me with vampire venom without my consent?

I'm ashamed to admit that I think part of me went along with the ceremony because I knew that if I became a vampire, I would lose any chance to ever be with Van.

So by the time LaRue said she was ready, silver chains bound me to the other chair and an IV needle was stuck into the crook of my arm. Plastic tubing ran from the needle into the cauldron. Van made quick work of putting a similar IV needle into Marek's arm, explaining that it and the tranquilizer darts were made of silver so they could penetrate Marek's flesh. The darts had contained concentrated wolfsbane, the same stuff LaRue had sprayed at Marek and Grace's car when we escaped from Deep Ellum.

Van hadn't explained what was about to happen, or what I could expect afterward. When I asked, he and LaRue exchanged a look that didn't inspire much confidence.

Owen had stood quietly, his back against the doors leading into the bar and the row of dogs at his feet. Overall, he had seemed to be handling the situation quite well. At least until now.

"Vampires? Werewolves? Neighbors with guns wandering around the house? I'm pretty sure I have taken the train to crazy town, but I've gone with the flow. I helped you drag a guy in here and chain him up next to an altar, for God's sake. A guy that you've drugged, which can't be legal. Laramie, I've kept quiet despite the scary black magic vibe going on in here. I've even watched you get chained up. But I'm not going to sit back and let you take part in some type of bloodletting or exchange, or something just as crazy, without more answers."

"It's voodoo," LaRue responded stiffly. "I don't practice black magic, so you can set your mind at rest about that."

"Oh, I feel so much better now," Owen said sarcastically. "Look, I see an altar and I hear talk about blood. I don't think you can get much blacker into the magics than that. I know what I'm talking about. I read stuff." The last part was said a tad belligerently.

I have learned over the years that some people don't handle scared well. So they channel that fear into anger. I was touched. Despite the secrecy and the agenda Marek claimed Van had, I truly believed Van was looking out for me. But he was a steamroller. I was glad Owen was pointing out the sort of obvious issues that I was too punch-drunk to articulate clearly. It also reminded me that I hadn't told him how I came to be involved in this.

"Owen," I said, cutting off a very pissed-looking Van, "The short story is that I was attacked by werewolves Friday night. They left me for dead. And I would have died, but Marek injected me with his venom. That saved me from dying from the werewolf attack but it will turn me into a vampire within seventy-two hours of the bite if we don't reverse the effect his venom is having on me."

Owen stared at me for a few long moments as if he was trying to determine whether I was pulling his leg. He took a deep breath, released it on a long sigh and said, "Well, why didn't you just say so?" He leaned back against the door.

With that, LaRue tapped her iPhone and the familiar drumming music filled the room.

"It is a cleansing ritual," she said to no one in particular. "His blood is cleansed before it enters Laramie, in the hope that it will counteract his vampire venom in her blood."

In the hope? Aw, hell.

LaRue circled the chairs that Marek and I were chained to, her body swaying to the drumbeat. Her lips moved but, as in the laboratory, I couldn't make out the words. Each circle took her by the candle-laden altar, where she passed her hand through the flame of the largest candle. On her third circle, the flames on all the candles flickered. I looked down at the plastic tubing to see if anything was happening. Blood, much darker than human blood, was oozing through the tube, leaving Marek's arm and headed toward the cauldron. The closer it got to the vessel, the stronger grew my feeling that what we were doing was wrong.

The first drop of Marek's blood fell into the debris in the cauldron. Smoke filled the cast iron pot and an ominous hissing began. It sounded like it was filled with angry snakes. With growing dread I noticed that a thick black sludge had begun to ooze from the cauldron and up through the tube attached to my arm. I'd known the ceremony would involve a transfer of blood from Marek to me, but this was way creepier than I was prepared for.

Marek jerked in the chair. His eyes opened and his gaze swept the room, then fell to the table and took in the cauldron and tubes between us. Horror contorted his features and he struggled to break free from the chains that bound him. He was too weak to fight the silver and after several moments his struggles stilled.

"Don't . . ." he said in a hoarse whisper. It was all he could manage.

I looked down again and saw that the dark substance had almost reached the IV needle in my arm. It looked thicker and blacker than it had traveling from Marek's arm. Panic overwhelmed me at the thought of it entering my body. I began to struggle, and finally realized why Van had chained me too.

Van knelt beside me and wrapped his arms around me. "I know it is scary, but stop fighting it. This is going to fix everything." He held my hands to keep me from pulling the needle. As terrified as I was, his touch reassured me.

"No . . . will make everything worse." Marek could barely push the words out.

"It will fix it! What the hell were you thinking, injecting her with your venom?" Van leapt to his feet to confront Marek.

Marek ignored Van. He kept his gaze on me and, when our eyes met, he stared deeply as if trying to plumb my depths. It took the last of his strength to say the words but he managed them, loud enough for us all to hear over LaRue's chanting and the drumming that pulsed from her phone.

"I didn't. It was Jad."

34

WELL THAT CHANGES EVERYTHING

24 Hours
(Midnight Sunday)

All movement in the room ceased. Well, almost all of it. LaRue stopped dancing and chanting. Owen's hand froze mid-stroke on Bo's head. Van quit breathing. You know what didn't stop? The most important thing. Marek's blood had completed the journey through the stretch of the plastic tube leading from the cauldron to the needle stuck in my arm. It entered my bloodstream with the accuracy and force of a heat-seeking missile.

My scream of pain broke the stillness of the room. When I looked down at my arm, I expected it to have incinerated from the fire that traveled up it. The pain passed through my shoulder and then coursed through my neck. There was a roaring in my ears and the world around me slowed. I looked at Van, but his back was to me. He faced the bay window that overlooked the front porch of The Madam, although the curtains were drawn.

"Van . . . ," I whispered. I knew I was dying and I wanted

to tell him . . . what, I'm not really sure, but I wanted him to be with me when I drew my last breath.

As the pain coursed through my body and I waited for the end, I realized that I had been lying to myself for months, maybe years. The secrecy, the lies, even the possibility that Jad might be out there; none of it mattered. Van was the only thing that mattered to me right now. I willed him to look at me, but he continued to stare intently at the curtains covering the window.

LaRue had sprung to action with a loud cry and fumbled with the plastic tubing in my arm, her tiny, fairy-like fingers suddenly clumsy. How convenient for her, I thought. She had never liked me and now she would get to watch me die. It pissed me off more than a little that things were going to end happily for her.

A fresh barb of pain shot from my shoulder across my chest. When Marek's blood hit my heart, it would either stop it or it would be pumped through the rest of my body. Either way, I would die. I couldn't withstand that much pain coursing through my body.

Van's hand was only a few inches from my left hand. My arms were still chained to the chair, but I tried to stretch my fingers to touch his hand. I wanted to be touching Van when I died.

A howl broke through the drumbeats. Even in my agony I was embarrassed, because it must have come from me. Then I realized that it had been Yella, and she now stood next to Van, focused on the window.

The first arrows of pain hit my heart and I soundlessly mouthed, "Van."

The room dimmed. My heart pounded so hard I was sure it would explode. I lowered my fingers back to the chair. As my vision dimmed, I focused on Van. I wanted to him be the last thing I saw. My eyelids were heavy and they shut, casting my world into darkness.

The shattering of glass dumped enough adrenaline in my system to allow me to force my eyes open. Grace O'Malley stood in the room, window glass raining down around us. She was crouched, her fangs extended, gripping a sword in one hand and a dagger in the other. She looked from Marek to me and growled. She was pissed!

She was glorious.

The avenging angel of death had come for me for what I'd done to Marek. I managed a slow smile. Grace would also kill LaRue, for her part in it. My eyes closed again as I slid toward oblivion, not quite a happy woman, but one somewhat at peace knowing that her frenemy wouldn't get to enjoy watching her die.

THE BAT CAVE

**12 Hours
(Noon Monday)**

When I regained consciousness, a miniature high school band was using my skull as a parade ground and a pimply teenager enthusiastically banged his mallet against my brain in lieu of a bass drum. It had to be daytime. It was the same headache I'd had during daylight hours since the attack.

That I wasn't dead came as quite the surprise. How had I survived the avenging angel of death, AKA Grace O'Malley? With a supreme effort, I pried open my eyelids, dreading the carnage left by Grace.

"Hey, honey! Glad you could join us," Owen said. He sat in a chair to my right. Bo lay on the ground beside him.

"Where are we?" I croaked, my voice more frog than bat.

"We're underneath The Madam. Did you know that she has a cave attached to her basement?"

I felt punch-drunk. Trying to move as little as possible due to my throbbing head, I took in my surroundings cautiously. We were in a cave. A very nicely furnished one, but still a cave. It was about twenty feet wide and maybe forty feet long. A large wooden door set into bookshelves was at one end and large wooden cabinets with doors lined the other. In between were several chairs, desks, filing cabinets, and even a couple of beds. In one area, the flagstone floor was covered by workout mats. Weightlifting equipment circled the mat along with other exercise items such as balance balls and jump ropes. The weapons were the most interesting aspect of the cave's décor. Rows of swords, knives, crossbows, clubs with spikes and a few things whose purpose I was clueless about lined one of the walls. Electric lights dangled from the twenty-foot-high ceiling at intervals. Electrical cords snaked throughout the space: along walls, over the flagstones and, in some places, under the rugs that dotted the floor. It was quite cozy. I shuddered.

"A cave?" I asked and then, "Really?" when I realized I was still chained to the chair from the ceremony.

"After that shit show upstairs, the White Knight and the Voodoo Princess weren't sure what kind of mood you would wake up in. They decided you were better off chained up for their own good."

"That isn't strictly true."

When I rolled my head in the direction of the voice, the tempo of the rollicking pain party sped up. LaRue sat slumped in a chair against one of the cave's walls, cradling the big-ass shiny six-shooter in her lap. Some things, or people in this case, never change.

"How long have I been out?"

"The full twelve hours," LaRue said.

I understood the significance.

"Does that mean that Marek's blood counteracted the venom?" I looked from LaRue to Owen.

Owen shrugged in the universal 'I don't know' gesture, but wouldn't meet my eyes in the universal, 'you're screwed' gesture.

"Or now you have a double dose of vampire. Or it restarted the seventy-two-hour clock. Or it sped up the entire process and you could change at any minute." LaRue was always a dose of sunshine.

I looked at LaRue while I tried to think of a scathing retort. Her face was blotchy and swollen. She gave a loud sniff and released her clutch on The Cannon long enough to rub her watery red eyes.

An involuntary smile crossed my face. LaRue looked like she would be one of those girls who would get prettier and daintier when she cried, but nope, she was an ugly crier.

I looked around the cave and my small lift of happiness faded.

"Why are you crying? Where is Van?" If that crazy redhead had touched a single hair on his head, I would kill her with her own sword. Once someone unchained me, that is.

"Van is fine," Owen hastened to tell me. "He is out looking for Tom Harner and Austin Crockett and . . . Jad."

Marek's words from the ritual came crashing back.

Owen, with his usual uncanny ability to read me, said, "Girl, we need to catch you up."

"How about you take these chains off?"

Owen rose and started toward me, but a small sound from LaRue stopped him.

"Come on, Princess," Owen cajoled with a smile. "She is obviously herself and in control. What's the point in keeping her chained up like a dog? No offense, Bo."

LaRue shook her head in response. When Owen took another step toward me, the barrel of the revolver rose from her lap. He looked at me regretfully. Bo, who had raised her head at her name, looked from face to face and then dropped it back onto her crossed paws. She sighed like she was the most put-upon creature in the entire world. Yet I was the one still chained up.

I leaned my head against the chair, thankful for its high back, and wiggled around within the chains until I got comfortable. Based on how loosely they'd bound me, the chains were there more for the vampire-stopping properties of the silver than the binding strength they would have on a human.

"So honey, when Grace O'Malley, vampire extraordinaire, made her amazing entrance, I was sure she was going to kill us all." As he talked, Owen waved his hands about to help him tell the story. "She freed Marek, getting some pretty harsh silver burns in the process, then she dressed down Van and Miss Voodoo Princess here like you wouldn't believe. But nobody died."

That didn't get the rise out of LaRue that I thought it would, but I think she was shell-shocked. The blank expression on her puffy face didn't register Owen's comment and she continued stroking The Cannon. She was the image of a distraught and pissed-off woman plotting murder. If Wikipedia had a page titled "Woman Thinking About People Who Need Killing," LaRue's picture would have been on the sidebar.

"Then, even though Grace didn't owe us any explanation, she caught us up on what she and Marek have been up to." Owen shook his head like he couldn't believe her generosity. When I didn't say anything he asked, "Well, aren't you going to ask?"

"What have they been up to?" I asked politely, even though my head was pounding.

"Well, after your Aunt Hattie died, your creepy neighbor approached them wanting to sell his house and The Madam. He told them that you were selling it to him."

When Owen paused for effect, I feigned shock.

"Marek and Grace wanted both properties and when it looked like Tom wasn't going to get The Madam, they tried to approach you, but you weren't having any of it. Meanwhile, they heard what your business was going to be and wanted in. The Dragonfly is a dog-friendly hotel, so having a place like this right next door was a win for them. They tried to let you know that they would support the business, but you wouldn't meet with them."

Owen stopped long enough to shoot me a reproachful look.

"Well, how was I supposed to know that?" I asked huffily.

"By picking up your phone when they called."

"All this business talk is all well and good but there's something else—or someone else, as the case might be—that's a higher priority for me." I looked to LaRue. "What about Jad?"

Owen shot me a look to let me know he didn't appreciate me trying to change the course of his story.

"Okay, but I have to go back a little bit first. Marek and Grace knew about Jad working with the Van Helsings. When he died they thought he might have been murdered, but they felt that was on Van to figure out. But when rumors started up about an Evil, out-of-control vampire about six months after Jad's death, they figured they should get involved. Marek has been tracking the vampire's trail but he hasn't been able to catch up to him.

"Is it the vampire who killed Jad? Or . . . ," I trailed off, unable to voice the alternative.

"Oh, for God's sake! Jad is the vampire! How did you miss that?" LaRue said.

"Is it true? Owen, is Jad definitely alive?" I asked.

"Um . . ." Owen looked to LaRue for help, but she only stared back defiantly. "I don't know if being a vampire is actually considered alive or not, but there is a lot of evidence that he may be up and moving around. He's most likely the vampire they're tracking."

A small sob escaped LaRue.

Owen rolled his eyes at me and then continued. "Then, with the vampire running amuck, the widow of said vampire—you, Laramie, in case you haven't been paying attention—turned up practically on Marek and Grace's doorstep by way of inheriting The Madam. They surmised, correctly, that you were totally clueless about the supernatural world. They heard that Tom and Bernie were trying to put the kibosh on The Whine Barrel. They were determined not to become involved in 'human matters,' but then Crockett got involved. I never liked that guy," he added. "Van and Jad didn't either. They knew he was a vampire, but it was more than that. They thought he was involved in something shady and were investigating him. Van told Grace all about it last night."

"But Grace has been working with Crockett!" I interjected.

"Oh, honey! That tall drink of firewater has been acting as a double agent," Owen said. "She and Van had it out over that last night. Apparently, our Grace has a long history of playing fast and loose with the right and wrong line. So when Marek and Grace were trying to figure out why Crockett was involving himself in your affairs, it wasn't a stretch for her to play along with him to find out what was what."

Our Grace? Had I only been out twelve hours?

"But I found her hair in the dumbwaiter." I refused to give up on Grace as a suspect.

"Yeah, she stopped by to look for clues after the police left," Owen explained, dismissing my find with a wave of his hand.

So much for my sleuthing abilities.

"So Grace took Marek back to the Dragonfly. Van searched the house for Tom, but found nada. Then he brought us down to this amazing lair. You really didn't know this was here? You haven't been holding out on me?" Owen asked me suspiciously.

"I had no idea," I was starting to feel as shell-shocked as LaRue looked.

More was said, but I was having a hard time keeping up with Owen's drama and flourishes. The main thing was that Van and Jad had known about the cave. It was connected to

The Madam's basement by a secret door. They had used the cave as a sort of headquarters for their sup-hunting activities when they didn't want to deal with the Van Helsings, en masse, at The Compound. Since they and Hattie were the only ones who knew about the cave, we would be safe here until Van's return. After getting us settled in Van had left, determined to locate Tom before he fled the country—if it wasn't already too late.

"That's it?" I asked Owen. LaRue had gotten up somewhere toward the end of the story and exited the cave through the door in the bookshelves, which I believed led into the basement of The Madam. She had shuffled from the room hunched over like an old woman. She had even listlessly placed The Cannon on a shelf next to the door as she walked through it.

"There are some pretty big holes in that story," I said to Owen.

"I'm telling you everything I know."

The enormity of the situation hit me. Jad was alive and had injected me with vampire venom. Since we hadn't used his blood, there was no way to know what would happen to me. Oh, Jad, I knew you didn't really love me, but why would you have done this?

"What about Temple and the True Cross? Am I still going to turn into a vampire tonight? And, and . . ." I faltered, knowing that several other big points were floating around out there. ". . . Why did Tom kill Bernie for Crockett? How does that fit into any of this?"

"I think I can answer that," Tom said, looking at us down the barrel of his black semi-automatic.

36

THIS IS NOT THE WAY I'M GOING OUT

**11 Hours
(1:00 p.m. Monday)**

Tom stood inside one of the floor-to-ceiling wooden cabinets that lined one end of the cave. I gaped at him as he stepped out of it and moved toward me. Owen hurried over to stand beside my chair. Bo walked stiff-legged to my other side, her gaze locked on Tom and her fur raised.

Tom stopped ten feet from our little group. He took in my chains with a sneer.

"Look at Laramie, all chained up and nowhere to go."

As much as I wanted to, I refused to rise to the taunt in his voice. He had entered the cave through the opposite end from the door LaRue had left through. With The Cannon sitting on the shelf where she'd left it, she was unarmed. We had to keep Tom talking until she returned. If she overheard him, she could call Van for help. Plus, I wanted answers.

"I'm definitely a captive audience, so why don't you give us some of those answers you just promised? I have a couple of new questions, too. Like how you found out about the cave and how long you've been hiding in that cabinet."

"Oh honey, you are still clueless, aren't you? Here you've been running all over town the last two days, playing sleuth, and you still aren't any further along. Tsk, tsk, tsk . . . I will fill you in on some of it while we wait for your associate to come back from the little girls' room. Hopefully she will have taken the time to wash her face and fix her makeup. She looks dreadful," he said with a slight comedic shudder.

Maybe it was because of my low self-esteem issues, but I've never been able to stand being called stupid. Despite my determination not to rise to the bait, I couldn't keep quiet about what I knew.

"Well, I know you're not the successful writer you want everyone to believe you are. You're dead broke." When he clenched his jaw, I knew I had scored a direct hit. "You've lived off your mommy for years and now you are living off loans. And I know you killed Bernie, although to be fair, you told me that last night."

"My first book was very successful, and when I sold this place to Cerny I would have been successful again. You know this property should have been mine after Hattie died, don't you? My mother was her closest friend. She dedicated her whole life to her. She cooked and cleaned for her. She never had any kind of life outside of The Madam. Mother looked after Hattie until she was so weak from cancer she couldn't get out of bed. Then she made me go check on Hattie and wait on her. Like I was an errand boy rather than a brilliant novelist. Uh, uh, uh," he said to Owen, shaking the pistol's barrel at him the way you would shake a finger at someone for being naughty. Owen had gradually been moving behind me and to my right, closing the distance between them. "Don't think you are going to get close enough to grab my gun. Didn't anyone ever tell you not to be a hero?"

Owen shook his head sheepishly like he had been caught. But I noticed that his movements had caused Tom to turn his back to the door LaRue had used. Now she would have a chance of reentering the cave without Tom seeing her. Owen would be getting a bonus in his next paycheck.

"But Hattie signed over your house to Maria years ago," I protested. "She loved Maria like a daughter and nursed her too." When Maria's cancer had gotten bad, Hattie spent more time looking after her than Tom had. She'd told me that she had spent hours sitting by Maria's bed while Tom was locked in his room, writing.

"Ha! Mother was only a servant to Hattie, and I was even less than that. When Jad died I tried to talk to Hattie about what she was going to do with The Madam. When I asked if she was going to leave it to me, she laughed. Laughed! Then, when I offered to buy it, she seemed insulted. Like I wasn't good enough to live here."

I almost felt sorry for Tom. Almost. To believe yourself a part of the family and then be laughed at would be horrible. I would have been heartbroken. But Tom hadn't been heartbroken; he'd been offended that Hattie hadn't seen his greatness. Plain and simple, he was a textbook narcissist, or maybe a sociopath.

"As for me telling you that I killed Bernie, that was a mistake. I don't make many of them, but that was one. I was going to kill you last night and make it look like a suicide. Your friend here keeps getting in my way." Tom motioned at Owen with the gun. "First he nearly caught me in the storeroom on Friday night when I let myself in to meet Bernie, and then he showed up last night. But I'll take care of both of you, and the little sad girl too. I always have a Plan B, or in this case, Plan C. Get it? Plan C for cave."

"Or is it C for Crockett?" I said.

Tom looked so shocked it was almost comical. I had to get him off this talk about killing us and find out why he was doing Crockett's dirty work.

"Jad was suspicious of Crockett before his death," I said.

"If you used the tunnel between your house and The Madam left over from prohibition days . . ." I raised my eyebrows in a question. "You overheard Jad and Van talking about Crockett and went to him with the information."

"I did go to him, but not until after I did some research myself on our good council member. All of his paperwork was in place . . . birth certificate, social security number, passport, and even school records. But when you check with the schools, from elementary on through law school, there isn't a picture of him anywhere.

"Oh, I didn't know anything about the vampire part of it," he continued. "Jad and Van, even in private, were fairly discreet with the terms they used."

I had kept my eyes glued to Tom's face during our exchange—no small feat when all I wanted to do was watch for LaRue's return. But I was afraid that any flicker of my eyes to the area behind him would remind him of her.

"When did you go to Crockett?" I asked between gritted teeth, a sick feeling in the pit of my stomach.

"Oh, about a week before your beloved husband, Jad, died in that tragic tractor accident." Tom's boyish grin was at odds with his grim words. "I have to say, the timing was certainly fortuitous. Crockett had only been on the council for a few months, but he was a rising star. There was already talk of him running for mayor. And then a young, handsome, deco-rated policeman dies in a freak accident right after I tell Crockett the policeman is investigating him? Well, I could pretty much set my sights on anything after that. As long as I stayed quiet, that is."

"You son of a bitch! You killed Jad!" LaRue screamed.

"No!" Owen shouted and flung himself at me.

Gunfire erupted around us. Tom fired several shots at us and spun to fire at LaRue. Two loud booms—that I swear to God sounded like cannon fire—bellowed from the door of the cave. I couldn't see anything except the ceiling. Owen's tackle had knocked me and the chair I was still chained to backward onto the floor.

Bo was barking but, thank God, it sounded like her mad bark, so I didn't think she was injured. I took the opportunity to wiggle out of the chains. As I had suspected, they were loose and I was able to push them over my head. I rolled into a low crouch, not sure where the biggest danger lay. The gunfire had stopped, or at least I thought it had. It was hard to tell over the ringing in my ears.

I looked first for Owen. He lay on the ground to my right. His face was contorted in pain and he gripped his side, red blooming between his fingers.

"Owen!" I exclaimed, and looked wildly around the room for Tom. He lay on the floor of the cave with his back propped up against the wall. His gun lay beside him. Two craters gaped in his chest. It was a grisly view.

Bo was in front of Owen and me barking ferociously, first at Tom and then at LaRue, who stood in the doorway with The Cannon still pointed at Tom.

I whirled on her. "What the hell, LaRue! What have you done?"

"You heard him. He got Jad killed and—and who knows what else!"

"We need answers, not another body!"

I crossed to Tom and knelt beside him. I used my knee to nudge the gun he still grasped away from his hand. The odor of fresh blood assaulted me. I'm ashamed to say, it smelled amazing.

"Someone call an ambulance," Tom said in a hoarse whisper, his eyes meeting mine. I looked back at LaRue. I didn't even know where my cell phone was.

"No!" LaRue replied, strangely calm. "We are going to let you die here. Just like you let Jad die out in that field."

"Hey ladies, I'm okay. It's just a flesh wound. I don't need an ambulance, but thanks for asking," Owen gritted out. He had pulled himself upright on the floor and Bo happily licked his face. His shirt was off and there was a bloody gouge in his side where one of Tom's bullets had grazed him, but luckily, no craters like Tom was sporting. That LaRue was a much better shot than Tom didn't surprise me at all.

"Owen, thank God you are okay," I said guiltily. Once I had seen Tom's injuries, I had completely forgotten about Owen.

Owen smirked at me, so I knew that he had grasped that Bo was the only one who had been thinking of him. He rubbed her big block head. She, in turn, wagged her tail so hard that her whole back end wiggled and gave him another enthusiastic kiss on the face. Owen pulled his phone out of his pocket and started to dial.

"No!" LaRue said and swung The Cannon at him.

"LaRue, I'm not going to let him die without trying to help and you aren't going to shoot me. Laramie, if you have questions you need answered, you better start asking them."

I turned back to Tom. He was struggled for breath, but he still managed an eye roll at me. He picked up almost exactly where he had left off before the gunfight.

"When you started trying to open your business, I knew it was time to call in my favor from Crockett." He coughed and a thin stream of frothy pink liquid escaped the corner of his mouth and trickled down his chin.

"Crockett brought in Bernie. They had worked together on several projects. Bernie would play bad cop, I would play good cop, and Crockett would be the mediator. Your paperwork would get held up and you would have to sell. To me." Tom closed his eyes.

"No!" I shook Tom's arm and his eyes opened. "Stay with me. Keep talking. You killed Bernie because he turned on you and wanted more money. But why did Crockett kill Jad?"

Tom tried to laugh, but couldn't manage it. "Bernie didn't

want more money. He wanted more power and he tried to blackmail the wrong person. Or vampire. Bernie hacked Crockett's email and discovered he was a vampire. He didn't believe it at first. It seemed so ridiculous. Crockett is working with a group of supernaturals trying to track down something that would give them unbelievable power. So Bernie copied all the emails onto an encrypted flash drive. He showed me some of them. He tried to blackmail Crockett into turning him into a vampire in exchange for his silence and returning the emails."

"Bernie as a vampire?" I broke in, even though I knew I shouldn't.

"It was never going to happen. Crockett told Bernie if he helped me kill you and gave me the flash drive with the emails, he would turn him. We came here Friday under the pretense of checking The Madam again, but you wouldn't let us inside. Later, when you went to the Dragonfly, I called Bernie and told him we had another chance at you. Crockett told me to get the flash drive from Bernie and take care of him. In exchange, he would make me a vampire and get you out of the picture so I could have The Madam. "

"And Bernie wasn't concerned you or Crockett would double-cross him?"

"I'm sure he was, but he couldn't miss his opportunity. He took a gamble and lost. I left the front door unlocked and then waited on the third story. I called Bernie up to meet me . . . I planned to push him down the stairs. We all know how dangerous those steps are," he said, giving me a knowing look.

A chill spread through me. "Not Hattie, too?" I asked incredulously.

"Now you're catching on." A fierce coughing fit rendered Tom unable to speak for several moments. It finally passed and he gasped, "Where is that ambulance?"

"It's coming," Owen replied tersely. I had heard him

mumbling on the phone, but I had been straining to hear Tom as his voice had gotten lower and lower.

"So, you had to shoot Bernie instead of pushing him down the stairs. Fine. What about Jad?"

"Before Bernie arrived, I had a flash of inspiration. Lots of people have guns. And there it was, right in your bedside table. I could kill two birds with one bullet. Well, several, but who's counting. The first shot barely nicked him, but it was enough to get him talking."

Dread washed over me. "When the police do ballistics, it'll show that my gun killed Bernie?"

Tom grimaced at me and went on like I hadn't interrupted. "Bernie had a flash drive containing all the emails, but he hadn't trusted Crockett completely. He handed over the flash drive but told me that if anything happened to him, a copy of all the emails would automatically be sent to your email account."

"Why Laramie's account if Bernie thought y'all were going to kill her?" Owen asked.

"So whoever was investigating her murder would find them and know Crockett was involved." Tom weakly waved a hand through the air, dismissing my planned murder as inconsequential to his story. "I shot him again, anyway. There was no way we could let him live at that point. We had planned to frame you for Bernie's murder but when he told me about the email to you . . . well, we couldn't take the chance that you would get them. So Crockett sent his guys after you, but they screwed up. They were supposed to drug you, follow you to your room and strangle you. Poor little Laramie picked the wrong stranger to celebrate her birthday with. That is what everyone would have said. But when you left the hotel the weres got . . . overzealous and then they weren't even smart enough to stay and make sure you were dead. Crockett has been going crazy trying to get you finished off."

"I'll just bet he has," LaRue muttered.

"Bernie had told me he kept an account that would send out emails if he didn't put in a stop code. For someone who had hacked email accounts for blackmail purposes, he was surprisingly lax. That was Bernie, though. He always assumed he was smarter than everyone else. The email account was on his phone and the account's password and the stop code were saved in his notes app. The flash drive was encrypted, but with access to the email account I was able to print everything out. It's all in the wall safe in my office."

"Tell me about Jad."

"Jad? You should be asking why me?"

"What? Why? You just told me that it was so I wouldn't get the emails!" I was dumbfounded.

"This goes way back to before the emails. They thought when they turned Jad they would be able to control him. They can't. He isn't like anyone or anything that they've ever dealt with. They were trying to use you, or the threat of harm to you, to keep him in line. A car wreck here and a riding accident there, just to remind him that you are human and can die. Fairly easily."

I gasped as I remembered my totaled truck and the spill after Deadwood spooked. LaRue had started sobbing softly, but I knew it wasn't over me.

"They overestimated Jad's affection for me. He couldn't care less," I said.

"Did they? Then why did he turn you after the werewolves tore you apart?"

I felt faint. I had tried not to think about Jad having done this to me, what it meant. But whatever his reasons, I didn't think it had been out of love.

"The other question you should be asking is 'what.' What were the emails about?" Even dying, Tom had to be in control.

"What?" I didn't want to play his game, but he was running out of time. We both were.

"The True Cross . . . take care of Dixie. Remember, she is the most important thing in the world to me . . . safe." Tom expelled a last slow, rasping breath.

37

WHY IS EVERYTHING ABOUT BLOOD?

**10 Hours
(2:00 p.m. Monday)**

"But what about Jad?" I whispered softly. I couldn't believe the gall of Tom, asking me to keep that little rat-dog Dixie safe after all the trouble he had caused me.

"Everyone down! Drop it!"

I have to say that none of our reflexes were that great. Nobody got down and LaRue definitely didn't drop The Cannon. In fact, she swung it around and pointed it at the open door that led from the basement into the cave. I held my breath and screwed my eyes shut, waiting for gunfire. I imagined a SWAT team getting ready to swarm into the cave.

But there was no gunfire and I heard Owen release the breath he had been holding. Thank God I wasn't the only ninny. I opened my right eye, slowly. The sight of LaRue and Van in a tight embrace made me want to close it again.

Van's eyes met mine over LaRue's head and he released her. He took several steps toward me but stopped when his gaze landed on Tom's body. He let out a shaky breath and, still staring at the dead guy on the floor of my cave, gave the order.

"Make the call."

"Are you sure? If things don't go well in other, uh, areas, this could be part of a cover story," LaRue said.

Van balled his hands into fists, closed his eyes and tilted his head back. His exasperated sigh practically echoed through the cave.

"Fine, fine, I'm making the call." LaRue set The Cannon back down on the shelf by the door and pulled her cell phone from a pocket of her leather pants. As tight as they were, I don't know how she managed to get a quarter in there, much less a phone.

"Is it just you?" I asked incredulously. "Where's the damn cavalry?"

"Man, are we glad to see you!" Owen broke in before Van could answer.

Despite my rude question, I seconded his sentiment. Then I saw that Owen's comment hadn't been directed at Van at all, but at Grace. She'd slipped in behind Van and was now leaning nonchalantly against a wall. Yella stood on her right side and the largest dog I have ever seen stood on her left. Not Worthless. The dogs were alert, surveying the room for threats.

I thought LaRue was going to jump out of her skin when she saw Grace. She couldn't get The Cannon back into her hands fast enough. "What's she doing here?" she demanded.

"And wouldn't I be the cavalry, love. Me and the beasts. Yella is one of you, and this is Finn. He's an Irish wolfhound and therefore owned only by himself, but he claims me as his. Don't be of a mind to make any sudden moves until he gets the measure of you."

The humongous, shaggy brown dog's focus was on LaRue's gun. Unlike Finn, Grace was unconcerned about the gun and motioned a release command. Both dogs rushed forward to greet Bo.

"She's helping," Van ground out between gritted teeth.

A slight smile danced across Grace's face at this, but she didn't add anything to his statement.

"Well, I'm ecstatic you're here. We need all the help we can get," Owen gushed at Grace. He was dazzled. Men are easily impressed. I refused to admit how impressed I was with Grace my own self.

Grace gave Owen a genuine smile. Had they bonded last night while I was in a vampire-blood-induced coma? I felt a twinge of jealousy, but I wasn't sure if it was because Owen wanted to be friends with Grace or because she had warmed up to him rather than to me. Well, when you thought about it, I had come on to her boss, or possible boyfriend, in her place of business. I had deserted her twice during werewolf fights, although in fairness, the second time she had told me to. I had broken into her office (I really hoped she hadn't found out about that) and I had taken part in stealing her boss's, or boyfriend's, blood. It was probably too much to hope that we would be braiding each other's hair anytime soon.

In addition to that, my traitorous diva dog, after happily greeting Yella and Finn with the required butt sniffing, made a beeline for Grace with her tail wagging hard enough to whip okra. Bo was sniffing her hands, legs, and feet for all she was worth.

"After I got Marek sorted at the Dragonfly so he could recover from the effects of your wee voodoo party last night, Van and I joined forces." At LaRue's indrawn breath, Grace swung her head in her direction, but continued, "Temporarily, anyway. Marek and I have been working it from our end, but we have had little luck. And," with a sweeping glance at our group, ending at Tom's body on the floor, "we may have underestimated the whole of you."

Owen practically said "aw shucks," and glowed with

happiness. LaRue visibly preened and dropped the barrel of The Cannon a few inches. Even I, reluctantly, felt a little stab of pleasure at her acknowledgment of our efforts.

"Me? You underestimated me? I would think my record speaks for itself." Van was the only one of our group who took offense to the backhanded compliment.

Grace just smiled her enigmatic smile. Then, when she realized that wasn't enough to charm him, "Aw love, you are a professional, but we never know what goodie-goodie roadblocks you will toss up. I will admit, this incident shows me that you are willing to get your hands dirty when it comes to the people you claim as yours." She glanced from Van to me and then back to him. "A trait I admire and support with all my heart."

So Grace wasn't all-knowing. Van had been willing to bend the rules to protect civilization from another vampire being inflicted on it and to honor a vow to a dead friend, not because he cared for me.

"They will be here in twenty minutes—thirty minutes tops." LaRue pushed the phone back into her pocket and, with a slight shrug, let the barrel of the gun point to the floor.

"You rang the cleaners?" Grace asked. Van nodded. "Another point in your favor."

"The cleaners? Are they the same ones The Shark, uh, Healy, called to take care of . . ." I trailed off and pointed upstairs. At Van's nod I squeaked, "But what about the body?"

"Love, they specialize in bodies. Most times they won't do a job without a body. They just handled your wee cleanup as a favor to, uh, The Shark," Grace said with a slight laugh.

"But, but, we have to call the police. And believe me, they are going to take longer than twenty or thirty minutes to process the crime scene and release it."

"Laramie," Van said slowly, "we can't call the police. They did a rush ballistics test on Jad's gun. It was the gun used to kill Bernie. They are getting a warrant for your arrest as we speak. What conclusion will they jump to when they see Tom's body in a cave full of weapons and chains below your house? Do you think they will believe your story? Any of our stories?"

"But you are the police," I responded lamely. "I know! We can move the body upstairs."

Grace and LaRue snorted in unison. I looked at Owen.

"Laramie, you told the complete truth about Bernie and look where it got you. Besides, they have ways of knowing that a body has been moved." Van nodded but remained silent. "This time you would have to lie, and sweetie, you can't lie for shit."

"But he admitted to all of it. He even admitted to pushing Hattie down the stairs. They will be able to see what kind of killer he was once I tell them that."

"It would only be your word that he admitted those things to you," Van said.

"But it wouldn't be, and I didn't kill him. LaRue shot him. She and Owen heard everything I did. And Jad; the police need to know about Jad."

"What about Jad?" Van cut in sharply.

I had forgotten that he didn't know what Tom had said. I considered how to go on, but LaRue took over.

"There is a secret passage between Tom's house and this cave. He overheard you and Jad talking about surveillance on Crockett. Tom went to Crockett and traded the information for a future favor. And Jad was turned into a vampire a week later, which we also can't tell the police." The last part LaRue said with a superior look at me.

"Son of a bitch!"

There was more cursing and not a little kicking of furniture from Van as we filled him in on the rest of what Tom had told us. Grace moved away from the wall as we progressed. Even the dogs quit sniffing each other and lay quietly watching us, almost as if they understood the gravity of what was being said.

When we finally got to the part about the True Cross, Grace gasped. I figured it was pretty hard to shock a centuries-old vampire, but apparently we had.

"There is no way Crockett has it," Grace said, looking intently at Van. "No way."

"Does it actually exist?" Van stared back at her. At her tight nod, he whispered, "Is it as powerful as the legends claim?"

"More."

WHO WILL I BE?

**9 Hours
(3:00 p.m. Monday)**

U tter silence reigned for several moments while Grace and Van stared at each other.

"We have to find the True Cross," LaRue said finally.

"LaRue, we don't even know where to start. We have to find Jad. His blood is our only hope of stopping Laramie from changing," Van responded.

"Van, I don't know if his blood will work after the ritual last night. I think we have to focus on the cross," LaRue countered.

"As much as it pains me to agree with the witch, I think that galleon has sailed," Grace said. "Laramie's die has been cast. We need to focus on helping the rest of mankind."

"Will someone fill me in on this True Cross thing?" Owen asked. Then he held up a hand. "But can I make a suggestion? I am bloody, tired, and hungry. Plus, I am completely over looking at, um, the body. Can we please continue this conversation upstairs in the kitchen while I clean up, and preferably over a glass of wine?" He shot me a look that let me know he didn't think much of my hostessing skills.

"Yes," I replied sarcastically. "Let's go upstairs and drink my stock. It isn't looking like I will need it for the business anytime soon."

My tone got everyone's attention. I figured since I had the floor, I should get it all out at once.

"Guys, I can't do this. I can't hide a body. I can't lie and pretend that because Tom was a murderer, his life meant nothing. That isn't who I am. I might hide from the hard stuff in life, but I follow the rules. I believe in doing what is right. I don't even recognize myself right now. I went along with taking Marek's blood, even though I knew with every fiber of my being it was wrong. What have I become? What will I become if I go along with these lies?"

"Laramie," Van said soothingly, "I know you are upset, but we are your friends and we have your best interests at heart." He took a step in my direction.

"No!" I said, raising my hand and taking a step backward. "No one in this room is my friend. Van, you have repeatedly lied to me and kept me in the dark about both my husband's life and his death. Grace, you did nothing but sit back and watch while Tom plotted to take my house. Neither you nor Marek felt like telling us that he wasn't the one who venomed me, even though you knew that was what we thought had happened." I raised my hand higher as Owen opened his mouth to speak. "No, Owen, even you kept me in the dark. You could have told me about your sister so I would have had some idea what I was up against with Bernie, but you didn't say a thing. And LaRue, you've done nothing but point that gun at me and hope to pull the trigger since the moment we met." I took a breath.

"Now I'm going to become a vampire and probably go to jail for Bernie's murder, because his actual murderer has been killed. Killed by my so-called friends."

Van looked stricken.

"What a load of shite," Grace said. "Who hid from us for months as we called and sent letters trying to meet with you. If you hadn't been so busy hiding, maybe we could have protected you from all of this."

"You refused to move to Dallas even though you knew that was where Jad was making a life and you're surprised that he didn't see you as enough of a partner to share that entire life with?" LaRue asked. "Hell, how often has Van tried to see you since Jad's death? You've pushed him away repeatedly. If you had deigned to be friends with him, he would have known that Crockett was lurking around you and could have prevented all of this."

Silence descended in the cave. I knew Grace and LaRue both had points, but I refused to admit it. I looked to Owen for support, but he was furious. When he saw my eyes on him, he added his two cents.

"Laramie, when would I have told you about my sister? Did you even once ask me anything about my life?"

"Owen, I didn't want to be intrusive," I responded. It sounded pretty lame, even to my own ears.

"Oh, like I always was?" I glanced guiltily at the floor, but he didn't let up. "Laramie, that is what friends do. They ask questions, they insert themselves into your life, they refuse to go away when you have had a bad day. I've tried so hard to be your friend. Just like Van has, and it even sounds like Grace and Marek were ready to be too, but you pushed us all away. You don't get to blame us for what's happening to you or for being kept in the dark about our lives, when all you had to do was let us in."

"But I don't understand," I said, my eyes filling with tears. "Why would any of you want to be my friend?"

"Oh, honey, I know your mama and your sister and yes, Jad did a number on you over the years, but the question you should be asking isn't why we would want to be your friends; it's why wouldn't we?"

Owen held my gaze and my vision blurred. A paw touched my leg and I bent down to wrap my arms around Bo.

"Oh, no," Van said quietly. He held his phone in front of him.

"What," LaRue asked.

"The police are on their way with the warrant for your arrest. We have to get out of here."

39

HOW TO CATCH A RAT

**8 Hours
(4:00 p.m. Monday)**

Van decided, and everyone except for me agreed with him, that I should stay in the secret cave. Owen would wait for the police so they wouldn't kick in The Madam's front door, and everyone else, including the dogs, would vacate the premises. The cleaners would be diverted to Tom's house. They could use the tunnel to access The Madam and remove Tom's body.

Van and Grace agreed that I needed somewhere safe to go through The Change. Grace said that she would arrange something and be back for me after nightfall.

Then, one by one, despite my harsh words, they hugged me and left the cave. Except for LaRue. There was no hug from her. She had been the first one out and without even a backward glance.

Van handed me the burner cellphone that he had taken, along with a charger, from one of the cabinets in the cave. He didn't want the police tracking mine. His eyes were particularly shiny, but he looked more resolute than sad. I knew he was still determined to find a way to stop The Change.

I hugged Bo and rubbed her tummy. She didn't want to go with them and in the end, Van was forced to pick her up and carry her wiggling body out of the cave.

A moment later, he returned to stand in front of me. I knew he had something to say, but in the end he only leaned forward and kissed my forehead. Then he left the cave and shut the door behind him. I heard the lock slide home and then movement on the other side, as if they were covering up the door.

And then I was alone. More alone than I had ever felt in my life, with only my thoughts to keep me company.

I'd always hidden from life, relationships, and love. Now that I might have to go into actual hiding and walk away from everything and everyone, I didn't want to. I wanted the life I had here, as messy as it was. I wanted my crazy family, this big old house, a chance at having real friends, the diva Bo, and Van. Most of all I wanted Van, and a chance to find out if he wanted me back.

Hattie had spent her life alone in The Madam. But she had surrounded herself with friends and, according to her, lots of lovers over the years. It devastated me to think that someone so kind, who had loved life so much, had been pushed down her own stairs by the likes of Tom. I looked over to where his body lay and shivered when I remembered his rasping last breaths.

Then I thought of his dying words about the information in his safe.

Everyone had been working so hard to save me. It was time I got back to work saving myself.

———

I moved as fast as I dared through the dank, dark tunnel for fifty yards or so, until it opened into a small cellar under Tom's house. That I survived the rickety stairs that led from the basement into the house's pantry was no small feat.

In Tom's study, the safe was easy to locate. I just picked the most pretentious painting in the room and checked the wall behind it. My only real trouble up until that point had been from Dixie the rat-dog. She had cowered in the living room when I entered the house, yapping incessantly and emitting the random low growl. Each time I turned my back on her, she darted forward and nipped at my ankles, only to retreat behind the nearest piece of furniture when I turned on her.

As annoying as Dixie was, she was the least of my problems. The safe was locked and I had no idea what the combination was. I was searching Tom's desk when The Cleaners arrived. They were dressed as actual cleaners and their van had a cleaning business emblem on its side.

I showed them into the tunnel and resumed my search of Tom's study, only to be interrupted approximately twenty minutes later by a rug salesman. His van was parked behind The Cleaners' vehicle and two workmen stood behind him with three large, rolled rugs.

"We are here to meet The Cleaners," said the salesman.

I motioned him and his workers inside and waved them down to the tunnel. They left two of the rugs in the hallway and took the other one down into the tunnel with them. Dixie yapped and growled the whole time, even managing to draw blood from one of the workmen's ankles.

I had almost completed a search of Tom's bedroom, when the salesman and his workers left the house with all three rugs. About ten minutes later The Cleaners came up from the cellar and walked out the front door toward their van. One of them paused before leaving the house.

"You want me to get rid of her?" he asked, motioning his

head to where Dixie's growls emanated from behind the hall tree.

Lord, but I was tempted to say yes. Then I remembered Tom's dying words: "Take care of Dixie, promise me." He'd died before I promised, and it wasn't like I owed him anything, but I still couldn't bring myself to let The Cleaners take her. It was in everyone's best interest for Tom's body to disappear, but I didn't think I could live with Dixie's blood on my hands, even if she was a vicious little thing. I shook my head.

"Suit yourself," The Cleaner said, then walked down the sidewalk to his van.

I peeped out a window that faced The Madam. The police were still there.

I turned to the growling hall tree. "I don't know what we'll do with you, but we will work something out. Although I doubt we will ever find anyone who loves you as much as Tom did. His last thought was about keeping you safe."

Dixie growled her response, but it was drowned out by my gasp. Tom's last words hadn't been to keep Dixie safe. They'd been that she was the most important thing, and to remember the safe. I ran back into the study and considered the safe's keypad. It required a numerical combination. I had already tried his birthday with no luck.

I sat at his desk and dug around in a drawer for a scratchpad and a pencil. Then I wrote out DIXIE and figured out the number each letter represented.

4-9-24-9-5

I quickly punched it into the safe's keypad. *Dang it!* I punched it in again more slowly in case I had messed up. Still nothing. I had another idea. I pulled out the burner phone and brought up the keypad. I wrote down numbers that corresponded with the letters on the keypad for Dixie.

34943

That didn't work either. I was stumped. I didn't know where to go from here, but I was sure the combination had something to do with Dixie. I opened the Internet browser on my phone and Googled the safe's brand and model number. According to the manufacturer, the code for that model should have eight numbers.

"Dixie is the most important thing to me." I took a deep breath, walked back over to the safe, and punched in 49249501. I heard the locking mechanism shift. I tried its handle and it turned. The door swung open without resistance.

Inside the safe sat a stack of white papers about an inch tall.

"Eureka!"

A growl floated up to me from behind an overstuffed chair across from the desk.

"Dixie, if I wasn't sure you would bite off my nose, I would kiss you."

I took the stack of paper out of the safe, sat at Tom's desk, and began to read.

———

When I looked up again the room was dark and tears streaked my face. I knew all of it now, except the why. Only Jad knew that, and he wasn't here to tell me why he had chosen to go down that road. But I thought I knew how to reach him.

I slowly withdrew my phone from my jacket pocket. I was shocked at the time. Four and a half hours had passed since I left The Madam. Van had entered the phone numbers for the group into the phone while it charged. I checked for texts. There was only one, and it was from Owen.

'The po po have gone—stay there til 9.'

'Found out some stuff—get the gang together,' I sent in response.

Next I logged into my email account using the phone's

Internet browser. I opened a blank email form and then slowly typed in the email address that had recurred repeatedly in the stack of papers.

In the message body, I typed in one word: 'Why?'

I hit send. Then I settled back to wait.

40

WINE FIXES EVERYTHING

**3 Hours
(9:00 p.m. Monday)**

"We don't have time to sit around drinking wine. Our number one priority is keeping Laramie from changing into a vampire."

All eyes at the table focused on me. I lowered my gaze to the glass of Texas cabernet I held in my hand. I still didn't like being the center of attention. I guess having a little vampire blood running through your veins doesn't change everything.

When I had walked into the kitchen of The Madam, clutching the stack of papers, Owen had been in the process of pulling a lasagna out of the oven. The gang had been waiting in the saloon and, despite some grumbling, Owen convinced us that the humans needed to eat and that everyone would benefit from a glass or three of wine. Grace had pushed together a couple of tables in the bar and set them with dishes and silverware. She seemed to be quite domesticated for a centuries-old vampire who didn't even eat real food.

"Jad asked for it. All of it," I said in a rush, afraid I would lose my nerve.

"What?"

"Why?"

"No!" Van, Owen, and LaRue exclaimed respectively. Marek and Grace remained quiet, but a look passed between them. They had known! Or at least they had suspected.

"These are emails." I placed my hand on the stack of papers I had brought to the table with me. "They are mostly between Crockett and several others, I'm not sure who, discussing Jad."

"I don't believe it!" LaRue stood up. "They're lying."

"Some of the emails are from Jad to them," I continued as though she hadn't interrupted. "They start from before his death and go up through a couple of weeks ago. That was probably when Bernie confronted Crockett and he quit using the email address that had been hacked."

LaRue collapsed back onto her chair.

"What do they say?" Van asked faintly. His jaw clenched as he waited for my answer.

I paused, unsure how to condense it all. "It looks like Jad approached them. He said that he had what they wanted and would give it to them if they changed him. The tractor accident was a cover for The Change, but somehow, they lost him after he was venomed. Afterward, there was a flurry of emails between Crockett and the others talking about their efforts to track Jad down. Not long after I crashed my truck, Jad contacted them again and said that if they left me alone, he would give them what he had promised. There has been a lot of back and forth, a lot of threats, but no resolution."

"But what about Tom tipping Crockett off? Once they knew Jad was investigating Crockett, they must have somehow coerced him into agreeing to The Change. He wouldn't have asked for The Change, but he would've agreed to it if they threatened one of us. You have this backwards," LaRue railed at me.

I tried to remain calm. "The best that I can tell, Jad had

already made a deal for The Change and a plan was in place for it when Tom went to Crockett about the investigation. Crockett contacted the person who was calling the shots, but he or she said the plan was already too far along to stop it. Tom didn't cause Jad's death, or whatever you would call it. Crockett just allowed Tom to think that rather than tip him off about the larger operation."

I looked around the table, trying to gauge how much everyone already knew. Owen was enthralled, Van and LaRue looked shell-shocked, and Marek and Grace looked guarded.

"He promised them the True Cross?" Van asked.

I nodded.

"Will someone please tell me what the True Cross is?" Owen asked for the second time that day.

"The True Cross refers to the cross that Jesus was crucified on," Van said. "Pieces of it are supposedly in churches throughout the world, although if it ever existed, it has been lost for centuries. Legend also claims that it has healing powers. It is of particular interest to the vampire community as it is rumored that if a vampire is in contact with it for long enough, it will turn him back into his human form."

"When supernaturals talk about the True Cross, we use the term to refer to one small cross made up of pieces of the crucifixion cross. The wood that Jesus's blood had soaked into—where his hands and feet were nailed and where his head rested, bleeding from the crown of thorns—was cut away from the rest of the cross. Those pieces were fashioned into a smaller cross and silver was molded to one side of it, possibly to hold it together or to make it more potent. The True Cross has only been missing for decades, not for centuries."

I tried to picture a wooden cross, stained with the blood of Christ, pocked with nail holes and embedded into a silver base. The look on Owen's face told me that he was having as hard a time as I was.

"Decades?" Van asked. "So we're back to World War Two?"

"Yes," Marek said. "Over the centuries since Christ's death, many factions have fought over the True Cross. There has been untold bloodshed in the quest to possess this miracle that is only supposed to bring healing to the world. Because of that, we worked hard to keep it out of the wrong hands. Regretfully, it was turned over to the Vatican for safekeeping and they had possession of it when the war began. The Pope traded it to Hitler in return for his promise not to loot Vatican City during the occupation of Rome."

"What did Hitler do with it?" LaRue asked.

"We will circle back to that. Do Laramie and Owen know about the supernaturals and what happened during World War II?" Grace asked.

I nodded. Owen said, "LaRue explained a little bit to me last night while we were waiting for Laramie to wake up."

Grace turned to me and asked, "Have they told you how you might be after you are turned? That you will be Good, Evil, or Dualistic?"

I nodded again.

"Crockett is a Dualistic," Grace said, as if it explained everything.

"Really?" Van asked in disbelief. "But he was captured with the Goods and tortured. I thought the Dualistics fought with the Evils."

"Dualistics are neither all good nor all evil," Grace said to me. "Reason rules their decisions. Sadly, reason, at the base of it, is whatever best suits the Dualistic in question. They will always choose the best path for themselves over what is best or worse for others. Because of that, Dualistics can never be completely trusted. Crockett can never be completely trusted."

"We moved our business headquarters to Dallas so we could keep an eye on him," Marek said. Then, with a look at Van, "We police our own."

"During the war," Grace said, picking the history lesson back up, "the Good vampires, and the werewolves who were aligned with us, along with many of the Van Helsings, were mostly killed. But a few of us, including Crockett, were captured and the Nazis conducted tests and experiments on us. They would draw our blood, mix it with different substances, and then put it back into us. Sometimes they injected it and sometimes they mixed our blood into our food sources."

"Food sources?" I asked weakly.

"Concentration camp prisoners . . ." At my horrified look, Grace became belligerent, "And I wouldn't be proud of what I had to do to survive. Most times I resisted, but they force fed me blood. The will to live increases and the ability to withstand the temptation of human blood decreases the hungrier you get."

She stared at me and I dropped my gaze. While I hoped I would never feed on a human, much less an innocent prisoner, I hadn't been in her situation and had no idea what I would or wouldn't be able to do.

"Before the war, all vampires reacted basically the same way to the same things. After the experiments, those of us who didn't die were changed. We were stronger, faster, and could withstand sunlight. We also found that we no longer needed permission to enter people's homes. Hitler was not only consumed with making a super race of Germans. He also wanted to create a super race of vampires. While most of the changes made us stronger, the one thing he did to make us weaker was take away our ability to change humans into vampires. He knew that the few of us left, only a handful by the end, would be hard enough to control. He didn't want us to create others who could rise up against him."

"I only know of Marek, Crockett, and you. How many others are there?" Van asked.

"That is on a need-to-know basis," Grace said pertly.

"We need to talk about what I learned at Tom's," I said impatiently. "This is all very interesting, but where is it going?"

"The substance they used to make us stronger." Grace sighed and leaned back in her chair.

"The True Cross," Marek said. He was still pale and drawn from last night's ritual, but he sat upright in his chair with perfect posture.

"My grandparents were captured, and experiments were done on them," Van said. "Why haven't they said anything about the True Cross?"

"Marek and I, ah, liberated the scientists' journals. We didn't want the information to fall into the wrong hands," Grace said.

"If they used it in experiments on you, it should have made you weaker, not stronger," Van mused skeptically.

"The blood," said LaRue slowly. "If they mixed shavings from the True Cross directly with your blood it could react differently than just holding the wood against your skin. The blood holds the particles in suspension. The combination makes you more human, so you can withstand sunlight, but without making you weaker. Blood is always the basis for everything."

Marek nodded at her and a look of reluctant admiration crossed his face. "Yes, it always comes back to blood. Plus, they added other things to the experiments and conducted voodoo, witchcraft, and even satanic rituals when they mixed the concoctions and put them back into us. We have no idea what worked, what didn't, or how; we just know that the True Cross, and blood, were the base ingredients of all the experiments. And . . ." Marek looked toward Grace. "We have underestimated at least one among their number."

"I told them earlier that we have underestimated all of them. If we had brought them in immediately after the attack, we might have already stopped The Change in Laramie."

"Should've, could've, would've," replied Marek with a

sardonic smile at Grace. "In life, as in business, it doesn't help to kick yourself over past mistakes. Instead, find a way to fix them and move forward."

"And wouldn't that be himself's way of saying 'You have the right of it, Grace,' but you'll never hear those words come out of his mouth," Grace pronounced huffily, but she cast Marek a small smile and then, seemingly unable to help herself, reached over and squeezed his hand.

Marek returned the squeeze and it was obvious that true affection existed between them. More than that? Who could say? They were two of the most beautiful people I have ever seen, not to mention two of only a handful of vampires who remained, so it only made sense that they would be together.

Van looked as if a storm was brewing inside him.

I looked around the table and took in the expressions of the others. Owen watched Marek and Grace with the same intensity I had, and not a little jealousy. I wasn't sure if it was for Grace or Marek or simply the bond they shared. I had never asked Owen about his dating preferences or relationship status. Just another failure of mine in the friend department that I hoped I would have the chance to rectify after this whole vampire mess blew over.

LaRue's eyes were locked on their clasped hands and she looked more than a little green. Her bias against vampires went much deeper than just dislike. She was going to have to get over that if she wanted to continue being a member of this group, whatever mad voodoo skills she possessed be damned. You can't trust someone with hate in their heart. It occurred to me then that LaRue would make the perfect new owner for Dixie. They had matching personalities and maybe they could teach each other a little about love and acceptance.

"But we are bringing them in now. It is all or nothing. We don't have a choice." Marek said the last part almost to himself, but Grace nodded.

"Tell them everything."

41

TEMPLE SENDS HIS REGARDS

2.5 Hours
(9:30 p.m. Monday)

"What do you know about Adam Temple?" Marek directed the question at Van and LaRue.

"I've heard the name and his story, but The Organization has never been able to verify his existence. To be honest, until today I've always thought he was something of an urban myth," Van responded. He cast a questioning look at LaRue for confirmation and she nodded in agreement.

"Temple was an American who joined the US Army at the start of the war," Grace said. His mother was German and he spoke the language fluently. Add in the blond hair and blue eyes he had inherited, ironically, from his American father, and the army saw his potential. They trained him first for Special Forces and then sent him through spy training."

"The Axis vampires had been watching for a good candidate who was a trusted asset on the US side, thus being in the perfect situation to be a double agent," Marek said, taking back over the story. "They turned Temple, and he agreed to work with them. When the Evil vampires went to Germany to fight the Allies in Europe, Temple was allowed to stay behind in the US. The US Army, not knowing he had changed sides, planned to drop him behind enemy lines. The Evil vampires didn't want him to blow his cover, and they figured he would join them once he landed. But before the drop could happen, the majority of the Evil vampires were trapped by the Allies and killed."

"That was fortuitous," Owen said, unable to stay quiet any longer.

"For us and your man," Grace agreed. "With most of the Evil vampires done in, Temple saw his chance. He deserted the military and, as far as we can tell, moved around the world. He took over the identities and fortunes, one after another, of the dead Axis vampires. In a small amount of time he'd amassed a large amount of wealth."

"So, once he realized he was one of the last bad guys, he left the game and focused on his own fortune?" I asked.

"Fortune and power," corrected Marek. "Because he knew he would be the focus of the Van Helsings and the Good vampires, he kept a low profile and amassed wealth without drawing too much attention to himself. He set himself up as a warlord in a small third world country in South America, where death was cheap and no one asked a lot of questions when people went missing."

"You think Temple was the vampire Crockett was working with to get the True Cross from Jad?" Van had gotten impatient again.

"Temple is the last remaining vampire, as far as we know, who has the ability to make other vampires. We believe he has killed the handful of Evils and Dualistics who survived the war. Crockett told Grace that Temple turned Jad, but as we've already established, Crockett can't be trusted. Still, we've always assumed it had to have been Temple. The message the weres gave Laramie during the attack confirmed it, and gave the reason."

"But why would Temple think I had the True Cross?"

"He doesn't." Grace looked thoughtful as she continued, "Temple is trying to bring Jad back in line and use you to get the True Cross from him. Crockett told us Temple turned Jad as a message to the Van Helsings. He didn't want us knowing that it had any connection to the True Cross because we would do everything in our power to keep him from obtaining it."

"I've been following every lead over the last," Marek looked at his watch, "seventy hours. I've had people tracking down any other vampires who could have turned Jad."

"And?" LaRue turned to face Marek.

"We can't find any. It had to have been Temple and I am convinced Jad offered him the True Cross, as the emails indicated, to change him. Temple hasn't made a lot of vampires over the years. He knows better than anyone that a vampire's biggest threat is another vampire. He has made several mates, but they have had short life spans."

I wanted to move the conversation back to Jad, but I couldn't help asking, "Why would his vampire mates have short life spans? What killed them?"

"The question wouldn't be what killed them, but the who of it," Grace explained. "Evils are incapable of love. Obsessed with someone or something, sure, but they cannot love. Temple's mates are but playthings to him."

Despite what I had heard so far, I felt a little sorry for this Temple vamp. Eternity sounded lonely without the ability to love. An eternity I could be facing if we couldn't stop The Change and I turned out to be Evil.

"Question?" Owen asked. "So, Temple has been hanging out down there in South America, doing his master and commander of his domain thing. He's killed off the other vampires, but other than that it sounds like he keeps to himself. I get the power aspect, but he has his own little kingdom. Why would the True Cross be so important to him?"

"He has lived that way from necessity," Grace said. "Drawing attention to himself meant risking the Van Helsings' ire and being hunted. The easiest way to kill a vampire is to separate him from his hiding place and let the light do your will. Wouldn't the sun be a vampire's greatest weakness? As for his desire for the True Cross, imagine living without feeling the warmth of the sun. Having to hide from it day after day. Living only in darkness," Grace said. "We did that, for centuries. That is Temple's life.

"Many of the Nazis fled to Argentina after the Third Reich fell. We fear that Temple may have the scientist who experimented on us in his possession. If so, and if he obtains the True Cross, he will gain immunity to sunlight. That will allow him to move freely throughout the world. And he could barter the cross's power to supernaturals and humans alike. He would be unstoppable."

"So Jad really is the key to all of this," I said slowly. "We have to find him to stop The Change, either with his blood or the True Cross. And then we have to keep it from falling into Temple's hands. Plus Jad is the only one who can tell us why he wanted to become a vampire."

"Do we really care?" Owen asked in a hard voice.

I stared at him, hurt to my core that he didn't care if I turned into a vampire. He added hastily, "Laramie, we all care whether or not you turn. I meant do we care why Jad wanted to be a vampire? He was turned and now he's trying to turn you, not to mention bringing all kinds of grief to your door. I say the hell with his problems. Let's find him and do what we need to do to stop your change."

I smiled at him weakly. I couldn't explain why, even to myself, but I needed to know why Jad had chosen the route he had and why he was forcing it on me.

I felt my phone vibrate in my pocket and hid it under the table while I checked my messages.

"Jad is the key," Marek confirmed. "I flew to South America yesterday to confront Temple only to discover he had just left to fly here. He has rented a large house in Dallas. I had planned to call upon him last night after I got Laramie to safety."

"You're just telling us this now!"

Van's chair overturned as he stood up. I thought he was going to climb across the table and strangle Marek. Grace leapt to her feet, putting herself bodily between the two. Not to be outdone, LaRue stood and moved around the end of the table to align herself with Van. Marek remained seated, appearing unconcerned.

I was too stunned to move. Not because of the bomb Marek had just dropped about Temple, but because of the email I had just received:

'Meet me at the dam as soon as you can get here. I'll explain everything. Come alone. Love you more than sweet tea. Just in case you were wondering if this is really me.'

42

A CLUE

**2 Hours
(10:00 p.m. Monday)**

Despite everything I had heard—and heck, even with my own memory of Jad leaning over me—deep down I hadn't really believed he was still alive. It wasn't a relief to discover he was—it was more heartrending than his death. Now I had to reconcile myself to the fact that the man I thought I knew had never existed. During the last two years I had come to accept that he had fallen out of love with me. Maybe he had never loved me the way a husband should love a wife, but I hadn't believed that he would purposely hurt me.

"Laramie!" Van said. From the tone of his voice, he had said it several times before I heard him. "Are you okay? We have to decide whether to put our resources into going after Temple or tracking Jad. I choose Jad, since he claims to have the True Cross. Stopping The Change is a long shot. We have to get the cross."

Each person at the table stared at me, waiting for my input. Five people who were ready to put their lives, mortal and immortal, on the line for me. I took a breath and tried to find the strength to tell them about the email. I opened my mouth to speak and then paused.

Should I tell them, or should I take my chances with Jad by myself? I didn't know why he had saved me from death by were, but I didn't think it was to kill me the next time we met. Besides, I had things to say to him. Things that I didn't want an audience for. Throughout our entire relationship I had smiled and nodded and went along. That Laramie was gone now, and Jad was about to figure it out.

From what Marek had told us about Temple, Jad was playing with a rough crowd. He might not care who got hurt, but I did. I had sleepwalked through the last two years—heck, maybe even my whole life. But when I looked at the faces around the table, I saw people who loved and supported me. Not Jad's wife, but me. I would be endangering them if I let them go to the meeting.

A warm, wet tongue slurped across my arm. I rubbed Bo's head and when I met her large, soulful eyes I was transported back to another time and place. A remote pasture where I had been completely alone with only Bo to kiss the tears from my face as I wept next to an overturned tractor. I had to go back to that place, but I never had to be that girl, all alone, again.

I sighed a long, heavy sigh.

It made sense to me now why I had resisted friendships for so long. Having friends is hard, y'all.

"You were right," I said, laying my phone on the table in front of me.

"Thank you," said Van. "Now we just need to start looking at places where we think Jad could be hiding. I—"

"No, Van," I interrupted. "I didn't mean about who we should go after, although I do agree we go after Jad. I meant you were right this afternoon. You were all right. You've all tried to help me during the last two years. I've refused that help because I didn't trust that any of you had my best interests at heart. I was too scared of the pain it would cause me if I let someone in and they betrayed me.

"Despite having how wrong I've been pointed out so force-fully this afternoon, I almost made the same choice again, just now, but for a different reason. I wanted to protect you all from harm. But real friendship is trusting people enough to let them into your life and letting them choose their path for themselves, no matter the danger."

I reached across the table and squeezed Van's hand in much the same way Grace had squeezed Marek's earlier. I looked into his eyes and let my bomb drop.

"I know where Jad is."

THE PLAN

**1.5 Hours
(10:30 p.m. Monday)**

I hated to admit it, but Marek had a pretty good plan. I guess being several centuries old helps one hone one's planning skills but, even so, I was impressed. If I had gone in alone, I would have made a hash of it.

Van had been impressed too, although he'd tried to hide it. He'd also fought my part in the plan, but he eventually had to cave. Poor Van. After tonight, his cool, controlled exterior might be gone forever. His hair stood on end from repeatedly pushing his fingers through it and he had the look of someone who was only one step away from totally losing his shit.

"I still don't like this," Van said to me as though he had read my thoughts. "I wish we could figure out some way to get there before him and set up."

Van and I were in the cave, and he was systematically filling a black duffle bag with every type of weapon imaginable. The others had stayed upstairs. Owen and Grace were scouring the emails from Tom's safe to see if I had missed anything that would be helpful.

LaRue and Marek, well, I didn't want to give that too much thought. I kept learning bits and pieces about being a vampire. The latest bit I learned was that Marek and Grace didn't require blood to survive, but drinking it helped them heal faster. Like almost immediately. Marek had completely recovered from the ceremony but he needed a boost before we met Jad. Each time I remembered LaRue's face when she followed Marek into that room, my level of dislike for her dropped a notch. She must have felt as horrible about taking Marek's blood as I had. It was the only reason I could think of that she would have agreed to be a blood donor.

"I know, but you agreed with Marek that with Jad's vampire senses he would know if anyone else was in the area." I didn't point out that it had been Van himself who had said that there was no way to get within fifty yards of the dam without being seen or scented. That would have been rubbing salt in the wound.

"I just wish we knew what he wanted with you. Why he did this to you." Van stopped loading weapons into the bag. His handsome face contorted with anguish and it was more than I could stand. I took his hands and stepped closer to him.

"I'm going to find out. And once we do, we'll figure out a way to stop this or change me back."

"Here." Van refused to meet my eyes. He pulled his hands from mine and reached into one of the cabinets. "Put this in one of your pockets."

He handed me a small capsule. It reminded me of the old black-and-white spy movies Jad used to watch. The spies were always given cyanide pills to take in case they were captured.

"Poison?" I asked as I drew back in horror. My future might not look bright, but I wasn't ready to end it all rather than become a vampire.

"No," Van said, and a ghost of a smile crossed his face. "Dramatic much? It's a GPS tracker. If this all goes to hell in a handbasket and Jad gets away with you, he won't get far."

That thought sobered me. "Do you think he's Evil?" The idea had been niggling at me all day.

Van put his arms around me and pulled me in close for one of his killer hugs. "After what I've heard today, I realized that I never knew Jad at all. I can't even begin to guess what he is like as a vampire."

When Van pulled back, I didn't know if I could stand on my own. My knees were weak as jelly from that hug. I've mentioned how good Van's hugs are, right? The thought that his sentiments about Jad echoed my own made me feel better, too.

So that was how I found myself, for the second time in two days, bumping down the rutted driveway of the house where Jad and I had lived during our marriage. My chest grew tight at the thought of my stop there yesterday and how Bo had acted. The new plywood covering all the doors and windows had told me that someone had been out to the house recently. Now I knew it was to keep sunlight out, not intruders. It gave me chills to think that Jad had been inside that house while I had obliviously walked around outside. Did vampires really sleep like the dead, as portrayed in the old movies? Or had he been awake and aware I was out there, just unable to get to me while the sun was shining?

If I'd only known that he had been hiding out at the house yesterday, all of this could have been over by now. LaRue could have performed the ceremony with his blood. The Change could have been stopped and we could all be together, figuring out what to do about Temple.

I smiled a little, in spite of myself, at the thought of Van and Jad working together again. I had referred to them as the Dynamic Duo, mostly jokingly, but sometimes sarcastically. I had been jealous of how close they had been.

My smile turned to a frown. Jad had asked to be turned into a vampire. He had brought all this upon himself. On us. I didn't think there was a chance in hell that Van and Jad would ever team up again.

44

SO CREEPY

**.5 Hours
(11:30 p.m. Monday)**

I parked facing the dilapidated house. In the early months of the marriage, driving up to it had made me feel like I was an adult and had given me a warm, accomplished feeling. By the end of it, feelings of failure and dread had swamped me each time I drove along the rutted track.

I had moved out as quickly as I could after Jad's death, even though it had meant moving back in with Mama and Daddy for a time. Anything had been better than staying in the house where my marriage fell apart.

The group had followed me out to my truck when I left The Madam. The humans and vampires had plastered varying levels of encouraging looks on their faces. The dogs were another matter. Finn and Worthless hadn't seemed too worried, but Yella and Bo's creased foreheads had reflected their concern for my ability to handle myself. I tried not to let their opinions shake what little faith I had in myself.

My job was to keep Jad in place long enough for the group to swoop in and snare him. Basically, I was the bait. What would we do with him after we had him? I'm not sure anyone had a definite plan; if they did, they weren't sharing it.

LaRue was going to take all her Voodoo Princess shit with her for the blood ritual. She wasn't sure it would work, but we were going to try if given the chance. We would be cutting it close timewise, but we didn't know if the seventy-two-hour window was even still in play after the ritual we'd performed with Marek's blood. I couldn't help but think that Jad had purposely timed his response to my email for that reason.

I just hoped I would have enough time to get the information I needed out of him before the cavalry came riding in. The Cabernet Cavalry, I corrected myself. Owen had dubbed our group that as we sat drinking my Texas cabernet and plotting this caper.

I texted Owen a smiley face emoji. That was my signal that I had arrived at the house. Because vampires have sensitive hearing and excellent sight, we wanted to stay off the phones as much as possible. I was supposed to be meeting Jad alone. If he saw or heard me on the phone it could scare him away. To anyone watching, using a quick emoji would look like I was just checking the time on my phone.

I would send a second smiley face when I arrived at the dam and a third one when Jad arrived. That third smiley would be their signal to start my way. I know, I know: real cloak and daggers stuff, right? Since I was new to this intrigue business they had picked the easiest possible code, something I couldn't screw up. Van was watching the signal from the GPS tracker. If I sent them two emojis together, they knew to go to my location, wherever it might be.

I sat in the truck and stared at the phone's screen to make sure the message sent. The cell rang, and Van's face flashed across the screen. This was the confirmation signal that my emoji had been received and that they were in position. I would only receive a callback for the first emoji. I reached out and touched his face on the screen, careful not to accidentally hit the 'accept call' option. I had never felt so alone. But I had wanted to do it this way so I would have time by myself with Jad, for closure. I allowed my fingers to rest on Van's face for two rings longer, then sighed and put the phone in silent mode.

I peered out into the dark surrounding my truck. For the most part, I had been paying attention to the area around the house. Really, I had been. Lighting up the car with my phone had looked like rookie move that let anyone watching the truck know I was alone. But if Jad was watching, I wanted him to see that I was by myself; maybe it would save me a walk across the pasture.

Not seeing any movement around the house, I stepped out onto the weed-covered driveway. I pulled the black duffle Van had filled with weapons across the seat and slung it over my shoulder. The metal clanking inside the bag stopped me. Who was I kidding? I didn't know how to use most of the stuff in there. With a sigh, I sat the bag back on the seat and rummaged through its contents.

I lifted out a small, black .380 pistol, sighed, and then shoved it back in with the other weapons. I couldn't shoot Jad, no matter who or what he was. The small crossbow with the silver-tipped bolts was also a no-go. I grabbed a wooden stake that was inserted into a sheath with an ankle strap and tucked it into the top of my black lace-up ankle boots, then secured the strap around my leg just above the boot. It would probably be a little uncomfortable when I walked, but I could manage.

I grabbed several bottles of holy water and stuffed them in my pants pockets. They were a little bulky, but it would have to work. I shoved my hands beneath the bottles of holy water and checked to make sure the tracker was still in my right front pocket. My fingertips brushed it. Thank God. If something went wrong with our plan, I knew Van wouldn't rest until he found me. Knowing that gave me the courage to do this.

I shrugged into my black jacket. I had dressed in black from head to toe in the hope it made me look like a badass. I wished the outfit magically transformed me into an actual badass. LaRue probably could have performed a ritual on it, but I hadn't wanted to ask and she hadn't offered. I slid my cellphone into the jacket's right pocket and then, after a brief pause, pushed another stake into its left.

Finally, I knew it was time to face the music. Or the ex-husband, or husband, or vampire or whatever. Labels are bad, right? I just knew that as of today, I was dropping my married name and going back to Harper.

I had been hopeful that Jad would be waiting for me at the house, but he had never been one to make things easy. The moon and a clear, cloudless night sky worked together to illuminate the pasture. At least Mother Nature was cooperating. Resigned, I forced my body between two rusty strands of the barbed wire fence that separated the overgrown yard from the pasture and struck off toward the dam.

I crossed the pasture, my boots raking through the brown stubble of grass, and entered the dark stand of trees that lined both sides of the creek. The creek was low and I crossed it by hopping from stone to stone, then trudged up the opposite bank.

Before leaving the concealment of the trees, I paused. The pasture where Jad's tractor had overturned stretched out ahead of me. With my improved eyesight I could make out the dark shapes of coyotes slinking across the far end of the pasture. Night vision goggles had nothing on me. My hearing had improved too: their high wails that pierced the night sounded different, less menacing somehow. In the past I would have been terrified to be out here sharing the field with coyotes, but after the last several days they were the least of my worries. Hidden by the trees, I sent the second smiley emoji.

I followed the creek across the pasture to where it opened

into a small pond. One of the Thompsons had dammed the creek years ago to create a watering hole for the livestock. I walked across the dam, the grass and earth springy under my feet. The water rose almost to the lip of the dam on one side, and there was a steep drop off on the other. The gouges the tractor had made in the earth when it rolled were no longer visible.

I pushed back the memories of the overturned tractor, the frantic emergency workers, and Bo kissing the tears from my face. No, I couldn't think of Bo right now, about what the future might hold for us or whether we'd even have one. I had to be in the present.

Jad had picked a good location, I'd give him that. The pond sat in the middle of an open pasture several acres square. Other than a hill at one end, it was all open, level ground. I was completely exposed.

I reached into my pocket and felt again for the GPS tracker that was my lifeline. Then I waited for my dead husband to arrive.

45

IS THAT A STAKE IN YOUR POCKET
OR ARE YOU JUST HAPPY TO SEE ME?

15 Minutes
(11:45 p.m. Monday)

I heard a whispering around me, like a breeze rustling the grass, and the small hairs on my arms stood at attention. The wind blowing the dried pasture grass is a normal sound in October in Texas. But there wasn't any wind. Steel bands wrapped around me and a familiar voice, one I had heard almost daily from the time I was sixteen years old until the time I was nearly twenty-eight, whispered in my ear, "Miss me?"

I would have jumped out of my skin, but Jad's arms restrained me. He pulled me close, his chest hard and unyielding against my back. He had always worked out, obsessively so, I had often thought. But he had never felt like this before.

"Is that a stake in your pocket or are you just happy to see me?" Jad asked on a low laugh as he removed the stake from my jacket. Only then did I register that his hands had been roving my body for weapons as his arms held me in place.

"Let go of me!" I pushed ineffectually at his arms and struggled to break free from his hold. He turned me to face him and buried his head in my neck. As I tried to push him away, my hands became entangled in his jacket.

"Laramie, you used to love it when I held you," he whispered into my ear. "You used to beg me for it."

My face turned hot with humiliation. I had begged for his touch. First when we were young. Then, as he became more and more indifferent toward me, it had been the only way to get his attention. I took a shot in the dark at something that had been niggling at me for the last two days.

"If I had known you had such a thing for voodoo princesses I wouldn't have bothered."

The lips that had been dusting a trail of feather-light kisses down the side of my neck stilled. A moment later, the arms released me and the wall of rock no longer held me up. I turned and was astonished to see him standing ten feet away, casually sliding the stake into his waistband. Like me, he was dressed all in black. Unlike me, he looked like a badass. The dark clothing matched his hair and contrasted with skin that, while not as white as Marek and Grace's, was lighter than I remembered.

"So, you know about that, do you?" Jad asked, unwittingly confirming my suspicions. Before I could respond he tacked on belligerently, "Who told you, her or Van?"

Pain sliced through me, along with hurt and embarrassment that Van had known about the affair. Had the three of them laughed at my gullibility?

Jad had added the line *I love you more than sweet tea* to prove to me that the message really came from him. I felt a little vindicated that neither Van or LaRue had understood its significance. LaRue had pointed out, a little superiorly, that Jad never drank sweet tea. Van had reluctantly agreed. When I had told them that Jad had loved sweet tea until he went off to Austin, where it was harder to find it in restaurants, LaRue had deflated. She had looked even more crestfallen when I told them that it had been our special term of endearment right up until he stopped drinking it. It had been the one message that he could send to me that no one involved in the supernatural world, not even his best friends, would know, because he had quit saying it before they met.

"You just did," I said. "Although compared to everything else you kept from me, a little thing like broken vows barely cracks the top ten."

"Oh Lar, don't be like that. I cared about you. Honest, I did. But LaRue . . ." He let the sentence trail off and, after a beat, smiled his trademark grin. The irresistible one that usually got him out of just about everything. Except that it had quit working on me at least two years before his death.

I didn't rise to the bait. He'd had me come out here for a reason and I didn't think it was to walk down memory lane or rehash past wrongs. He had always liked to tease or joke before he got down to the heart of the matter. I was done with that.

When Jad saw that his charm wasn't working on me, his smile faltered and I saw a tiny hint of sadness, but it was gone so quickly I might have imagined it.

He broke eye contact first and spun in a quick circle then turned back to me, the smile still in place, but not as certain as before.

"So, where are they?" When I didn't answer he continued, "I assume they're hiding in the tree line. I'm not surprised that I haven't been able to pinpoint Marek and Grace. They've been doing this kind of thing for a few centuries and, well, you know, vampires." He gave a short laugh. A laugh that cracked with nervousness.

Good, let him be nervous that the group was about to descend on him. I felt for my phone in my pocket and sent the signal that would bring the Cabernet Cavalry. It would take them awhile to reach us, but I still needed to work fast to get the answers I wanted from Jad.

"I'm surprised about Van, though. He is really, really, good at what he does, but, still, not a vampire. I was sure I would hear him crashing about out there. Did LaRue work a cloaking ritual on him or something?" Jad continued to scan the line of trees that would provide the only real cover for anyone approaching.

"You can relax," I said. "I'm here by myself. They aren't coming." Okay, so that last part was a teensy lie, but I wanted him focused on me, not waiting for the group to show up.

"Ha!" Jad's bark of laughter made me jump. "Do you really expect me to believe that? Laramie Harper Thompson, who wouldn't leave Faith to go to a real university? Who was so scared of her own shadow that she wouldn't even go to a movie by herself at night, for that matter? You really think I would fall for that? Tell them to come on out. I don't want to hurt anyone. We've got business to discuss."

"This is just between you and me," I said, narrowing my eyes in the way that used to signify to him that I wasn't playing around. "I want answers. Like why you always made fun of me for being scared, when all along you knew there were things out there to be scared of?"

Jad didn't answer, but he looked just a little bit scared himself. I was proud that my narrowed-eyes trick still affected him, vampire or not.

"I saw you before the attack; you were at the end of the alley under the streetlight," I said. Jad looked desperate but remained silent, so I asked what I'd come here alone to find out. "Why did you subject me to a life of blood and darkness when you could have stopped the attack?"

Still no response.

"Jad . . ." I pleaded, my voice breaking, "why?"

"Because I can't protect you any longer. Those accidents you had? First your truck and then your horse? That was Temple trying to get to me. I was there that night to protect you, but then I realized that turning you into a vampire was the only way I could give you a fighting chance against them."

"But, why? Why did you want this?"

"I had to, Laramie. I had to be a vampire to be able to rid the world of supernaturals, but I'm not strong enough to go up against Temple alone. I didn't think Van would let you out of his sight. And it's Marek's responsibility to keep Temple from getting the True Cross. Why aren't they here?"

My mind spun uncontrollably, so I latched onto the first thing I could. "Rid the world of supernaturals?"

"Yes, don't you see? With the True Cross, I can turn all the vampires and werewolves back to human. Then you'll be safe, and I can turn you back."

"If I change, the True Cross will definitely turn me back to human?"

"It should . . ."

"But?" I demanded.

"Well, the truth is . . . I don't actually have it."

"If you don't have the True Cross with you, then why would Marek protect you from Temple to keep it from him?"

Jad spun around and faced the trees, his head cocked as if he'd heard a sound. After a moment he turned slowly back to me. I didn't know if vampires could blush, but apparently, they could turn deathly white (pun intended) when they were frightened.

"Were you really stupid enough to come here by yourself?" he asked, barely above a whisper.

He turned back toward the trees without waiting for my answer. "We have to get out of here, now," he said urgently, his voice vibrating with a terror I had never seen him show when he was human. I fumbled the phone out of my pocket. Had I pressed the right buttons before? God, I hoped so.

Jad turned back to me and I shoved my phone back in my pocket without checking it. His expression frightened me even more than his voice had. His terror was only visible to me for a moment, then it was replaced by a sad resolve that settled heavily onto him. His shoulders slumped from the weight of it.

"Temple is here. I told him to meet me and I would give him the True Cross. At the very least, Van was supposed to be here with you to help me defeat him."

"Jad, where is the True Cross? We can take him to it." My heart fluttered at this. I didn't want to give an Evil vampire the powerful relic, but I also didn't want to die over a bargain that was never mine.

"How can you be so dense? I don't have it," Jad said, his voice so low I barely heard him. "I've never had it. I found enough information on it to make Temple believe that I had it, but I refused to give it to him unless he turned me."

"What the hell, Jad!" I screeched. "You've never had it? And now . . . and now, some vampire you've double crossed is going to kill us both?"

That he wouldn't meet my eyes gave me my answer. I hunched and shoved my hands into the pockets of my jeans while I waited for his response. But I didn't get one—in fact, he wasn't even paying attention to me anymore. The age-old story between husbands and wives. He looked off into the distance with his head cocked.

"I can't take you, Laramie. I'm sorry. I've protected you for as long as I've been able to, but the mission is more impor- tant. This is my fault, really. I counted on you being too afraid to come by yourself, but I forgot how hard it is for you to let people in. To ask for help. I would suggest you throw yourself on Temple's mercy, but I know firsthand that he doesn't have any." Jad looked at me again and shook his head.

"Jad, no!" I exclaimed. I wrapped my arms around him, clutching at his jacket.

"I had hoped we could rid the world of vampires together," he said regretfully, removing my arms as he stepped away from me.

Then he turned and was a blur of motion headed back toward the farmhouse.

46

THE SHOWDOWN

0 Minutes
(Midnight Monday)

The blur stopped abruptly after only a hundred feet or so. My heart lifted at the sight of four figures illuminated by the moonlight, standing fifty yards across the pasture from Jad. He looked around him in a frantic search for possible escape routes. There weren't any.

Then I realized that the four figures weren't the ones I had hoped for. This was so not-good. I fumbled my phone from my pocket and checked it. There was a red exclamation point next to my last emoji. *Failed to send.* Dang it!

I checked the signal bars. None! Double dang it! I held the phone up to the sky and spun around, hoping for a bar. Nothing! I punched Van's number and hit 'connect' on the off chance the call would go through. It didn't.

I looked in horror at the group in the distance. I could make out a large blonde man, a dark-haired female, and two more large, dark-haired men. The weres.

Dread stopped my heart in my chest for a moment, then caused it to pound so loudly that I was sure everyone in the pasture heard. My theory was proven when Jad glanced at me over his shoulder.

The world suddenly tilted on its axis and I dropped to my knees. My heart stopped for several beats and I was unable to catch my breath. My heart stuttered and thumped several more times before it stopped again. Was this a panic attack? It didn't feel like panic. It felt like death. I fell forward onto my hands, but no matter how hard I gasped, my lungs didn't fill with air. The pasture grew dark around me. I tried to focus on Jad. The bastard was smiling! He was going to stand there grinning like a loon while I died. I dropped my gaze to the ground between my hands and tried to focus again on breathing.

Then Jad was kneeling on the ground beside me. He rubbed his hand up and down my back in a soothing manner. "Don't fight it, Lar. Just let it happen. Slow your breathing. You don't need the air."

"My heart," I managed to gasp out. "I think I'm having a heart attack."

"You aren't, Lar, it's The Change. It's finally starting. Your lungs and heart are shutting down. Your brain doesn't accept what's happening and it's causing the panic. Just ride it out."

He was wrong. For the third time in three days, I was sure I was dying.

"We may have a chance now. I told Temple I would meet him after midnight, hoping that The Change would have already occurred and the others would be with you," Jad mused, almost to himself, "but at least it will be four against two now instead of four against one."

Just before the world went dark around me, I used my final breath to say what I had been thinking all night.

"Bastard."

———

"She is pretty, in a plain, girl-next-door kind of way, Jad. I can see why you just couldn't leave her behind."

I would love to say I fought my way back to consciousness, but it wasn't like that at all. One moment everything was dark, and the next I was lying on the ground with hay stubble, dry and sharp from the last cutting, poking me all over. And listening to the worst backhanded compliment I'd ever received.

The steady thumping of my heart felt normal and I took a small breath just to prove I could. Sweet air filled my lungs. I would never take breathing for granted again.

"Ah, sleeping beauty awakes."

A boot caught me under the stomach and rolled me over. It was attached to the blond guy I had seen across the pasture before my panic attack. Temple squatted beside me in a quick, fluid motion and grabbed my jaw with his hand. He twisted my head to one side as he inspected my neck. Then he jerked my face to his and stared at me. I stared right back. I could see why the US Army had thought he would make the perfect double agent. With his chiseled features, blond hair and blue eyes he could have been a model for one of the Nazis' Third Reich posters. Like the other vampires I'd met, his creamy skin looked ethereal, but the cruel twist of his mouth ruined the illusion.

"She has the mark but hasn't changed yet. Why didn't you speed up her change like you did yours?" Temple asked Jad, who stood on my other side.

Speed up The Change? My eyes flew to Jad.

"Oh, so she doesn't know?" Temple asked, correctly interpreting my look.

"No," replied Jad, "and I didn't come here to discuss that."

"Oh," replied Temple with a laugh, "you didn't come here to discuss how little your wife knows about your activities over the last . . ." He stood and turned to the dark-haired woman who waited behind him. She wore a low-cut shirt, tight pants, high-heeled boots and way too much makeup. Everything about her screamed bimbo. Temple snapped his fingers a few times, then asked her, "How long has it been, Allia?"

"Three years, give or take," replied the bimbo in heavily accented English. Mexican or South American? I couldn't be sure.

"Yeah, women never forget dates. That's just one of the reasons I keep her around." Temple turned back to gaze down on me. At that, Allia moved against his back and pressed her cleavage against him.

"One of the many reasons," Temple said with a leer at me when the bimbo wrapped her arms around his torso and her hands traveled downward to his waistband.

"Three years?" I asked. Jad had only been gone for two years. Then I remembered the emails.

"You bastard! You really did ask for this." It was old ground for us now, but Temple didn't know that. I had to buy as much time as possible for the others to get to us. I had to believe that they would come sooner rather than later.

"Ding, ding, ding! The little wifey finally gets a clue." Temple laughed again. The sound was eerie. Something wasn't right about him. Well, besides the whole vamp thing.

"Wanted this? Hell, he begged for it. He promised me my heart's desire if I made him a vampire. Then, he somehow managed to speed up The Change and separate himself from the werewolves I had sent to keep him, ah, safe. Neat trick, that—speeding up The Change from seventy-two hours to just twelve. Did you learn that from your voodoo girlfriend?"

Temple laughed crazily again when Jad flinched at the mention of LaRue. Jad had no secrets from this guy.

"Jad, why? How?" I said, playing for time.

Jad played along. "Van and I knew Crockett was a vamp and we also knew he had some pretty shady dealings going on.

I started surveillance on him, mainly because I was bored. Police work had become routine. It was obvious I wasn't going to make detective anytime soon. The supernatural world was quiet. Then . . ." Jad smiled. "Then I found an email account Crockett was using that we didn't know about. When I realized that he and Temple were emailing back and forth on a regular basis, I was just blown away."

"You flatter me," Temple said sarcastically, but his face told the real story. He loved that he had made such an impression.

"I had read in the Van Helsing's documents that they thought Temple had survived the war, but there was no real confirmation that he still existed. When I read the emails, I realized that I had found a vampire who could give me eternal life. Do you know what that means, Laramie? Only a few vampires still have the ability."

"Three," Temple said simply. At Jad and mine's looks he replied, "Three including Allia, you and me. Or four, depending on what happens with little wifey here. I killed the others, as I am going to kill you."

Gulp. In spite of the fear that Temple inspired in me, and despite not wanting to draw his attention, I had to keep the conversation going. "Why?" I asked Jad.

"I was always going to be in Van's shadow," he said resignedly. "I was never going to have his money, his family's prestige, his fighting abilities—any of it."

I opened my mouth to contradict him. This wasn't what he'd told me just a few minutes ago. Jad silenced me with a look. I guessed that his plan to wipe supernaturals from the face of the earth with the True Cross wasn't for general knowledge. So which one was the truth? Eternal life, or getting rid of all the vampires?

"And don't even try to point out that I had you. I never had you. Well, not from the moment you laid eyes on Van."

That was wildly unfair. I hadn't realized for years how I

felt about Van. It wasn't right for Jad to throw it out there as an excuse to become all undead and everything. Even if he was just saying it for Temple's benefit.

I stuffed my hands in my pockets in annoyance and my fingertips bumped against the small bottles of holy water. I wasn't positive of the effect it had on vampires, but in the movies it always slowed them down, what with the burning of flesh and the smoke coming off them. Well, every little bit helped. As Jad continued talking, all eyes focused on him, I tried to loosen the lids on the bottles without removing them from my pockets. Not an easy job.

"Plus, I knew you were planning to leave me."

I jumped when he said that. I didn't think at that point in our marriage that Jad had noticed anything I did. When I saw that everyone's eyes were on me, I quit fiddling with the lids on the bottles and tried to think of something to say.

"You . . . you did?" Lame Laramie, just lame. I was finally getting the answers I wanted and that was the best I could come up with? The truth was that the answers were no longer important. I just wanted to live.

"Yes, Temple wasn't supposed to change me for another month, but I knew I had pushed things as far with you as I could. I wouldn't be surprised if you already had a suitcase packed when I died."

I felt the blush bloom across my cheeks, but hoped the moonlight concealed it from everyone. Jad's sad smile let me know that it hadn't. Damn that vampire night vision.

"It was important to fake my death before you left me, so you would get the insurance money. As much as you and Van made googly eyes at each other whenever you thought the other one wasn't looking, I knew you would never end up together. Van has too much honor to step in on a friend's wife. Of course, I knew he would try his best to look after you, but I also knew you wouldn't accept money from him. So I had to make sure you were taken care of, financially, at least."

"How generous of you," I said dryly. "You had me all along. Jad, I would have stayed with you forever. You were the one who pulled away. You were the one who decided I wasn't enough."

"Jad, I would have stayed with you forever." He mimicked my statement in a high, cruel voice and then gave a harsh laugh. "Just what every man wants to hear. No matter how much I loved you, you were only going to stay with me because it was your duty."

"You're a fine one to talk about duty, when you married me knowing you didn't love me. Then you carried on with LaRue behind my back for I don't know how long. Maybe years!" I practically yelled the last point.

"Ah, so she does have claws. I was beginning to wonder," Temple interjected. "But I don't buy this lovers' quarrel. You want me to show her mercy when I kill you, but I won't. Your time is up. Either produce the True Cross or you are both going to die."

Temple gripped Jad's left arm. One of the weres moved behind Jad and wrapped his arms around Jad's neck. The second were gripped Jad's right arm. Then Allia stepped in front of Jad and pulled a stake from her boot.

47

IN FOR A PENNY, IN FOR A POUND?

**+15 Minutes
(12:15 a.m. Tuesday)**

"Wait!" I exclaimed, before I could think better of it.

They stared at me. I cleared my throat as I tried to think of something to add. Something that would buy Jad some time. Not that I cared about his miserable hide, but they would turn on me next.

Temple raised his eyebrows at me.

I took a deep breath and cleared my throat. Again. This would either buy me some time or get me killed ahead of Jad. I opened my eyes as wide as they would go and made my voice as guileless as possible.

"I'm just wondering how a brand-new vampire got away from such a powerful vampire like yourself? I would think you would want to hear that from Jad before, well . . ." I made timid gesture at the stake Allia held with its tip pressed against Jad's chest. "I mean, don't you want to hear how he outsmarted you, so you don't make the same mistake with someone else in the future?"

Temple initially reacted with a slight flaring of his nostrils.

But by the time I had finished my act of idiocy, a wash of red covered his face. Then the red washed away and his mouth compressed into a thin, hard, line. He stayed that way for a few moments, obviously struggling for self-control.

You know that feeling you get when you top the first big hill on a roller coaster? You want to keep your eyes open because you are either about to have the ride of your life or you are going to die. That was the exact feeling I got while I watched Temple struggle for control. Involuntarily, just like on a rollercoaster, my eyes snapped shut. I couldn't watch what was about to happen.

Temple's eerie laugh echoed across the still pasture. My eyes sprang open. He was bent over with his hands on his knees, laughing so hard I thought he would start gasping for breath any second. Then I remembered that vampires don't breathe.

When Temple finally regained control of himself, he stood up and wiped his hands over his face like he was wiping away tears. But there were no tears. His face was oddly composed and smooth, like those Hollywood types who have injected their faces with so much Botox, they couldn't show a true emotion if their life depended on it.

"God, I needed that! I haven't laughed that hard in at least a decade. I'm starting to understand what Jad sees in you. I might not kill you after all. I may keep you around for entertainment."

At his statement a strange, terrifying sound, a cross between a growl and a hiss, erupted from Allia's throat. Her eyes became blood-red and she dropped into a crouch. Terror washed over me with the realization that I had become her target. I might have even peed myself a little.

"Allia!" Temple barked. She froze in place, but her eyes remained eerily red and fixed on me.

"No matter what, you will always be my favorite, mi corazón." Temple practically cooed the words at her. "Maybe

I will even give her to you to play with occasionally." Allia rose from the crouch and her eyes returned to normal. Well, almost. Red rings still encircled her coffee colored irises. She gave me a tight smile that promised all kinds of torture in my future, then returned to her former position with the stake against Jad's chest. I shoved my violently trembling hands in my pockets.

"Actually," said Temple, regaining everyone's attention, "my little country bumpkin has a point. I would also love to hear his version of how he escaped from my men." He finished with a pointed look at the weres. The implication was clear. If either of them had fudged the slightest bit in their versions of the events surrounding Jad's escape, there was going to be hell to pay.

Jad's eyes closed momentarily in relief at the reprieve, but he quickly became his cocky self again. "May I have a little breathing room please?"

Temple considered the request, then gave the were goons and Allia a slight nod. They released their holds and stepped away from Jad, but Allia did not sheath the stake.

Jad made a great show of straightening his clothing.

"I have always been fascinated with becoming a vampire. The Van Helsings have been producing their own reports for several centuries and have also amassed quite a library from other sources. In my years of working with them, I spent as much time as possible researching the process, or trying to." Jad was really getting into the story and his volume increased with his excitement. "There were tons of references on stopping The Change, or the quickest way to kill a vampire after The Change, but—"

"Shut up!" Temple ordered Jad and held his hand up for silence. He cocked his head.

A distant whomp, whomp noise reverberated through the air. My hearing had greatly improved since the bite, but I was still nowhere near these guys' league.

When I met Jad's gaze, he winked at me. Cheeky bastard!

As the noise increased, I recognized it. I scanned the horizon, but it was still too far away. Jad nodded imperceptibly when our eyes met and he lowered, just barely, into a crouch.

"Why the hell is José coming?" Temple asked Allia. "I haven't given him the signal. Call him!"

Allia pulled a cell phone from her pocket and walked a few steps away from the group, phone in the air, trying to find a signal.

Damn. I had been sure it was Van's helicopter bringing the Cabernet Cavalry, and from the resigned look on Jad's face, he had thought the same. Now it was anyone's guess if it was Van or José, but with everyone's attention diverted, Jad mouthed one word.

"Run."

Jad sprung at the werewolf closest to him and with one quick motion, twisted the were's head so hard I thought it would tear from his body. The bones in his neck snapped. The were fell to the ground and began flopping like a fish out of water. The other were's anguished howl reverberated through the air around us at a pitch that I was sure would make my eardrums bleed. Jad delivered a powerful punch to his throat and the howl became a wet gurgle. The were dropped to his knees, clutching his throat with his furry hands.

Frozen, I watched the weres' death throes. They had tried to kill me several times over the last seventy-two hours, but I didn't wish them dead. Not like this.

"Laramie, damn it, run!" Jad's command was followed by a loud crunch as Temple tackled him.

Temple straddled Jad and pounded his face with his fists, the blows cracking like a sledgehammer hitting a boulder. I didn't want any of that action. I spun desperately, looking for the best direction to run. With the moonlight glinting off its rotors, I could just make out the dark form of the helicopter swooping toward us.

I took a step in the direction of the copter, only to pause. Did it contain friend or foe?

I turned away from it, but I couldn't make my feet move. Jad had knocked Temple off him and was attempting to stand. Before he could gain his feet, Allia flew through the air, striking him. They landed together in a heap. Jad rolled Allia over so that he was on top of her. Temple sprang toward them, covering the distance in a single leap. It sounded like two boulders colliding as he crashed into Jad.

I couldn't have asked for a better chance to escape. The weres lay motionless except for an occasional full-body twitch. Temple and Allia were intent on beating the hell out of Jad. I could barely hear the helicopter over the sound of their punches, hisses and growls.

The helicopter was closing fast, but was too far away. If it held Van, he would arrive too late to save Jad. And once Jad was dispatched, Temple and Allia would turn on me. If it was Temple's helicopter, they would be preoccupied with him. I might be able make it to the distant tree line and if I could, they would never find me. I knew this land like the back of my hand. But if I wanted to live, I had to go now.

I turned my back on the noises coming from the vampire pile and looked longingly at the trees. I sighed. My ex-husband was a huge pain in the keister, but I couldn't leave him like this.

I shoved my hands resolutely in my pockets and turned back to the vamp dogpile.

THE ANGELS SANG

**+30 Minutes
(12:30 a.m. Tuesday)**

J ad had told me that once, when he had been in a fight for his life with a crack dealer and had to put out an assist officer, that the first police car siren in the distance had sounded like angels singing. He knew it was about to rain police and he just had to hold out long enough for them to get to him.

The noises from the helicopter were getting louder as I walked toward the vamps. If it was our people, Jad and I just had to stay alive long enough for them to reach us. If it wasn't, then I had to be the cavalry for us instead. Allia and Temple both had their backs to me and were focused on making Jad pay for the trouble he had caused them. He was barely moving, but I hoped that if I could get them off him he would make a quick recovery.

I pulled my hands from my pockets as I walked. Here goes nothing, I thought, and then threw the bottles of holy water as hard as I could at Temple's back. The glass bottles shattered against the rock-hard bodies of the vamps and the water doused Temple and Allia.

Screaming and pandemonium ensued. Well, at least for a few moments. My aim has never been that good, so even though Temple had been my target, the majority of the water hit Allia. The smoke billowed from their burns. A slight breeze picked it up and carried the smell of charred flesh to me. Allia hopped in circles, flames snapping in her hair. Temple, his shirt hanging in smoking strips, slapped ineffectually at her burning tresses while trying to keep the fire from spreading to himself.

I couldn't believe my luck. Fire is one of the few things in the world that's deadly to vampires. Were they really going to go poof after a little dousing with holy water? Was it really going to be this easy?

Yeah, it wasn't. As quickly as it had begun, it was over. Temple ripped a shirt off one of the weres and threw it over Allia's flaming hair, suffocating the worst of the fire. Then he turned on me.

Oh, Holy Mother of God, he was ripped! Okay, I shouldn't have been ogling a guy's chest right before I was about to die, especially since it belonged to the guy who was going to kill me, but damn! It might have been the best one I'd ever seen in person. His abs were . . . But I digress.

"My eyes are up here."

I dragged my gaze to his face. In spite of my terror, it was hard not to laugh. His left eyebrow had been singed completely off, and there were still smoldering spots on his head. While his chest might inspire awe, his face no longer did. In addition to the missing eyebrow, his cheeks and nose were misshapen. Jad had been able to get a few licks in before he ended up at the bottom of the pile. I suppressed a giggle. I needed to work on my tendency to laugh at the most inappropriate moments. Maybe it was hysteria, but it was damned inconvenient.

"You really are entertaining, and obviously more than a little crazy," Temple said, his voice tinged with awe. "I had almost convinced myself to let you live, but you are too dangerous to keep around."

"Adam, he's gone!"

Temple swung around and I stared at the empty ground where Jad had been. I guess he had taken his own advice. I searched the pasture. He was about a hundred yards from us, but he wasn't running. He was frantically waving his arms at the helicopter.

"That isn't José," Temple said matter-of-factly. "Friends of yours?"

I grinned. Those whoomp, whoomps sounded sweeter than angels singing. We were saved!

"You take care of her, then meet me at the pickup point."

"Gladly," replied Allia, not taking her eyes from me. Temple ran toward Jad. I glanced over at the weres. Though still on the ground, they were moving more than they had been, recovering from injuries I had thought were fatal.

My gaze swung back to Allia at the sound of dry grass under her feet. She circled me in a low crouch. A cat playing with a mouse. She smiled and leapt.

Once, when I was a teenager, Monty had thought it would be funny to sneak up behind the horse I was working with and pop a plastic bag. If there was any justice in the world, the horse in its fright would have kicked the bejesus out of Monty. But horses, especially that horse, being 'flight' rather than 'fight' animals, didn't provide me any justice. It barreled over me to get away from the huge monster, in its mind at least, that was attacking it from behind.

Allia slammed into me with a force that made me think the horse had just been a large dog. If this had happened before I'd been venomed, I'm sure the impact would have crushed my chest. Even with the new and improved body that the start of The Change had provided me, ribs cracked. I lay on the ground trying not to writhe in agony. Instead of finishing me off, Allia was toying with me. Once again, she circled me in a low crouch, a sadistic smile on her face.

I pushed myself to my feet, groaning involuntarily when broken ribs shifted. In a move a mixed martial arts star would have been proud of, Allia propelled herself through the air and collided with me again. We crashed to earth some distance away, with me on the bottom. On impact with the hard earth I felt my hip bone give way. Her fist connected with my face and I heard more than felt the crunch of my cheekbone.

I thought about lying there. Just giving up. It would have been so much easier than continuing to fight. But here's the thing, y'all: I'm not a quitter.

My vision dimmed, but I struggled to maintain consciousness. If I went out, I was a goner. Not that I wasn't anyway, but by God, I was going to make her work for it.

My eyes tracked Allia's progress as she circled me, waiting for her next leap, while my mind took stock of my injuries. The broken ribs scraped against each other, and my face was the consistency raw hamburger. Surprisingly the hip didn't feel too bad, but not surprisingly, the leg connected to it wasn't working. To make matters worse, the ankle of the other leg was fractured. I could feel the bones sticking through the skin just above the top of my boot. I didn't want to lie there waiting for her to finish me off, but with both legs out of commission I couldn't stand. I only had one option. It was a long shot, but it was the only shot I had.

I groaned loudly, not having to fake it at all, and curled into a fetal position. Well, a half-fetal position, as I couldn't seem to pull up the leg connected to the broken hip. Luckily it was the other leg I needed. Still groaning, even louder now with the pain of moving my body, I grasped my ankle, concealing it under the other leg. I tried not to gasp in relief when, instead of bone, my fingers grasped wood.

"Laramie!" Van's voice carried across the pasture, but he was too far away to save me. Allia knew it too.

"Your friends are more concerned about Jad than you," she said. "They set the helicopter down by him. They will never make it to you in time. It will be nothing to finish you off and meet Temple to be picked up. We will laugh about you when we have sex tonight." And with that, she leapt.

49

IS THAT A STAKE IN YOUR POCKET OR ARE YOU JUST HAPPY TO SEE ME? PART 2

**+40 Minutes
(12:40 a.m. Tuesday)**

I barely had time to roll over to meet her attack, much less get the stake up. In what felt like slow motion, Allia's body slammed into me. I had wrapped both hands around the stake and held it in front of me, pointy end up. I felt both arms break as the force of her body hit them. The blunt end of the stake slammed into my sternum and the bone first cracked, then caved in under it. Panic washed through me. What if I staked and killed both of us at the same time?

Then, peace washed over me. If I was going to die here, then so be it. I hadn't given up, I hadn't backed down, and I had held my own. I could die happy (well, semi-happy) knowing that.

The weight of Allia's body lifted off me, taking the stake with it. My hands lay useless on my chest. It had a concave shape, but I didn't feel a hole. I was in a world of hurt, but I wasn't dead. Unfortunately, neither was Allia.

She was on her knees, frantically clawing at the stake embedded in her chest. Her look of total disbelief would have been comical under other circumstances. Small glowing cracks crisscrossed her face and arms. They widened into fiery fissures.

"You bitch," she croaked.

The orange fissures deepened into hellish crevices and then, poof, Allia disappeared. She just imploded into herself. Even her clothes combusted. A small pile of ash sat unobtrusively where she had been. If not for the rising wisps of smoke and the charred stake protruding from the heap, I would have thought it was a fire ant mound.

I stared up at the star-filled sky, breathing in small, shallow, gasps—caused, no doubt, by a punctured lung. My sternum was crushed into my heart, but its ragged beat proved I was alive and still human. I could hear the gang calling my name. It sounded as if they had spread out while searching for me. They would find me soon. I would just close my eyes for a little while and rest until they did.

I wasn't sure how much time had passed when I heard a noise off to my right. Which one of them found me, I thought dreamily? I hoped it was Van. Maybe he would gather me into his arms and kiss me. Several times. Long, passionate kisses.

I rolled my head toward the sound and slowly opened my eyes. Fifteen feet away, one of the werewolves had made it to his feet and was facing me. The other one was sitting up and trying to get his legs under him.

"Oh, fuck me." I could barely whisper the words.

I gave the were the same advice that Jad had given me. "Run," I whispered. It was the best I could do. It had no effect on him. In fact, he took a menacing step toward me.

I tried to take a deep breath so I could yell for help. Nothing happened. My lungs wouldn't work. My heart was motionless. I had panicked earlier, but now I was at peace. My pain receded like an ebb tide slipping out to sea.

I could feel my bones mending, even shifting to knit together. I wasn't up to fighting the were yet, but it wouldn't be long. He took several staggering steps toward me. He wasn't a hundred percent either.

"Run," I said again, my voice clear and strong. He and the other were, who was finally standing, paused. Look at that! I made two weres think twice about attacking me.

The first were swung away from me. I barely had time to register what I thought was my victory when a white blur struck him in the chest and rode him to the ground. Growling, snapping and grunting filled the night. Bo's grunting. What the hell?

When the second were moved to help his friend, I tried to spring up from the ground to protect Bo. I screamed with the effort and fell back to the earth. The hip wasn't healed yet. I rolled to my stomach and, using my hands like claws, pulled myself across the uneven ground. I had to get to Bo before the other were did. But I wasn't going to make it; they were too far away.

The second were reached the fighting pair while I was still several feet from them. He was unsteady as he leaned forward to pull Bo off his buddy. His hands were mere inches from her fur when a yellow airborne missile knocked him sideways.

"Yella," I groaned with relief. Then Finn was there with his teeth sunk into the were that Bo was still giving what for.

"Great job, guys," I got out weakly. Yella had the second were down and was dealing with him by herself. I raised my head and looked for the rest of the gang. Worthless was ten feet away, sniffing at what he seemed to find a particularly interesting clump of grass. While the fight between his friends and the weres raged on nearby, he nonchalantly hiked his leg and peed.

"Hey," I said sharply, "a little help here."

Worthless looked at me, tongue lolling out of the side of his mouth in a lopsided grin, gave a yip of recognition, and then bounded into the fray. I lowered my head back onto the grass, completely spent from the effort.

I briefly passed out again, but was brought back to consciousness by passionate kisses. From Bo. I managed to roll onto my back without screaming. I wrapped my arms around her and pulled her close.

She still loved me. It didn't matter to her what I was now.

And then Van was there. He held me in his arms just like in my fantasy. Well, not exactly like my fantasy because he wasn't kissing me, and Bo was lodged happily between us.

"Thank God, Laramie! You're alive. I thought I had lost you forever."

"No, I'm still here, although it was touch and go there for a little while." I laughed weakly. "What took you so long?"

"You, you idiot. We were waiting for the third emoji."

"No bars."

He pulled me closer and held me like he would never let me go. I was good with that plan. Van's body was warm and he smelled musky and manly and something else I couldn't quite identify. I never realized before how good Van smelled. When he drew back our eyes met, and he leaned in again. This was it; he was going to kiss me. I raised my face to his and closed my eyes.

They sprang back open at a loud slurp, just in time to see Bo's wide, pink tongue slide across Van's face. He wrapped one arm around her and pulled her from between us. He leaned toward me again but stopped when a throat cleared behind him. Dang it! We might as well be at the Mesquite Championship Rodeo on finals night, what with all the people and animals milling about.

I peeked over Van's shoulder to see who had so rudely interrupted us. Grace and Marek stood several feet away, two extremely disheveled and chewed-up weres in tow.

"Temple escaped, but we have to do something with these lads. Should they be taken back to the helicopter?" Grace asked, a mischievous smile playing across her face. Crazy wench. She knew she had interrupted my moment.

"Sure." Van replied to Grace's question without taking his eyes off me.

Finn stood on point next to Grace, Yella by Marek, and Worthless danced in circles around the lot of them. Marek rolled his eyes, then pulled a tennis ball out of his pocket and threw it a distance that a professional baseball player would have been jealous of. Worthless barked a joyous woof! and then chased after the ball. Marek grinned while he watched his goofy dog bound across the pasture. Unconditional love lit his face. He didn't care that Worthless wasn't the brightest bulb; he loved him for what he was. Grace and Marek, werewolves in tow, struck off across the pasture.

I glanced toward the helicopter and saw that Jad and LaRue stood just beyond it. I couldn't make out what they were saying, but she looked pissed. I didn't envy him that conversation. I had a feeling that LaRue could make him squirm much more than I ever had. Good, it served the smarmy, cheating bastard right, I thought with a small, fond smile. After a few false starts, at what he thought was truly the end he had sacrificed himself in an attempt to save me. That had to count for something.

"Do you still care about him?" Van asked.

"No," I said, and my eyes met his. "It's been you since long before Jad died. I just couldn't admit it to myself. I couldn't believe that you could ever feel the same way."

Van closed his eyes in relief. Now kiss me, you fool. But nope, still talking.

"It was you the second I met you. It was like a freight train hit me."

"Or a vampire." At Van's look I continued, "It's a long story, don't let me interrupt you."

"The last three days have been hell. I never thought you would be mine, but there was always a distant hope. Then you were bit and I thought you were lost to me forever. But when Jad met the helicopter tonight he told us that something had stopped The Change, but that we had to get to you or Allia was going to kill you. I was so happy and so scared all at once." He glanced over at the pile of ash. "How did you kill her? I know that you've gained some strength since The Change started, but how did you manage to kill a vamp? You know what, never mind, just know that you always continue to amaze and impress the hell out of me. I love you, Laramie. If you had been killed tonight, I wouldn't have been able to survive. You are all I want in the world."

My future had faded like a watercolor in a rain shower, each of Van's words washing more of it away. He was saying everything I had hoped to hear, but it no longer mattered. I wasn't the same Laramie that he thought he was saying it to. Then, of course, he finally kissed me.

When his lips met mine, they were warm and soft and oh so perfect. I opened my mouth to tell him no, but he deepened the kiss, effectively silencing me. I raised my hands to his chest to gently push him away, but somehow, they got tangled in his shirt and I pulled him closer. He felt wonderful, and tasted even better.

With a gasp he jerked back and put his hand to his mouth. When he pulled it away, his fingers were red with blood. He gaped at me in horror. I tried to close the distance between us, but he pushed against me.

"Van," I tried to say his name, but something in my mouth kept me from pronouncing it correctly. I ran my tongue around the inside of my mouth. It encountered two sharp protrusions along my top row of teeth, and I knew the truth.

Fangs.

Unable to stand the way he looked at me, I dropped my gaze from his face and focused on the vein in his neck, pulsing madly. We could discuss this. He loved me, right? Love meant accepting the sum of the person. But I wasn't a person anymore. My body throbbed to the beat of Van's pulse. How strange, I thought dreamily and leaned in for a closer look at the suddenly fascinating vein. My hands were still wrapped in his shirt and, almost effortlessly, I pulled him closer. I barely noticed the way he struggled. No, that wasn't true. I'm ashamed to admit that his struggles excited, maybe even aroused me. Almost of their own accord, my fangs slid into the vein in Van's neck. He fought harder to break free from my hold. I heard yelling in the distance, but the throbbing in my ears was louder. Van's struggles grew weaker and then subsided all together.

And the throbbing? It stopped along with his struggles.

50

A LITTLE TEXAS RED

Tuesday Night

I spent the day after I killed Van at the Dragonfly. Regret and sadness have blurred my memories of the time, but this is a mixture of what I remember and what I've been told.

Marek and Grace had pulled me off Van. Off Van's body, that is. Luckily, before I completely drained him. I had only stolen enough of his blood to stop his heart. Only. A vampire hasn't bitten a Van Helsing in at least sixty years, but mission SOP (Standard Operating Procedures) still required that they carry several pints of blood and medical gear on every mission. Van's father and Owen restarted Van's heart with the help of the onboard AFIB machine LaRue boosted with voodoo.

LaRue wouldn't speak to me or make eye contact. As surely as she used chicken bones in voodoo, she regretted not killing me back at her shop when she had the chance. I wasn't sure Van wouldn't have agreed with her at that moment, too.

Van's father, who had been roped into flying them out to Faith, hadn't looked so happy with me either. Mr. Anderson flew the humans, the dogs, and the restrained weres back to the Anderson compound in Dallas. No doubt I was persona non grata there now. They wouldn't let me see Van, even a glimpse, before the helicopter took off.

I had been so distraught and exhausted that Marek had carried me back across the pasture to the farmhouse and my truck. It had felt so good to just close my eyes and let someone else carry my load, literally, for a little while.

During the excitement caused by my attack on Van, Jad had slipped away. The good news was that I had managed to drop the GPS tracker in his jacket pocket when he had embraced me in the pasture, so the Van Helsing bumpy-hunting machine had sprung into action, ready to track him to the ends of the earth. Jad might not have the True Cross, but he was searching for it and we wanted to know what he knew.

I woke at sundown locked in a room. It was a lovely furnished room, but still locked and inescapable all the same. Marek and Grace arrived to spring me from my gilded cage before I had time to work up a good panic. It turned out that the room was in a hidden basement under the Dragonfly. I wasn't the only one with a bat cave.

I felt fine. I had healed from the night before, due in no small part to the blood I had stolen from Van. My eyesight and hearing were off the charts. I could count the stitches in the weave of the bed linens from fifteen feet away. And through the room's thick stone walls, I had heard Grace and Marek whispering outside the door when they arrived to release me.

I had woken hungry—well, more thirsty than hungry, but for what, I didn't know. Grace had brought blood and several types of human food for me to try. She told me that all vampires craved blood and were stronger with it as a part of their diet. But most of them, the Good ones anyway, abstained from human blood as much as possible. They could survive on regular food in small quantities, but what worked for each vampire was unique. No one knows why, but the theory was that it was probably linked to what they liked to eat before The Change.

About that Good, Evil, Dualistic thing . . . I still didn't know what I was. Marek and Grace said that it might take months for my true nature to develop. She assured me that my attack on Van didn't mean I was Evil. She went so far as to say that she didn't think an Evil vampire would feel as bad about it as I did, but it was too early to know for sure. We also didn't know if sunlight would kill me or not. LaRue suggested that because of the blood ritual with Marek, I might be able to survive small amounts of sunlight like he could. I figured she was trying to kill me by sending me out in the sun.

Van had sent a single text message that asked me to meet him at The Madam when I woke up. Grace and Marek tried to push food on me again. They stressed that I shouldn't see Van hungry, but I couldn't force anything down. Everything they brought, even the blood, had looked revolting.

Grace and Marek walked me home. The October night was cloudy and blustery, but The Madam's soft, white glow beckoned me. The sight of her, as always, gave me chills and goosebumps. Who knew vampires could get goosebumps?

All of my friends—I loved the thought that almost overnight I had a group of people around me I could call friends—had been productive while I had slept the day away. Owen, though, won the gold star. He had used his superior computer skills to hack the good Council Member Crockett's email account. He emailed the police department, from Crockett, confessing to Bernie's murder with details, based on Tom's account, that only the murderer or the police could know. In the email, "Crockett" had also confessed to Tom's murder.

It had been Grace's brilliant idea for The Cleaners to drop Tom off at Crockett's house. Surprise, surprise, The Cleaners' skill set extended beyond just cleaning up scenes. They could create them too, if need be.

Crockett? He was in the wind, as was Temple. For now. Marek and Grace said that they would turn up again at some point, like bad pennies.

Word on the street—Owen had found the information in the police department's database, but word on the street sounded so much cooler—was that the police had canceled the warrant for my arrest.

The Madam's front door stood open when we arrived. Van, wearing the same clothes as the night before, sat slumped at a table in the saloon with a half empty bottle of Dingle Irish whiskey and a single glass in front of him. His hair stood out in every direction, and his eyes, when he raised them to meet mine, were bloodshot. Small lines creased around his eyes and mouth. I'd never noticed them before—was I only seeing them now because of my improved eyesight, or were they new?

My mouth was dry, and I didn't think I could form words even if I knew what to say to him. I mean, what do you say to the man you love after you've killed him? A white streak made it halfway down the stairs and launched herself at me. I caught Bo and held her close while her tail beat my side like a switch. Her tongue cleaned every inch of my face. Gratitude that at least this remained filled me like wine poured into a glass.

When I raised my head from Bo, my gaze met Owen's. He watched me from the bottom step of the grand staircase. Grace held up a hand to stop him, waiting to see how I reacted to Bo before he was allowed closer. I smiled uncertainly at him and he flung himself at us, enveloping both Bo and me in his embrace.

It ended up being a wet reunion on both of our parts, with Bo licking our faces. And the good news? Not even a twinge of desire to sink my fangs into either of them.

A low growl broke into the reunion. I pushed Owen and Bo behind me and crouched to meet the threat. Dixie bared her teeth at me and growled from her position at the top of the staircase. I swung to face Owen.

"I couldn't leave her at Tom's, and I've been wanting a dog . . ." Owen said sheepishly. As memories of our deal to let him live at The Madam and have a dog surfaced, he continued, "She and Bo get along. Dixie has only drawn blood on Bo once and that was just a superficial ear wound." At my ominous look he added, "She's so small. How much trouble could she be?"

I narrowed my eyes at him, but I had been the one who had told The Cleaners not to make Dixie disappear. No good deed goes unpunished.

A clink of glass broke into my stare-down with Owen. With a slight raise of his eyebrow and a jerk of his head toward Van, he took Bo and walked out the front door. His look over his shoulder told me they would be right outside if I needed them. Dixie ran down the stairs and followed them out. Not to be cowed, she made a snapping motion at my ankle as she went by. I jumped back at least a foot. *Dang rat-dog!*

Grace and Marek stood as silent sentinels a few feet away but made no attempt to hide their amused smirks. After a quick self-check, I nodded slowly at them. They followed Owen through the front door of The Madam, leaving it cracked open in case I needed them. Well, in case Van needed them, really.

Then I focused fully on Van and just let my eyes soak him in. He should have looked awful with the bloodshot eyes, disheveled hair, and rumpled clothes, but he looked amazing to me. I took a slow step toward him and then another, and another. I was halfway across the saloon when the smell hit me. The glorious smell. As the thirst washed through me, I knew what I craved, and this time there was no stopping me. I would not be denied. I realized I had broken into a run only when the room blurred around me.

Van, to his credit, didn't so much as twitch as I flew past him on my way to the bar. I slid to a stop in front of the closest crate of Texas red wine. I'm not sure how I even got the first bottle open. I may have bit off its top. I do know that I drank it straight from the bottle. After that, my hunger eased. I opened the second bottle the good old fashioned way with, a corkscrew. I took it, along with an oversized wine glass, and joined Van and his whiskey.

"Laramie, everyone knows that Texas red wine is just a step up from swill," Van said. He attempted a crooked smile.

"Van Helsing Anderson, I declare, you are such a snob," I joked in return. The wine coursed through me and after guzzling the first bottle I was a little tipsy. That was probably a good thing. You know, liquid courage and all that.

"Van, I'm sorry I killed you," I said. *Very eloquent, Laramie.*

"You should be." Van sighed. "I'm sorry for all of it. I'm sorry I brought Jad into this life, because you got pulled into it too. I'm sorry that I kept you in the dark and I'm sorry that I couldn't protect you. I'm sorry that you are now this . . ."

"No, Van. Look, I didn't make it easy for either Jad or you—"

"Don't take up for that bastard!" Van exclaimed. He slammed his hand on the table with enough force to make me, and the bottles and glasses, jump.

"He is a bastard, isn't he?" I mused with a smile. "We can agree on that."

"Yes," Van replied. He poured two fingers of whiskey in the glass and leaned back in his chair.

"Van, I'm done blaming other people for where I end up in life. My decisions and my choices brought me here." I looked around The Madam and took in all the work I had done. I could hear Bo tearing around the front yard, Owen chasing her to get her worked up, and Dixie yapping at God knows who or what. I could also hear low murmurs from Marek and Grace on the front porch. A warm feeling flowed through me. I had friends, a beautiful home, and I was alive (well, sort of). What more could I ask for? I took Van's hand in mine before continuing, "And here isn't so bad."

Van looked at me and I knew that he didn't agree. The more that I could ask for in my life was Van, but I didn't think he was ready to be a part of it. After years of trying to push him out of it, now I couldn't bear to think of a life without him . Like Scarlett, any true Southern girl's hero, I vowed to put it out of my head until tomorrow.

But I figured that as long as I had killed the mood, I might as well ask some questions.

"So, have you ever known a vampire to drink wine instead of blood?" I asked.

"There are accounts of vampires drinking wine . . ." Van trailed off, looking as though he was searching for the proper wording. "But I think they drank it more for dessert than for the main course, if you understand my meaning."

And I had worried that I had killed the mood?

"Van," I whispered, unable to ask the question in a regular tone. "Do you think I'm Evil?"

"Matthew six, thirty-four," Van replied.

"What?" I asked when I realized he wasn't going to say anything else.

"Sufficient unto the day is the evil thereof," Van quoted. "In laymen's terms, you are doing okay, you aren't killing people. Well, anyone since last night. Let's deal with what we can and not take on any additional worries."

"So, we are going to Scarlett O'Hara it?" I asked. To his puzzled look I replied, "We'll worry about it tomorrow."

Van nodded, then slid a folded piece of paper across the table to me. When I started to unfold it, he laid a hand over mine.

"My men were able to follow the GPS signal from the tracker you planted on Jad to a small airstrip in East Texas.

They found the letter and the tracker in place of small airplane that Jad had liberated. The letter is for you."

"Have you read it?" I asked. When Van nodded, I slid the piece of paper into my pocket to read later.

I was surprised Van hadn't asked me about what happened in the pasture. What Jad wanted from us. But now wasn't the time. Van was exhausted and not a little drunk. Tomorrow, I reminded myself.

But I had one burning question that couldn't wait, so I threw it out there before Van either left or passed out.

"Van, I have an extremely serious question to ask about all of this vampire stuff."

"Okay," he answered resignedly. "Go ahead."

"Am I right in assuming that The Change started the instant the vampire venom entered my body?"

"Yes, that was how your blood could immediately start regenerating itself. Why?"

"You don't understand what that means?"

Van frowned. "No, I can't say that I do."

"It means that technically, I died before I turned thirty. I'll be twenty-nine forever!" I told him with a grin.

Van's face lit with a smile as beautiful and as welcome as a rainbow after the rain.

And just like that, life—or death, depending on how you thought about it—looked pretty good.

EPILOGUE

Laramie,

Once again, I underestimated you. In my defense, it came from years of watching you underestimate yourself.

You have that indefinable quality that draws people to you and makes them loyal. Hattie left you her house. Tom killed Hattie and Bernie but could never bring himself to kill you. Grace, a pirate queen from a bygone era, is ready to have sleepovers with you so y'all can braid each other's hair. Even Marek, centuries-old Marek, who has been through all the wars and hasn't gotten involved with human dealings in over sixty years has aligned himself with you. And Van, well, just please take care of my friend. He has loved you for years and he will still love you when the dust settles.

If you brought that quality with you into the supernatural world, you could be the one to tip the balance between Good and Evil. You may not have ever been a rodeo queen, but I think you have exactly what it takes to be a vampire queen. You have a talented group around you. Use them to find the True Cross.

Be careful who you trust.

I'll be in touch.

J.

ENJOYED THE STORY?

Thank you for reading Dying in Dallas. If you enjoyed Laramie's journey, please consider leaving a review where you bought the book. I appreciate your help in spreading the word, and reviews make a tremendous difference in helping new readers find the series.

Join my newsletter, **The Night Club**, at jckeough.com for notifications of giveaways and new releases, along with personal updates from behind the scenes of my books. To sweeten the cauldron, you will receive my short story "Dinner with the Delaneys" for free.

ABOUT THE AUTHOR

J.C. Keough is the creator of Laramie Harper Chronicles. Jamie is working on the second book in the Laramie Harper Chronicles and the first book in a new series named The Texas Tender Mysteries. The Tender Mysteries will combine beer, boats, murders, and ghosts.

Jamie lives in a small town on the Southwest coast of Ireland with her husband and their two fur babies.

You can find out more at www.jckeough.com

 facebook.com/jckeough

 twitter.com/jckeough

 instagram.com/jckeough

 pinterest.com/jckeoughauthor

Made in the USA
Coppell, TX
14 August 2020